MEMENTO

Michael M. Mooney

DOUBLEDAY & COMPANY, INC.

GARDEN CITY, NEW YORK

1979

The character of Suzanne and the character of her biographer are both inventions; together with all the other personalities of this fiction, they bear no resemblance to any persons living or dead; only the city is real; and even so, New York is no more than the focus of illusion.

Library of Congress Cataloging in Publication Data

Mooney, Michael Macdonald, 1930–
Memento.

I.   Title.
PZ4.M8184Me   1979   [PS3563.O566]   813'.5'4
ISBN: 0-385-14474-1
Library of Congress Catalog Card Number 78-7762

For Anne

Memento   pl. -TOS, -TOES. Late ME. (Imper. of L. *meminisse,* to remember; see MIND.) 1. *Liturg.* Either of two prayers, one for the living and one for the dead, beginning "*Memento.*" 2. A reminder, warning, or hint as to conduct or with regard to future events, as in "*memento mori.*"

ACT III
La Princesse Lointaine

ACT I

Golden Girl in the Golden Land

1

Le Magistral

1970

SUZANNE telephoned the first week of October 1970, during the early part of the week. As I remember, she called me at the newsweekly where I labor as a senior editor, and she said she wanted to meet for lunch at Le Magistral: "On Saturday, so we will have time to talk." She had already calculated for me that Le Magistral was no more than a two-block walk from my office at 488 Madison. She promised she would have "an incredible story to tell," and her bait was phrased, "if you need any excuse, Mr. Editor." As always, she disguised her hook in sparkling laughter. Although I had not seen her for five or six years, I had loved her once upon a time and then followed her amazing career at a distance. So I knew her style: one trick of her success was that she always challenged her fish with some pretty reason to catch the angler. Nevertheless I agreed to Le Magistral at one o'clock.

On Saturday the two-block walk over to Fifth Avenue then to Fifty-second Street was a delightful relief from the gloomy paragraphs with which I had been wrestling all morning. Instead of still another dismal jeremiad upon the city's destiny, I could lift up my eyes to a pretty fall scene. Crowds of enthusiastic women were turned out to pursue their winter supplies. They were pressing on their voyages through a blustery gale—clear, dry, bright blue air down from Canada at last, its lulls edged in arctic chill and its puffs violent from the northwest. Its effect was to quicken every step, and all the women I could see were as excited as the day. The sun sent reflections caroming along the mirrored walls of the city's soaring, glacial towers. It took me a moment to adjust from the glitter of New York at its happiest to the sheltered cove inside Le Magistral's double doors: in dimmed incandescent yellow light among deep red decorations and salmon-pink linens, hushed preparations were continuing against the arrival of the lunch crowd.

Suzanne would not appear until she was at least thirty minutes late, of course; in the meantime, I had to be prepared to wait. While a table was still available, I took a banquette offered by Monsieur Paul and ordered my scotch and water. Although his clientele for lunch on Saturday would not be so very different from the fashionable crowd who were his regulars during the week, they would tend to linger on a weekend. The result would be hardly any turnover at the tables. Once Le Magistral filled, latecomers would have an interminable wait at the bar, regardless of their reservations. Before the scotch I ordered could be returned from the bar, Le Magistral began to fill with a rush.

Monsieur Paul placed his arrivals efficiently, rubbing his palms together as he settled one group behind its patch of salmon-pink tablecloth, returned to the arch marking the boundary between the tables and the bar, retrieved his next party, and guided it to its assigned place. Within ten minutes he had managed to fill his arena—even the shallow mezzanine, up two steps at the back. His long center stage was filled with tables for twos and fours jammed chockablock. Each banquette, ranged beneath the mirrors along both walls, held its pair. In the two alleyways between the center-stage tables and the banquettes, captains and subcaptains hustled drinks and presented menus, although no one seemed in any hurry to order.

Boisterous talk and every appearance of gaiety blustered up from time to time just as the whirlwinds had outside. A man's hacking laughter soared up above the hubbub. A woman trilled.

Because the room was now so busy, voices had to be raised when ardent expressions were to make themselves heard. Rising up with the gales of talk—and perhaps because of it—clouds of tobacco mixed with mysterious perfumes: the essences of crushed flowers and marvelous powders and heavy musks and dense ambergris. And if at any moment attention should wander from the fascinations available at every table, these favored few could inspect each other in the mirrors set along the walls. They could see at a glance that they were among the anointed: the rich, the powerful, the famous, the eminent, the distinguished, the adept, the beautiful people, the fortunate, the clever—and the subjects every so often of the city's admiring gossip. They could see all that for themselves.

They preferred Le Magistral among the many baroque French restaurants they might choose because Monsieur Paul had earned their favor. He played the part of a modest physician. He was perhaps about fifty, gray-haired, of middle height, all smooth and round and solid. His speech and manners were exactly those of a grave but sympathetic doctor required to attend the infections of an army on campaign. He could say yes with such sibilance that he appeared to have considered his response with great care. Even when baffled, he was always easy and informal—but exactly correct—with his army's commanders and the women in their baggage train. If he loaded the menus of Le Magistral with traditional cures, he always stood by over the table to watch the results of his prescriptions. His restaurant was a sanitarium for the noted few. Monsieur Paul himself insisted upon calling it "my little hospital."

He insisted because he understood how much his patients wanted to believe—if only for a lunch or a dinner—they might find sanctuary from the unidentified terrors that followed them. Although most were adventurers, or served as *condottieri* for powerful corporations, their courage sometimes failed them. They were generally raffish, cynical and worldly, but they could be as startled as children by the most ordinary circumstance. Since they were experienced gamblers, they should have known how much their success was the result of nice odds and good luck. Certainly they believed the incredible continent set out to the west of them—its mountains and plains and valleys and people—might still be plundered for enough treasure to ensure their futures. Yet they were uneasy and had to "keep busy," as they explained it. Above all, they were reassured by the company of others just like themselves. Yet Monsieur Paul would get exhausted every so often by their complaints. When his own despair welled up, he dealt with it by fleeing to Vegas on the night flight and not returning for two or three days, or for as much as a week.

One of his patrons caught my attention in the mirror across from my banquette, and I exchanged nods with the movie critic vested by the city's most popular magazine. Beside him, a wistful little blonde at least forty years his junior waited patiently for his attentions, but she would have a long wait. At the table for four near the center, a thirty-five-year-old beauty was having better luck with her companions. When she sent back her head in laughter, she exposed a marvelous white throat hung with an emerald necklace, and the men at her side flushed. At the next table, the stout woman of sixty was the empress of a Paris banking fortune that had survived the German occupation. Although Mme. Empress never wore anything but what she called "simple little dresses," her couturier, who now sat beside her for lunch, clothed her with all the fond care she deserved, and she always headed the list he presented on Seventh Avenue as his credential of success.

Another of that designer's displays sat in the banquette directly behind him—a listing for whom he provided great quantities of silk and linen and batiste in size six. She was the wife of an ambassador to the United Nations, ambitious and hard-working, determined to locate the center of all that mattered socially. It was her duty to find it, and if all the intimate dinners she had arranged and all the indexed lists she had cross-checked had not yet secured the place she so fervently desired for her country, her husband, and herself, she was not yet ready to admit it did not exist. She was lunching with the anchorman of a network evening news, and surely the sage all America knew so well would be able to give her the directions she needed.

As fish and meat in spiced and creamed sauces were brought in, Monsieur Paul's happy few bubbled over with the pleasures of their good fortune. Their celebration was reaching its height when, as if prompted by a cue from an unseen stage manager, Suzanne arrived to make her entrance. She stood, with a vague and tolerant smile, on the frontier between the jammed bar and the vista of the main stage, waiting for Monsieur Paul to abandon some lesser mortals and the flaming dish he had prescribed. Since he was bent over its portions, he had not seen her yet. As she stood, counting the members present from her constituency, every woman in her audience had the opportunity to inspect her wool Chanel suit—in soft pink checked with white and piped in deep pink. I suppose she knew exactly how long it would take each man to catch refractions of light playing upon her lustrous red hair; and how soon each would wonder how she moved.

Only one or two heads actually turned to stare. The beauty whose whisper was notorious bent her head to the ear of the man on her right. He was apparently startled by the secret she had imparted, because he looked up sharply. The empress of Paris banking tapped her wineglass with a long red nail, demanding that it be refilled, and her designer obeyed instantly, but not before he stole a glance at Suzanne in the mirror. Whether there was really any pause in the babble of conversation or not, Monsieur Paul looked up, left his foursome to a captain, and went to greet Suzanne.

She allowed him to bend a kiss over her hand, then followed him through the aisle. To make room for her passage, waiters snapped to attention, but she took her time. She sent a distant wave to an old lover at a table she could not reach. She stopped beside a table where four men had to abandon the intricacies of their deal for her smiling approval, and to introduce to her the only one she had not met. She paused again to promise the senator's wife at the next table to compare notes within the week. At last she focused the blaze of her attention at the banquette where I stood waiting, napkin in hand. She still was not quite ready to let her court resettle itself to its pleasures. She wanted both her cheeks kissed, and then she took my hands in so firm a grip that I could not move, stepped back half a pace as if to get a better view, and convinced Monsieur Paul that I had not changed a bit. For Monsieur Paul's crowd it made a charming scene, not dissimilar, I was to understand, to being chosen from the lists for knighthood.

She settled into our banquette without pausing in her enthusiasms. She kept Monsieur Paul waiting in attendance, and he apparently was willing to let the balance of his customers go if only
Suzanne would improvise some little drama for him—perhaps
even with a speaking line of his own. His expectations soared
when she would not order a drink until she had consulted his
menu. Using it as her only prop, and brushing back the deep red
coils of hair from her brow, she concocted with great economy a
pretty scene, conveying to him that some mysterious voyage was
about to begin, an escape to secret islands, a journey postponed
too often—yes, that was it: we were about to embark on the first
adventure she had been able to arrange for us both for some
time. Surely such a departure required at least champagne,
didn't Monsieur Paul agree?

Having established for him that lunch was to be a drama, and
without waiting for his consent, she explained that more than
five years had elapsed without a single secret passing between us
—didn't Monsieur Paul agree that was far too long? She made
him smile and shake his head at my folly, and as soon as he had
played the part she had assigned him, she let him go with an
order for white wine. He left us, convinced he had chosen the
wine himself, to go with gray sole amandine—the best of all the
possibilities he had considered for her.

Then she sent waves of gaiety in my direction, and soon we
were both laughing at the silly histories we had made of our
lives. There was no question, in her opinion, that the more ma-
ture man, the man with some experience, the man who could be
"serious," was really after all the most attractive man to every
woman: didn't I realize how important that was?

Since I was being enveloped in her perfume—it was still Calèche—none of these emanations of charm and flattery seemed to
be a bit exaggerated. Her eyes gave every assurance of vital concern for my welfare. They searched my own relentlessly, without
shyness. If they seemed a bit brilliant with delight, or if what really lay beneath those long, dark lashes was flecked with pep-
pery amusement, it didn't matter at all—she was just as fascinating as she had always been.

I could remember when freckles had spread across the bridge
of that straight nose, distributed in a thin band from one high

cheekbone to the other; but the freckles had long since been subsumed under the incredible complexion for which they must have been the harbingers. Strawberries and cream was the cliché, but she could have been colored by one of Disney's artists, and it was her extraordinary complexion that had earned her the nickname "Snow White."

There had been a time when Suzanne, a.k.a. Snow White, had also been known as "Rapunzel." The nicknames she had earned were suggested by the obvious: she had thick, lustrous, dark red hair that was once so long it fell below her hips. Since then, her necessities had changed. She no longer wore hair that could be uncoiled like that of a princess in a tower, but set it in loose waves to the shoulder, a style almost suitable for a suburban matron. It still framed with its russets her advantages: a complexion of moist pearls, hard brown eyes, an apparently generous mouth, and even, white teeth she bared for her untamed laughter.

Despite the fame of her beauty, and all its uses, she had learned to carry it easily, as if it were no more than one of the many costumes she put on. There had never been anything frail about her, and she had never pretended to any man there might be. She was an athlete in the way she moved. Her breasts were small and firm, her back and neck just a shade too long, and her shoulders slightly too broad, because they were strong. To describe her as boyish in figure would be to distort the picture entirely, but she did give the impression that any man who wanted her would have a chase to run, and that the only men to catch up would be those for whom she chose to pause.

She had always walked fast, with a combination of a glide and a slight hesitation, as often seen in the peculiar walk of sprinters or hurdlers. Her long calves and tapered knees were not at all like a dancer's. She loved movement for its own sake—all the free rides like skiing, surfing, water-skiing, as well as swimming and skating and tennis and dancing—because she guessed that if there was any center to her at all—if she thought about it—it was the location, the nucleus, of some mysterious energy. If she sensed that this ancient force had been concentrating itself within her as each successive year had passed, and if it ever frightened her, it was also the source of certain advantages.

For example, many of her admirers would not believe she had

reached thirty; others said she was "near thirty"; and some
guessed she was well past thirty. These guesses were all based
upon reasonable external evidence, and the only lines on her
face were the crow's-feet that appeared at the corners of her eyes
when she was amused. But guessing her age from external details was like guessing the age of an Abyssinian cat: nothing on
the surface had anything whatever to do with the essential mystery—she was only the immediate example of something like five
thousand years of continuous development. Anyway, I knew she
was forty when we began to see each other again in 1970, because when we were both sixteen we used to tell each other that
I was an "older man." Since I was born in May 1930, and Suzanne not born until September 21, but in the same year, it was a
lovers' joke exchanged between innocents in the teeth of the
facts. In the evergreen optimism of our youth we had loved the
potentials of Suzanne's strange charm.

At lunch that October we laughed again at summers past until
Monsieur Paul reappeared with his cart of sweets and pastries.
Then it seemed that Suzanne had accomplished all her introductions. With coffee it turned out that the "incredible story"
she had promised by telephone would be none other than her
own. She wanted me to help her write her biography: didn't I
think that would be an amusing idea?

Of course it would, but I could foresee some practical difficulties.

She swept them aside. She would not be put off by a list of the
problems the events of her career might raise. She was determined; she said she would be delighted by the scandals she
might create. She laughed and tossed her head the way she always had when light glanced from the foaming crest of one of
her own inventions.

"I don't care if it is all true," she said. "I want to leave something behind me. Something permanent. I have never fallen in
love, and I have never written a book. Those are the only two
crimes which have escaped me."

I suggested that we might make a novel of it, fictionalizing the
main characters in such a way that no harm would be done. Besides, by treating her story as a novel, the romance of her career
could eventually be turned into a marvelous movie.

She would have none of that. She wanted history, what she said would be a "proper biography," and she was prepared to argue that if secretaries of state who had accomplished nothing, and chairmen of corporations who were no more than vain, and songwriters and aging actresses, and even companies like Bell Telephone could have their histories set down, then she had a right to one of her own.

"What I have to say," she concluded, "is more truthful about how we live than their silly stories."

In any event, playful fencing was over: she had come to lunch prepared. It was soon obvious that her intelligence network had supplied just about all she would need to carry out her objective. She had probably spent no more than thirty minutes calling her sources to collect the information about my divorce. She had gathered up an estimation of how many evenings I spent "just reading."

"You won't find what you are looking for by reading all those books. Anyway, you should leave something permanent too."

She knew I had the necessary freedom, and she had at least some detail—all that was necessary—about every woman I had seen over the past six months. She tossed the mass of red hair again and laughed at me; giving me time, I suppose, to consider all the adventures I had not yet attempted. She was even prepared to analyze my restlessness at work: wasn't it a fact that after a few years, every senior editor at a newsweekly could easily get "depressed"?

She rephrased "depressed," softening it to "a bit bored," as if she were allowing me to plead guilty to a lesser charge, rather than stand trial. Yet the essentials of her indictment were perfect, and she was happy to summarize them: the business of weekly journalism was an endless cycle, every Thursday another middle-class crisis invented for the week, always solemn and judicious in its opinions, "instant bourgeois history, packaged for your subscribers like so much Velveeta cheese. Just the same," she allowed, "you are afraid at the moment to give it up, but you wouldn't have to, don't you see? We will meet only on Saturdays for a few hours."

After that she had clear sailing. As to the practical difficulties, she agreed: "If we must fictionalize it, or at least disguise the important people, we will—if you decide that would be more sensible." By then it was nearly five o'clock and Le Magistral had emptied, its staff already setting up for the theater crowd. Only Monsieur Paul remained to attend our exit. Outside, in the gale beneath the canopy on Fifty-second Street, we agreed to begin the next Saturday on what she called "our biography."

By the end of October, I had settled into playing her court historian. Our collaboration was soon routine. At two o'clock every Saturday afternoon I presented myself at her penthouse apartment on the twentieth floor of 30 Central Park South. In the beginning I was met at the elevator doors by her secretary, Margaretta, and shown directly to the library. After I was an accepted visitor, I was sometimes met by her maid, Nicole; or by James Moriarity, her chauffeur and bodyguard. I would arrange the campaign desk in the library with my notebooks and the tape machine, and Suzanne would walk in, give me a kiss, make earnest inquiries about my health and happiness, then take her place on the blue velvet couch. She would start talking for the tape recorder exactly where we had ended the Saturday before.

She had arranged to have no interruptions, she never wasted a moment, and she seemed intent on finishing. From time to time I would interrupt her to ask questions if it seemed to me she was wandering too far or if I believed she was lying. At exactly four o'clock Nicole would appear with the tea tray. Suzanne poured, then we would continue until five o'clock. We rarely ran past our deadline, but on one occasion she brought in her daughter, Angelique, who was then nineteen, for introductions. Later I asked Suzanne whether she didn't think her biography might be a source of embarrassment to Angelique, and I remember distinctly that her answer was a scathing, "Why should it?"

Between our sessions, I used the research facilities at the magazine to check the names, dates and places, because the accuracy of her story began to be something of an obsession. I would dig through published materials or morgue materials to check on her. The amount of time I spent "just reading" at home increased considerably. During the Christmas holidays, we missed two Saturdays, and we missed three in a row in February when she took Angelique skiing. By May 1971 we had met twenty-five times; I had seventy-six hours of tapes, eighteen spiral-bound college theme books of my own notes, plus a considerable accumulation of related materials stored in five cardboard cartons.

I have no reason to doubt Suzanne's original intention to complete her "book project." She simultaneously commissioned Enrique Cardinale to draw the plans for what she called her "museum" in Saratoga. In the same way I had been engaged that fall to play the part of her biographer, Enrique was playing the part of court architect. We began work at about the same time: October 1970—sufficient proof, it seemed to me, that her purposes then required the services of both an architect and a historian.

The only difference was that Enrique could, and did, complete her "museum" in secret. By May 1971, however, both Suzanne and I knew that her biography had no chance of being published, precisely because no publisher would risk the libels her truths would raise. In any case, she finally did fall in love that year—with André de Montreuil—and perhaps from her point of view one crime superseded the other. They were married November 2, 1971. The arrival of de Montreuil marked the end of Suzanne's devotion to "history."

After her strange funeral I discovered something in my notebooks—something she said after tea one Saturday afternoon. At the time, I believed it unimportant. My notes show we were in the middle of an entirely different topic—an account of her success in suborning judges—when she suddenly veered off in a new direction: "After we die, I suppose, we must have a very different view of things, if we have any view at all. Don't you think that would make a marvelous business—some sort of service for the dead?"

I had not yet caught up with her.

"Well, something halfway between lawyers, who collect a fee for reading off the last will and testament of the deceased, and Western Union, which sends flowers and telegrams with good wishes to the mourners. I should think in many instances bad wishes would be a much better business."

As she warmed to the idea she began to decorate it: she changed its name from Posthumous, Inc., to The Repository, Inc. She was delighted with the idea that it might be advertised as "The Company That Will Give You the Last Word." She was intrigued by the possibilities she could envision: there would have to be a schedule of variable fees, depending upon the difficulty of the request, but the fees could be agreed upon in advance. The contracts would cover the performance of tasks for the dead that they couldn't, or wouldn't, do for themselves while they lived. For example, a man could turn informer with impunity after he was dead. "Take the case of a racketeer who wanted to tell the district attorney how to prosecute: he couldn't do that while he lived, because he would be afraid of being rubbed out, wouldn't he?"

Suzanne was sure The Repository could get an impressive board of directors: men who were above reproach, perhaps a respected district attorney, and a minister, and a doctor of philosophy from some university. Didn't I see the advantage of the whole thing? The living can never reply to those who are laughing at them from beyond the grave. "For example, we would charge no more than a minimum fee to wives who wanted to inform their husbands about the true identity of the father of each child. Wouldn't that be fun?"

Beyond the entertainment it provided her that afternoon, I didn't think she had pursued the idea. It appeared as an aside—an unexplained meander—in my tapes and notes. They lay untouched—my private morgue—until Suzanne was reported drowned.

2

Memento

1976

THE *Daily News* reported that she had drowned late Saturday night, August 28, 1976, "in the private lake on her summer estate near Saratoga Springs, N.Y." On Monday, local and state police were said to be "investigating the mysterious circumstances of her death," and the lake had been drained in an unsuccessful attempt to locate her body, "which has not yet been found." Despite confusion in the early reports about exactly what had happened, and the obvious fascination of the *News* with "society beauty's death still not determined," no follow-up stories appeared after the coroner's report was accepted Tuesday: "accidental death by drowning." The *News* gave her age as forty-two in the obituary, on page three Tuesday morning.

The New York *Times* gave her age correctly—as forty-five—but ignored the mysterious details of her death. Instead, on Tuesday morning the *Times* ran a prim and proper obituary, as dull and dreary an entry as any listing in Who's Who, and perhaps largely taken from it. The obituary might have been written by a young reporter attempting to sharpen his skills, or perhaps by a rewrite man with an idle hour on Monday afternoon. The materials in the *Times* morgue were probably thin, and the editors apparently believed she belonged in the minor orders of fame. She had avoided controversy, she was not sufficiently eccentric—at least not publicly—she had always been shy of accepting certifications of public acclaim, and so it appeared she was not famous enough to be graced by flashes of perception in a handcrafted obituary written by Alden Whitman.

Instead she appeared under the headline "Countess de Montreuil Dead. Leader in Many Civic Affairs." A sober report containing no more than the bare facts followed. She had died Saturday in Saratoga at age forty-five. She was born Suzanne Benson, September 21, 1930, in New York. She was the daughter of the late Mr. Porter C. L. Benson, an investment banker, and of the late Mrs. Porter (Mary Hadley Stewart) Benson, of Boston and socially prominent in New York.

The *Times* noted that Miss Suzanne Benson had made her debut at the Junior Assemblies in New York in December 1947; that as the Countess de Montreuil, she had been active in business, in politics, and in the city's charities, and had entertained frequently. In addition to her home in New York City, she maintained houses in Nassau, the Bahamas, on Q Street in Georgetown, Washington, D.C., and during the thoroughbred racing season, near Saratoga Springs, New York.

Two paragraphs followed with a conventional listing of the corporations of which she had been an officer or director. Their names were so obscure that their cumulative significance was easily lost. Many appeared to be related to real estate, but the list also included two small state banks, a public relations company, a corporation evidently in the business of selling cut flowers both wholesale and retail, and several investment corporations with names that could have been interchangeable.

The succeeding paragraphs summarized her political associations, and they gave a better approximation, by inference, of her civic activity. She had served as a committeewoman for the New York State Democratic party and had been a delegate to several national conventions. She had served as a member of the party's State Caucus Committee. For the sake of the Democratic party she had served as an adviser to: the National Committee for Court Reform; the New York State Welfare Conference; the New York State Civil Service Commission; the State Commission

for Prison Reform; and the New York World's Fair Advisory
Committee. In addition, she had been a member of the White
House Conference on Education, 1958–68; the President's Ad-
visory Committee on International Relations, 1961–63; and an
Advisory Committee to the Commissioner of Internal Revenue,
1960–68.

One paragraph summarized her charities and academic associations, and the list was typical of any successful city woman: the
Garden Club of America, the Horticultural Society of New York,
the American Crafts Council, the Business Committee for The
Arts, the Association for Aid to Crippled Children, United
Cerebral Palsy, the chairmanship for two years of a Red Cross
corporate fund-raising committee, and a committee place on
three charity balls. Like many others who had made quick fortunes, she appeared as a trustee of two obscure colleges, one in
Maine and the other in Ohio.

Her survivors were her husband, Count André de Montreuil; a
daughter by a previous marriage, Miss Angelique Lyle; and a
sister, Mrs. Stanley Hutchinson. At the bottom of the column, funeral services were announced as private and scheduled for
eleven o'clock, Wednesday, September 1, at St. Thomas More's
R.C. Church, East Eighty-ninth Street. "Contributions to the
Harkness Pavilion, Columbia Presbyterian Medical Center, were
requested by the family in lieu of flowers."

Yet St. Thomas's dainty country-Gothic church could barely
contain the flowers that had arrived by Wednesday morning.
Nor did there seem to be anything private about the occasion.
By eleven o'clock the crowd present resembled the mob at one
of those media funerals so popular with the six o'clock TV news.
Every pew was filled. Behind the railing in the back of the
church, every space that might contain mourners was occupied. Late arrivals stood on the steps outside the church. There
were no TV cameras present, but St. Patrick's Cathedral would
have been a better choice. Perhaps de Montreuil had not expected so many to abandon summer vacations and return to the
city for an event in the week before Labor Day. Perhaps St. Patrick's had not been available to him: no one could have presented a shred of evidence, as far as I know, that Suzanne was,
or ever had been, a Roman Catholic.

Fortunately de Montreuil had arranged to have the New York Police Department on duty. A half dozen blue uniforms were doing their patient best to create some order among the line of arriving limousines, or at least arrange matters so that when the services ended, the funeral cortege would be able to get out of Eighty-ninth Street. Since I arrived a minute late myself, I had the opportunity to see an ambassador to the United Nations and then the governor of New York arrive at the steps of the church, be let out of the depths of their limousines by their chauffeurs, but have no place to go except to edge into the jam on St. Thomas's steps with others in black suits and black hats and black dresses. Mingled among the mourners on the steps were other chauffeurs in black caps who had successfully double-parked their Mercedes around the corner—somewhere on Park Avenue.

Drivers and celebrities stood together in the sun, some murmuring responses to the congregation's intonations barely heard through the open doors. Unable to advance through the crowd at the doors of the church, I reversed my field and cut through the rectory entrance. I squeezed into a place along the jammed east wall next to Frank Fitzgerald, staff director of the National Committee for Court Reform. We exchanged nods. Suzanne had supported his organization for a number of years: raised money for him, given cocktail parties for his benefit in her penthouse, organized the committee's annual dinner at the Waldorf. She had once explained to me that she thought it was "smart money to support all the good-government causes, regardless."

Frank grabbed my elbow between his thumb and forefinger—the accomplished politician's confidential grip—gave me the big wink, and whispered that he had counted "twenty-seven judges in here. That's half your story."

Frank's success was always the big wink: passing on a secret everyone already knew to confirm to them the singularity of their own importance. Maybe Frank had counted right. He'd have been the one to know. I could recognize only four judges, but I exchanged nods with Sean Murphy in the nearest pew. By his own account, Sean was "the world's greatest jewel thief."

There could be little doubt that everyone else was occupied in much the same way: looking for faces they would recognize at a major public event. Although they all held in their hands the pamphlet provided by the church so they could follow the requiem mass and make the appropriate responses to the priest's incantations, their responses were ragged at first, distracted by inspections of each other's attendance. When the priest sang out the final words of a prayer, heads bowed down in unison to the pamphlets at hand, searching for the appropriate "Amen." Then one head after another came up again to continue counting the house.

Their responses to the priest improved as the mass spun on. They were, after all, accustomed to appearances at public ceremonies. They were present to propitiate fate, and so they conducted themselves with the appropriate straight-backed rectitude. They had also come out of admiration for each other. If grief lingered anywhere among them, it would be tucked away in a secret corner. They did not believe losses should be displayed. They had come not to weep but to see and be seen. Since they were all practiced survivors, they were curious, and just as often filled with wonder, about how the trick had been done. When the priest gave them the cue, the congregation of worldly success rose up to hear a reading of the Good News from the Gospel.

Once all were standing, I could no longer see Suzanne's coffin at the altar rail. Too many perfectly barbered heads and little black hats with perfect black veils intervened. But a shaft of light came down from a window to illuminate the occupants of the first pew on the right side, and I could see Angelique's bare head. It had a shape like her mother's, but Suzanne's rich auburns were softened in Angelique's hair to burnished copper highlights over honeyed gold. She had grown considerably taller than her mother, and I would have to guess she was five feet seven, maybe even a shade more. She had her mother's high cheekbones. She was lithe, and stood with a languorous ease instead of the compact athletic energy that Suzanne always appeared to be about to release. Angelique was certainly striking. She could have modeled, if she wanted to. She would be about twenty-five.

In the pew with Angelique stood her stepfather, André de Montreuil, recognizable to everyone from behind by his head of perfectly trimmed salt-and-pepper hair and by an entire inch of white, handmade French shirt collar showing above his well-tailored gray London suit. He appeared, as he always did, turned out in precisely the style the occasion required. The Count de Montreuil never failed to attend a ceremony with anything less than studied, even polished, devotion.

In the pew behind him, Suzanne's sister, Mimi, was partly obscured from my view, but I could easily see her husband, Dr. Stanley Hutchinson, M.D., Ob-Gyn. Next to "Hutch" were his sons: Franklin, eighteen; Waldo, fifteen—called "Sonny," as I remembered; and Bruce, twelve.

"The Lord be with you," said the priest as he concluded the reading from the Gospel. "And with your spirit," replied Suzanne's audience.

After consulting their pamphlets, they settled into their seats, taking another opportunity to have a look around. They were expecting to hear a sermon, some moral lesson drawn from Revelation, but there was no eulogy. The congregation had to rise again immediately to recite the Nicene Creed. When they finally were allowed to sit, they had to relocate their place in the script by observing the priest, already busy mixing the water and the wine. Since I had no pew, I remained standing along the wall, and at last I had a clear view of Suzanne's polished mahogany coffin.

Gloomy thing: Philippine mahogany, rusts and reds, sanded and varnished and polished, with bright brass rails and handles—all to be sunk in the ground? An odd thing to do in obedience to God's will—if that was what He commanded: buy a small chunk of real estate and bury an expensive box in it? What would Suzanne have made of all this?

"Silly, darling," would be my guess. "Too proper, too many long faces."

She often dismissed pretense with a wave of the hand and "Poof!" The shadowed interior of a reconstructed medieval church would have given her reasons enough for a "Poof!" Yet she would have enjoyed the show—the staging itself—of a requiem mass. She would have studied the priest's vestments: Look there, how threading with gold and trimming of white lace made the effects of the blacks even gloomier. Look how banks of blue and yellow candles flickered, and waxes floated up to mix with women's perfumes and the overwhelming sweetness of too many flowers.

Her catafalque was surrounded with a massive display of white roses—the kind of thing de Montreuil would choose. I would guess that if she'd had her choice, she'd have said daisies: "Field daisies—why not?"

Although she no longer had the opportunity to improve her staging, she'd have been proud of the crowd she had turned out and delighted by the vista of the whole lot of them down on their knees. According to the instructions given them at the beginning of the canon of the mass, they were being asked to remember in their prayers all those present and departed "whose faith and devotion to the Lord were known to Him."

It was a scene she would have savored: "Look at them! On their knees—marvelous, no?"

Offering up a sacrifice for themselves, families and friends—that's exactly how the pamphlets read: "For the good of the souls, for their hope of salvation and deliverance from all harm."

To which she surely would have answered: "Nonsense!"

It was a shame that *Women's Wear Daily* didn't cover funerals, because the gossip columnists would have been breathless at the "names" attending Suzanne's last benefit: besides the governor, and the missions represented from the United Nations, and the distinguished judges counted by Frank Fitzgerald, among those kneeling were Mr. Chairman of the Board of a communications conglomerate and his third wife; the owner of a famous art gallery and his boyfriend; the landscape artist for whom the gallery was the agent; various solemn officers of museums, of banks and of retail chains, identifiable by the practical wives they kept at their sides; an overrepresentation of smooth-faced lawyers—the sort who were involved in the delicate arbitrations necessary for pension funds, city unions, sports stadiums and tax shelters; and sprinkled among them film producers and fashion designers and public relations advisers.

Kneeling uncomfortably in one pew was the face of America, seen at seven o'clock eastern and six o'clock central every night on the network news. Not two pews away was an artist who created "happenings," seen only by an invited few in a Houston

Street loft. Directly behind the artist was a lady whose husband had unfortunately died, leaving her a fortune in mouthwash, who now spent liberally the proceeds of germ-free breath on Democratic candidates who "cared" and was therefore received as a duchess in the party's councils.

Dukes and duchesses. Princes and barons. Lords, bishops, men at arms, monsignors and petty curates, jugglers and fools of the city's empires. Scattered among these were some who perhaps had an intimate reason to love Suzanne: old Amedeo Scutari and his wife, Marina-Christina; sharing a pew with them and equally at home with the mass, Hermes Antoniadis, dealer in flowers—wizened and shriveled, well into his nineties. There were those, too, from her personal staff: secretaries, building managers and accountants she had tyrannized for years but who remained faithful nevertheless. And there were, I could see, at least two lovely representatives of what she called her "Escadron Volant," the practiced beauties of the "Green Book." The thin brunette was Diane—Mrs. Thomas Miles; the long-haired blonde was Annette—Mrs. Howard Ryan.

As the mass was nearing its end, I caught the eye of John Tallman. He was standing along the crowded west wall exactly opposite my own place. I had worked with John on a Saratoga jewel robbery story in 1966, when he was chief of the Capital District (Albany) Bureau of the FBI. We nodded to each other.

At the end of the mass the blessing was omitted, but I believe it always is at requiem masses. Instead the priest came through the gates of the altar rail and intoned a string of prayers over the coffin. Then he walked twice around the bier, sprinkling it with holy water. Then twice again, swinging clouds of sweet incense. He began the Lord's Prayer: "Our Father . . ." and the congregation picked it up. I could not help but remember that Suzanne had once said: "Do you suppose that if someone repents at the last minute, at the very last instant of life, that would count?"

I had answered her that according to the ancient doctrines of almost every faith, any repentance was supposed to be sufficient. She had laughed and said, "Fiddlesticks!"

The mass was ended. The congregation was directed to go in peace, but they had to wait until the professionals from Campbell's funeral home had gotten the coffin out the door and through the crowd that still clogged the steps. Once Campbell's men had slid the mahogany box into the hearse, her mourners could begin to disperse, nodding to each other, exchanging solemn sighs, shaking hands as if joined by death into some common bond.

They came out from the dimmed aisles into bright sunshine on St. Thomas's steps, squinting at a scene of confusion. The order of the limousines behind the hearse had been hopelessly scrambled by the city's police, and although the governor got away quickly, many of the self-important had to wait somewhat longer than they had planned for their chauffeurs. Some cars did not get away until nearly twelve-thirty, which would make their occupants late for their lunch dates.

I hung about for a moment outside the church's doors. I had time to linger: at the magazine, I was supposed to be writing a "special report" sizing up presidential candidate Jimmy Carter, but it was not scheduled until the September 13 issue. I had a week's grace before deadlines began to close in on me.

Mimi Hutchinson arrived at my side with her husband and her three sons in tow. "Thank heavens I found you. I have been unable to reach you, and both Hutch and I have tried at your office and at your home. You know you are supposed to come along with us, don't you?"

I did not, nor did I know where it was they were going.

"Suzanne left complete instructions for everything. Wouldn't that be just like her? Well, that's exactly what she did. And her instructions are quite clear that you are to be one of the witnesses—you're to be in the party going to Saratoga."

Mimi passed on the instructions with such enthusiasm that I sensed she was not as distressed by Suzanne's death as she was excited by it. Nor was there any clue in Hutch's somber manner; Dr. Stanley Hutchinson was as serious, sympathetic and thoughtful as a practicing gynecologist would have to be. Mimi's sons stood by, trained to wait politely until their mother had finished her transactions.

"We'll drive back tonight, but that will get us here quite late. Meet me at Thirty Central Park South—but of course you know exactly where. I shall be there in half an hour. There's to be a

light lunch, and we will all have a chance to prepare ourselves
for the drive. It's at least three and a half hours, you know."

I knew how long it took to get upstate, but I did not quite understand what was to take place: was there to be a burial in
Saratoga? A ceremony for an empty coffin?

"Just meet me at Thirty. We'll share a car to Saratoga—it's all
been laid on. We'll have time enough to discuss everything on
the way. I'm going to see Hutch and the boys off to Bernardsville."

She led her squad away toward Madison. I loitered for a few
moments on St. Thomas's steps to watch the stragglers, then
caught a cab at the corner of Eighty-ninth Street and went down
through the park. Mimi had achieved every objective she had set
for herself. No one could have faulted her on a single choice.
She had married the right man, obviously, a man she was convinced she could always love. In return Hutch had advanced until
he was a highly respected doctor—he worked in association with
two other men at one of the very best clinics in the city. For
Hutch she had raised three sons, and aimed them all down the
right tracks: Frank was already at Harvard, she'd said, and Sonny
at Andover, and Bruce was probably in a school that Mimi had
calculated as "just right for him." When Bruce was ready for Taft,
he'd be given the choice to go wherever he thought he'd be
happiest.

The Hutchinson home, in Bernardsville, New Jersey, was at a
distance from the city that was not too inconvenient a commute
for Hutch, despite the odd hours sometimes required of obste-
tricians. Mimi's neighbors would surely describe her house as
"couldn't be more attractive," and if the biggest bill Mimi paid
each month was from Bloomingdale's, she could argue that she
liked to keep things looking "bright and cheery." She kept herself in shape too, played tennis regularly at the club in the summer, and met Hutch twice a week in the city during the winter.
Hutch could say with a justifiable pride that Mimi had a "solid
backhand."

On the drive through the park I wondered how much of Suzanne's career Mimi knew. I was to discover that Mimi may have
lacked many details, but she understood well enough what Suzanne had been after. By the time my cab pulled up to the can-

opy it was fifteen after one. In the lobby Suzanne's secretary, Margaretta Cooper, sat at a card table facing the door. Standing at parade rest behind her was Suzanne's bodyguard, James Moriarity, his fields of fire covered. Margaretta recognized me without consulting the list of names spread out before her, and she waved me toward the penthouse express elevator. James had his make too, but he would give me no more than an impassive nod.

Coming out of the elevator into the pink-and-black marble foyer, I was surprised by a wave of loss—a nostalgia for my Saturday-afternoon expeditions in biography. Fortunately the scene in the penthouse was an entirely different ceremony from the requiem conducted at St. Thomas's. Laughter and boisterous talk bubbled across the sixty-foot living room, and the crowd, with drinks in hand and salmon sandwiches, could have been the same list to whom Suzanne had habitually introduced Democratic party hopefuls year after year. I edged my way through shoulders and elbows until I could pay my respects to de Montreuil.

The Merlin of finance stood immobile by the windows, receiving quietly each man and woman to arrive in his presence, chatting with each about some affair he knew might absorb the guest for a moment. He did it in a style they could appreciate, for they were all accomplished too, and André de Montreuil was an expert at his craft: the discreet and quiet word. He had aged.

The chairman of Providence Holding Company had placed himself with the light behind him. He stood before floor-to-ceiling windows, shut tight to take advantage of the air conditioning and creating for him a backdrop with its own circumspect and sanitary hum. Each applicant for his audience waited until those favored by his attentions moved on, and while waiting everyone could see behind the Count de Montreuil a magnificent view of the city painted across the humming windows. Under a blue-white summer sky, Central Park appeared in the center of a marvelous glass fresco, its luxuriant summer greens colored by a slight yellow haze, and its perspectives on left and right so long that the gigantic façades of Central Park West and Fifth Avenue seemed small. As they extended off somewhere into the Bronx, the effect was to imply that the city's scale was not really so gigantic after all; that if so much could be encompassed in this single view, perhaps understanding all the city's complexities would be only a matter of having the right perspective.

Against the background of this romantic vision, the Count de Montreuil easily gave each visitor the impression that every assurance should be taken literally, and that he himself had never guaranteed his good will without meaning every word he said. In honor of his wife's "passing away" he wore a black armband on his gray suit, because gray was always his color, including even the Countess Mara tie, its colors balanced exactly to impeccably neutral.

He chose the color of his wardrobe, and for that matter the color of his limousine and his chauffeur's uniform and his office carpet and walls, because he believed that tones of gray suited the effect of grave neutrality he so carefully maintained. He was sixty-five, and his eyes so pale a blue that in certain lights they, too, appeared gray—and to great effect, because their expression was absolutely flat.

He did everything, when he had his choice, precisely. He had a slight overbite, and so his smile came frequently and gave the impression that everything he heard might well be benign, which was exactly what he meant to convey. He once told me that he was five feet eleven inches tall, extending that fact with such finality that he created by the way he said it a temptation to get out a measuring tape and find out if perhaps he was really five feet ten and seven eighths. Perhaps as he had aged he had shrunk just a little, as people often do.

Yet there was no reason to doubt him: whatever he said was spoken with conscientious earnestness. As he delivered each phrase, or inquired thoughtfully into the next detail, he stood quite still, and easily. He was trim and fit. His long, delicate fingers were manicured by experts. Receiving the necessary condolences, he held a drink in his left hand as comfortably as he would have held five cards. Anyone could see that if he happened to draw to an inside straight his expression would never waver. At his side by the window, imitating his confidence because the opportunity required it, and adopting the role of hostess in her mother's place, was his golden-haired stepdaughter, Angelique.

But it was obvious that de Montreuil and Angelique were going to have to share their billing as hosts, because Enrique Cardinale had arrived. While they stood by the windows to accept the good wishes of the city's most respected men, Enrique rushed through the crowded room among the women. They had unpinned their hats and put aside their veils. They still wore the same simple little black dresses in which they had knelt in the gloomy pews, but in church it was difficult to distinguish one woman from the next. In the brilliant room, a bracelet of heavy gold links illuminated a narrow wrist; a pin of worked gold leaves caught the light on an attractive breast; a double strand of pearls decorated a neck like a swan's; and an emerald ring set on a band of tiny diamonds caught the eye. It was to these attractions that Enrique hastened.

Before each new discovery, his hands fluttered, scattering up like pigeons from a remark or a glance, then settling again before they dared reapproach. He looked as if he, too, might be in his sixties, but his apparent age was the result of weariness around the eyes, a dissolute mouth, and having his hair dyed as gray as de Montreuil's so that he would look old enough for Suzanne. He was actually only forty-six, but he had insisted gray hair would make him dignified and therefore a more suitable escort when Suzanne wanted him to appear in public with her.

For the funeral he had found a black suit, but it did not fit him, and he wore it like a costume for a part in which he knew he had been miscast. He could be heard telling one woman that he thought it was too black and that he had always been especially sensitive to color, that he had a very good color sense, and that he really liked only bright colors. Like de Montreuil, Enrique had blue eyes, but Enrique's eyes were unclouded: a baby blue, dancing with innocence and curiosity at any bright object as soon as it appeared in his field of vision. Like de Montreuil, Enrique took very good care of himself, and manicured his nails faithfully, but apparently for different reasons: Enrique's fingers were never still, always reaching to touch the newest object of fascination. Although de Montreuil was guarded, even modest, about what his business might be, Enrique would be delighted to explain to anyone who would listen that he had been trained "in architecture." Depending upon the circumstance, Enrique would be happy to modify his occupation from "architect" to "designer" if he found it necessary to certify himself as an expert on jewelry, or the printing of patterns on sheets and pillowcases, or choosing just the right colors for bedroom décor. He didn't generally emphasize it, but as a matter of fact he had also been an experienced window dresser—before Suzanne had rescued him.

According to her version, he had been a professional skater—under a different name, of course—in the chorus of the Canadian Ice Follies. While the show was playing at the old Montreal Forum in 1966, he was arrested and accused of a murder. The story came to Suzanne's attention; she arranged bail for him; and for a number of reasons the case never came to trial. Suzanne's explanation was that she didn't think Enrique had been solely responsible anyway—in her opinion the whole thing was really quite unfair. In any event, the publicity about the case had been so lurid that a fair trial would have been impossible. Her conclusion was that anyway Enrique had always been devoted to her, and he was useful, "and great fun." Since Suzanne was so often the star of her own entertainments, she needed a master of ceremonies, and Enrique gloried in the part.

For her sake he was continuing to do what he knew best: concentrating upon the women in the crowd, moving from one to another, whispering a compliment, noting some detail of fashion or costume, consenting to a confidence, arranging secret codicils to the published treaties. He interrupted his travels for a moment when he sighted me, rushing up to take my hand between both of his, and gushing how pleased he was that I was finally there. Real tears welled up in his eyes, and it occurred to me they were the first I had seen that day. Before we could both be embarrassed, he had sighted Gail Fowler. Promising that we would have a chance to talk—to have a real talk—he explained that he needed an immediate word with Gail and he was on his way again.

Mrs. Eric Fowler was an assistant editor of a glossy and oh-so-chic fashion magazine—a stylish widow in her thirties, exploiting to its limits the pleasures of her independence. She moved through a schedule of dinners and outings and openings, and was reported to have been seen on the arm of a brilliant young producer in from the Coast for a screening, or having dinner at Pearl's with an assistant secretary of commerce up from Washington for the evening. Her name appeared regularly in the gossip columns, and she had been given private lessons by Suzanne.

Although Suzanne shunned publicity for herself, because she said she had nothing to gain by it, she had taught Gail Fowler how to be all the more desirable to some men by being understood as a public property. Each mention of Gail Fowler's name in "Suzy" or *Town & Country* or *New York*, Suzanne had taught, excited the imagination not only of the lovers Gail had already passed through but of many more who had not yet called. Since there were men who needed above all the prestige of a well-known woman, Ms. Gail Fowler was one of the leading ladies of Suzanne's Green Book and a privileged member of the Escadron Volant.

Unsurprised by Gail Fowler's presence, I was confused by the appearance of Lydia Hopkins—a researcher at the newsweekly where I worked. She was, I would have assumed, out of place among Suzanne's crowd, but I had never seen her without her eyeglasses. I thought Lydia was faithfully married to Frank Hopkins, a lawyer downtown, and managing two children as well as her career, and all that. I had never heard her talk about anything except the current issues, and women's rights, and what the children were doing at school. I caught up with her at the bar, and in what I thought could be passed off as office banter, remarked upon her display of emeralds—an extraordinary bracelet with a matching pin. They were, I would have thought, somewhat beyond the range of editorial salaries, and I asked if they were family heirlooms.

Ms. Lydia Hopkins dealt a quick answer for oafish curiosity, but she was generous enough to soften her reply with an easy smile: she said she kept two uniforms, one for home games, one for away. Then she laughed at me and said I had better update my research: "Wouldn't you think Suzanne added new faces to the Green Book from time to time? Tch. Tch."

She turned away, back into the crowd. While I was getting my drink refilled, John Tallman appeared at my side at the bar. He was direct: "This a story for you?"

"Maybe. Is it a case for the FBI?"

"Maybe. Are you on assignment?"

"In a way. At a news magazine we look into many stories, even if we don't publish every one of them. Is your interest because you suspect the drowning was not accidental?"

Big John paused before he answered, turning to the bartender to refill his scotch. I remembered that while the reporters waited for developments in the Saratoga jewel-robbery story in 1966, Tallman had entertained us hour after hour with stories of the days when he had worked for a circus. He had traveled with it through the South, and he could adopt circus patter as his own, playing a roustabout or a barker for the sake of his story. And I remembered, too, how he could interview his listener as he talked, reading his suspect's eyes for reactions—a carnival trick useful to a detective.

When the bartender had fixed the scotch to John Tallman's satisfaction, Tallman picked up again in circus-patter style, mixing grins and winks with an exaggeration of the polite and deferential public servant, an FBI man mocking his own report: "The Bureau has taken an interest in this case, sir, only because it has come to our attention that in addition to the lady we honor here today, and who we were unable to find in the lake, our dredging turned up one white male, age 32, approximately five feet seven, one hundred sixty pounds, identified from prints by the Police Department of the City of Detroit as Jacob Bernstein, a.k.a. Jake Brown, a.k.a. Little Jake, charged once grand larceny, auto, three times on murder one, but no convictions."

Tallman ended this piece of news with a bow, sweeping his hand and arm as if inviting me into his imaginary tent, all with a half grin.

"O.K., John. In other words, a hit man?"

"Exactly, sir. Exactly. When we pumped the place out, we found no lady in the lake, but instead we found this-here-knight-from-the-Detroit-roundtable, drowned to death but still clutching a United States Army forty-five-caliber-automatic."

"Fired?"

"No. Not fired."

"So the lady was not shot."

"Apparently not by Jake Brown."

"What else?"

"Nothing else, like I said, for now, Mr. Editor. How are you doing the story—as a national event for the magazine, or as a friend of the family?"

I tried to explain that I wouldn't necessarily do the story at all. John Tallman had me there: "Ah, c'mon."

I didn't understand how the hit man got himself drowned. Tallman's answer did not clear the matter up: "Mr. Brown got himself caught inside the Countess's temple, and apparently could not find his way out."

"What was he doing in there?"

"Chasing her, as I understand it."

"He chased her into the temple, and then couldn't get out before he drowned? What the hell is that story, John?"

"That appears to be about right, sir. That's how we reconstruct it."

"Well, then, what evidence is there that she drowned?"

"The coroner's report, Mr. Editor. And it's official."

"Based on what?"

"Eyewitness reports."

"Whose?"

"Your friends Mrs. Burns, Mr. Cardinale, Mrs. Burns's friend Adam Shepherd."

"You're telling me something, Agent Tallman."

"No sir, I'm not. I thought you might tell *me* something."

"You mean she might still be alive—she hasn't—she didn't drown at all?"

Before Agent Tallman could supply any further details, Suzanne's sister, Mimi Hutchinson, reappeared. Although I introduced them to each other, Mimi was not interested in Agent Tallman from the Federal Bureau of Investigation. She was arriving with marching orders.

Everything was running late, she said, and she thought I should be sure to go to the bathroom, because we were going to be escorted all the way to Saratoga by the state police and they were not going to stop. I was to meet her in the lobby. I was to ride with her in the second car. There would be just the two of

us, since Hutch had taken the boys home. "It's just not necessary
for them to attend this kind of thing. You have ten minutes to be
downstairs."

Others had apparently received the signal simultaneously, creating a delay at the elevator until de Montreuil was summoned.
He spoke up, requesting that those who were going to Saratoga
be allowed to depart first, and that all others step back for a moment. He apologized that there was only one elevator. He was
sure everyone would understand the necessity of getting the funeral cortege on its way. He directed those who were doubtful to
consult Mr. Cardinale: Enrique had in his hand Suzanne's own
instructions regarding who should attend the ceremonies in Saratoga. He said Suzanne had left behind explicit instructions in
case of her death: "As you all know, it was just the kind of thing
she would do." He assured everyone that Suzanne would have
wanted them all to attend, but she had thought out the limita-
tions of the facilities, and the great distance, and since these
were her very own instructions, he was certain everyone would
agree to abide by her wishes.

The elevator filled with the first load of those checked off
Enrique's list, and disappeared for the street. Again the Count
de Montreuil announced to those waiting that anyone on the list
for Saratoga should depart immediately. He soothed those who
would remain behind—it simply would not have been practical
to include all of Suzanne's many friends. He announced that he
himself would not be going to Saratoga, that he would keep
company with those who had to stay in the city, that in fact he
would be grateful to those friends who would linger with him
for a while, "right here in the apartment Suzanne loved so well."
When the elevator returned, de Montreuil gave Angelique a
farewell kiss before he dispatched her on the same descent in
which I had squeezed as a passenger.

It was two-thirty by the time our cavalcade pulled away from
the curb on Central Park South. We moved toward the West
Side in a string of limousines behind an escort of sirens and
flashing lights on three motorcycles and a lead car—state police,
Mimi assured me smugly, provided by the governor. By three
o'clock our convoy had picked up the hearse, which waited for
us at the George Washington Bridge plaza. By three-thirty we

were being waved through the toll gates on the New York State Thruway. At the speed we traveled, we were probably picking up lost time on the schedule.

Enrique and Angelique were the only two passengers in the lead car, and Mimi and I shared the car that followed them. Behind us, I would guess there were fifteen more cars filled with passengers, some black limousines provided by the mortician and others privately owned, all with their headlights turned on to indicate their immunity to the speed limit. I wondered if Suzanne had expected to die—there were so many instructions for everyone.

"No, I don't think she expected it," Mimi answered, "but you know how she was: she was always preparing for everything. She left a packet of letters, all very exact, with— Here, see for yourself; this is the one for you."

From her purse Mimi took a cream-colored envelope. Suzanne's initial was embossed on the back, and my name was on its face in Suzanne's script. When I had opened it, the card inside read:

> Mon petit lapin blanc,
> Now you can publish, or perish.

It was signed with her "S," and underneath her signature she had added in parentheses an afterthought: "President, The Repository, Inc."

I saw no reason not to hand it to Mimi. Her reaction at first was to ask me if it was one of Suzanne's secret jokes. I explained that it was only partly a joke, and described something of our interrupted biography—the Saturday afternoons on tape.

Mimi was distressed at any biography: "You know, of course . . . surely you know what an habitual liar she was."

I had to agree with her, but I pointed out that I had checked nearly everything Suzanne had spun into the tapes, and I was reasonably sure of the accuracy of most of it. In any case, I would check again every piece of her story, and I would certainly be grateful for the details that Mimi might add, especially about their childhood.

"That won't do. My sister just loved to lie. She would lie for the fun of it. She would lie when there was no need to lie. I could never understand it."

I could guess what Mimi feared, and so we watched the Thruway speed past for a while. Mimi had devoted her life to doing all the right things. She had built her Bernardsville nest stick by stick with an absolute certainty about what was "proper." She had always been shocked by Suzanne's heresies, and frightened by them, but Mimi could tolerate them as long as she never had to admit she knew about any of it. She thought the New York *Times* obituary had covered everything quite sensibly. Wouldn't that do?

Her second line of argument came up along a rising curve of anger: "The story of Suzanne's life should be suppressed. Look here: it won't do anyone a bit of good now, and it could do many people lots of harm. She's dead. She's gone. Why should she have the right to create trouble even after she's dead? Why should my sons have to have their schoolmates, or anyone else, whisper about them behind their backs?"

I didn't think anyone would. I didn't think she need worry a bit; neither she nor Hutch nor her sons were involved in Suzanne's adventures, and no one would have the right to make them guilty by association. Anyway, I thought she was overrating the whole thing. Even if I did complete Suzanne's biography, there were many stories like Suzanne's appearing every day, and within a week or a month they were soon forgotten and gathering dust.

She was unimpressed.

I took a chance and asked her what gift Suzanne had left to the family of Dr. and Mrs. Stanley Hutchinson of Bernardsville, New Jersey.

She considered her answer for some time, and then, wearied by alternatives, finally answered: "I suppose you'll find out anyway. Three trust funds of five million dollars each for my sons, to be managed by the Bank of New York."

We traveled the rest of the Thruway in silence, each in a separate soft corner of the limousine. As we turned off the Northway at the second Saratoga exit, she leaned across and patted my hand. "All right. The fact is I've always . . . well, done is done. . . . I suppose I've really always envied her, and if you must know, there are days now in Bernardsville when I wonder if she didn't have the right idea all along." She added that if I needed details she would help: diaries, albums of old photos, some clippings, wedding pictures, "and that kind of thing, up until Dick Lyle died."

If Mimi had never had all her sister's charm, she must have once been able to do a good imitation of it. Mimi's thick brown hair and occasional rosy blush were reflections of Suzanne's deep reds and pale whites, but the same brown eyes that Suzanne had flashed with black challenges appeared in Mimi ready to make peace. The energy Suzanne always displayed flickered dimly in her younger sister, and it could be said that, having accomplished all that custom and tradition had required of her, Mimi now waited patiently with nature's fires banked. She smiled at some interior dialogue, and shared it when I said her offer of details on Suzanne was generous: "Oh, hell, you're probably right. Nothing will ever wake up Bernardsville."

As we drove through old Saratoga, she asked our chauffeur to turn off the air conditioning. We rolled down our windows, and the resins of Adirondack pine sweetened the air. When our cavalcade passed down Union Avenue we had a glimpse of the old race track on our left, and I was prompted to say something to the effect that Suzanne certainly loved the horses. Mimi shrugged. "She loved every gamble."

In the center of Saratoga we had to pause at the stop light by the Adirondack Trust Company. Getting through the left turn at the light our string of cars broke into sections, and so on the far side of town on Route 9N we stopped again by Stewart's Dairy until the convoy could be reassembled. At Stewart's our escort of state police left us, and we went on without them along the narrow Adirondack blacktop roads. We turned left at South Corinth and began the climb to Suzanne's farm. We drew up to the entrance of the main house and alighted before double front doors in shining black enamel and polished brass, tended by a butler. Above the doors there was a magnificent American eagle, originally carved for a clipper ship's prow, with arrows clutched in both sets of his talons.

The passengers from the city were directed by the butler to bathrooms where they could "freshen up." A maid escorted the ladies up an oak staircase to the guest suites on the second floor. The men were to use the powder room downstairs, just off the library. We were told we could gather in "the old bar" at our convenience. By then it was six o'clock, and we were reminded to present ourselves upon the lawn at the back of the house at "six-thirty promptly."

A plaza ran across the length of the back of the house, with a low granite wall and plantings along its balustrade, but it was interrupted in its center by a grand staircase which descended to the lawn itself. From the staircase, the lawn sloped away gently for about one hundred yards to the edge of the sizable lake, and by six forty-five some sixty men and women were disposed across the sloping lawn. One or two groups of those waiting were composed of five or six talking together, but most held themselves separate from each other in twos and threes. By then the sun sent long shadows extending from each cluster of shoes half hidden in the grass. In most cases the shadows would not stretch far enough to connect one group to the next, and so the distances between them were exaggerated.

If those waiting had looked behind them, their perspective from downhill up the sloping lawn would also have exaggerated the height of the balustrade running along the plaza at the back of the house. They would have understood how the house had been placed upstage upon the brow of the hill, how the balustrade and its plantings formed the front of the stage, and where the footlights were hidden. But Suzanne's audience had turned their backs to her house.

They studied instead the lake which spread from the lawn below them. On its far side they could see a low modern building, almost concealed by pines, sided in weathered cedar, with skylights set in a two-story tower—what Suzanne had called the "studio." Rising above it, an old, slope-shouldered Adirondack mountain loomed—thick with pines and gathering long shadows into her folds before settling down for another weary night. Running out from the spot at the mountain's base where the studio nestled in the pines, a road appeared on the far side of the lake at the spectator's right, then came across the top of the dam that contained the lake, then disappeared again on the near side, curving away behind the barns at the extreme right hand of the view.

The road was blacktopped and fit exactly the width of the dam it crossed. The dam was the earth-fill type, its slopes faced with riprap of granite blocks and timber, except near the center, where the road bridged a sluice constructed of concrete abutments and doors of steel. The four gates of the sluice stood open above water level, and it was obvious that the dam was filled nowhere near to its lip: the lake's waters poured away over the sills of the sluice, rushing to catch up with the stream that fell far below. Inevitably the eye traveled from the height of the water at the bottom of the dam's gates to the height of the lake lapping at the low shore of a pretty little island set in the lake's center. From the lawn, the island was about a half mile away, but even if distances over water deceived, the island appeared to be so low that if the dam's gates were closed, it must be inundated.

At the extreme left of the view the lake narrowed, then disappeared around a corner that hid the stream that fed it, and so the eyes of all those upon the lawn were drawn again to the island in the center. As dusk advanced from the east, the old mountain cast down her reflection upon the lake's glassy surface, and the black mirror of water made a vivid contrast to what could only be described as a brilliant white temple on the little island. Even at a half mile's distance it was an impressive structure, with a radius of at least one hundred feet, perfectly circular, with slender columns around its perimeter supporting a flat white roof. No entryway or doors could be distinguished in its façade: they must have been hidden by the circle of columns; and although its design might have been drawn from classic sources—especially in the use of white marble—it gave the sense of being in the center of itself; just as modern a museum as Suzanne would have demanded.

Like everyone else waiting on the lawn, I was fascinated by the sight of it rooted to the spot in a kind of dreamy contemplation. I stood alone because I had been abandoned by Mimi from the moment we arrived. She had said she would have to change her costume. Absorbed by my speculations about Suzanne's temple, I was startled by John Tallman at my elbow, and I jumped.

"Easy does it," he said. "Want to know how it worked?"

I most certainly did.

"Right. In the house up there, in the countess's bedroom, there's a control panel. It's in her desk. By inserting a key to unlock the controls, and then merely turning a switch, the gates of the dam over there can be closed. The sluice doors are pulled up by cables—the motors are electric, just like a draw bridge. As soon as the sluice gates start up, so does the water, and presto, as the level of the lake rises that pretty little temple is flooded and disappears entirely beneath the lake."

I looked again at Suzanne's temple: that was the "museum" she had commissioned Enrique to design at about the same time she wanted me to write her biography. John Tallman answered my question before I could ask it: "Yes, the water comes up fast. Which explains why a hit man from Detroit might get trapped and drowned inside."

But it did not explain how, or whether, Suzanne had also been trapped and drowned—if she was.

Again John was ahead of me: "That's right, Mr. Editor, she might still be alive."

"Then, this is all—that funeral at St. Thomas More"—I couldn't help but laugh at the idea, it was so typical of Suzanne—"all this folderol is nothing but a charade!"

"Perhaps," John said. "Perhaps. We have the sworn testimony of Mrs. Burns, Enrique Cardinale and Adam Shepherd that they saw Suzanne enter her temple, that Jake Brown rowed out into the lake after her and also entered the temple, that the sluice gates of the dam were then closed by persons unknown, and that the water then rose up."

"The Repository, Inc.," is what I said.

"What?" John asked. When I didn't answer, he provided the obvious question: "Want to know how many keys there are?"

I did.

"One."

"Who used it?"

"Unfortunately, sir, the Bureau has been unable to answer your question. On Saturday night any number of her good friends could have used the key. All deny doing so. When we wanted to drain the lake Sunday morning, Enrique showed us where the key was—just where it should have been, hung on a hook beside her desk in her bedroom. We used it ourselves—no problem, emptied the lake by lowering the sluices, took the boat out to the temple, and found Jake Brown about halfway into the center of the place with the forty-five in his hand. There was mud in there of course, but it's all been cleaned up. Since Sunday, that Enrique has had a crew working day and night. But no body."

"In a case where there's no body, doesn't the coroner usually have to delay—to make sure the deceased is dead and gone?"

"Yes, that would be it, usually. In this case, however, there seemed to be a number of important people who'd just as soon have your countess declared officially dead. And if she had any objections, she had time to state them, if you see what I mean."

"The local coroner was impressed by the opinions of powerful folks from the city, John?"

"I would say that he had been impressed to make up his mind without delay."

"And so in the opinion of the FBI what we have here is a case in which death may have been accidental but perhaps was not, and a woman who if she was not murdered may be having a grand time somewhere, which we will know about if she shows up but which we won't if she doesn't."

"That's about the size of it. Want to know what's inside the white marble temple?"

I certainly did.

"You're never going to believe it."

I assured him I was quite prepared to believe what was inside, but before Tallman could tell me what he had seen, we heard a bell—like a dinner bell—begin to tinkle. Along with everyone else, we turned to look back at the house, where the sound of the bell was getting louder. "Well, that's it," he said. "I see it's finally time for your lady love's boyfriend to do his production number. Give me a call when you get back to the city. We'll have a talk, sure enough."

He turned away, heading up the lawn with long strides toward the kitchen side of the house. As Tallman disappeared around the corner, an extraordinary procession began descending the grand staircase to the lawn. Twelve women came down

the steps two by two. They were dressed as if they were bridesmaids, in long flowing green chiffon dresses that nearly covered
green satin slippers. They wore broad picture hats decked by
wide bands of green silk ribbon that fell behind them to their
waists. Each carried a bouquet of field daisies and yellow mums
tied with matching green ribbon, and as they swayed in step together down the lawn, they smiled broadly at every man their
eyes could entice. They marched toward a little timber dock at
the edge of the lake, and as they approached it they drew the
separated groups upon the lawn in with them as if they were
pulling closed the drawstrings of a purse.

Simultaneously, the black hearse came around from behind
the barns on the right, driving across the lawn slowly, with four
sturdy mortician's men trotting beside it like secret service men
beside a President's car. The hearse stopped at the dock a moment before the bridesmaids arrived. From the front seat two
men joined the four runners, and together they lifted Suzanne's
polished coffin from the back of the hearse, carried it to the dock
and set it down.

Moored beside the dock was an odd little barge—perhaps
twenty feet long and with a beam of about six feet. It could have
been modeled from the design of a Boston Whaler, but its
varnished wood made it almost a match for the coffin. Three of
the mortician's men stepped into the barge, and after they were
ready they heaved together with the men still on the dock until
by stages they had the coffin placed in its ship. Then they all
disembarked and went trotting after the hearse as it was driven
away up the lawn.

No one had said a word. Nor was a word spoken as the twelve
bridesmaids took their places in the barge, seating themselves six
on each side, facing each other across the coffin, holding their
bouquets in their laps, and continuing to smile as if they were off
on a picnic. Since the slope of the lawn formed a kind of amphitheater for this odd scene, and since everyone's attention had
been centered upon the difficulties of getting the coffin from the
dock into the barge, no one had noticed the arrival of Enrique
Cardinale. He edged his way through his audience to the dock,
and he was the last to step into the barge, taking up a position at
the stern as if a coxswain, where—incongruously—he began to

pull on the starter cord of a small outboard motor. He was dressed as the Fool of the tarot cards, with a silly red-and-blue stocking cap, knee breeches of red and yellow, and bells at his stockings. By the time he had finally started the outboard and his crew had cast off their lines from the dock, nearly everyone on shore was smiling as broadly as the women on board. When Suzanne's ship and crew were halfway out into the lake, someone whispered a joke to a near companion and the first real laugh broke the silence of the spectators.

Jokes and gossip and talk increased steadily upon the shore, as if an orchestra were tuning up. Out on the lake the barge arrived on the island on the downstream side. At that distance, it was difficult to see clearly, but it appeared that the women had some sort of winch and cable device to help them roll the heavy coffin off the bow of the barge and into the temple. From the shore, we could see them disembark, then move back and forth at a series of tasks, then accompany the low silhouette of the coffin as it rolled toward the temple's columns. The coffin disappeared inside, the women followed it, and we waited.

Perhaps fifteen minutes elapsed. Conversation on shore was in full swing; the band of talk and chatter had struck up. If the community invited to serve as witnesses for Suzanne's last drama believed it was attending anything unusual, it was apparently already bored by the newest sensation. No one even commented upon the women designated to serve as the barge's crew. In the circumstances, I myself did not remember the order in which they had appeared in their march down the lawn, except that the first pair included Suzanne's sister, Mimi, and Suzanne's daughter, Angelique. Thereafter, the other ten included: Mrs. Ellen Burns, often called "Aunt Nellie" and well into her sixties; Miss Lucille Friedrich, always called "Miss Freddy" and in her fifties; the others were somewhere between the ages of thirty and forty, all members of Suzanne's Escadron Volant: Ms. Margaretta Cooper, Mrs. Howard (Annette) Ryan, Marie de la Rochefoucauld, Mrs. Lewis (Nadine) Reeves, Mrs. Thomas (Diane) Miles, Mrs. David (Nan Sears) Kaufman, Mrs. Frank (Lydia) Hopkins and Ms. Gail Fowler.

Out on the island we could see these bridesmaids taking their places in the barge once more. We heard the outboard kick and start. Simultaneously we heard the gates of the dam to our right begin to grind, and as we turned to look we could see the sluice doors closing, then clanging shut. No water rushed across their sills any longer. All talk among the witnesses had stopped just as finally. Before the crew of Suzanne's funeral barge had returned to shore, the lake had already risen enough to submerge the dock. Enrique had to make his way forward to the bow of the barge to hand the ladies of the Escadron off to the lawn. Everyone retreated together from the rising water. From the balustraded plaza behind the house we watched as Suzanne's white temple was going down into the waters of the lake. Behind a mountain ridge to the west the sun dropped from view, and above us the sky's night blue deepened. Within five minutes the temple had disappeared. The lake was like a mirror again; not a ripple showed anywhere on its black surface.

3

Mlle Modiste

1930-38

SUZANNE's birth certificate confirmed that she was born at 8:15
A.M., Sunday morning, September 21, 1930, in Doctors Hospital,
Eighty-seventh Street and East End Avenue, New York City. I
understand that her mother and father were filled with joy at her
birth, just as any other parents would be, and they celebrated
their daughter's arrival by observing the traditional ceremonies.
On the Saturday after Suzanne's birth she was christened at St.
James Episcopal Church, Madison Avenue and Seventy-third
Street. Then a small reception was held at her parents' apartment at 120 East End Avenue. Throughout the reception in her
honor, Suzanne slept—in a bassinet of white silks and pink bows,
on sheets of salmon lisle, and under a crocheted coverlet
trimmed in white lace. She was guarded by Rose, the new
French nurse, who agreed enthusiastically to every compliment
showered upon the daughter of Mr. and Mrs. Porter C. L.
Benson.

After making the appropriate remarks about the miracle they
had come to inspect, sixty or seventy intimate friends circulated
through the Bensons' apartment—one of those roomy, floor-sized
"flats," arranged in some twelve rooms on the sixth floor of a

grand old building. From the windows along the east side of the building, visitors could look down on Carl Schurz Park. Beyond the park they watched tugs working through the East River currents. On the far side of the river they could see the landmark they all knew well: the Pearl-Wick Hampers sign in Queens. Besides confirming the features of their landscape and being comforted by the very sensible decoration of the Bensons' apartment, all those present at Suzanne's first reception were quite certain that the baby girl they had just approved would take her rightful place, eventually, in the orderly society of which they themselves were certified examples. Indeed, not one of them would have questioned the good fortune or the credentials of any daughter of Mr. and Mrs. Porter C. L. Benson.

Suzanne's father was as tall and handsome as any father could have been in 1930; with black coarse hair, pale white skin, a good, aristocratic nose, even teeth, a broad chest, strong arms, and a kind and forgiving smile. At the age of thirty, when Suzanne was born, he had all the assurance, confidence, quiet manners and easy humor of success. He could afford his good fortune, because it came to him by inheritance, and it never required him to look back for something that might be catching up. Instead he could look ahead with confidence, because he was the product of a peculiar system, a unique education that as far as he knew had never failed: Phillips Academy, Andover, 1919; followed by Princeton, class of 1922, and membership at Princeton in the eating club of Ivy; capped by Harvard Law School, 1925, and editorship of the *Law Review* in that year. From his exemplary record at Harvard Law he stepped easily—almost as if by common consent—into a responsible position in the Foreign Department of J. P. Morgan & Company, where each day at Wall Street's "corner" he dealt judiciously with the problems presented him by Dawes Plan bonds and other European complexities. He was fluent in French, and soon managed commercial affairs well enough in German when he had to. If the pay at Mr. Morgan's bank was outrageously low, especially considering the considerable responsibilities he already carried, Porter Benson's salary could be supplemented by the dividends he drew from his own holdings in Pennsylvania, Kansas Pacific, Burlington & Chicago, and Bath Iron Works securities. By 1930, of course, his stocks and bonds were priced at fearful discounts at the exchanges upon which he traded, but Porter Benson was sure the prices of his securities must eventually recover because, as he explained, "This country is fundamentally sound."

In the long view Porter Benson's estimation of the national strengths might have been correct, but by 1930 the newspapers were reporting confusion in the national purposes. Some of the reports bordered on anarchy: distressed farmers in Iowa rioting against foreclosures, teachers battling police in the streets of Chicago over insurance, mobs surging against the locked doors of banks, and demagogues of every stripe demanding crazy schemes for change. A few of Benson's acquaintances in Wall Street had committed suicide—a pointless thing to do in his opinion, because it solved nothing. All these dislocations, he said, were temporary; and in any case, they were being sensationalized by what both Porter Benson and his wife always referred to as the "popular press," a source with a long history of inaccuracy derived from doubtful motives. The "popular press" always exaggerated. The country would survive, as it always had, "by keeping to fundamental values, and with good leadership."

In 1930 Suzanne's mother agreed wholeheartedly with her husband on the fundamental values, and for almost similar reasons. At twenty-three Mary Hadley Stewart Benson was still hopeful, because her "background," as she called it, was "the same as Porter's." She would point out, however, one minor difference: her family—the Hadleys and the Stewarts—came from Boston. It was a distinction she did not really believe she had to explain. She thought what she meant by "Boston" should be obvious in every gesture: it included the ability "to control oneself in difficult situations"; it also required ladies to sit up straight; and it was clearly indicated by the breadth of her concern for world affairs. If some peculiar twist of fate brought into her drawing room the odd stranger who did not appreciate Boston's place in history, she was surrounded by evidence she could introduce to correct his misunderstandings. Her tea set had come down to her through generations of suitable marriages. The Coromandel screen that stood in the dining room had an important history of its own. She could produce Chinese porcelains,

Japanese watercolors, an extraordinary collection of silver, and several lovely pieces of Chippendale—all of which had been unloaded on the docks of Boston or Salem from sailing ships captained by grandfathers and uncles and cousins. Nor could it be said that her understandings were shallow, because the leatherbound volumes set upon the library shelves included not only the Waverley Novels of Sir Walter Scott, not only the poetry of Pope and Byron and Keats and Shelley but also the *Meditations* of Marcus Aurelius and the *Dialogues* of Plato.

Yet she carried the weight of so much history, so many important cousins, as lightly as her husband displayed his credentials. An habitual modesty had been one of the central purposes of her education. Miss Mary Hadley Stewart had attended the Beaver Country Day School, then Abbott Academy, and had been presented at tea for her debut in Boston during the Christmas holidays in 1924. Because she had shown some talent and much diligence, she was sent off to study at L'École des Beaux Arts in Paris, where everything was arranged so that she could live with a married second cousin who had a house near the Parc Monceau. In the early part of the summer of 1926 she returned to Boston and summer vacations at her family's shingled house on Buzzard's Bay. The winter of 1926–27 passed a bit slowly for her, and she considered returning again to the Continent, but when summer came around again her social acquaintance widened satisfactorily. Then she had the good luck to meet Porter Benson when the New York Yacht Club cruise delivered him into Marion Harbor for a clambake.

They were married in Boston on a rainy Saturday, June 23, 1928. After a lazy, three-month tour of the châteaux of the Loire and three weeks in Rome, Mr. and Mrs. Porter C. L. Benson returned to New York and announced by Tiffany cards that they would be "at home" at 120 East End Avenue. During the summer of 1929 they purchased and began to remodel a "summer residence" on Centre Island, Oyster Bay, on Long Island's north shore. After Valentine's Day, 1930, Mary Stewart Benson no longer doubted her pregnancy. While waiting for September, she named the son she expected for the husband she admired so much: the boy would be Porter Benson, Jr. She had to cast about for a name in the event that it turned out to be a girl, but no name suggested itself. Only after the baby was delivered and would be a girl forever did her mother choose. A Stewart clipper-ship captain had brought back a wife from Bordeaux to Dedham, no one else in the family had ever named a child for her, and she would do. Suzanne Stewart Benson was entered in the records in the rectory of St. James in New York, christened on September 27, 1930.

Two and a half years later, March 9, 1933, a second daughter was born; she was christened Mary Hadley Benson but was always called "Mimi" to distinguish her from her mother. Various difficulties complicated both the pregnancy and the birth of Mimi. Although Mary Benson had hoped for a son, the possibility was never fulfilled. After 1938 Mary had to admit that she would have to depend upon her daughters to secure her future.

Suzanne and Mimi remembered the years between 1930 and 1938 as one long summer of golden days for golden girls, spent on sunny, hot beaches and splashing about in warm salt water. They must have passed through winters too, but what they remembered they saw from their rooms on the third floor of the house on Centre Island—a summer's view through the leafy branches of oaks and maples to the west harbor of Oyster Bay. They recalled the mornings they ran down the stairs, charging the screen doors and letting them bang closed behind them, their headlong assault carrying them across the lawn to the beach. Then they would spend the day in the sand building castles, digging tunnels and constructing dams to channel the rising tide. If the sun baked them dry, they moved into the water, surrounding themselves with fountains of splash and spray, until the skin of their fingers was all wrinkled up and Mademoiselle Rose, who stood guard over them all day, said they had to come out for a while.

As each summer was replaced by the next, they could not distinguish one from another; nor could they remember any order to their adventures. At low tide they often walked along in the smooth sand until a clam spurted, and then chased him down with clam rakes, digging frantically until they had him. They learned to row, but Mimi was always losing both oars because she would forget to ship them as she should have. From the dock that stretched out from their beach into the bay, they fished for snappers. To catch weakfish, they had to use a net, which was much more difficult. They turned horseshoe crabs upon their backs, and the thing to do was to jam their tails into the sand or else the crabs would get away. They walked a net between two poles through shallow water at high tide to catch whitebait, but catching silversides always ended up in an argument about whose pole had let the school escape. One day, having discovered that Mademoiselle Rose couldn't swim, Suzanne turned the canoe over deliberately, swam under the capsized boat and into the air pocket inside, and pretended she was staying under water forever. Mademoiselle Rose, watching from the beach, was hysterical by the time Suzanne consented to appear.

On a mooring off the beach was Daddy's Garwood speedboat, *Mlle Modiste*. He had named it for the Victor Herbert show; he could sing all the words to the song "Kiss Me Again." He sang in a beautiful tenor voice that always made their Mother dreamy. He would tell the people who came for weekends that *Mlle Modiste* was "very fast," in such a way that it would make everyone laugh, and he would explain over and over how she had been used as a rumrunner before he bought her. *Mlle Modiste* was fifty feet long, but very narrow-beamed. Her varnished brightwork gleamed because it was washed down with fresh water and a chamois every day by Cap'n Johnson. Daddy said that the engines were twin "Hall-Scotts"; that each engine had "twelve cylinders in line," and that was very important.

When Daddy decided it was "time to go for a spin," Cap'n Johnson would row out to the mooring, start the engines, and maneuver *Mlle Modiste*, all growling and throbbing and churning, into the dock to pick everyone up. If Suzanne and Mimi were quick enough, Cap'n Johnson would take them along in his rowboat and they could help him cast off. When *Mlle Modiste* was away from the dock and cutting her gorgeous wake down the bay, Suzanne and Mimi would ride on the bow, their backs against the glass of the bow cockpit, their hair flying behind them in the gale. They would have been goddesses, they knew, if only they had not been forced to wear their bulky, ugly orange life preservers.

They couldn't go unless they did; that's what Cap'n Johnson always said. He had been the captain of a real ship that had sailed on the ocean, but something happened to his ship, so he worked for Daddy. He wore white pants and a blue jacket and a captain's hat, and he had a voice like a foghorn and pretended to be all gruff and mean, but he wasn't. He let Suzanne and Mimi help him polish the brass on *Mlle Modiste* and showed them the right way to use the cotton waste, and how to avoid spilling the polish and ruining the varnish. During the week, when Daddy was in the office all day, Cap'n Johnson taught them how to sail. He waited patiently while they struggled to bend the sails on the Wee Scot sailboat which was theirs. He just sucked on his pipe while they sailed back and forth in the west harbor, and then eventually around Brickyard Point past the yacht club. In the summer of 1938, when Suzanne was seven, Cap'n Johnson declared she had won her master's ticket and was competent to handle her Wee Scot alone—with Mimi as crew—as far as the black lighthouse that marked the channel into Long Island Sound, but no farther, and provided the girls wore their life preservers. He knew, and they knew, that the moment they were out of sight around Brickyard Point, no one could enforce the life preserver rule any longer. Cap'n Johnson was Suzanne's favorite instructor.

The Benson girls had many other teachers. From Mr. Callahan they learned to swim properly at the Creek Club's pool. Mr. Callahan, they agreed, was the hairiest man there ever was. The thick mats of black curly hair that covered him from head to toe made him, in Mimi's opinion, ugly, ugly, ugly. Suzanne said that ugly did not stop Mr. Callahan from being the best swimming instructor in the whole world. He showed them how to breathe evenly with each stroke and not toss their heads, and to keep their eyes just below the level of the water and their elbows high, and to pull their hands all the way down and all the way through. They spent three hours every week improving their kick, pushing flutterboards back and forth across the Creek Club pool.

They were chauffeured to the Creek Club by James Moriarity, Daddy's chauffeur, who came back to pick them up after he had left Daddy at the Locust Valley train station in the morning. James Moriarity had been in the Marine Corps, and in a war in Nicaragua, and had been a sergeant first class, and he knew how to stand at attention better than anyone. Every time he did something different for Daddy he had a different uniform: at the breakfast table he stood at attention behind Daddy's chair with a white jacket on—that was his "mess jacket"; the moment Daddy started for the train, James disappeared, then reappeared instantly to hold open the door of Daddy's car—by then he was wearing a chauffeur's jacket and cap. Actually, Suzanne explained to Mimi, he just changed the jackets; the pants were always the same.

It was James Moriarity who took them to East Norwich to Johnny Gilbert's Riding Stable for their riding lessons. He waited for them until they had finished two hours of walking, and posting, and keeping their hands down and their backs straight and their heels down and their toes out. During the summer of 1937 Suzanne was entered in the Piping Rock Horse Show, and so all summer long, three days a week, Johnny Gilbert marched around the ring on his bandy legs yelling at her—especially about leaning into her canter as she approached her jumps. Late in the summer, as the date for the horse show neared, Johnny Gilbert took her for gallops through the fields behind Rothman's before he would finally allow that she might be ready. In the beginning some of the gallops terrified her.

On the day of the show, Suzanne was set up on a stupid little pony she had never even seen before—borrowed from another customer of Gilbert's stable. Instead of being asked to demonstrate all she had practiced, she was walked into the ring on a tether held by her coach and then required to sit there along with six other little girls and look pretty. After much nodding of heads by the three judges, a woman came up and handed Suzanne a yellow ribbon with white lettering that said: "Piping Rock Horse Show, Third." Suzanne was furious at anyone who came within her range: at Johnny Gilbert, at her Mother, and she even let James Moriarity have it when he tried to console her. Through her tears she told them all it had all been stupid, it was a waste of time, and she was never going to any more riding lessons, ever.

The only ally Suzanne could find who would understand the injustice of what had taken place was Mademoiselle Rose, who had once been the nurse and was now called the governess of the Benson girls. She was their companion, their confidante, their friend. As a matter of fact, from the moment they were born neither Mimi nor Suzanne had ever known a day or night without Rose nearby. It was Rose they hugged when they needed to, and Rose who hugged them. It was Rose who brushed their hair, and made them brush their teeth, and chose their jumpers and party dresses, and sent them off to school, and met them when they came back, and sat with them at their own little table where they ate supper early, long before the grownups. It was Rose who made them take their elbows off the table, and Rose who stopped the game of firing butterballs at the ceiling with their butter knives. When they had questions they thought should be secret, they asked Rose in French, unless they were in Paris.

There was one summer when Rose did go away for a month. According to their Mother, Rose had to go to the city because her brother was ill; but it was not clear how soon she would be able to return. A substitute arrived to take Rose's place. Within two days the substitute was complaining to their Mother that these little girls were ill-mannered, ill-tempered and just not to be controlled—"little barbarians, nothing more." By the end of the month the substitute had quit in a huff, and Rose had returned. The Benson girls sensed they had won a significant victory, and they preserved their gains by several months of model behavior.

They would have thought it very strange indeed if for any reason Rose had disappeared again. They would have been even more uncomfortable if their Mother had attempted to usurp Rose's place in their lives. Their understanding was that their Mother was supposed to be their father's companion, coming and going according to a schedule determined by the overriding priorities of his needs. Their Mother's duties therefore were perfectly obvious: to appear beside her husband in fairyland costumes and marvelous perfumes; to put her arm through his when they stood side by side; to concentrate all her attentions on making him smile; to maintain the unique beauty of his life when all the people he knew came and went through their apartment in New York for dinner, or stayed at their house in Oyster Bay for weekends, or wherever Daddy had to be.

For example, on summer Sundays Daddy organized tennis

tournaments for everyone at the clay court down near the beach. To attend these important affairs, Rose dressed Mimi and Suzanne in white linen dresses and they wore white shoes with straps that buckled. After they were dressed and their hair combed and their ribbons tied, they walked down to the tennis courts and sat for a while with the other beautiful ladies. Just as the grownup ladies did, Suzanne and Mimi sipped iced tea with mint in it and clapped their hands when the men made a fine shot. If Mimi and Suzanne got bored, they could be excused and escape to the beach and swim, but their Mother had to stay until the tennis was over.

After tennis, Daddy always was the leader in the troop from the tennis court to the bathhouse on the beach. The ladies changed on one side, and the gentlemen on the other. In Suzanne's opinion not many of Daddy's friends were very good swimmers—they just paddled around a bit and then went and sat with Mother on the beach, sunning themselves; but Suzanne stopped any other project she had in progress to watch her father swim. He headed straight out into the bay, swimming rhythmically, until she could hardly see him any longer, just his arms still flashing. He would stop out there, probably resting on his back as easy as you please. Although she knew better, she would find herself rehearsing a script in which she would have to save him. She would need Mimi's help to drag the rowboat down the beach. Then she would tell Mimi to stay ashore, because it would save weight. She would row with every ounce of strength she had, and she would keep the handles down and the backs of her hands flat, the way Cap'n Johnson had taught her. She would reach her father just in time, and she would see in his eyes as he reached for the safety of the rowboat how grateful he was. One difficulty with her scenario was that she could never figure out how she would get him aboard, up over the gunwales, because he would obviously be much too heavy for her. She wondered a great deal how heavy he would be, and if she pulled and he lifted himself—if they worked together—would they be able to get him into the boat? The only other solution she could imagine was the one in which she got a rope under his arms and then towed him.

She rehearsed this peculiar drama to herself in absolute secrecy, particularly since she had not one single reason to doubt his ability as a swimmer, and the doubts she expressed—the situation in which he needed her—constituted, she believed, a frightening disloyalty. Nevertheless, on one occasion her compulsion overwhelmed her. Flushed with shame, she bullied Mimi into accepting the urgency of getting the rowboat afloat by pretending that she had sighted a shark cruising offshore. Unfortunately it happened to be low tide, making the distance between the high-water mark and the shallows, where their lifeboat would finally float, more than fifty yards. Two desperate little girls heaved together, their shoulders bruised by the boat's gunwales and their bare feet digging trenches behind them in the sand. By the time the lifeboat had been floated by its panting crew, their father was striding toward them through the shallows, prepared to give their little project—whatever it was—a helping hand. Water dripped from his powerful round shoulders, and a wake like an ocean liner trailed behind the thrust of his thighs as he came ashore. Suzanne pretended to him that they were just going for a row in the bay.

In addition to golden memories of the beach on Oyster Bay, the Benson girls could also reconstruct events from their childhood winters. Yet what happened in winter lacked the intense yellows and blues, the brilliant focus, and the sweet, soft, salty taste of southerly breezes that suffused their summer afternoons. Despite the handsome view from the windows of the Benson apartment at 120 East End Avenue, the city was a place of gray shadows. Roller skating in Carl Schurz Park under Rose's close supervision had its excitements, but it lacked Oyster Bay's variety. In their city routines they were constantly being protected from forces around them that were substantially beyond their competence. As a result, they felt diminished. The authority over their own lives they worked so hard to establish every summer was denied to them again in the city every fall.

Besides, the city's season presented subtleties for which reasonable explanations from their Mother were always being postponed. A stunning example was presented to the Benson girls one October afternoon in 1935. They were being chauffered with Rose from the apartment to Best & Company to buy new shoes. James Moriarity had stopped their limousine for a red light at the corner of Eighty-sixth Street and York Avenue. Waiting for the light to change, they saw a ragged band of boys with dirty faces running toward their car. Before anyone realized what had happened, a brick came sailing through the window, shattering glass all over the back seat. Rose screamed. James Moriarity gunned the car away, but not before Suzanne clearly heard one little boy's furious shout: "Economic royalists!"

They had to pick pieces of glass from each other's hair, but no one was hurt, not even a scratch. They had not had a chance to be frightened, because it had all taken place so quickly. Their reaction was more or less an excited curiosity. When they were safely home, however, their Mother made a great fuss about it, calling Mademoiselle Rose and James Moriarity on the carpet with Suzanne and Mimi as witnesses, as if somehow it had been the fault, all along, of their guardians. After their Mother had dismissed Rose and James to meditate on their carelessness and the good fortune of their employment—although they would be forgiven in this instance—Suzanne wanted to know what "economic royalists" meant.

Her Mother fended off any explanation, but Suzanne was not going to let the question go. She badgered her Mother to exasperation. She was told she could ask her father when he got home. That night, Porter Benson picked his daughter up for extra hugs, held her in his lap to hear her questions, and replied that it certainly wasn't anything she would ever need to worry about. And that was that. His evasions only whetted her appetite for answers, but she was required to go to her room because it was time for her father's dinner.

At bedtime Rose took up the task, trying to satisfy both Suzanne and Mimi. They were very rich, said Rose, with a beautiful Mother and a handsome father, which had made those dirty little boys on York Avenue jealous. Not knowing what to do, they threw the brick. Yet Rose could not translate the meaning of the words "economic royalists" very clearly in either French or English. To illustrate what she was attempting to explain, Rose constructed parallels for her girls she supposed they might recognize: they were in many ways little princesses themselves, with lives not so different from those of the princesses in the stories she had been reading to them at bedtime.

Rose's pretty picture delighted Mimi. It bemused her, because Mimi could imagine all sorts of advantages a princess might have. But the idea of being a princess did not entirely soothe Suzanne: perhaps because until then Suzanne had dreamed of princesses who lived far, far away, and she would not want to accept any nearby example of the difficulties she knew princesses were always being called upon to solve; or perhaps because Suzanne sensed that being a princess might be another way in which the city, or winter, or growing up, was going to diminish her freedom. In any case, the message sent to the Misses Benson by brick through the limousine window in the fall of 1935 grew clearer.

They began to collect information on Daddy's "business," and whatever that might mean. It was "investment banking," and according to their Mother, Daddy was "the managing partner of Benson, Salas and de Sales." When the mysteries of "business" were being discussed, it was referred to as "The Bank." They understood correctly that The Bank was Daddy's own bank. They found out he had started it in 1932, that the managing partner was "the most important one," and that The Bank specialized in "European transactions," which was somewhat enigmatic but was the reason they were always going back and forth across the Atlantic on the ocean liners. Daddy's bank had offices in New York, London and Paris. Mr. Salas was the man Daddy had to talk to in London. Monsieur de Sales was the fat man who came to see them at the George V in Paris.

They traveled constantly in the winters, starting from 120 East End Avenue by packing the steamer trunks, which were like little bureaus. They were experts on the differences among the various liners, on the advantages and disadvantages of the *Normandie* and the *Rex*, the *Europa* and the *Bremen*, but they liked the *Bremen* best of all. It had a special playroom with an oversized wooden train set upon wooden tracks that went around the room. It was not quite large enough to ride upon, but it could be pushed up and down painted hills and through pretty little mountain villages with cows and sheep and marvelous chalets with tiny window boxes set under their windows.

They were worldly travelers, sophisticated about Atlantic gales, and knew the most curious things: the tea was bad on the

Dover boat; Swiss border guards spoke German; French children
wore tops on their bathing suits—even the boys; the English had
electric buckboards; instead of having the luggage under the letter B, it was better to get it placed under the letter Z on the pier,
because customs would clear it faster. Yet they knew nothing at
all about the national catastrophe in their own country. They
never saw one man selling apples or a single woman shining
men's shoes. If they heard anything else they could remember
that seemed to have any significance beyond the caravan their
family made as it shuttled to and fro, it was something about
Chancellor Hitler, who was considered to be a very bad man,
and the Germans, who were "being difficult" in some way that
was bad for The Bank.

Because their favorite boat was the *Bremen*, Germans-who-
were-difficult was an item of education not easily digested. In
their experience it was the French who were always difficult and
invariably causing noisy scenes. Yet there was certainly something peculiar going on. They had learned the words to "Who's
Afraid of the Big Bad Wolf?" and they sang it for Daddy. It
made him laugh and laugh and laugh. Then Rose said they were
not to sing it any more on the *Bremen*, because it "might make
some people mad." She allowed it would be all right to sing on
the *Normandie*, a distinction so fine in its meaning they had to
conclude that some people thought Chancellor Hitler was the
Big Bad Wolf. When they asked, Rose said they were correct; it
would not be dignified to sing it any more on a German ship—in
either French or English.

They had no opportunity to test their discoveries in politics,
however, because one afternoon in August 1936 their Mother
required their presence in her bedroom. She was in a tea gown,
propped up against the pillows of her bed, her legs stretched out
on the counterpane. By a nod she indicated that Rose should be
seated on a chair, and she patted the bed beside her, making a
place for each of her girls. She said they should sit quietly, because there were important things to discuss. It was absolutely
necessary for them to start their education in American schools,
she said, to learn America's traditions, and have American
friends of their own age, and learn to read and write and add
and multiply. She had to agree they already knew how to read

but said there were a great many other things they must learn.
They could not continue traipsing like gypsy girls all over the
world. A good education was so important that they would be
staying with Rose in the house in Oyster Bay all year round, because Suzanne had been entered in the first grade of the Clearbrook Country Day School.

Things in Europe were getting to be very difficult. There
might be a war; not right away, but there might be one, just the
same. Daddy would have to be gone for as much as one or two
months at a time, because of The Bank, and she thought they
could understand that she should be with their father. She assured them their father would always be with them for Thanksgiving and Christmas, and all summer long, just as he always
had.

If Suzanne and Mimi suspected they were being abandoned to
the care of Rose in the big white house on Centre Island, every
doubt was canceled by some benefit. The city was to be avoided
anyway. Because Suzanne was going to be away at school all
day, Mimi would have Rose to herself. And Suzanne was excited
by what sort of stage school might present, and what leading
roles she might be required to play. Before school could begin,
Suzanne was taken to the second floor of Best & Company,
where she was outfitted with an entirely new wardrobe of
jumpers, gray pleated skirts, a plaid skirt fastened by a big safety
pin, blouses and soft sweaters, and six different pairs of shoes—
the various costumes certifying that what Suzanne was about to
begin was important.

The Clearbrook Country Day School turned out to consist of a
pleasant group of brick buildings just off 25A, a half hour's drive
from Centre Island. Each morning after breakfast, James
Moriarity drove Suzanne to her official appointment with education, and she sat in the front seat of the car on the right side, just
the way Daddy did. Although school buses transported most
children to the public schools of Long Island, all transportation
to Clearbrook was as private as the school itself. Every morning,
Suzanne's car was one of the many limousines driven by
chauffeurs that circled the school's flagpole to discharge their
miniature passengers. Every afternoon, a line of Cadillacs and
Chryslers returned, their chauffeurs lolling in groups beside the

cars until their charges burst from the school's doors. There were
some plainer autos, driven by governesses, and a few wooden
Ford station wagons driven by interested mothers, but not a majority.

To understand who these children really were, three special
codes had to be deciphered. The first of these codes was the happiest: the children knew each other only by their first names,
and to that extent they were very much like other children. Further, their chauffeurs and governesses not only knew their own
children by their first names but knew their children's friends'
first names too, as if in a democracy of spirit.

The second code was more difficult, but it had its reasons and
they were substantial ones: Teachers addressed their students
only by their last names, a practice followed so rigidly that if it
happened that two or more children from the same family were
to be distinguished from each other, regardless of sex, their report cards read something like "Morgan I," "Morgan II," "Morgan III." If, in addition, two or more families of the same last
name had a number of children at classes, the report cards might
read "A. Roosevelt II" to distinguish the child from "P. Roosevelt II." In such a case, the deciphered code meant both Roose-
velts were the second child, but distinguished by the initial letter
of the first name of the father, not the child. The reason for what
at first might have seemed a complicated system was, upon further inspection, quite sensible: the Clearbrook School was convinced that its business was to educate the leading families of
America.

The fundamental values to be inculcated by education, above
and beyond any other principle or purpose, formed the matrix of
Clearbrook's third code. Educating heirs to a long-established
system was a solemn duty: gigantic corporations, banks, insurance companies, brokerage houses, shipping lines, railroads and
vast tracts of real estate were at stake. If the nation was to fulfill
its promise, a certain style must be understood. Even the boisterous comedies of kindergarten could provide lessons to those who
might be the proconsuls of an empire, and Clearbrook's teachers
were sure of what would be necessary. Decency and neatness, of
course. Sobriety and careful speech. Slow, patient and steady
work was rewarded, because brilliance—on its own—was no

longer required. Clearbrook taught how Europe and classical Greece provided both treasures and lessons from the past. From history Clearbrook drew the moral attitudes useful to the responsibilities of power. Clearbrook was pious, but it had clear objectives: sound minds and healthy bodies, to be trained by following Plato's principles in general but tempered by beginning each school day with an "assembly," at which a devout and humble reading from the King James was offered, followed by a lusty singing of hymns such as "Holy, Holy, Holy."

What Suzanne learned at Clearbrook Country Day was only slightly different from what the curriculum suggested. In the first grade, during the fall of 1936, Suzanne was among those arranged by Miss Little in a circle on the floor. Miss Little was reading aloud to her class the story of Rapunzel. Because Suzanne adored Miss Little, she had already decided to become a teacher one day. Wholly absorbed by Miss Little's account of Rapunzel in the castle tower, and terrified by the part of the story in which the prince climbed the ladder only to find the old witch in the tower, Suzanne was unaware that she had her middle finger, to its second knuckle, inside herself. She would never have been conscious that anything was wrong if Miss Little had not picked up the ruler from the floor beside her and smacked Suzanne's bare knee with it.

Suzanne was not really embarrassed, but a rush of blood flushed her cheeks. She felt an excitement for which she could not account. Miss Little continued to read as if nothing had happened. Miss Little didn't even look up. Suzanne never did it again at school, or anywhere else, except sometimes when she got into Rose's bed at night for a cuddle, or in the bath by herself after locking the door. In the second grade, in January, she was subjected to the same flush again, and again was surprised by its pleasant effects but could not account for its intensity.

Suzanne did not think she was responsible at all for what happened. That day, she was one of the last ones to leave class. It was snowing heavily outside and Miss Evans instructed the children to put on their galoshes before going home. Suzanne did not think she needed them, because she knew James Moriarity was waiting to pick her up the moment she emerged from the school's door, but in the hallway outside Miss Evans's classroom, where the lockers stood in a row, Suzanne sat down on the cold marble floor to obey her teacher's orders.

The galoshes, however, did not fit so easily over Suzanne's saddle shoes. The rubber soles of her shoes prevented her from doing any better than inching the rubber of the galoshes over the shoes fold by fold. As she struggled, frustrated almost to tears by the efforts of her twists and turns to improve the angles at which she pulled, she was suddenly aware that old Mr. Turner, the school's principal, was standing at the wall opposite her, watching. By then the corridor was deserted.

He did not move, but leaned against the wall with his arms folded, smiling down at her over the top of his glasses. Once again the blood rushed into her cheeks, along her arms, and at her throat. This time she attempted to prolong its arrival, perhaps to study its effects, and she worked at the galoshes more deliberately. She stole a look to see if Mr. Turner was still smiling, but he was not. He had pursed his lips. When she had finally fitted the galoshes over her shoes perfectly, she paused to study her accomplishment, examining each foot in turn for its fit. Mr. Turner still had not moved.

Finally she pulled her skirt down over her knees and stood up. After she had latched her locker closed and had her book bag in her hand, she could have left immediately. Instead she stomped the galoshes on the floor, as if she were making a last improvement in their fit, and then looked up directly into Mr. Turner's eyes.

She had him pinned there, stricken almost like the Greek warrior she had seen that very morning in *Stories of Yesteryear*—shown in the drawing with his shield swung open and half the javelin that had caught him sticking from his chest. She felt the flush surge to a new height before she turned and let Mr. Turner go free.

On the drive home James asked the little girl who was his only passenger the question he asked every afternoon as they passed the graveyard by the Brookville light: "How many people would you guess are dead in there?" According to the tradition they had established between them, Suzanne was supposed to answer, "They're all dead," but on that day she would not answer him, even after he had asked her twice for their password. He had to leave her alone to her concentrations. When she got to the house, she went directly to her bath without prompting. She locked the bathroom door even against Rose, and stayed in there for a long time.

In the spring of the same year, near the end of the second grade, Suzanne was taught another lesson—one she said she never fully understood until years later. One of the games Clear-brook's teachers had devised for recess on the playground was a variation of tag: the boys from a class arranged themselves in a wide circle, and the girls stood inside the circle; at the teacher's whistle, the boys began to pass a basketball to each other around the outside of the circle until the moment was ripe, and then one of the boys would throw the ball at a girl he had targeted inside the ring. The girls could duck or dodge as much as they pleased, but if a girl was hit by the ball, she was "out." The game continued until a time limit had expired, or until all the girls were "out." Then the sides were changed, with the boys on the inside and the girls in the ring around them. The team that won was the one with the least "outs." It was by far the most popular game on the playground, and the noisiest, each shot and every escape punctuated by shouts and screams and blood-curdling yells.

During recess on a warm morning in May the teacher who normally supervised the sixth grade was absent from the play-ground. Apparently by mutual consent, the twelve girls and fifteen boys of the sixth grade conducted themselves to the tennis courts just east of the macadamed playground. The courts were surrounded by a high chain-link fence, and the fence had but one door as entrance. Outside the fence, a thick hedge of juniper pines shielded the courts from the wind, and also hid them from the playground and its basketball boards, its teeter-totters, its swings and Junglegyms. On the playground, word soon spread that there was something to see in the tennis courts. Why the same news never reached any of the teachers until much later, no investigation was subsequently able to discover. In any case, children slipped away to the courts in twos and threes.

By the time Suzanne joined the spectators behind the screen of junipers and had pressed her nose against the court's chain-link fence, the sixth grade inside the court was in the grip of a marvelous frenzy. Hidden away from any supervision, they were playing their own version of basketball tag. Two of the biggest boys blocked the only door through which any of the girls might escape. A dozen other boys had collected five or six basketballs among them, and in groups of two or three they would corner a single girl at one end of the court, or against the fence, and then at close range fire basketballs at the victim with every ounce of strength they could summon. Whether the ball actually stung as much as the girls pretended was part of what puzzled Suzanne, but then she watched two boys catch a girl and spread-eagle her wrists against the fence, and a third boy fire a basketball directly into the girl's stomach, pick it up as it bounced away, and fire it again, and again. The girl was sobbing, and Suzanne concluded that it must actually hurt.

What was more mysterious, however, was that although every girl trapped in the court was weeping, the strange affair was being conducted almost silently. When the same game was played out on the open playground, boys and girls together shouted and screamed and yelled, but in the enclosed tennis court all were silent; the boys looked grim, and the girls wept, and sometimes smiled oddly even as they wept, but they all kept silent. Suzanne could not imagine why the girls did not make a group attack on the two boys who guarded the court's door. She did not see even one girl attempt the exit.

Equally astonishing was the group of three girls who had linked their arms together in a half circle with their backs against one of the net posts. A pack of five boys menaced them, harassing them by firing one vicious shot after another, not one of which missed. Yet the girls stood open to each salvo with tears streaming, helpless to the boys' assaults, without separating their linked arms or raising their hands as shields to the oncoming basketball. They would not let go of each other.

Exasperated, the boys decided to pry them apart and get them up against the fence one at a time. They wrestled one girl away from her fellow prisoners, then dragged her on her back by her arms to the fence. When they attempted to stand her up against the fence for what they called her firing squad, she wriggled away, but she ran right back to link arms with her sisters at the net post. The sequence of bombardments from which she had just escaped could then begin again, and the same attempts to wrestle away one girl from the defiant group. The scene Suzanne was watching rooted her to the ground beneath her feet. Goose pimples crept up her thighs, mixed with the flush she already knew along her upper arms.

She watched one determined boy stalk a pretty girl who was weeping but half smiling simultaneously. As the boy advanced he held his ball cocked and ready to fire; the girl retreated from the threat of his shot by no more than a half step at a time—pretending, as she ducked and feinted first one shoulder then the other, to be about to dance away. A second boy approached as if he wanted to join their match, but they shooed him away, stopping their affair to hiss at him until he understood theirs was a private match. Then they locked eyes upon each other again, and resumed their deadly advance and retreat. Once, her young lover let fly with his ball and missed his target, and it seemed to Suzanne that the girl was free to run at last, to fly away. Instead the girl stopped and waited while the boy scrambled along the edge of the fence after his lost ball. When he had retrieved it, and defended it against the claims other boys made upon it while she taunted him, they rejoined their waltz almost exactly where they had left off.

Then Mrs. Burke, a mean, white-haired old lady who taught third grade, came marching through the court door. The game came to an instant halt. Every sixth-grader, boy and girl, froze in exactly the spot where he or she stood. Basketballs rolled away by themselves, untouched. The trio of girls at the net post finally unlocked their arms. Mrs. Burke shouted at them all: they were to go directly to their homeroom, instantly, that very minute. As they filed out obediently, one or two of the girls had to straighten stray hairs, or refix a ribbon, or wipe from a cheek the stains of tears that remained as evidence, but their demeanor did not suggest a single clue to what had just passed. Suzanne searched every girl's face, but every one was as smooth and modest and composed as it habitually was, just as if she were singing hymns at assembly: "Holy, Holy, Holy."

Mrs. Burke's face, however, was bloated with fury. Her eyes bulged as she toured the court's perimeter along the inside of the fence, shouting through it at all the children who still lingered to go directly to their classrooms. Her eyes blazed with such fire that Suzanne suspected she would have choked every child she could see, if only the innocents on the other side of the fence were not beyond her grasp. Each child vanished the moment the blind anger in Mrs. Burke was understood. Suzanne agreed with her classmates that Mrs. Burke was crazy.

School ended soon after for the summer vacation of 1938. Faithful to the promises her Mother had made, Suzanne's father returned from the business of The Bank in Europe, commuting instead from Oyster Bay to his office in the city. At the tennis tournaments on the weekends, everyone noticed Suzanne's new fascination with the game. When Mimi complained of Suzanne's absence from the beach behind the court, Suzanne withered her younger sister: baby games. All the sand tunnels they could ever dig would end up being pretty much the same, and as far as Suzanne was concerned, she was bored with them.

At the beginning of the summer Suzanne had little to do except hang about on the chairs under the umbrella beside the court, sipping iced tea, swinging her legs, watching and waiting. She followed the mixed doubles with as much pleasure as anyone else among the spectators, but it was when the men played that at all times Suzanne knew the score to the dot, in points, games and sets. Her Daddy let her call out the scores, then taught her how to be the "ball boy." She scooped up wasted serves along the fence. She saved extra balls until the server called for them. She stood as still as a little mouse against the fence when play was in progress. She was rewarded by her Mother with a white tennis dress of her own, and Rose fixed her red hair behind her head in braids to keep it out of the way. One day, Daddy brought back a sunshade hat from the city as a present so that Suzanne could be presented in a costume just like Alice Marble's. At the end of a day's matches, Daddy always thanked her for her participation as "our ball boy," giving her a gallant bow from the waist and leading the polite applause from his other guests. Rose helped Suzanne practice a pretty curtsy with which she could reply to her Daddy. He said she did it like a princess.

While Daddy was away at The Bank in the city during the

weekdays, Suzanne took her Mother's Wilson racket from the sports closet and practiced at the bangboard day after day. The summer of 1938 ended before she could entice her father into their first match, but she had a promise from him that they would play together when summer came around again; he swore he would, crossed his heart and hoped to die. Thereafter, in her dreams, her Daddy always came to her in his tennis whites; in his pleated white flannel trousers; running and sliding, leaving skid marks behind him on the clay court; his sweat matting to his chest his short-sleeved, open-necked shirt and making the hair glisten on the backs of his wrists. When he came to the umbrella for a towel to wipe his forehead and the back of his neck, he would smile at her. Sometimes she couldn't look at him, he was so beautiful. When he went out on the court to play again, the towel he left over the back of the chair smelled just like him, and like his Vitalis.

4

Princess

1938–48

"My Daddy had promised me he'd play," Suzanne said. "And so every detail of the fall of 1938 became an indelible memory." Clearbrook Country Day School reopened on Wednesday, September 14, but for the first time she did not look forward to the school year. "I was assigned to the third-grade section taught by Mrs. Burke, and I did not care for Mrs. Burke."

Besides, Mimi had also started school, which meant that Mimi now also had adventures and enthusiasms to report to Rose at supper every night. Suzanne had to share not only the honors of school itself but its privileges—shopping for school clothes and sitting in the front seat of the car each day on the way back and forth. Sitting in Daddy's place while being chauffeured by James was not the same as going to school with Mimi. In any case, the winter would be a seasonal interruption from the main business of her life: her summer objectives. Although the tennis matches her Daddy had promised her had been postponed, Suzanne devoted herself to the next summer—which would surely arrive in its time—and she planned to practice her strokes at the bangboard after school every afternoon through the fall. She promised herself to keep at it no matter how cold it got; she had cal-

culated she would be able to continue into November before it
became too dark. She could start again in March. During the
first week of school, she concentrated on her backhand. She
had planned to alternate weeks—backhand weeks and forehand
weeks.

Wednesday morning, September 21, 1938, marked the beginning of the second week of school—a forehand week. It was also
her eighth birthday, and she could anticipate the presents she
knew her Daddy had left behind for her. He was away in Europe
on his fall trip for The Bank, but she would open his presents at
her party that afternoon after school. The girls from her class
would come at four o'clock. She'd have a cake. She'd make her
secret wish and never tell anyone—Women's Singles Champion
of the Whole World—and then blow out every candle. When she
was dressed for school and her book bag packed, she went down
to breakfast early.

Her Mother had already left the table and gone to the living
room again to sit beside the Philco radio, listening for news from
Munich. Her Mother had been sitting beside the radio just about
day and night since Sunday. For the first time, Mary Benson had
not traveled to Paris with her husband. She explained the exception to her daughters and assured them there was no need to
worry. There might be a war, but America would not be in it. It
would be a war between Germany on one side and France and
England on the other, but no matter what happened, their father
would be all right, because he was an American citizen. Mary
Benson said there were many people who thought the war might
be avoided if the Germans would be reasonable. There was a
meeting going on in Munich to make peace; that was the news
she was listening for on the radio, and she was waiting for bulle-
tins.

It had been raining since Sunday: only a light, misty drizzle at
first, then steadily more, day and night, all Monday and all Tuesday. After breakfast Wednesday morning, James Moriarity interrupted Mrs. Benson's radio watch to inquire whether he should
take the girls to school as usual. It was his opinion that they
were in for a heavy northeaster; perhaps the girls should be allowed to stay home for the day. Mrs. Benson said she saw no
reason why the girls should not be driven to school as usual. Ac-

cording to the radio news there would be rain, then it would turn cooler.

On the way to school, West Shore Road was flooded by the spray from angry easterly waves breaking against the sea wall. James told the girls about equinox storms—there was one almost every year. Then they saw that big branches were down at the Mill Neck light, and James had to turn up over the hill to go around through Locust Valley. Arriving late at school, they ran for the school's doors through sheets of driving rain. At about eleven o'clock Mr. Turner sent messages around to each classroom. School was being closed. Their parents had been called to pick them up. They should wait quietly in their classrooms and work ahead in their workbooks until their cars arrived. James appeared almost immediately at the door of Suzanne's classroom with his hat in one hand and holding Mimi with the other. Instead of returning to Centre Island, James had waited for them.

Just getting to the car, they were soaked again. When they began to prattle, he spoke sharply and asked them to be absolutely quiet, because he had to concentrate on driving. He looked grim enough to silence them. Rain spread across the windshield so heavily the wipers could not sweep it away; Suzanne helped by wiping the fog on the inside for James, and both girls peered ahead to watch for things that might be in the road. They meandered through a long route toward home through fallen branches and some trees that were already down, but if the Bayville Causeway was the long way around, it turned out to be clear. Getting across the windswept causeway was scary. Gusts of sand blew off the beach and rattled against the car. The tide had risen so high on either side of them, they could imagine how bay and sound would soon be joined and the car cut off. On the sound, long white rolling combers came up almost to the road. The wind shrieked in the worst gusts, blowing the tops of the waves away, making it impossible to see anything at all and causing the car to sway, but they made it home by twelve-thirty. They rushed to their Mother in the living room, soaking wet, dripping water from their slickers, dancing with excitement about being let out of school and their trip home through the storm. Mrs. Benson did not want to be interrupted, because radio reception was very poor; Columbia's network was not getting anything through at all, but she expected WEAF would provide a bulletin from Munich momentarily. Her daughters should change their wet clothes immediately and have lunch. She was sorry Suzanne's birthday party had to be canceled. Perhaps the party could be arranged for Saturday. Yes, Suzanne could open her presents tonight anyway.

Before Mrs. Benson could get the news from London, her radio would go dead. It would never tell her the reason why CBS was having such difficulties with transmissions across the Atlantic. By the time Mimi and Suzanne finished their lunch, the center of the "disturbance" was about 120 miles south of them, off Atlantic City, and coming fast. By then the storm the Benson household believed was a mere northeaster actually spread across a half million square miles of ocean. It had been created weeks before, on a warm, lazy, sweet afternoon over the sparkling blue water in the Atlantic's zone of soft blue trade winds. It had appeared among the million fleecy white cumulus drifting harmlessly west. Against all calculable possibility, some moist draft of wind had gusted up for reasons of its own, and another after it, and when night fell, drafts continued to waft upward. Despite the probabilities, rain fell from it the next day, and the day after as well, and on the surface of the sea, winds picked up to thirty knots, and then sometimes even a bit more. As if to express some unspoken need, it began to unleash lightning upon the earth below, heated strokes of white and rosy fire, seeing the surface upon which it had once smiled as a place to send devastating negative charges. As an odd little tropic storm of no consequence continued to drift west through the trades, a diameter of a mere three or four miles would no longer satisfy the furies it contained. Thunderbolts flashed incessantly, but its passions could not be slaked. Whirlwinds rose up to seventy knots, and then more. Once it abandoned what might have been its gentle purpose, it became insatiable: sucking moisture from the sea below into a soaring, seething, darkening mass of clouds, multiplying its anger geometrically. Yet inside the center of this frenzied tower of catastrophe there always existed a zone of peculiar calm.

All around the calm eye, winds howled—chaotic, arbitrary, voluptuous, and indifferent to the placid concerns of the landscape over which it would pass. It was first sighted three hundred and fifty miles northeast of Puerto Rico on September 16, and reported by the freighter S.S. *Alegrete*. It stood off Jacksonville, Florida, on Sunday, and made slow passage toward Hatteras Monday. Wednesday morning it started moving again—toward Long Island's south shore at sixty miles an hour. The winds around its eye gusted to two hundred. The lights went out in the Benson house at 2:19 P.M., and Mrs. Benson, forced to abandon the radio news from Munich, finally noticed the extraordinary winds buffeting her house.

Genuinely alarmed at last, she gathered her children and her servants from the kitchen and the pantries into the library—a command post Mrs. Benson deemed would be the safest place. The turbulence of the wind around them continued to increase, rising at times to a shriek. Ferocious gusts pressed against the house and drove rain in white cascades against the windows. Lightning flashed incessantly, but the thunderclaps that should have followed could not be heard in the uproar. Mrs. Benson had a hurricane lamp lit to oppose the gloom.

At first, Suzanne and Mimi ran from window to window to report what they could see, but then their Mother forbade them to go near the windows. She ordered that all the curtains be drawn against the possibility of flying glass. In the dim glow of the hurricane lamp, Mimi was satisfied to settle into Rose's lap, but Suzanne could barely be controlled, could not be made to sit still, was not at all awed, and seemed to love it. She repeated to everyone who would listen how she had seen trees falling out there, crashing to the ground, without making a sound because it was so loud, so noisy. Suzanne thought it was terrific. "Just terrific. Isn't it terrific?"

At about four o'clock, it stopped, "just like that." The house ceased to shudder, the wind was silent—"as if God had snapped his fingers."

When James pulled open the library curtains, the sun was shining—a peculiar, glorious, orange-and-yellow light that played marvelous reflections from the water still dripping from all they could see. Mild zephyrs blew across an appalling scene of wreckage. Hardly a tree stood on the back lawn. Trees had gone down every which way, like jackstraws. The oaks and maples and willows had splintered, but the locusts had blown down straight from the roots. Blue sky showed above them.

Some of Mrs. Benson's household left the places they held at the library's windows and began to wander toward the pantry and kitchen for better views. Then they heard the roar coming again. The sun disappeared as if covered by a saucer, and before they could scurry back to the library, the first gust beyond the eye hit the house from the northwest. With it they heard above their heads, on the second floor, the windows in the green guest room shatter, a door slam like a cannon shot, and the sound of wood splintering. The moans and shrieks and complaints and ecstasies of the storm were now in the house with them. James Moriarity volunteered, took a flashlight with him, and went upstairs. He returned to say he thought it would be all right: a lot of water coming under the green room's doorframe, which had been blown right out, but the damage could be cleaned up.

By about six o'clock they all sensed the din around them had slacked. There were intervals between gusts when not much more than a winter's gale blew, and the intervals grew successively longer. Beneath the wind's assaults the house still trembled every so often, but now it shuddered as if relaxing. By seven o'clock the winds had abated to a fresh northerly, and the rain came only in spastic squalls. By nine o'clock, it was gone entirely. There was no longer any frenzied excitement; nothing but a delirious memory.

The Benson household ventured outside eventually, standing in a cautious group upon the back porch. The silence surrounding them was in many ways as magnificent as the storm had been. What they had survived had spent its passion and, finally exhausted, had closed its eyes. A black night lay around them, a languor in its air, like a weakness in nature after all—clean and fresh to the taste but slightly salty. There was enough light from a canopy of stars to see the blasted trees on the lawn. Yet in the trees' shattered disarray there was something—some mysterious glory—as if their destruction contained something even more spectacular than the freedoms that had swayed them in gentler days.

Beyond the trees, down at the beach, the bathhouse was gone, swept away by the splendid gusts. If any plank or two had tried to resist, it had been snatched away to oblivion. Beyond the emptied beach the bay rested, as smooth as glass, twinkling pinpoints from an indifferent Milky Way reflected on its black surface; a bay now as placid and calm as on an August night, without any sign of the seething excitement in which it had been seized. From its waters an ancient power called. By common consent, and without saying a word to each other, the members of the Benson household were drawn toward it, down the lawn through the wrecked trees, just to have a look. Before anyone could find a path that would reach the beach, they were required to halt, then retreat as fast as they could walk, and finally to run for the safety of high ground.

Perhaps the tide only meant to answer whatever it was they had desired: and so it began to rise. It came up past the seaweed which usually marked the boundary for high water. It kept summoning itself, in an eerie and irreversible advance, past where the bathhouse had stood, up the lawn toward the house. It came through the trees splayed across the lawn, submerging them branch by branch. No wave accompanied it. No ripple bothered its glassy black surface. Nothing was going to stop it. Fascinated by what was coming toward them, the Benson household made for the safety of the big house they presumed would be their shelter. Then they had to consider what they planned to do if the tide continued to rise. At the very moment horror began to flood up in them at a rate equal to the tide's advance, the waters stopped as if surprised, paused as if deliberating alternatives, then obediently began to recede. Suzanne was the one, they would all agree later, who broke the terror that gripped them: at its cresting she had laughed, then started to applaud. Everyone had joined in Suzanne's applause, as if they were at a tennis match, because, they would say, at the time it seemed to be the appropriate thing to do.

After that, Mrs. Benson sent her servants back inside. They chattered to each other like starlings as they lit candles and lamps and began to mop up where the water had come through. Mimi and Suzanne were sent to bed: it would be the best place for them to be, it was late, and there certainly would be no electricity or any lights until morning. Her Mother agreed that at breakfast Suzanne could open her birthday presents from her father.

There were other presents, of course, but the two Suzanne opened last were the only important ones. The first came in a small grained leather box of its own. Folded exactly into the box's cover was her father's card: "Porter C. L. Benson" in engraved script, and underneath, "Benson, Salas & de Sales"; on the back, in his own hand, he had written: "To my princess. Love, Daddy." On a cushion of red velvet lay a brooch; a double pearl was held in the center of its elliptical outer ring by a spider web of crafted gold threads. Suzanne said she would not wear her brooch until Daddy came home.

Once it was unwrapped, the second present turned out to be an unusual sort of diary, bound in dark green morocco leather and arranged inside in such a way that Suzanne could review on the same page five years of her life at a time. The days of the week were not printed in but left open for her entry; instead, six ruled lines on each page had been provided to note the major events of September 21, 1938; and then beneath them six more for September 21, 1939; and then, successively, six more for each year—1940, 1941 and 1942. The record she began on her eighth birthday she kept faithfully for the rest of her life.

She began her diary by noting that, because of what turned out to be "the hurricane," there was no electricity and therefore no light, no pump to raise water to the house, no telephone, nor any news from Mother's radio, until Monday, October 3. The Benson house on Centre Island was cut off at the ruined Bayville Causeway from the rest of the world. To regain access to the mainland, crews of men worked until dark with chain saws at the tangled trees blocking the road, and the days were punctuated by the crumps of the dynamite the men used to blast the stumps. There was no school either, an event Suzanne noted in her new record book with a happy exclamation point. Suzanne and Mimi helped to carry water in buckets from the well house at the beach. Since everyone else was too busy at more important matters, Suzanne enlisted Mimi for the task of attempting to clear the tennis court of the seaweed and debris that had been caught in its fence by the outgoing tide. Working with rakes and a wheelbarrow, they almost completed their self-appointed work before school was announced as possible the next day. The road would be clear Monday morning, October 3. Life would be returning to normal schedules.

After school on Monday even the electricity had been restored. Suzanne ran upstairs to dump her books on her bed; while there was still light she might work on the tennis court again. She was surprised to find Rose waiting for her in her room. It looked to Suzanne as if Rose had been crying. Rose said Suzanne should go to her mother's bedroom immediately: "Your mother has something important to tell you."

Suzanne hesitated at the closed door, then knocked, and a man's voice answered her knock. As soon as she had entered, her mother introduced her to "Mr. Putnam, who is a very dear friend to all of us."

Mr. Putnam rose from the chair he had pulled up beside her mother's bed and took Suzanne's hand with great solemnity; then he sat down again, crossed one leg over the other and folded his fingers in his lap. Suzanne sensed that he was a man who always waited politely. He would not meet her eye, and she did not like him one bit. He could have been her father's age, but he was already going bald. He was able to cross his legs too easily—they must have had thin shanks. Between the Louis XV chairs by the window there was a tea tray on the table, with two empty teacups and two blue napkins rumpled up on it. Her mother and Mr. Putnam had not eaten all the petits fours.

Her mother was propped against pillows, lying on top of the bedspread, wearing a tea gown; but her hair was fixed and her face made up as if she were about to go out to dinner. Mimi was already snuggled up against her, and her mother patted the place on the other side of the bed she expected Suzanne to take. When Mrs. Benson had encircled each daughter with an arm and they had agreed they were comfy, she attempted to begin: "Ten days ago, your father was . . ."

Suzanne felt a dew start above her upper lip. To wipe it away she attempted to free herself from her mother's embrace.

Her mother had not finished. She cleared her throat, and began again: "Your father was found . . ."

Unable to see her mother's face, Suzanne searched the eyes of

Mr. Putnam. What she saw was cold and far away, despite the sympathetic expression he had arranged upon his face.

Her mother had turned to him: "John . . . you explain it."

John Putnam took his time, looking first at the fingers with which he had made a church in his lap. "Girls, the fact of the matter is your father has died. We didn't know about it until today because of the storm. He died in Paris ten days ago."

Suzanne felt her mother's arm tighten around her shoulders; she was trapped on the bed, but she knew she would have to get away. A wave of irresistible exhilaration was coursing through her—she could have skipped, she needed to jump, she had to run. Instead she was being forced to listen to her mother and Mr. Putnam. They were explaining things, they said. Things that didn't matter at all. About being realistic, what would be practical. Going to Paris to bury your father there, many other things to attend to. No reason to be worried; certain changes would be necessary. Mr. Putnam was only there to help, only there to help. If there was a war, The Bank would not be able. Practical. Being realistic. Like little soldiers. Christmas together just as they always had, chin up. Realistic. Through the sounds of their babble, Suzanne could hear her sister sobbing. As Rose said later, it was Mrs. Benson's attempt to wipe away Mimi's tears that caused her to relax her grip upon Suzanne for only a moment.

In an instant Suzanne was off the bed and running. She shot through the door before anyone could stop her. She was down the hallway and up the stairs two steps at a time to her own room. When she reached her sanctuary, she slammed the door behind her, went to her dresser, brushed her hair until she was bored with it, reset its ribbon until it was perfect. She straightened her blouse, tucking it carefully into her skirt again, took off her shoes and put them away neatly in their place in the closet. She turned down the cover of her bed, arranged the pillows against the headboard and sat up against them, stretching out her legs and crossing them at the ankles just as her mother had done. She smoothed her school skirt down over her knees and folded her hands in her lap.

Rose went in to see if anything could be done, but Suzanne would not turn to look at her. Sensing that nothing ought to be done immediately, Rose took up a seat in the armchair opposite the bed to stand guard, and to wait. Within a few minutes Mrs. Benson opened Suzanne's door and would have entered on tiptoe, except that Rose's eyes blazed at her with authority. Rose was able to wave Mrs. Benson out again.

Hour after hour, Suzanne continued to stare into the distances ahead of her. She would not speak, never moved, nor did she shed one tear. Her stilled pose suggested that at her center she was calm, but a sodden wretchedness flowed out from her, black gusts of despair swirled about her, and a cold rain fell—illuminated from time to time by furious lightning—on the horizon her eyes desperately searched. Against the powers of the storm raging in the heart of the child, Rose prayed to the Virgin Mary—and to St. Lucy as well—that her little girl might cry.

Suzanne never did. In the near hours of dawn her eyes finally closed from exhaustion—still dry. Rose pulled the yellow comforter up to Suzanne's chin, covering her just as she was, fast asleep but sitting up. Then Rose switched off the light, pulled the curtains and closed the door.

"You've got to remember," Mimi said years later, "that I was only five then and barely understood half of what was happening. I do recall that there was some sort of an argument between Rose and our mother. Rose insisted that Suzanne be allowed to sleep it off. After Suzanne had spent something like a day and a half sleeping, mother said Suzanne had passed through it, after all, like a little soldier. Those were mother's words."

According to Mimi their mother left for Europe on the *Rex* with John Putnam soon after their father died. "They buried Daddy in Paris. They did what they could to straighten out the affairs of The Bank. It was not until long after the war that Suzanne and I realized how much mother really did for us.

"The Bank had been having difficulties. I think mother and John Putnam only learned about them for the first time when they got to Paris. It all had to do with Hitler going into Austria and Czechoslovakia. Anyway, it was no easy matter to straighten out, because when Daddy was found dead in his room at the George V the insurance company would not pay. His cause of death was listed as suicide at first, so they said the insurance didn't apply.

"With the help of Monsieur de Sales, mother and Mr. Putnam

arranged to have the prefect of police change the cause of death to murder. Then the insurance could be paid. After that, mother and Mr. Putnam had to settle up accounts with Daddy's partners. It all took forever to get done. They didn't get home until the day before Christmas.

"Well, I think the murder was supposed to have been by poison, but I don't think that's true at all. Paris was crazy just before the war. I think they paid whoever it was they had to pay so that mother could collect the insurance. Of course, I didn't understand a bit of it at the time, but in retrospect I think Suzanne's reaction was peculiar. I can tell you that I was the only witness, and an accessory after the fact, to what must be listed as Suzanne's first crime."

Perhaps because Mary Benson and John Putnam had been away too long, they returned with too many gifts for Mimi and Suzanne. When the sisters were finally allowed downstairs on Christmas morning, the number and variety of presents they discovered under the tree exceeded by far the cargoes delivered upon any Christmas past. The girls tore paper from boxes for more than an hour. Suzanne's two "big" presents could not be wrapped, however, but stood by the tree, decorated by lengths of wide red ribbon. The first of these was a canary in its cage, a gift of love, according to its card, from her mother; the second came from Belgium, a gift of love, according to its card, from John Putnam—the dollhouse that Suzanne had always wanted.

It stood almost three feet high and four feet wide; Suzanne could look through the windows of both its floors from the front; and in the back it was cut away for easy rearrangement of its neatly decorated rooms—chairs and tables and beds and bureaus. Suzanne was on her knees looking into the tiny bedroom upstairs when she heard her mother say, "I think you should thank John properly for your present, Suzanne."

Suzanne rose and did as she had been told. She gave John Putnam a winning smile, her best curtsy, and then a kiss upon his cheek from tiptoe, which made him blush. He hugged her in return, to which she acquiesced. He told her earnestly how glad he was that they could be friends.

After a long Christmas lunch, with John Putnam sitting in her father's place, her mother suggested that the girls might want to be outside for a while; that she and John wanted to be quiet and chat in the library about things that would not interest them very much; that since it had just started to snow perhaps they might want to try sledding; and that they must bundle up.

Suzanne obeyed readily. She was soon busy on a project that required Mimi's assistance, yet with ultimate ends she would not reveal. As Suzanne's plan unfolded, Mimi began to object, but Suzanne would brook no insubordination. Mimi quickly realized she had better do what she was told. Terrified by Suzanne's determination, Mimi helped get the Flexible Flyer out from the shed under the kitchen, struggled as best she could with her end of Suzanne's new dollhouse as they loaded it on the sled, waited patiently beside the sled until Suzanne returned from her second raid into the house, and then kept the canary's cage and the dollhouse balanced on the sled as Suzanne dragged the rope of her cargo toward the beach. By then the snow was coming down hard.

With Mimi's help, Suzanne set the canoe upon its bottom, then slid it across the snow-covered beach until its bow was lapped by the bay. They fetched the dollhouse first, setting it across the gunwales of the canoe. Suzanne ordered Mimi to stand watch at the canoe while she brought the canary's cage down the beach and set it amidships, between the seats. Suzanne then rebalanced the dollhouse on the gunwales, facing the open portion of the house toward the bay and away from the snow being driven at their backs by the easterly. She had to make several attempts to catch the terrified canary by its back inside the cage, but when she finally had a firm grip she had no problem at all getting it up inside the dollhouse in the little bedroom on the second floor. With the easterly blowing snow across the dollhouse roof, the canary was apparently satisfied by the shelter it had found. Then Mimi was again ordered to keep the house balanced until Suzanne had launched their ship out to sea.

They watched at the water's edge, stamping their feet against the cold and pulling their snowsuit hoods up around their ears. The easterly gradually blew the canoe away from the protected shore. The boat began to rock with the waves that formed beneath it, but still the house and its passenger stayed balanced across the gunwales. One puff turned the canoe sideways. The next drove it on with increasing speed farther out into the bay. Wind and wave began to combine, and at last it seemed the dollhouse might have shifted slightly, but snow obscured their visibility, and the canoe was farther and farther offshore. When they lost sight of it, it was bobbing and rocking; although the dollhouse should have gone over by then, it still held on. Perhaps it was partly frozen, said Suzanne. In any case, she was satisfied they had done all they could. On the way back up to the house she warned Mimi one more time: if she ever told anyone, she would be punished too.

When the loss of dollhouse and canary was discovered later that afternoon, eight-year-old Suzanne appeared to be as distressed as everyone else, and five-year-old Mimi cried fearfully. Although suspicions brimmed in many hearts of the Benson household and there was accurate gossip among the servants, Suzanne insisted to John Putnam that she could not imagine what had happened to her favorite presents of all. In the circumstance, her mother believed it would be best to let the matter drop.

Suzanne recorded Christmas 1938 in her diary with disarming brevity: "Nice dollhouse from John Putnam—yellow canary from Mother." Her diaries, it should be said, never contained the extravagant secrets or the foolish enthusiasms of most young girls. On the contrary, they disguised nothing, probably left out nothing, were never sentimental, told exactly how things worked, and may have been absolutely realistic. If they lied at all, they lied only by economy—in the sense that "dollhouse from John Putnam" and "canary from Mother" did not quite cover all that had occurred.

Suzanne could not have started her journals until after her eighth birthday and after the hurricane, which would explain why neither event was recorded. On the day she was informed of her father's death she slept for eighteen hours, and therefore her entry was brief, but forgivable: "Must let hair grow." She was not required to comment upon her father's death at all, and it is reasonable to assume that the one word she entered for that day must have been inscribed later: "Never."

These two enigmatic exceptions having been noted, it should be said that she kept her notes faithfully thereafter. Each day's entry usually filled all the space allotted. In creating her history she satisfied several purposes for herself: her diaries were her own manual of instructions, her assurance to herself that she was not wasting time, an annual record of her education, and an analysis of the social landscape through which she was required to march. They were all these things simultaneously, like the journals of a surveyor or an explorer, and therefore if their style was strange or their quality peculiar, she had her reasons. Unlike other young women, Suzanne never speculated on her conscience, or indulged herself in the comforts of remorse, or was debilitated by silly guilts. She recorded the geography she explored as it was: unadorned. With a marvelous indifference, she described accurately what she saw.

Suzanne's first diary covers the years from 1938 to 1942, and just as John Putnam and her mother had forecast, practical changes were necessary as a result of Porter Benson's death. In January 1939, the Bensons moved into New York City during the winter, and they moved from 120 East End Avenue to a "more convenient" flat at 655 Park Avenue. The girls were transferred from Clearbrook Country Day School to the Spence School, at 22 East Ninety-first Street. Since Mimi and Suzanne could take the bus to school, it was no longer really necessary to employ James Moriarity as chauffeur, and he had to be let go.

Because the widow Benson was required to return to Europe again and again to salvage what she could of The Bank before war closed all frontiers, Rose continued to supervise her little girls, both in the city during the wintertime and at the house on Oyster Bay during the summers. Until December 1941, and Pearl Harbor, their mother was rarely at home. She spent most of her time in Paris, and was required to use circuitous and time-consuming routes to get back and forth. Going from Paris to Spain to Lisbon, and then waiting for the Pan American Clipper, for example, took seven weeks just to get home.

Nevertheless, with Rose as their chaperone, confidante and companion, Mimi and Suzanne followed the course of education laid out by their mother. Besides the necessities taught at the Spence School during the winter, they had lessons in piano and then dancing. Although summers at Oyster Bay no longer sparkled with the same brilliance, Suzanne continued her tennis and took lessons at it. On the rare weekends during the summer when Mary Benson was at home, she was visited by John Putnam and a wide variety of other interesting—and some not so interesting—men. Suzanne indexed every one of them in her diaries with annotations on their occupations, an estimation of their probable wealth, their mannerisms and their weaknesses. Sometimes an interesting quote was recorded in answer to Suzanne's inevitable interview. After Pearl Harbor, Mary Benson had no reason, or any way, to travel any longer, and despite her attractions, the number of available men diminished. The war made charming weekends at Oyster Bay impractical, and those who came to call at 655 Park Avenue for drinks and the theater afterward were, in Suzanne's opinion, "nothing but leftovers." In the summer of 1942, Suzanne began to note in her own simple code, by marking X's with no other comment, how many martinis her mother drank at the end of each day.

Beginning with Suzanne's second five-year diary, in 1943, some reading between the lines would be justified in assessing the extent to which Suzanne and her mother found it difficult even to sit together in the same room. Although they maintained an habitual courtesy—it could have passed as a genuine fondness, an enthusiasm for mutual concerns—their backs arched invisibly when they were in each other's company. If they had been cats instead of women, they could not have disguised the hair they caused to rise on their opponent's necks, nor the thickened tails they would have waved. Perhaps some antipathy was to be expected between mother and daughter, because by 1943 Suzanne was being asked to concentrate upon the meaning of transcendental mysteries: her breasts had begun to grow; her first period arrived; at a dance at the Piping Rock Beach Club she discovered some of the powers she might exert when she pressed Billy Vail's erection back at him through her summer pinafore. On a night race conducted by the Junior Yacht Club she experimented with lingering kisses. She discovered how to drive Bimmy Thompson to distraction, and she knew she could do it again whenever she pleased. On the issues of lipstick, shoes, party dresses, even school dresses, and on the subject of her red hair, which by then hung to her waist, it seemed her mother considered her something of an asset but perhaps a liability at the same time. Suzanne discovered she could raise both fury and fear in her mother's eyes by failing to wash her hair and then insisting she would never, never cut it. Fortunately peace came to Paris in August 1944, and Mary Benson was soon required to travel again. By then Suzanne had been registered as a freshman at Wavertree Hall, the most exclusive—and admired—boarding school in America, dedicated to the education of young ladies, and situated in the rolling hills of western Virginia, near the hamlet of Wainscott. She might just as well have attended Foxcroft, Miss Porter's, Westover, Ethel Walker's, St. Anne's, Madeira, Rosemary Hall, or the like, but she was fortunate enough to get her first choice. Although mother and daughter were relieved of each other's constant proximity as every school term began, they always said good-bye at Pennsylvania Station with what appeared to be an affectionate embrace.

There were interruptions necessary for summer and winter vacations, but Wavertree Hall was the center of Suzanne's life from the fall of 1944 until she was graduated, in June 1948. In addition to a curriculum of academic excellence, Wavertree Hall promised everything Suzanne desired: an examination of her strengths, a development of her powers, an improvement of her skills, then a certification that she was prepared for life's adventures, and even a substantial guarantee of the self-assurance necessary for success. All these expectations were fulfilled in the company of approximately 120 young ladies much like herself, selected as carefully, and constantly available to each other for inspection, imitation and comparison. Absorbed by the values offered by Wavertree Hall, a fourteen-year-old adventurer left the world in which her mother had exercised authority for a new world. Suzanne arrived at Wavertree Hall late on a Tuesday afternoon in September 1944. Before supper in the dining hall was over for the new arrivals, she had made her first friend for life, Mei Mei Wilson, daughter of a Boston investment banker and a Chinese mother who had been graduated from Radcliffe. Mei Mei's mother was the daughter of a Chungking war lord, which was very romantic in Suzanne's opinion, and it was pleasant, Suzanne believed, to be able to choose one's own friends.

There was, in addition, more than friendship to be explored. Wavertree Hall was the creation and an expression of the iron

will of Miss Elizabeth Morgan, headmistress. By the time Suzanne arrived, "Miss Elizabeth," who was never called anything
else, was in her sixties, as spare and straight as an oak rail and
said to be five feet ten in her stocking feet. Actually, her height
was perhaps exaggerated, and could only be estimated, because
no one had ever seen her in anything but high-button boots
under long black skirts, or in her riding habit and riding boots.
By 1944 Miss Elizabeth's hair had turned snow white, and she
wore it close-cut and mannishly brushed back. It was rumored
that she had once been a stunning beauty, which was easy to
see, and had dealt with innumerable lovers. Her students found
it simple to imagine her past as tumultuous, but difficult to picture what kind of man would have stood up to her. Because of
what she herself called "good carriage," which she constantly
reminded her young ladies to imitate, she was an imposing
figure.

Every spring, Miss Elizabeth supervised the riding lessons
conducted in the rings at Wavertree Hall's own stables. Each
one of her young ladies was assigned a horse and then required
to perform the meanest tasks in caring for her horse's feed, tack
and stall. General Lee's cavalry had no better care, because
every fall, Miss Elizabeth had a major foray to lead: the Al-
bemarle County Hunt, which she required all her young ladies
to join. They came streaming after her through the rolling Virginia farms, chasing a running fox, doing their best to keep up
and "behave themselves decently." Fox hunting terrified Suzanne at first, but she could keep up, cursing between her
clenched teeth, because of bandy-legged Johnny Gilbert. She
remembered the lessons he had shouted at her for the sake of the
Piping Rock Horse Show. In his memory, she held her hands
low, her heels down, pressed her knees forward into each jump,
and kept her eyes up and out ahead—where the headmistress of
Wavertree Hall could always be seen leading the field.

Miss Elizabeth rode sidesaddle, in long black dress and top
hat, seated like a ramrod upon a massive black brute of a geld-
ing. Her hunter stood better than sixteen hands high, and it
was said she alone could handle him. She went sailing over rail
fences one after another, and then she would pause in the chase
to trot beside one of her ladies for what she called "a nice little

chat." She delivered short moral lessons without finding it necessary to catch her breath. Her panting students were left with an impression that they had been visited, in the midst of the hunt, by a goddess. She offered maxims of proper conduct as if she were only putting things in their rightful places, and her advice came wrapped in the cadences and soft syllables of old Virginia.

Her calm authority had an inexorable logic behind it. Miss Elizabeth had not one single doubt about what her duties were. As far as she was concerned, it was perfectly obvious that her responsibilities—indeed, all responsibilities—were inherited, just as land had to be. Although history might take twists and turns, because men could never control their passions, history's continuity from one generation to the next would be determined by purposeful women. Revolutions, wars, governments—good and bad—might come and go, just as they had in Virginia, but turn matters this way or that and young women would still marry. Then they would provide, for better or for worse, the manners of the household they ruled. They inevitably bore children. They alone would be responsible for the education of those children. It must be obvious that if the texture of society was to have any quality to it—"quality" was Miss Elizabeth's most important word—then the nation's best young women must have the right education.

Miss Elizabeth was so confident of her theory that she never felt she needed to argue it or shore it up by citing history's examples. Certain truths were, after all, self-evident. She only used the stories she knew so well from the romantic history of Virginia, or from England in the regime of the Whig aristocracy, by way of illustration. As an heiress of a great tradition, she was absolutely clear as to her own responsibilities. The Civil War had left two duties to a Christian Virginia lady: first, to care as best she could for the generations of "darkies" who still depended upon the mistress of Wavertree Hall; second, to inculcate gratitude to God for the favors bestowed upon Mr. Jefferson's republic in the hearts of the daughters of Yankee capitalists. Although the War had been lost, peace might still be won.

Riding to hunt was only one of the ceremonies upon which Miss Elizabeth insisted. Alert minds and healthy bodies were developed by a Spartan regime. The attractive young barbarians with whom she was charged would benefit immeasurably by sleeping outside in barracks under the roofs of screened porches. They were protected against rainfall, and snow if it did not drift in, but they would sleep outside in the bracing weather nevertheless. They were young and strong, Miss Elizabeth said, and they need not be coddled.

Moreover, if democracy was necessary—and Mr. Jefferson seemed to think it was—then it could survive only if the best of its citizens never wavered of their purposes and understood the meaning of discipline. Therefore, the student body of Wavertree Hall was organized like an army company, in four platoons of thirty students each, with a chain of command running up from the lowest privates—unevaluated freshman girls—to the company's Commander—an appointment every senior desired with all her heart. Lest any student misunderstand, or grow inattentive to the benefits of Miss Elizabeth's system, the entire school was drilled and marched, underwent inspections, and stood parade in white gloves with wooden rifles upon their aching shoulders. As a reward, Miss Elizabeth used her not inconsiderable connections to convince real generals of the United States Army —men whose names were legend in Pacific jungles and famous to the Normandy countryside—to come down from Washington to Wavertree Hall and review her troop. Some may have arrived embarrassed; all went away impressed.

As Miss Elizabeth saw it, her ladies had to be "prepared": they might themselves be wives of generals of the United States Army, or discover themselves in diplomatic posts at the Court of St. James's, or in Paris, or among the wild tribes of Mahomet at fringes of the American empire. The history of great nations was written in the biographies of warriors and statesmen; given the fortunes inherited by the ladies Miss Elizabeth was required to educate, she thought it perfectly reasonable that biographies would appear in due time that would mention her students' early education at Wavertree Hall. Her young ladies were the best this nation could offer, Miss Elizabeth said, and they must not be soft.

Experienced in the management of young women, Miss Elizabeth complemented her military scheme of four platoons with a sophisticated parallel social organization designed to absorb other potent young energies: the four "flower" sororities. In a twinkling the Wavertree Hall company could redirect itself toward more feminine concerns. Poetry was represented by The Daisies, music by The Daffodils, drama by The Lilies and dance by The Roses. Performances were prepared in each of these arts throughout the school year, then given in the spring during a week of celebrations, initiations, pageant and holiday. Everything was carried off in full costumes, expertly rehearsed and fabulously staged.

To support such an immense extracurricular labor, each new freshman girl was assigned to the sorority of her choice, and then as a "slavey" to a senior "mistress." Since the capacity of young women for cruelty was known to be almost unlimited, there were complaints of excess in the hazing of slaves by their mistresses. Perhaps in one or two instances the humiliations were carried too far or got a bit out of hand. Yet the effect of the entire system had to be considered beneficial; the mistresses were responsible for the initiation of their slaves in the spring, and generally were immensely proud of those they sponsored. Moreover, each mistress tutored her slave toward her eventual role in spring's Dionysian pageants; yesterday's "slavey" was inevitably tomorrow's mistress; and if appalling scenes were sometimes reported, probably exaggerated, every freshman suffered for the sake of the greater common good and waited until her turn came. Surely the flower societies were an accurate miniature of life itself.

From the leaders of the four flower sororities, from the platoon lieutenants and company officers, from the academically superior and from those few who could ride at the forefront of the hunt, Miss Elizabeth chose ten each year to be her "companions" on Sunday afternoons in April and May. Without a shadow of a doubt, the single greatest honor conferred at Wavertree Hall was to be among the ten thus honored by Miss Elizabeth. They were invited on Sunday afternoons to her house, where behind a boxwood hedge Miss Elizabeth had constructed her own shooting range. She taught each honor student to disassemble, clean and reassemble a Colt .45-caliber army automatic. She reviewed its eight safeties. She showed her ladies how to load a clip, how to bring sights down to the target, how to squeeze off each round,

how to wait until the evaporating kick, of its own accord, brought
the sight down again to the target. She allowed them to blast
away at a range of fifty yards until they could center seven out
of eight shots into the silhouette of a man. Miss Elizabeth quoted
Jefferson: "Eternal vigilance," she said, "is the price of liberty."

Before the ten were graduated, Miss Elizabeth had a chance
to talk with them again, to remind them that a lady's responsibilities to the nation were unending, that they must know how
to pour tea for great company, hold their reins lightly, keep a
firm seat in the saddle and know how to shoot. Although Suzanne lost the competition for appointment as company commander to her best friend, Mei Mei Wilson, she was selected as
one of Miss Elizabeth's honored companions in the graduating
class of 1948. Suzanne Benson was the commander of a platoon,
mistress director of The Lilies, academically fourth in her class
over all, but first in history, which was taught by Miss Lucille
Friedrich.

Perhaps Suzanne's success at history was inevitable. On the
day in 1944 that Suzanne arrived at Wavertree Hall she caught
the eye, and thereafter the fond attention, of "Miss Freddy." As
a result, when Suzanne Benson was a freshman she was assigned
as a slavey to Leslie Bond, the senior who was mistress director
of The Lilies. Mei Mei Wilson found herself slavey to Marianne
Shipman, mistress director of The Roses. Since Leslie Bond and
Marianne Shipman were the favorites of Miss Freddy in 1944,
they no longer lived in the barracks but had moved instead to a
comfortable suite in Miss Freddy's house—one of the former out-
buildings of Wavertree Plantation. Although no rule explicitly
stated as much, it was generally understood that if Mei Mei Wilson and Suzanne Benson could survive their initiation by Leslie
and Marianne, the younger girls had an excellent chance to replace the graduating seniors as boarders in Miss Freddy's comfortable, and privileged, lodgings.

Miss Freddy's position at Wavertree Hall was peculiar: she
was not only the school's instructor in history, and director general of spring's pageant, and faculty adviser to all the sororities,
and coach of field hockey and basketball, but also, in her special
way, an antigen to Miss Elizabeth. That is, Miss Elizabeth was
in her sixties, white-haired and from Virginia; Miss Freddy was

only twenty-six in 1944, her hair was raven black and shone with youth, and she was from New York.

Miss Elizabeth derived some of her authority from the elegance of her severe simplicity, while Miss Freddy's attractions depended upon various displays of folly—perhaps the colorful scarves she habitually knotted at her left wrist, or perhaps the variety of incongruous slouch hats she apparently collected and then wore every so often to express her whim of the day. Miss Elizabeth stood up straight for classic virtues; Miss Freddy's beauty was an example of older mysteries. Her complexion was as perfect as the gloss on good china, except that at the crest of each of her high cheekbones she had been blessed at birth with symmetrical beauty spots. These tiny triangles provided young girls with the materials for endless debate: Miss Freddy actually pasted them on each morning; no, they were natural; no, they were anomalies; no, they were curses put there as a result of old and terrible secrets. In the dining hall, when gossip turned around the question of why Miss Freddy would have left New York to shut herself up in the Virginia countryside, one answer suggested that she had put money into Wavertree Hall—most of the money that kept it going, as a matter of fact, because Miss Elizabeth's family was "ruined." Those gossips who pretended to be well informed, and to have the best sources, compared Miss Freddy's endowment of the school to the dowry nuns conferred upon nunneries when they took the veil. If that analogy left Suzanne's curiosity unsatisfied, eventually a senior finished off further questions with a smirk by saying, "You'll see."

Miss Freddy was respected. She was held in as much awe as Miss Elizabeth, because she was equally self-contained and confident, and perhaps because Miss Freddy's lessons to the daughters of Yankee capitalists better suited their tastes. Despite all there was to admire in the example set by Miss Elizabeth's "Christian Virginia lady," there was something about her that was arcane, foolish and, in the end, not-very-sophisticated. For example, Miss Elizabeth had an adjutant minister on duty to teach her pupils Christianity, Church of England style. On Sundays, Dr. Roswell Spaulding thundered from Proverbs and St. Paul, and led the congregation in "Onward, Christian Soldiers." While none of Wavertree Hall's young ladies would ever have laughed at Miss Elizabeth, Dr. Spaulding drew sniggers and mimicry and outlandish pantomimes.

He did not deserve every jibe. He preached that men of good will would inherit the earth. He enlisted half the school in support of the United World Federalists, and he could prove that when One World was established, and saw its interest in common peace, it would have its headquarters in Nice, France. None of this did any harm, and after Dr. Spaulding had bored everyone in church, some girls would be invited to visit Miss Freddy's house for tea and talk. They would discuss the operas of Wagner, the poetry of Mallarmé and Baudelaire, and the philosophy of Nietzsche. After church Miss Freddy produced readings from Molière's plays. Since she also cast the parts for spring's big productions, it had to be admitted she was just more interesting than Dr. Spaulding—that's what it came down to: "just more interesting."

Her house was fascinating too: she had "done so much with it." It was a frame cottage set apart a comfortable distance from the school's main buildings and barracks; when the plantation was working, it had been the overseer's house. Behind her cottage, Miss Freddy had designed and nurtured a marvelous garden, surrounded entirely by boxwood to a height of seven feet—a magic and secret space. She had spent a great deal of money to completely rework the house itself. The salons she conducted took place downstairs in a handsome sitting room with a grand fireplace and hearth. Next to the kitchen was Miss Freddy's study—large enough to contain her library and her grand piano, upon which she played Chopin's exercises constantly. Her plan downstairs also provided a separate entrance leading to a small bedroom for her two privileged boarders. It was said that she had her own bedroom upstairs, and another sitting room. Only Miss Freddy's senior boarders had seen what was upstairs.

As slaveys to Miss Freddy's honored seniors, Suzanne and Mei Mei were required as freshmen to spend their free hours on Saturdays and Sundays, and to snatch minutes from their weekday schedules, to haul wood for the fireplace, till and rake and mulch the garden at the back, sweep and tidy the kitchen. The moment they could complete a task, Mistress Leslie or Mistress Marianne thought of another to keep their slaveys running ragged. What began to frustrate Suzanne and Mei Mei more than anything else was that Miss Freddy never spoke to them at all. She would speak only to Mistress Leslie and Mistress Marianne, and Miss Freddy pretended that Mei Mei and Suzanne did not exist. She carried this design further than they had expected.

In November of the year of their service, she included them for the first time at an afternoon private tea. Their hopes soared, because they believed they would be joining a privileged association. They arrived at Miss Freddy's house with their hair done "and looking decent." But as soon as they passed through the gates of paradise, they were humiliated by being told to answer, "Yes, mistress," to whatever was required of them. When they were not fetching tea, or more cream, or more cookies, they were ordered to sit on their hands, palms up, on the floor and be silent. In the sitting room downstairs Leslie and Marianne and Miss Freddy then had themselves a nice afternoon's talk about Wagner's Ring Cycle and pretended not to notice their servants.

The next step in their education baffled them even more; they were required to memorize endless passages from a gardening encyclopedia. If they failed to recite what was assigned in its entirety, Mistress Leslie and Mistress Marianne demanded that they kneel on the palms of their hands, which was awfully uncomfortable, and toll through the list again: herbs—anise, basil, borage, burnet, caraway, chives, dill, fennel or sweet fennel, garlic, lavender. . . . By one device or another, the initiates were always at fault and had to begin again on their knees. Miss Freddy would not yet notice their presence. She always seemed to be somewhere behind their backs. By the time their freshman year had passed into February, Suzanne and Mei Mei were exhausted by the tasks their tormentors set for them, yearned for any kind word from Miss Freddy, and on the other hand, constantly promised each other to "see it through."

By then they understood, even if imperfectly, what was expected of them. If they feared it, which they were meant to do, it was mysterious and secret and exciting. There was never any privacy on the sleeping porches of the barracks, but Mei Mei and Suzanne found times to whisper to each other the rationalizations they constructed. They would not entirely admit what

they wanted, but they agreed that sleeping in the barracks
"ought to be out." They calculated that Miss Freddy's system
provided her with two new girls every three years. They would
be moving into her house as sophomores and they could stay
there until they were graduated. They would initiate their replacements when they were seniors, just as Mistress Marianne
and Mistress Leslie were initiating them. They concluded they
were just lucky to have arrived at the moment when Mistress
Marianne and Mistress Leslie were due to graduate. They
laughed over "just lucky." They began to review for themselves
exactly what they imagined Mistress Marianne and Mistress Leslie and Miss Freddy might have in store for them. They prepared themselves as well as two fourteen-year-old girls could. Finally, on the first of April, Mistress Leslie interviewed Suzanne,
and Mistress Marianne separately questioned Mei Mei. Both initiates were sworn to secrecy forever and ever. Both were promised they could back out at any time, but the oath of secrecy
would still hold. Both agreed to obey every wish of their
mistresses. Both repeated the secret word, "Shemhamforash."
Both received invitations to be at the door of Miss Freddy's
upstairs sitting room at exactly eight o'clock Friday evening,
"washed, anointed, bathed in lavender."

The bid they had hoped for had finally come. They washed
their hair, pressed the blouses of the Wavertree Hall school uniform, chose their best panties, tied the scarves at their necks just
so. They were at a loss about getting "anointed," but they
believed they had solved the problem of lavender with Yardley's
soap in the shower. They would be entering the upstairs rooms
in Miss Freddy's house—the suite none but the most favored at
Wavertree Hall had ever entered.

When their timid knocks were answered, Miss Freddy's secret
den exceeded in its luxury the scene they had hoped for. Scented
candles flickered when Mei Mei closed the door behind them,
then held steady again in a sweet and heavy air. Giant tapers set
upon iron stands cast their own shadows upon the walls, and the
girls could see at a glance that all four walls were entirely covered by folds of rich, dark green silk. Upon their right as they
entered stood a massive seventeenth-century bed, like one of the
official beds of France's royal court, raised up as if it were a

throne itself, canopied, with green velvet curtains tied back at its corners. What a cave it would be when its ties were undone!

Ahead of them, upon a Récamier covered in yellow silk, Miss Freddy reclined in a tea gown, fastened high at the neck and apparently cut from the same green velvet that hung from the bed's high frame. She had crossed her legs at her ankles and wore sandals of gold, much like those everyone would wear in the spring pageant. She was smiling faintly, probably at their awkwardness. On each side of her stood her favorites, costumed in linen and lace with girdles at their waists, and deep-cut blouses, like those they would be using in this year's production of *The Threepenny Opera*. Each of Miss Freddy's favorites was holding across her thighs her riding bat. They gave their first command nearly together: "Kneel."

Then Miss Freddy finally began to speak to them, in a voice so sweet, with such tenderness, that it took her initiates somewhat by surprise. "Know this," she began. "The Universe runs itself. Do you agree?"

Her pupils, anxious to please her at last, answered yes with all their fervent young hearts.

"And Nature prohibits nothing. Do you agree?"

Under the circumstances in which they found themselves, they could never have thought of any alternative.

"Nature knows nothing of the silly little rules made up by men on earth. Do you agree?"

They agreed. They answered yes step by step to Miss Freddy's catechism. They saw clearly for the first time how manners and morals were arbitrary affairs. They consented to all Nature's commands. They promised they would never equate chastity with virtue, any more than they would equate hunger with bliss, or thirst with happiness. They understood perfectly that love was Nature's garden. They saw vividly that a garden would be ruined if it was not cultivated. They realized why Nature must be spaded and hoed, weeded and tended, and then harvested. They did not think fruit should be left to rot on the vine. They knew at last why apples must be picked. They believed every flower should be cut. And arranged, too. Miss Freddy asked if they would like to go home now. Mei Mei trembled, but said no, with her eyes downcast. Suzanne said, "I have no home."

Miss Freddy was silent, measuring Suzanne's reply. Then she said with considerable authority: "Just an obedient yes or no will do, slave. Do you want to leave?"

Suzanne looked her lover straight in the eye. All time collapsed into the second that stood between them. Suzanne answered, with half a smile, an obedient, "No."

Mistress Leslie gave the order that they should rise. Standing, the novices were stripped of their clothes by their priestesses; next each had a green velvet ribbon tied around her neck; then their wrists were tied with lengths of velvet cord behind their backs. Together Mistress Leslie and Mistress Marianne unpinned Suzanne's long hair and let it fall free. When their victims were ready, the older girls stood before them. The formula they followed required them to say, each in her turn, to her novice: "I give you the first password, perfect love," followed by a sweet kiss upon her novice's lips; then: "I give you the second password, perfect trust," followed by a longer, lingering kiss upon the lips; and then finally: "I give you the third password, a kiss," whereupon each mistress took her slave in her arms for a kiss which gave Suzanne the sensation of how soft and sweet her own body must be.

Miss Freddy spoke again, saying that the slaves must kneel. After their mistresses had helped them to their knees, they were blindfolded. They heard Miss Freddy say: "Now is the ordeal."

Mistress Leslie must also have gotten down onto her knees, because from beyond her blindfold Suzanne took new instructions. She was asked to repeat the first password. After saying, "Perfect love," she received a kiss as before, and then was told that there would be three stages to the initiation; that this night was the first, a week from this night would be the second, and the third night would follow a week later. Did she consent? She did. She could hear Mei Mei agree just as she had.

Then she was asked to repeat the second password. After saying, "Perfect trust," and getting another kiss, she was told she must be purified as follows: on the first night, three times and seven; on the second night, eleven; and on the third, twenty-one times. Did she consent? She did.

There was a rustle, a pause, and Suzanne heard a bell tinkle. Her mistress guided her forward, until she was positioned with her thighs against the edge of the Récamier she had seen. Then she was pushed down until her breasts were pressed into its silk. She guessed that Mei Mei was being positioned exactly as she was, and that they were now facing each other across the Récamier's lower length. Again it was Miss Freddy who spoke: "Will you always be prepared to keep secret the arts of your sisters?"

They would be.

With an awful whir and crack, the riding crops they had feared all along came down three successive times. Mei Mei screamed at the first blow, probably mostly from surprise. But Suzanne had to admit to herself that the crop did sting, and the sting lingered across her bottom cheeks, burning with fire. At the third swipe, Suzanne was not as brave as she had supposed she would be. Despite the promises she had made to herself, tears welled up in her eyes and ran down from under her blindfold. "Three times you are purified," said Miss Freddy. "What now is the first password?"

After answering, "Perfect love," Suzanne felt strong hands take the hair behind her ears, and her face being raised, and a kiss given to her lips. This time it was Miss Freddy, and Suzanne answered her ardently. When Mei Mei had been given her kiss, Suzanne agreed without any regrets to be purified seven times, even if gritting her teeth would not save her from finally breaking into sobs.

But, that first Friday night, nothing else happened. They were dismissed after no more than passwords and kisses and "perfect love" and "perfect trust." They were sent back to their barracks and the sleeping porch with all the other common herd. They had to wait through an entire week, hiding the black-and-blue lines the crops had left upon their buttocks from any inquiries by their classmates. They had to fear what eleven "purifications" might make of them and the abandon Miss Freddy's ceremonies might produce. They sat in mild discomfort through an entire week of pointless classes, drills upon the parade grounds with make-believe rifles, and earnest chatter from other young ladies, who neither knew nor could be told anything at all. The two of them could only imagine in restless daydreams what had happened upstairs after they were dismissed.

Not until the second Friday night of their initiation, after eleven awful blows from the riding crop, were they required to masturbate until told to stop by their mistresses and Miss Freddy. A week later still, after the last night's incredible ordeal of twenty-one "purifications"—which left marks upon them both for a month—did two sobbing fourteen-year-old novices get to give and receive all the ecstasies for which they had suffered.

Thereafter, as their freshman year neared its end, Suzanne and Mei Mei continued to play the roles of slaveys, but took part in every scene that was played out in the secret suite upstairs. Miss Freddy remained loyal, more or less, to Miss Leslie Bond of Greenwich, Connecticut, and Miss Marianne Shipman of Llewellyn Park, New Jersey, but neither of the two initiates was jealous or impatient. In fact, they understood implicitly Miss Freddy's loyalty to her two departing favorites. Upon their graduation, in the spring of 1945, Miss Mei Mei Wilson of Boston and Chungking and Miss Suzanne Benson of New York and Oyster Bay would succeed to the private room on the first floor of Miss Freddy's overseer's house, and presumably to all her attentions in the suite upstairs.

Upon their return to school as sophomores in the fall of 1945, their expectations were fulfilled entirely. In the following three years they took the education, academic and moral, offered by Miss Elizabeth's Wavertree Hall, but lived apart—tutored in every voluptuous nuance, as well as in history, art and music, by Miss Freddy. They continued to ride to hunt after Miss Elizabeth, and they drilled up and down the parade ground with wooden guns at their shoulders, but they learned from Miss Freddy skills that might be invaluable: how to make up their eyes; how shadows and liners and lashes could be combined to create a mood; how perfumes called up various images; how a costume could be improvised by stitching a different hem or twisting a scarf into it. They tended the garden and tried every herb whose name they had memorized in their initiation. They brewed spiced soups, tasted wines, arranged flowers, and twisted blooms into each other's hair. They studied the qualities and the luck they might expect from rare jewels they planned one day to buy or have set at their feet. They painted each other's toenails.

To explore all their bodies might contain, they adventured through scenes they staged for themselves, playing for each other as if they were hidden in fragrant woods of leafy tenderness, but also rehearsing the pleasures they might discover in a desert of dry terrors. They explored every sensation nature had provided for them: every soft stroke they could send through each other's hair; every thrust that might make a heart pound wildly; every sweat they might raise up from each other's pores; every tear they could pull down from a victim's eyes; every groan or sigh or scream they could draw from each other's throats. By the time they were ready to initiate replacements, introducing two innocent freshmen through the ordeals of purification they had once enjoyed, they had exhausted each other. They could demonstrate without any flicker of embarrassment an attitude not much different from what they argued was nature's own: a wicked smile upon their lips, their shaded eyes thrilled at a new violation, their breasts and bellies shining in excitement at any degradation, captives of any miserable pleasure, capable of making one insatiable demand after another.

As soon as replacements were initiated into Miss Freddy's tutorial, Suzanne and her friend were ready, they believed, to experiment on the world itself. For their graduation, in 1948, Mei Mei's family came down from Boston and Suzanne's mother picked up Mimi by car from Miss Porter's School, where Mimi was a sophomore, and drove down to Virginia. The graduation ceremonies included a review of the Wavertree Hall Company Troop under the command of Captain Mei Mei Wilson, and the review was inspected by General Johnson McNair, a great friend, it was said, of Miss Elizabeth.

After the parade, General McNair spoke to the members of the student body, their parents and friends, assembled on folding chairs before the reviewing stand. He reminded them of the greatness of America, and how the American Dream was founded, in the final analysis, upon the American Family. In his opinion, the great Republic which he had been given the honor to defend in war had always been based upon its honored family traditions, and he called upon them to do their duty in the years to come, never forgetting the very special education they had been privileged to receive. General McNair said he knew from his own sad experience at war—and war was so terrible—that for evil to triumph, in the words of the great philosopher, it was only necessary for good men to do nothing. In conclusion, he was sure they would all agree "that those wise words were meant to include women too."

His remarks were answered by hearty applause, led from the dais by Miss Elizabeth and Miss Freddy, and joined by those seated upon the parade ground. Afterward, the Wilsons and their daughter and Mrs. Porter Benson and her daughters had dinner together at the Old Virginia Inn before returning to New York.

5

Green-and-White-
Striped Tents

1948

"MY MOTHER was appalled." Suzanne smiled with satisfaction at the memory. "I had made only one good friend at Wavertree Hall—and a Chinese girl at that!"

Suzanne would remind her mother that Mei Mei was only half Chinese—a distinction that only increased her mother's fury: "Half Chinese amounts to the same thing." Suzanne's assertion that Mr. and Mrs. Wilson were from Boston did nothing to soothe her mother's dismay: "Perhaps Mr. Wilson is from Boston, but Mrs. Wilson clearly is not."

Since Suzanne and Mei Mei Wilson were constantly demanding to visit each other during vacations, Mrs. Benson complained to a circle of sympathetic friends that she was "practically being haunted by that little yellow peril." Not one Christmas or spring or summer vacation could be scheduled without the two girls each insisting upon a week at the other's house. Mary Benson attempted to fend off as many of these exchanges as possible. During Suzanne's first two years at Wavertree Hall, she had sought to discuss the matter with her daughter "in a reasonable manner." But talks between mother and daughter on the subject of Mei Mei Wilson somehow always seemed to get off the track.

Suzanne would be adamant that she had a right to choose her own friends; her mother would say she didn't see why Suzanne couldn't choose less exotic friends; certainly there were many girls at Wavertree Hall from good families with whom Suzanne might find something in common. The argument became a ritual.

It always began in much the same way: Suzanne would have to apply to her mother for permission for Mei Mei to come and stay. It always ended with a long lecture by Mrs. Benson about "the importance of friends and family in life." Sometimes after Suzanne and her mother had exhausted each other, Mei Mei would be allowed to visit. Sometimes everything would have to be rearranged and Suzanne would go off to Boston, or in the summertime to the Cape, because Suzanne was always welcome in the Wilsons' house. There were no new developments in the dispute until the fall of Suzanne's junior year at Wavertree Hall.

Then, one evening, Suzanne waited until her mother had finished her second martini before bringing up the subject again. Suzanne was prepared for the usual discussion about all the wonderful girls whose parents her mother knew quite well and who could come to visit instead of Mei Mei, but in the midst of her mother's usual examination about who Suzanne's other friends might be, Suzanne said something to the effect that the Wilsons were "unbelievably rich."

"Money," said her mother, "has absolutely nothing to do with it." She reminded Suzanne that the year of her debut was approaching; that, thank heavens, society was not yet beholden to money. What with the war and all, there was a café society and all that, "but the real New York society had stood up quite well, just the same." Suzanne would soon want friends with whom she had "things in common," and although Mei Mei was a good friend at Wavertree Hall, there would be other associations and friendships in life that "would be far more important in the long run than those made at school."

Suzanne replied that she thought Mei Mei would be having her own tea to be presented in Boston; that if the old fuddy-duddies who ran the cotillion at the Copley couldn't stand to see a beautiful Chinese girl in the cotillion line, the Wilsons had enough money to have their own party. "And you can bet that just about everyone will come, too."

Her mother could hardly imagine that anyone would ever see Miss Wilson being presented at the Copley in Boston. Nor did she think it likely that Miss Wilson would be seen at the Grosvenor Ball in New York, or at the Junior Assemblies either, for that matter.

Yet Suzanne could hear in her mother's voice a passport she and Mei Mei might use, and she gambled for it: Mei Mei Wilson was going to be presented at the International Debutante Cotillion in New York, Suzanne said, and the Wilsons had enough money to give Mei Mei her own coming-out party wherever she wanted it—in Boston, on the Cape, or in New York—in December or June or any other time she felt like it.

Mrs. Porter Benson sniffed at the thought of the International Debutante Cotillion: "A ball for perfume manufacturers and Rotarians." Nevertheless, Mei Mei could come and visit for a week that Christmas, and her opposition to "that exotic Chinese beauty" seemed to soften—in fact, it seemed to be evaporating. At a suitable moment, Mrs. Porter Benson even agreed to have dinner at a restaurant with the parents of her daughter's friend. Perhaps, she explained, by having dinner with them she might "get to understand the Wilsons' point of view."

Mary Benson's point of view, she knew, was "sound." As a widow, she was entirely responsible for her daughter's education, and seeing to it that "the right thing was done." God knows, Suzanne was her only concern. She had seen her through this far, and she would see to it that she did the proper things, what was necessary, until she was married. After Suzanne was married, there wouldn't be much Mary Benson could do, but until then her responsibilities were clear.

In Mary Benson's opinion, Suzanne should not question the rights and wrongs of how society—good society—conducted itself. In New York, society was a simple, practical system—just a certain way the right families went about doing things. It allowed young girls to meet and get to know the young men they were likely to marry in any event. And she could assure her daughter that at seventeen or eighteen no young girl knew what was best.

It had to be understood there was nothing Mary Benson could do about Miss Wilson at the Junior Assemblies or the Grosvenor

Ball. If, on the other hand, Mei Mei was in fact going to be presented at the International Cotillion in New York, and at her own tea in Boston, then perhaps it would be all right if Mei Mei and Suzanne jointly had their own coming-out party in Oyster Bay after they were graduated from Wavertree Hall. "After all," said Mary Benson, "the girls have become such good friends."

Subsequently, over a series of dinners and theater evenings and careful visits back and forth, Mrs. Porter C. L. Benson of Centre Island, Oyster Bay, and New York, and Mr. and Mrs. Desmond H. Wilson of Boston came to an alliance and made treaties and selected a suitable date for the coming-out party to be given jointly in honor of their daughters, on Thursday, June 17, 1948. They agreed that the Benson house on Centre Island, Oyster Bay, was an ideal place. After walking through the rose garden south of the house, they also agreed that its space was perfect for the tent that would be erected to contain the thousand young people they expected. There was no need to spell out that Suzanne's social credentials in New York society were being traded for Mrs. Wilson's inheritance of treasures won in inscrutable wars on the Chinese mainland. Instead they met those delicate crises that did arise in connection with the party's provisioning by a generous acceptance of the other partner's contribution to the joint venture. Since the site of the party was at Suzanne's home, "a truly lovely setting," according to the Wilsons, the very least the Boston couple could do was to write checks for "this or that small necessity." The total contributed by the Wilsons was an uncounted amount somewhere between fifty and one hundred thousand dollars—a sum roughly matched by Mrs. Benson in a capital contribution consisting of Suzanne, her background, bloodlines and credentials.

Once constituted, the Benson-Wilson partnership was a busy affair. Besides the issuing of fifteen hundred handwritten invitations, there were at least a thousand other details that went into a successful coming-out party: reserving the twenty-two-man Lester Lanin orchestra; erecting the gigantic green-and-white-striped tent; constructing an oak dance floor the size of two basketball courts; ordering truckloads of champagne sent out from Sherry's—which had to be unloaded early; renting four hundred gilded chairs, seventy-five round tables and linen, three steam tables to keep food hot; and having twenty-five hundred stemmed glasses unpacked and washed by Day-Dean's caterers. Ten days before the date of the party, the lawns around the Benson home on Centre Island looked as if Barnum & Bailey's circus were being unpacked. Mrs. Porter Benson wandered through the scene somewhat dazed by the number of practical questions she was required to answer. The dance floor extended somewhat farther than planned; could the rosebed at the west end of the garden be dug up? Would it be all right if the apple orchard across the road was used for the guests' parking? Could the guy wires for the tent be tied down at the base of that oak? Did Mrs. Benson's liability insurance cover part-time help? Suzanne's mother smiled vaguely through all this. She was comforted by the constant presence of her old friend John Putnam, and by starting the champagne, she admitted, a bit early.

Suzanne and Mei Mei, who had come to stay two weeks in advance, steered clear of her. They had schedules of their own to meet, and Suzanne's younger sister, Mimi, acted as their lady in waiting. The two debutantes were busy every night except Sunday, attending ten coming-out parties in a row, celebrating the introduction to Long Island Gold Coast society of other seventeen- and eighteen-year-old women like themselves. They attended parties under green-and-white-striped tents upon lawns in Locust Valley, Glen Head, Lloyd Harbor, Mill Neck, Oyster Bay Cove, Peacock Point, and on Snake Hill Road, overlooking Cold Spring Harbor.

The society to which these young women were introduced was, curiously, a society they already knew quite well. The name of each young woman could be found in the junior or senior class lists enrolled at a handful of schools, not all of which were exactly like Wavertree Hall, but none of which was very different either.

They danced every night with young men with whom they were entirely familiar. Many of their partners were the same ones with whom they had practiced the box step at dancing class when they were ten. The names of these reliable beaux could be found among the students enrolled at schools such as Andover, Exeter and St. Paul's School. In the nature of things, some dancing partners had to be slightly older and therefore had already gone on to studies at the appropriate Ivy League colleges. In order to provide what was invariably called "circulation," at each dance there had to be an excess of young gentlemen to young ladies in a ratio of approximately three or four to one. A massive stag line "made for a better party."

Good parties depended upon a good list. Drawing up the list of who should be invited, and who should not, was the work of specialists. Extracting the right values from a family background to find suitable young people was not a matter that could be handled correctly by just anyone. Prominent among the specialists at drawing up the right list were Episcopal ministers and their wives. They were uniquely qualified for their task by long tradition, on the one hand, and by the objective of "coming-out parties," on the other: the certification in due time of a suitable Christian marriage. Logically, therefore, no Jewish boy or girl fit the requirements of any list. On some lists the children of a few prominent Catholic families had to be included because they were neighbors, or perhaps associated in an inextricable way in business, or members of the same clubs. Obviously, Episcopal sextons of lists faced no easy task, but they persevered.

In any given year, the Junior Assemblies in New York was the high point on the presentation calendar, offering the debuts of about sixty young women. Arranging suitable lists of young gentlemen from among New York's limited population of designated heirs to great capital funds might not present any special problem for the Junior Assemblies. Yet in the same year there were always individual parties given by doting parents for their marriageable daughters which were to include—as did the Benson and Wilson affair—two hundred young women, and therefore something like eight hundred young men, if the right proportions were to be maintained. Obviously not all the students at Harvard, Yale and Princeton qualified. Among those who did qualify, some would not accept. Consequently the lists of Mrs. William de Rham's dancing classes at the River Club had to be searched again. The Social Register was, of course, a standard source, but sometimes it did not supply all the names necessary—particularly if there was a competing event. The girls themselves often came up with suitable names and their mothers constantly added others. In many instances the list used at one party could be patched into another. Summer vacations created new discoveries. A few young men might be enlisted during the winter while skiing, but not many—a mere handful from the Foster Place at Stowe, or perhaps from Mrs. Ryan's lodge at Mont Tremblant.

Once they were added to the lists, the young men and young women followed a reasonably standard procedure over a period in June of about three weeks of days and nights of debutante parties. Small dinner dances were scheduled at eight o'clock each night. At the dinner dances the proportion between young men and young women was about equal and they ate and danced in pairs. To these dinner dances the young women invited their favorite beaux, or their mothers chose escorts for them. During dinner, mothers and fathers, interested aunts and uncles, or sponsoring godparents could be seen and appreciated. Since their efforts were understood to be at an end, appropriate champagne toasts were made to the aged for bringing into the world "a really marvelous girl." After the dinner dance, at about eleven o'clock, the appointed escorts would shepherd the really marvelous girls to the main stage—the big dance already begun under the tent.

At last all the effort of collecting lists was put to its final test: the stag line, outnumbering the available females by four to one, crowded along the edges of the dance floor. Identically dressed in black-tie uniforms, they surged between the tables near the edges of the tent or hovered in black clumps around the poles that supported the tent at its center. For ancient but forgotten reasons, the poles were always disguised with vines of smilax and ivy and hung with balloons. Around these venerated symbols, the stag line sipped from glasses of champagne, setting them down wherever they pleased when they spied an attractive girl being whirled by.

Once the girl had separated a potential partner from the herd, she had sacred tasks to perform. As he advanced toward her, weaving between the shoulders of other couples, she had to keep his attention with her eyes until she could induce him to tap upon the shoulder another gentleman indistinguishable from himself. Then, as her next partner gathered her waist to his belly, she could adapt her step to a different style, swing her arm over a new shoulder, smile up into fresh eyes, and pretend that she adored—at least for eight bars of music—all the possibilities he might represent. Her turn with each lover probably lasted no more than one minute before another took his place. To the extent that she could display all the excitement, all the variety, all the advances and enticements, all the delights of the sex she represented, she could expect an almost endless succession of partners. No matter how much her feet hurt, not one of these young women ever voluntarily gave up the dance floor for even a minute.

They danced continuously, in long white dresses. They two-stepped to choruses of bouncy show tunes. They knew by heart Cole Porter, Gershwin and Kern. They had practiced for so many years the turns and whirls they were required to do that they could have fox-trotted in their sleep. When they waltzed, they were swept around the floor in the galloping Vienna style; when they sambaed, they were marched in a step straight from Rio. They smiled and laughed and flirted. They were led to believe that the long hours they passed upon the dance floor were spent searching profitably for the right man, the one who would make them happy—for richer, but not necessarily for poorer, in sickness and in health, until death did them part. If they were not overly concerned with the "poorer" part, it was because their long white dresses were expected to be convertible—within the near future—into wedding gowns. Until that day the music would never stop—at least not before dawn.

Then the cars would be brought up to the door of whoever owned the house and had given the party, and the escorts appointed for the evening would drive the debutantes to their homes, or to the homes of the friends with whom they were staying. On the way home it was not unusual to have to turn on the windshield wipers to clear the dew and morning fog that accumulated. There might be good-night kisses at the doorstep, but by then everyone was too exhausted for passion. In any event, the broad, warm light of sunrise contradicted every promise—except that they would dance together once more that very night.

Exhausted virgins slept until midafternoon, washed their hair yet again, and saw to it that another dress was pressed and ready. They fitted a new pair of dancing shoes on their swollen

feet and set off again for the next dinner dance at eight. For ten
days, more or less, they lived on the crest of a wave. After that,
according to their own estimation, they would be "on the
beach." Exactly why they believed that the story of their life was
to be contained in so fleeting a season, they hardly ever questioned.

Suzanne, too, sensed on the evening of June 17 that her ap-
prenticeship was ending. For her own coming-out party she had
selected a white dress of batiste, trimmed at its hem with ecru
lace. The skirt was full, and decorated horizontally with row
upon row of white ribbon. The waist was narrow; the bodice
fitted tightly over her breasts and was held by ribbon straps over
her shoulders. With Mei Mei's help she wound her red hair up
off the nape of her neck, and when her mother asked if it all
wasn't a bit older in its effect than Suzanne meant, Suzanne
paused before answering so that her mother would understand
the new authority she was claiming. "No," said Suzanne. "That's
how I want to look."

To honor the occasion, Suzanne took from her bureau drawer
a small grained leather box that she had not opened or touched
in ten years. Her father's card still lay in it. From the red velvet
cushion she took the brooch with the double pearl in its center
and pinned it above her heart. Mei Mei said she thought Suzanne was the most beautiful woman who had ever lived.

The dinner dance they attended first was hosted by the Wilsons at the Seawanhaka Corinthian Yacht Club. Suzanne's escort,
Nick McKay, answered handsomely the Wilsons' toasts to Suzanne. By the time Suzanne arrived back at her mother's house,
Lester Lanin's orchestra was already thumping away at show-
tune choruses. John Putnam took the part of her father
and waltzed Suzanne around once. Thereafter Suzanne never
stopped dancing, except to eat scrambled eggs twice, until after
six in the morning.

Lanin's orchestra quit playing, but Mr. Wilson paid them
overtime to go on. When overtime ran out and Lanin's men
packed up to leave, a Princeton boy sat down at the piano and
provided another half hour of music. At about seven o'clock, the
last fifty or sixty people wearily abandoned any more of it. They
left a dance floor across which the long rays of the morning sun

threw strange shadows from the legs of the chairs and tables standing empty along its edge.

Suzanne's mother had passed out at about three o'clock and John Putnam had carried her to bed. Mei Mei had disappeared somewhere. Nick McKay had lurched away—"Gotta go to the john." Suzanne realized that she was entirely alone except for the caterers' men, who were breaking down the steam tables and starting to clean up. She found a half-filled glass of champagne left at a table and drank it. She saw another and wandered over to finish it off too, when one of the caterers' men called to her: "I got a full bottle, sweetheart, if you want it."

"Bring it to me," Suzanne said. She stood in the center of the dance floor, waiting for him to obey.

Apparently he didn't quite understand her at first, because he hesitated. She repeated her command, and with an embarrassed laugh he did as he was told. He must have been fifty, she guessed. He had an anchor tattooed on his arm with a name in the banner. She gave him a smile like the ones she had been flashing all night: "What was her name?"

"Mary Ann," he answered. He was awkward.

"Marvelous," she said, and then allowed him to stand there while she used his shoulder for support to balance first on one leg and then the other while she untied the straps of her dancing shoes. When she had got them off, she handed them to him as if she were paying him for his bottle of champagne, took the bottle from him, then turned her back, walking toward the west end of the tent. She ducked under a guy wire and set off down the lawn toward the beach. He called something after her, but she could not hear it distinctly.

The morning dew on the lawn chilled her toes. When she arrived at the gate of the tennis court, she swung it open. It squeaked on rusty hinges. Inside the fence the grass needed to be cut under the spectator chairs. The cast-iron chairs and the table in which the umbrella would have been set needed paint and showed flecks of rust. Along the inside of the fence, the honeysuckle should have been trimmed back. The net was rolled away around the far post, and she could see that its tape was frayed. At the end of the court on the bay side there were strands of beach grass at the foot of the fence—as there always would be in spring—but no one had swept them up. The chalk lines of the court itself had not been painted for at least a year, and the clay surface had not been rolled. Suzanne walked down toward the bangboard, where the roller had been left up against the fence, took a swig from her champagne bottle, then set it down to start the roller. But the roller was rusting too, and its axle had not been greased, and it screeched when she pulled on it, starting hard. She dropped the handle, left the roller where it was, and looked around the court once more for something she could play with.

6

La Rue

1948

BY JUNE 1948 Suzanne's mother suspected her daughter of being rebellious—perhaps mutinous might have been the better word, except that Suzanne made no overt challenge to her mother's system. Mary Benson could never precisely define, or perhaps would never admit, exactly how Suzanne was collecting the arms of revolt, but she was sure of it just the same. There was always something about Suzanne in the presence of her mother that had the air of a "clear and present danger." Mary Benson spoke to John Putnam of her fears: Suzanne was always "so restless," but in John Putnam's opinion it was "just youth having its day."

Suzanne felt her mother was being overly protective, as usual. Suzanne's objectives—to the extent she thought about them— were the same as every other woman's, and no different from her mother's. Suzanne had learned the gentle arts of poise, manners and dancing, just as she was required to do. She had also learned how to challenge a boy with her eyes—at the beginning she pretended she would fight with him if he wanted—and if her challenge was sufficient, it would deliver the boy to her side as if by magic. And so she studied her eyes as an experienced painter would, from various distances and in various lights, and tried upon them mascaras, lashes of various lengths, creams added on and wiped off, pencil doodlings of all shapes and lengths. She had been asked to perform certain social tasks; she thought dancing was great fun, provided she had partners; attracting partners was a necessary skill, and therefore she learned it obediently.

Her mother had sent her off to Wavertree Hall, where she learned that the society of young women like herself was indeed a pleasure. She learned all the nuances and fathomed all the delights of the pleasure to which she had been delivered. When she came home for vacations, her mother had seen to it that she should attend the progressive cotillions by which young ladies were expected to widen their acquaintance. The result was that she had fascinated a list of something like two hundred young men. After the dances, many of her beaux wanted the kisses that custom and tradition agreed they ought to have. Therefore, Suzanne ran a long series of laboratory experiments before the mirror upon her full and sensuous mouth—trying out the various shapes and colors and sheens, the tricks that her lips might do for her.

To her mother's purposeful training and to the education she had received at Wavertree Hall from Miss Elizabeth and Miss Freddy in the uses to which her beauty might be put, Suzanne faithfully added the results of studies she made on her own. For example, she examined the magazines published for women and rehearsed all the many ways she could arrange her extraordinary hair. It still grew to below her waist, thick, deep-red, strong hair, for which she was required to develop techniques of arrangement and programs of maintenance of her own—all of which took great skill and devotion. Moreover, she was a scholar of all the ways that she might care for or improve her lustrous skin. She knew soaps and scrub bars and sponges and blushes and rouges. Although she glowed with good health, she took nothing for granted and reviewed systems to improve all that nature had provided. She was never troubled by pimples, blackheads or oily skin—difficulties that appeared as threats in a thousand advertisements—but she considered seriously all the prescriptions she might use in case any of these calamities should ever visit her.

Just as she had learned from Miss Freddy all the heady

powers that perfumes could add to voluptuousness, she observed with a shrewd eye her mother's example, and the examples provided by her mother's friends, of the science of decoration—of furniture and table settings and linens and curtains, and how great houses, or interesting ones, could be managed. She shopped the windows along Fifth Avenue and Madison as if she were going to buy as she pleased. She looked carefully at fabrics and colors. She knew good furniture from imitations. She never failed to pause and meditate on what Tiffany had arranged in its windows as rewards for the successful woman.

She made notes and collected sketches on clothes and fashion. She read *Vogue* and *Harper's Bazaar* and *Town & Country* with the devotion to which they surely were entitled and with a scissors nearby, ready to cut out and add to her files any ideas she calculated as especially suitable to her particular case. How she looked and what she wore and where she went obviously mattered; everything she read and saw and heard in the world that she inhabited plainly said so. The curriculum she followed was purposeful; her studies would be rewarded soon enough; and the objectives of every woman she knew were invariable—to make themselves pleasing to men. Far from rebelling against her mother's standards, Suzanne embraced them entirely. She enjoyed to its utmost being "marketed" as a debutante. She was exuberant that something over six hundred young men had been delivered to her at her own coming-out party and that good manners required every one of them to dance with her. If she was an asset to be displayed, as were the jewels arranged artfully upon cushions in Tiffany's windows, she thought it only reasonable to discover as much as she could about who the customers were.

Suzanne soon realized that coexisting with the institution of debutante parties supervised by socially adept Episcopalian ministers there was another institution called La Rue, a nightclub situated between Madison and Park on the north side of Fifty-eighth Street, supervised by swarthy Italian proprietors. In fact, green-and-white-striped tents and La Rue were heavily dependent upon each other, although at first the politesse of the situation might seem confusing to the uninitiated. Fortunately, before

I took Suzanne there for the first time, I had been through the elaborate rites La Rue entailed on innumerable occasions.

An elaborate comedy was required. When I picked up the young beauty I was to escort to The Senior Get-Togethers, or whatever dance was scheduled for the Ritz or the Plaza that night, I would be asked whether I planned to return my prize to her family's home immediately after the dance.

"Oh, yes," I was supposed to say. "However," I was allowed to inquire, "would it be all right if we stopped for a moment after the dance at La Rue?"

The girl's father might then frown slightly, but in the end he would invariably allow that as long as it was La Rue, "That would be all right."

Then, as we waited for the elevator we would all shake hands, and the girl's parents would give her a hug and urge her to have a good time, and I would be reminded again that La Rue was approved, but any other nightclub was forbidden—the cause perhaps of ruination to their precious flower. I could reassure them by repeating, "Just La Rue," as the elevator doors closed.

All of which was odd enough in itself but particularly strange because La Rue was said by some informed sources to serve as the headquarters for not one but two rings of prostitution. The second of these rings was alleged to handle only girls under seventeen. Surely these allegations must have been considered false by thoughtful parents.

Inside its double doors La Rue had a hatcheck concession situated at the immediate right, and it was staffed by a plump fifteen-year-old blonde who was desired by at least half the graduating classes of Princeton, Yale and Harvard. Unfortunately Reni was rumored to be "reserved" by the club's manager "for older gentlemen." Perhaps Reni was always busy later because she was a favorite among Racquet Club members, or perhaps she went home to her mother in Queens. Whatever the facts really were, or the rumors may have pretended, Reni was sexy enough to engender such wild stories.

Beyond Reni's hatcheck bay, an antechamber of blued mirrors, indirect lighting and black ceilings was blocked at its far end by a maître d's velvet rope. On almost any night, a crowd of Texans with money or Chicago grain merchants with their wives were firmly being turned away. Yet after the designated dance any debutante and her escort could slip quickly by a crowd of disgruntled out-of-towners. The rope barring the way would be unhitched, and they would be sent directly to the bar and promised a table by the dance floor as soon as one was available. The members of New York society were easily distinguished by the look of feigned boredom composed on their faces, and they could always be said to have just come from some important affair. Consequently most men were in black tie, and almost all the women in long dresses.

Two orchestras provided continuous dancing: Eddie Davis played a magic violin across show tunes in the two-step beat that society insisted upon, varied from time to time by a lilting waltz; and a relief band played rumbas, sambas and tangos. During the Latin interludes most New Yorkers abandoned the dance floor to return to their tables or the bar. What was most curious was that at La Rue—and only at La Rue—gentlemen could "cut in" to dance with ladies they presumably knew, and no fuss was ever made about it. "We're old friends" was the password, and if a young man cut in on a married woman, the decent thing for the husband to do was to retreat, smiling, to the bar. After a dance, the lady was returned to her table or to her evening's companion at the bar, no questions asked.

It was a club: dancing at La Rue was a continuation of other dances at other times in other places; on almost every night half the patrons had "known each other for years." It was a haven: husbands and wives came to relive their youth and rekindle the future. It was a safe place: if a man brought someone else's wife or a pretty young thing he happened to meet on his travels, there never seemed to be any need to pass that kind of news along to the city's gossip columnists. It was a retreat: lawyers stopped by after working late over a stock prospectus; bankers arrived who had not yet closed their deal; contractors came to sketch up plans; public relations men hovered at the bar to have a drink with new connections. To Suzanne, who had been tucked away at a girls' school in distant Virginia, La Rue looked as if it might be the beachhead to the real world.

After a dance at the Plaza that ended at 1 A.M., I took Suzanne to La Rue during Christmas vacation in 1946. It was her first

time. She was sixteen and I was wildly in love with her. She had
sworn that she loved me too, and for Christmas had presented
me with a pair of orange and black socks which she claimed she
had knitted for me. "Princeton's colors," she said with pride.
When I was taping her biography in the fall of 1970 I asked her
if she remembered the orange and black socks. She admitted she
did. They had been knitted by her freshman slavey at Wavertree
Hall.

I hoped that by transporting her to La Rue I could avoid
being tapped upon the shoulder every minute by another stag-
line competitor. We walked from the Plaza across Fifty-eighth
Street, and made our way through the crowd of tourists barred
at the door by the velvet rope. Although to the captain who
stood guard at the rope we were both obviously underage, he
sent us to the bar.

Around the semicircular bar there was a crowd three deep.
Near the corner a man of about thirty gave up his stool and
offered it to Suzanne. Since he could get the bartender's attention, I had no choice but to allow him to order the drinks for us—
the advantage I had held as "an old La Rue hand" was dissipat-
ing. The crowd pressing around the bar made it difficult for me
to find a place, and after the drinks arrived and John David Garraty had introduced himself, Suzanne and her new friend engaged in a conversation too distant for me to join. Every so
often, Garraty would call out over intervening shoulders and
heads to me: "How ya doing, pal?"

I answered by taking Suzanne out on the dance floor, but the
moment the Latin band came on, she said she wanted to return
to our drinks. No sooner did I return her to the barstool Garraty
had guarded than he asked her to rumba. He handled their departure so smoothly that I could find no way to object.

By three in the morning the crowd at the bar had thinned
enough so that we had the place almost to ourselves. Suzanne
danced with me, and with John David Garraty just as often. I
was increasingly impatient, but Garraty had all the time in the
world. He could talk without stopping, and she was apparently
fascinated by him. As he stood at the bar, stories about himself
poured out. He told them all with deprecating laughter. He said
he had studied history at Columbia, and he did imitations of

what I was supposed to believe were his professors on the intricate relations among the crowned families of Europe. He did French, German and Italian accents, and an Irish brogue that did carry a certain charm.

He explained that he was from a family of black Irishmen, great liars and inventors, every one of them; that he had worked as a reporter on the *Herald Tribune;* that he now did public relations—which he said meant translating the grunts and groans of inarticulate businessmen into serviceable English in press releases.

"If my release appears in the paper, I sometimes get paid by my clients."

"How can they be clients," Suzanne asked, "if they don't pay you?"

"If the release appears in the paper, and I can get a Bachrach photo of the son-of-a-bitch printed along with it, then I always get paid—especially if it runs in the *Times.*"

"Businessmen pay to get their pictures in the paper?" It was hard to tell if Suzanne was really incredulous, or leading Garraty on.

"That's what I do, by jingo. Make history for a fee. I prove to them that they exist. If they don't appear in the *Times,* they are afraid they might not be here at all."

He reeled off a list of clients he claimed he represented, and the restaurants to which he took each one—which, he said, was how he got to be so fat and happy. He was no more than five feet ten and he must have weighed at least 230 pounds. He said he ate well, slept well and had a hundred friends. His job was to make business seem like fun, and it really was, it really could be. He always had tickets for the Yankees, and for the Ranger games at Madison Square Garden, and for the fights—would Suzanne like to go to the fights? "I'll give you a call when there is a good fight coming up."

Suzanne said she'd go to a fight, but she liked hockey games better. With what could have been generosity, she said she was sure that I would like to see the Rangers play. She explained to Garraty that I had played hockey for Andover—in the Garden, too—against St. Paul's School.

"Just call, pal, that's all you have to do. I'll have tickets for a

Ranger game for you and your little lady whenever you want them. Give me a call. Anytime."

When I finally got Suzanne out of La Rue that night, she kissed me passionately all the way home in the taxi—which soothed my pride somewhat. After that first night, whether I was the lucky one or some other blessed escort had been designated to take Suzanne to a cotillion, as soon as the dance was over she insisted they go to La Rue, where she always sought out John David Garraty. "But you were just boys," she would explain years later.

In 1946 and 1947 she used La Rue to meet some of Garraty's friends. At the bar one night in the fall of 1947 she met a former New York City cop who said he was also "in public relations."

Suzanne wanted to know, "What kind of public relations?"

"For unions," said the Irish cop.

"What kind of unions?"

"The bartenders, maybe the steelworkers, electricians—guys like that."

"What do you do for them?"

"I work things out. I get the union guys and the company guys to sit down and talk things over. Maybe we go fishing for a couple of days. Maybe we take a yacht and go cruising down Long Island Sound, play a little poker, give everyone a chance to relax."

"Do you take girls on the yacht?"

"That could happen," said the Irish cop. "That has come to pass, but not girls like you, Miss Debutante."

"Well, now, Officer," said Suzanne, imitating a thick Irish brogue. "I've heard it said that Rosie O'Grady and the colonel's lady are sisters under the skin. Do you think that's true?"

"Glory be," he answered in a brogue slightly more legitimate than her version. "I'd surely like to find out."

Suzanne did not explicitly state that she was prepared to conduct what both she and her new admirer agreed would be "scientific experiments" upon the matter of Rosie O'Grady and the colonel's lady. But on the nights when she arrived at La Rue with some baby-faced prep-school boy and found the Irish former cop standing there at the bar, she quickly brought the subject up again. She would ask if he had been conducting any experiments lately. He would answer that he had not yet begun the series he had in mind, but he was anxious to start. It was not long before Suzanne had him convinced that he would soon have every reason to be proud of himself; that if his experiment could not be tested today, there would be a tomorrow when it would be.

When they danced together, the former cop usually hummed along with the show tunes the band played. Late one evening, when La Rue was beginning to empty, Suzanne asked him to sing for her: "You have such a beautiful voice."

"What song would the colonel's lady choose to have dedicated to her?"

"'Danny Boy,'" she said.

"That's a song an Irish father sang for his youngest son. It's not to be sung to ladies."

"Sing 'Danny Boy' anyway," she said.

He began to sing quietly at first, in the bar, and against the two-step music in the main room. As his tenor voice gathered force, the bar conversations died away. Then others came from the main room to stand in the archway between the bar and the dance floor to listen and watch. Eventually Eddie Davis brought his orchestra to a stop too, so that there was nothing left in either room except "Danny Boy" coming around for the second time. Those who could see as well as hear had a view of a seventeen-year-old girl perched upon a barstool, her legs crossed comfortably, dressed like a debutante, with thick red hair that hung straight to below her waist. In front of her a space had been cleared, and about eight feet from the girl was a big black-haired man with both his arms extended wide, their palms out toward the girl. He was singing to her in a tenor that rose up from the pit of his stomach, and his eyes were glistening. Her eyes were as moist as his. When he came to the end of his song, their audience applauded as she rose from her stool to meet him halfway across the space that had separated them. She put both of her hands upon his cheeks, raising her own face to kiss him upon his lips.

He answered by folding his arms around her, and it looked as if she would disappear into the wall of his broad chest. There were witnesses who also said she reached up and drew her index finger across his lips, as if she was sealing them into silence. She said something to him, he laughed, and he nodded his head in a resigned way.

According to John David Garraty, what she was supposed to have said was, "Never," and what the Irish former cop had answered was, "All right." Garraty claimed that his fellow practitioner in the arts of public relations told the story on himself. "That broad," the singer of "Danny Boy" would say, "was too much for a simple Irish lad like myself. I am glad I had the opportunity to sing to her, but I could not have made a general practice of it."

There were others Suzanne met in La Rue who were less modest in their hopes. Garraty introduced Suzanne to a fifty-year-old man who waltzed beautifully, and who Garraty said was "in black-market steel." The steel trader pestered Garraty about Suzanne constantly, claiming that in his entire life he had never held a waist so supple. "I've made a fortune in two years," he assured Garraty, "and I'd give it up for a night with that little piece." Garraty passed on the compliment to Suzanne, who answered that the steel trader wouldn't give up a penny to a blind man—which Garraty had to admit was probably true.

Garraty told Suzanne that Peter Dickerson ran the most important real estate brokerage business in the city—Dickerson, Rolfe and Streitfeld. Dickerson liked young girls—the younger the better. He told Garraty he had never seen so slim a figure and so cute a bottom as Suzanne's—like a boy's! "Mr. Dickerson is cute too," said Suzanne, "and he can think whatever he likes."

"John Carter," said Garraty, "runs the hottest ad agency in town." When Carter gave his card to Suzanne, and said that she should model, and that he would help to get her started, Carter explained that the agencies were looking for the "all-American-girl type." Fashion models were an entirely different thing, Carter explained. They had to be skinny to show the clothes well. The agencies needed models like Suzanne, models who would look natural pushing a vacuum cleaner through the house, or washing venetian blinds up on a ladder. Suzanne had great legs, said John Carter, and the scrubbed, fresh look every agency was going crazy to find. In his opinion, Suzanne could make a hundred grand a year as a model. "Thanks," she said. "But it's not something I need right now."

Henri de Puyans, the American representative of the French banking family, did not see Suzanne as an "all-American girl." He laboriously explained to her that manners in Paris were quite different from those in America; that it was quite common for husbands, who were perhaps a trifle bored with their marriages, to have a good friend to whom they would be faithful for years. There were many such cases in Paris. It was considered foolish in France to get a divorce over nothing. It was more practical for the marriage to continue, because the wife need not be insulted. On the other hand, the mistress enjoyed many advantages too. In the opinion of Henri de Puyans, as long as the man could afford it, there were many opportunities for a young woman who had perhaps a small apartment of her own, yet was free to meet the more important men and women of politics and business—and banking, of course. Particularly, as in his own case, where the banker was required to travel extensively. It gave a young woman the opportunity to travel, to entertain, to broaden her perspectives, to polish her education. "Style," said Henri de Puyans, "is, in the end, everything."

"According to Monsieur Puyans," Suzanne said, laughing, "I have style, panache, verve, good manners, perfect teeth, small breasts like apples, and know which fork to use first. Which do you think, John David Garraty, is the most important of these for a woman?"

"I'm an apple man, sweetheart. Let me have a bite of them ol' apples every time."

"You are a barbarian, John David. I think Monsieur de Puyans is correct. Forks are very important."

Whether it was De Puyans, or John Carter, or the waltzing steel trader, or Peter Dickerson, or any of the others, John David Garraty introduced Suzanne to them all as if he were the secretary of a club that met each night at La Rue. Within a year, Suzanne was such a well-recognized regular that she was greeted by the captain at the rope by name—"Miss Benson"—and automatically shown to a stool at the bar, together with whatever young gentleman she had dragged along as an escort from New York society's certified cotillions.

After the Grosvenor Ball at Thanksgiving in 1947, Suzanne arrived at La Rue as usual. She spun off her escort for the evening, George Macdonald, by introducing him to her old friend Garraty; and Garraty in turn soon had poor George trapped in a conversation with still another old pal at the bar. Once John David had Suzanne out on the dance floor, he announced there was someone he wanted her to meet.

"Another one of your pals who wants to show me his suite in the Hotel Elysée tonight?"

"No," said John David defensively, "not this time. You'll say yes sooner or later, but this time it's a woman."

"Is she a client of yours?"

Garraty said that she was not, but he wished she were. "She is the world's richest woman, and she has a finger in every pie in town. She has her own racing stable. She inherited two hundred million dollars of some sugar company's stock, and the word is she's improved plenty on that. To be invited to one of her intimate little dinners for twelve is to be seated at the table of the gods. She's one of those women who make this city go round and round. She supports the opera, the Metropolitan Museum, six other charities, two stockbrokerage houses—"

"And a partridge in a pear tree," said Suzanne. "And exactly what does she want from me?"

"Ah, c'mon," said Garraty. He could not imagine that Mrs. Ellen Burns needed anything, or anybody. He concentrated for the moment on their dancing—through two choruses by Eddie Davis's orchestra 'of "Fine and Dandy."

Then he picked it up again. Mrs. Burns had seen them dancing together and had asked him to introduce Suzanne to her. She wasn't a monster. She just liked to meet new people. In fact, she had a reputation for spotting talent. She had singled out Suzanne, and Suzanne ought to be flattered. "I'm going to learn you how to table-hop, pal," said Garraty. "We'll just stop by her table and say hello."

That's all there was to it. Mrs. Burns was at a table of six next to the dance floor. Suzanne was introduced to an English couple, Lord and Lady Somebody, who looked as if they had been embalmed; and a Mr. and Mrs. Gould—Mrs. Gould said she was an old friend of Suzanne's mother. Mrs. Burns's friend—a Mr. Phelps—said nothing.

Mrs. Burns did not invite them to sit down, and Suzanne did not see anything about her that appeared remarkable. She was in her late thirties; her simple little black dress was decorated by no more than the customary single strand of pearls; her manners were sanded smooth and varnished, just like those of a dozen others who were friends of Suzanne's mother. "For some reason, young lady, everyone calls me Aunt Nellie, and I hope you will too. I knew your father before the war, and someday perhaps we can talk about that. When the horses are running you must come and visit me in Saratoga."

Then Aunt Nellie's interview was over. John David Garraty escorted Suzanne back to the bar, where Suzanne had no alternative but to agree to dance with George Macdonald, who was, after all, the beau of the evening. George believed—perhaps with some justice—that he had a right to some of Suzanne's time.

A month later, George Macdonald once again had the bad luck to be cast in the part of Suzanne's shill. He was the designated escort for the Colonies, a dance scheduled for December 26, 1947. It came after the more important cotillions, such as the Junior Assemblies and the International Debutante Cotillion, for each of which Suzanne had been required to appear with two qualified young gentlemen, certified as socially acceptable, in white tie and tails. But for the Colonies, after Christmas, Suzanne could call up her second string, and so George Macdonald appeared at Suzanne's apartment in black tie, doing his very best to play out the game according to the rules. He thought Suzanne was "a super girl." He assured Mrs. Benson that he would return Suzanne immediately after the dance was over, especially since it was already snowing hard and taxis might be difficult to find at the St. Regis after midnight.

After midnight, however, the city was being snowed under by a major blizzard. No taxis were to be found at the St. Regis, or anywhere else. Snowplows passed by on Fifth Avenue from time to time, but they were not able to clear the streets, and the drifts were gaining. Suzanne loved it: her solution to being stranded at Fifty-fifth and Fifth Avenue with George Macdonald was to insist they walk three blocks north into the teeth of the freezing

gale, then downwind to La Rue. George thought her mother
might be worried. They had promised to come straight home.
She was probably waiting up.

"Never," said Suzanne. "She's alone tonight. No Mr. Putnam
to hold her hand. She was at the martinis the moment we were
out the door, and she kept at them until she stumbled into bed.
She's been snoring for an hour." When George complained that
La Rue would probably be empty, Suzanne's answer was: "All
the better."

It was not quite empty; one couple had the dance floor to
themselves, and about four tables in the main room were still
filled. Happily, John David Garraty was holding court in the bar,
even if his audience was but one handsome man of about thirty,
whom he introduced as "Mr. Sam Harper, Jr., rising star of the
law, partner in the distinguished firm of Fletcher, Mahoney,
Browne and Adams, stranded this wintry Friday night from the
warmth of his hearth in Greenwich, Connecticut, and the solace
of his faithful wife, by the worst blizzard since eighty-eight. The
New Haven trains are snowbound."

George Macdonald's lips pursed into a thin line, but Garraty
soon had distracted him with an involved estimation of the
Rangers' chances for a Stanley Cup season. Since George had
played defense for St. Paul's School, Garraty assured him he
must be an expert. He questioned a smiling authority on every
nuance of good defense. In fact, it was soon Garraty's opinion
that Lynn Patrick, the Rangers' coach, should have the opportunity to hear Macdonald's analysis.

Meanwhile Sam Harper had asked Suzanne to dance. By then
they were the only couple on the floor. She wanted to reconfirm
that he was married. He would only answer "Mmmm." Where
would he spend the night, then? At some hotel? "Mmmm." He
was a superb dancer. Despite all the experience she had gathered from hundreds of stag-line partners, she was required to
concentrate upon his rhythms. He was tall, which made it easier
for her; he kept his steps small, and she could keep her toes inside the arches of his shoes; he was strong and sure of himself,
and the hand that led her from the small of her back was absolutely confident that she would follow where he planned to turn.
Over his shoulder she could see that Eddie Davis was bending

his violin and his orchestra to them, and grinning. "Listen, Sam Harper," said Suzanne, "you really should tell me something about yourself."

"Why?" He grinned, and leaned back from her, and started a series of whirling turns around and around the dance floor, so that if she was not to get dizzy she had no alternative but to keep her eyes fixed on his. Each time they passed the same spot in front of the bandstand, he asked her again with a marvelous grin: "Why?" until finally she said: "All right. Stop!"

She took him by the hand back to the bar, where Garraty was now attempting to keep George amused with complicated Irish jokes. Towing Sam Harper by the hand, Suzanne arrived to interrupt. With an authority in her voice developed as a drill sergeant upon the parade ground of Wavertree Hall, she gave Garraty his orders: "Take George Macdonald home, now."

Poor George imagined he could protest, gracelessly asking what Suzanne intended to do.

"Good night, George." She offered him her hand, and he automatically returned her handshake. "Thank you," she said, "for a wonderful evening."

Fortunately Garraty understood immediately what she wanted. "Let's go, George, old pal; we're on our way out into a beastly night." He already had George standing up and aimed for the door. Without letting go the firm grip he had established upon George's upper arm, John David leaned toward Suzanne and gave her a kiss on the cheek. He embroidered the sentiments in his eyes with his make-believe Irish brogue: "Ah, well, may the best man, they say. In any case, my little tempest, may the angels visit you in your dreams."

While Garraty bustled a reluctant George Macdonald from the scene, Sam Harper took Suzanne back to the dance floor one more time. By then they were the only couple left, but the orchestra was flattered and continued to play for them. "Waltzes, please, Mr. Davis," said Suzanne's hero. "Do you reverse, my princess?"

Suzanne would only say, "Mmmm." She could fit the top of her forehead against his chin. She could close her eyes into the crook of his shoulder. As they waltzed, she drew in through flaring nostrils all she could smell of him. She guessed there would be no fat on him, and it would be wonderful to watch him swim. He had strong hands, but long, delicate fingers. When they could assume they were finally free to leave without any further delays, they stopped to thank Eddie Davis, then got their coats and started out into the storm. Sam Harper put an arm around her shoulder to shield her from the wind blowing from Madison down Fifty-eighth Street. They huddled together and ducked their heads against the driving snow. "Where are you taking me, Sam?"

"Does it matter?"

Recollections varied about what then happened. Suzanne would maintain that she had been a virgin until Sam took her to the Plaza. Sam Harper would later say that if Suzanne claimed it was so, then he was complimented and honored to hear such news. He thought it detracted nothing from her reputation to say that theoretically, he supposed, a technical definition of virgin might be applied, but if Suzanne was a virgin that night there certainly was no evidence—material or otherwise. He never knew any other woman who was so joyous in bed. There were no boundaries to her exuberance.

Of course, there would not have been any way that Sam Harper could know about the training Suzanne had received at Wavertree Hall. Yet Suzanne would be the one to point out that Miss Freddy's schooling had nothing to do with the games she played with men; one thing had nothing to do with the other. "When women make love," she would say, "they reflect to each other the pleasures of which they are capable. When a man and woman meet, there are pleasures to it—God, they can be fantastic—but they are trying to kill each other with love."

Whatever memories they may have saved, it was a fact that Suzanne kept Sam Harper at his task until something past noon the next day. Then they slept until teatime Saturday afternoon, took the elevator down to the Palm Court, drank daiquiris and ate chicken sandwiches, and returned to their musky room until Sunday morning. "The amusing thing," Sam Harper would remember, "was that from Friday night until after breakfast Sunday we never actually looked outside, partly because all Suzanne had to wear was the long dress she was wearing when she left one of those silly dances. Besides, our suite was one of the old small ones at the back. Our only view was of the air shaft between buildings. Suzanne called her mother Saturday morning to say that because of the storm she was staying with a friend. I called Babette in Greenwich—she was my wife then—with the same story. We both assumed that our excuses were probably a bit shaky and no one would believe us, but not at all. We had not exaggerated one bit—it was actually the worst blizzard to hit New York in almost a century!"

When they finally took the time to look out the windows of the Plaza, a brilliant sun was shining again on a city in dazzling white—clean and fresh and bright. Here and there snowplows shoved at gigantic drifts. Crews of men straggled about with shovels to clear small paths. Cars left at the curbs were completely buried: almost twenty-six inches had accumulated while Suzanne was exhausting Sam Harper. As soon as the lovers realized their excuses had been accurate, they returned to their rumpled room to play with each other again. Sam Harper remembered that when Suzanne first let down her hair and turned to him naked, he had blurted out, "Rapunzel!" He said he was in love with her from that moment on, "and I've never regretted a moment of it."

It was certainly true that Suzanne provided Sam Harper, Jr., with something he desperately needed, but the substance of what it may have been was a mystery. Perhaps Suzanne relieved him of his sweet habits of reason, or let him escape now and then from his rational designs. Sam Harper's wife, Babette, apparently thought so and eventually sued for divorce. Thereafter Sam lived at the University Club and never remarried. In some odd way, Suzanne gave back to every man who loved her exactly what he asked for—neither more nor less, and wildly different for each man, but as if she could recognize instantly the design of his secret key and accommodate her lock to its turn.

It was Suzanne's genius to adapt her designs to her lovers' needs without stinting, never holding back in any secret reserve some shadow of a doubt about her lovers' illusions. After 1948, John David Garraty and Sam Harper remained forever as Suzanne's faithful lieutenants. What she delivered to each of them was quite different, but all they desired; in a sense, they loved

her not for what *she* was but because she understood completely
who *they* were. To say, for example, that Sam Harper's later success was a result of Suzanne's patronage was to confuse what
was exchanged between them. Long before he fell in love with a
seventeen-year-old girl with long red hair, he was recognized as
having the kind of mind that would be superior at the intricacies
of the law. He had grown up in Charleston, South Carolina,
where law was revered. He was an honors graduate of the Harvard Law School. He had clerked for two years with a Supreme
Court justice. Before he was thirty he was made a full partner in
his firm.

He had the cast of legal mind his associates described without
embarrassment as "beautiful." He was scholarly without being
pedantic; solved the problems brought before him with an easy
grace. He kept his distance from the emotions of every issue and
avoided pointless discord. He turned every difficulty this way
and that, as if it were a Chinese puzzle, and by examining between the tips of his long fingers what someone had cleverly
constructed, Sam Harper would eventually feel out a reasonable
way to understand how the thing was put together.

Although many of the problems brought to his attention—particularly those Suzanne sent on to him over the years—involved
ferocious and sullen passions, he never abandoned his devotion
to careful study. He did everything dispassionately, as a scientist
of the law's requirements and a clinical student of what lay at
the boundaries of "any reasonable doubt."

Suzanne's other faithful servant after 1948, John David Garraty, was far easier to understand. He never slept with Suzanne,
but didn't need to, and was always her lover anyway. He wanted
no more than to be connected to the big events of his day and
say, "Hi, pal," to the important men, and sometimes have them
say, "How're you doing," in return. "Public relations" to John
David Garraty meant that he would have a connection at the top
—to the key man, the inside deal, the "real" story, the hot news
that would hit the papers in that afternoon's edition—with which
John David Garraty could assert some association even if it
might be a bit remote. The newspapers, therefore, were to be
studied, beginning on page one, then right through to the stand-

ings of every baseball team, including their won-and-lost columns and the games behind.

There was, of course, much news on page one that John David Garraty had to forgive the newspapers for publishing—stuff about African countries and trade conferences in Geneva and what some bozo in the Kremlin had to say. He supposed they printed foreign news because they had to keep up appearances. He could be generous with newspaper editors and their fascination for remote stories, because he was grateful for news of the city's professional sports. Garraty knew as much as anyone alive about the working details of Ranger defensemen, Yankee pitchers and Giant quarterbacks. He nearly always managed to have a pair of tickets in his wallet pocket, with which he would generously part to some "pal" he had just met at a bar. He was proud that he could stand at the bar at Toots Shor's during lunchtime and wave at Horace Stoneham slumped at the corner table, and that after a while the owner of the Giants would wave back. John David Garraty was honored to do "public relations" for Suzanne for nothing, because he guessed that she was an event in herself. His judgment was confirmed when Suzanne was only seventeen and "Aunt Nellie" Burns had also spotted her as "talent."

During the summer of 1948, Suzanne added mobility to her ambitions by forcing her mother—after six months of bullying—to buy her a powder-blue Buick convertible. She used this "graduation present" to drive from Oyster Bay to the city at least three days a week. Sometimes she met Sam Harper for lunch. Sometimes they could not meet until five or six o'clock. Sometimes they went tea-dancing at the Savoy Plaza. Sometimes they went directly to bed. Suzanne added a marvelous variation to their meetings by inventing a game Sam Harper could not resist.

She went to Woolworth's, bought a wedding ring for one dollar and a gigantic glass-diamond engagement ring for fifty cents. It was obviously fake—if it had been real it would have been fifty or sixty carats. Then she would drive to a hotel she picked almost at random, with an Hermès traveling bag as a prop. She would deliver the bag to the doorman and hand him the keys to the car, ordering him to have it parked. She would sweep into the lobby, register at the desk, without pausing, as "Mr. and

Mrs. Sam Harper, Jr., for just one night," and be shown to the
small suite she demanded. She would then telephone Sam at his
office, saying that she was at the Madison, the Stanhope, the
Murray Hill, or wherever it was that she had alighted, and waiting for him. If the hotel manager at the desk hesitated for a
moment, or if he eyed the fake diamond doubtfully, or asked a
discreet question to indicate any delicate suspicions he may have
been harboring about the seventeen-year-old girl who was claiming to be a Mrs. Harper, Suzanne would retell each such danger to
Sam later in theatrical detail.

At first Sam scolded her. Couldn't she see the *Daily News* headline: LAWYER TRYSTS WITH TEEN-AGER IN MIDTOWN HOTELS;
GREENWICH WIFE PICKS UP TRAIL? Yet, each time he asked her to
stop, they were already in bed. The only time he expressed his
objections before he reported to the hotel she had selected, she
broke off their conversation, saying, "I'll have to call you back."
She made him wait by the phone in his office until nearly six
o'clock. When she finally called, she said she was in the tub, and
she was masturbating. She would tell him what it felt like when
she came. How long would it be before he could get to room 517
of the Volney?

Only rarely could Sam stay overnight. He had to take the late
train to Greenwich, which meant that after he had ordered Suzanne's blue Buick convertible taken back out of the garage, and
paid the bill for the room, Suzanne often had the opportunity to
wink or wave good-by at the same desk manager she had passed
just hours before. She said she liked the small residential hotels
best, because at the big hotels they worked in shifts, and after six
there was never the same clerk.

As soon as Sam resigned himself to the complications Suzanne
could invent for the hotel game, she upped the stakes. The last
train he could catch for Greenwich left Grand Central at three
minutes past midnight. At about eleven o'clock, therefore, Sam
would eye the watch he placed upon the bedside table, then
move from their rumpled bed toward the shower he thought was
necessary. Although he wouldn't admit it, he feared carrying
Suzanne's Calèche into Babette's house.

Suzanne's answer at first was simple: she rolled over on top of
Sam the moment his eyes strayed toward his watch. Then she

caught him coming out of the shower with the hotel's towel still wrapped around his waist, and by stretching herself out upon the edge of the bed with a pillow clutched between her thighs she was able to make Sam miss another train. As she went along, her tactics at the game of beat-the-clock became more complicated. By starting at five o'clock in the afternoon she could exhaust him so that he slept beyond the last train. By holding him off until the last possible moment, she would let him have his choice: take the train or stay. But it was not until the end of summer that Sam moved to a bachelor's room at the University Club and his troubles with Babette really began. In the meantime, Suzanne was always back at her mother's house in Oyster Bay before dawn, and if her mother was convinced that her daughter was conducting an affair in the city, she had no reasonable grounds upon which to object.

There were two subjects Mary Benson admitted to her friend John Putnam that "we've never really been able to discuss." John Putnam, Esq., did not think he would be very helpful in discussing with Suzanne the dangers of sex, but he agreed to do what he could to explain the money situation. He would ask Suzanne to lunch, and they would have a serious talk about it. He would report to his client how it went.

Perhaps John C. Putnam, Esq., senior partner of the respected downtown firm of Webster, White, Moore and White, was justified in believing that he held worldly advantages over most seventeen-year-old heiresses. In the practice of law he was experienced, and at the specialty of trusts and estates considered to be a leading practitioner. Generally speaking, the daily routine of his trade was a thicket of complications, but with diligence its paths and byways could be learned, and the laws of inheritance, although confusing at first, had the advantage of being reasonably stable. Their application required a great catalogue of wills and codicils and testaments and notarizations, filings, forms and certifications. No estate or trust could be said to have been well managed unless the "tax considerations" had been "thoroughly studied," but all these mysteries and arcana could in due time be routinized. Modest John Putnam never pretended that his advice depended upon the forms he completed or the tax decisions he could quote by heart. Instead he implied that he earned his fees

—slightly higher fees than those charged by less respected counselors—because he stood, as he would say, *in loco parentis:* acting as a prudent father would have acted, if the man had only lived, for the security and happiness of the family for which he was responsible. "Property," said John Putnam, "never passes out of existence. It only changes hands."

At forty-two years of age, John Putnam considered himself worldly precisely because he knew intimately the continuous material results of birth and death, "in a practical way." If he had perhaps fallen into the habit of patronizing advice, it was a fatherly style he adopted because most of his clients expected it of him. He was required by the law to act as trustee of a great many estates, a serious responsibility after all, and in doing so he inevitably was involved in a wide range of personal and intimate problems. Hence he thought it would be practical to treat Suzanne as a grown woman, and he invited her to lunch at L'Aiglon "to talk business."

There were certain trusts left to her by her father, John Putnam said. Perhaps it was time for her to have some idea of how things were managed. She would be eighteen at the end of the summer, and the responsibility for her share of the principal amounts of the trusts would soon be hers alone.

Although she had to break a date with Sam Harper, Suzanne agreed reluctantly to meet her mother's lawyer at L'Aiglon. She also made sure she arrived a half hour late, dressed in the latest Dior skirt and shirtwaist and trailing a chiffon scarf drenched in a heavy perfume, suitable, John Putnam would have thought, for a much older woman. To his surprise, she seemed to know the restaurant's *patron* as well as he did. When Suzanne arrived at the table where her lawyer sat waiting, she immediately fell into the role John Putnam had planned to impose upon her gradually. In fact, she was exaggerating her part of the silly young heiress whose very existence depended upon the fatherly advice he would offer.

"Before you explain to me all those serious things I have to learn, John, you should have a drink. I know you love martinis; well, go ahead. It will make it so much easier for both of us. These money talks are always so confusing."

Suzanne occupied him with girlish enthusiasms until most of

lunch had passed, and it was late before the subject of money could be started. John Putnam had to plunge into the details without his usual introductory remarks. Essentially, he said, Suzanne should realize what a difficult position her mother had always been in. In his opinion, Mary Benson had done the best anyone could have done in the circumstances. When Porter Benson died in Paris, the war was approaching fast. He had certainly done the right thing for his daughters—all of his estate was left in trust for Mimi and Suzanne—but there were delays in Paris, as Suzanne probably knew, because the insurance companies would not pay a cent at first. Not until after the cause of her father's death was changed from suicide.

No, John Putnam had never believed her father had committed suicide. He loved his family too much. Putnam couldn't really say whether he believed her father had been murdered, either. Well, of course there were suspects, but with the Germans about to arrive in Paris, it was a confusing place. No one was being entirely sensible; surely Suzanne could understand that?

Even after they were able to collect the insurance, it was paid in francs, and the francs were in Paris and impossible to get to New York. In his opinion, Suzanne's mother had acted with great imagination, and at the same time prudently. "Well, actually, except for some personal items and title to the house in Oyster Bay, he didn't leave your mother anything. He left it all to you and your sister Mimi—equally between you until you are eighteen, which for all practical purposes is about now."

Yes, exactly: the money their mother collected in Paris was the money their father had left to his daughters. No, it was left in trust. There were two trustees: the Corn Exchange Bank and John Putnam. Trusts were commonly set up that way, but it wouldn't have made any difference if their mother had not been able to hide most of the insurance proceeds in Paris right through the middle of the war. She was able to do it because she realized she would never get the money out in time. It really was a very dramatic story. She bought gold jewelry at first and brought it home on the ships. Then she bought Post-Impressionist French paintings—Légers, Magrittes, Kandinskys and the like. The Germans hated them, didn't want them, said they were degenerate junk. She hid these paintings by leaving them with friends all over Paris, and how right she had been! In 1944 she was able to recover almost all of them, and sell them, and make a profit on every one, and bring back to New York a substantial sum of money that would otherwise have disappeared. Well, but in some cases the people to whom she had entrusted paintings later claimed they owned them. "There was nothing your mother could do about it, no way to prove the paintings really belonged to her daughters in New York."

Originally, the sum was about one million dollars, but Suzanne must realize that was in prewar francs in Paris, and a considerable sum had to be paid to various police and prefecture officials to get the official verdict of suicide changed. Of the remaining nine hundred thousand dollars, almost six hundred thousand survived the war and was eventually deposited into a trust account at the Corn Exchange Bank.

"Well, then, how much money do Mimi and I have now?"

Suzanne must understand that from the amount—the six hundred thousand or so—that was successfully transferred to New York in 1945 in either cash or paintings, there were loans advanced by the Corn Exchange Bank amounting to three hundred twenty thousand that had to be repaid.

"Why?"

Because that was what she and Mimi and her mother had lived on from 1938 until 1945.

"And now?"

In his fatherly way John Putnam patiently reviewed the cost of an education at Wavertree Hall for Suzanne and at Miss Porter's School for Mimi. The servants in the house at Oyster Bay were expensive. Suzanne's party in June had cost a great deal, despite the Wilsons' contributions for the major items. In his opinion Suzanne's mother had managed extremely well. Even if it might seem to be a dreary subject to a young girl of nearly eighteen, it was time she understood the facts of the matter. They were not poor, by any means, but the sum of two hundred eighty thousand remaining after the Corn Exchange loans had been repaid in 1945 really earned only five per cent after taxes, and after tax was the only realistic way to calculate.

The very best that he and the Corn Exchange Bank could do, and still act prudently, which the law required of them as trustees, amounted to twelve thousand in income after taxes. As against this, Suzanne should realize that the expenses of the Benson household ran about forty thousand each year—although he was sure she would agree they had a pleasant life and had received a really first-class education and had good value for the forty thousand spent. In an attempt to increase the amount of interest income they could receive after tax, he had arranged to have eighty-five thousand of their principal invested in a second mortgage on a really fine resort hotel on Saranac Lake, in the Adirondacks in upstate New York.

So, putting it all together, Suzanne and Mimi had between them the eighty-five-thousand-dollar Saranac Lake Hotel second mortgage, about one hundred fifteen thousand in other securities and cash, and income of about fourteen thousand a year, but the expenses continued to run at about forty thousand. "You are," he said, "two very expensive young ladies."

"We are also paying our mother's expenses, too, is that correct?"

John Putnam was sure they would both always want to see to it that their mother was comfortable.

"I want to go see that hotel."

He could assure her that it was being managed by top people —the Kirkeby chain managed a great number of hotels all across the country. They ran the Beverly Wilshire in Los Angeles and the Gotham in New York. They were very good at their business. Profitable, too.

"All the better, John. We can go in my new car."

He thought she would find it an extremely long and boring drive, way upstate to Lake Placid. Nearly as far as the Canadian border. A full day's trip. Over three hundred miles.

"We can go the whole way with the top down. If you don't trust my driving, I'll let you drive. When do we go?"

After lunch they parted on Fifty-fifth Street, with John Putnam finally consenting to check his calendar: he would see when he might possibly get two entire days free. It would be very difficult, he said.

Suzanne went directly to the Gotham. After doing her check-in routine, she took a bath, then called Sam. "We're trying the Gotham tonight. It's managed by Kirkeby. Very profitable, I'm

told. I'll be in the little bar downstairs at six. Pretend you're trying to pick me up."

Ten days later John Putnam found himself driving his client's
powder-blue Buick convertible north on 9W through Newburgh
and Kingston, to Albany and Saratoga Springs, where they
stopped for lunch; then past Lake George and Schroon Lake
into the Adirondacks. They passed through the village of Lake
Placid just before sunset and arrived, with the top down, before
the Saranac Lake Hotel at dusk.

They had been expected at the reception desk. While the only
clerk was making a fuss over their arrival, a Mr. Merz arrived,
identified himself as the manager, and explained that he had
held the dining room open for them past its usual hour: "Our
guests like their dinner promptly at six."

John Putnam and his client had dinner alone by candlelight in
an immense dining hall, capable, they guessed, of seating 300 to
350 diners at once. Mr. Merz stopped by repeatedly to inquire
whether everything was all right. Suzanne assured him the
chicken pot pie was one of the best she had ever tasted. As soon
as Mr. Merz had backed away, Suzanne leveled her gaze at her
trustee: "John, this is worse than Schrafft's. What the hell is this
place, anyway?"

He had to admit that perhaps it had seen better days. The
point she had to remember was that it was still profitable. Originally, back at the turn of the century, grand hotels were built
on the lakes of the Adirondacks so that great crowds of people
could get away from the city for the summer, or at least for the
month of August. When the Saranac Lake Hotel was built, it was
the center for a summer's social activity. Whole families came
with trunkloads of clothes. It was like the summer camps that
were being run for middle-class city children now, except that in
those days the camp included the parents—or at least the wives.

The husbands used to come up by train. There were special
trains that left Grand Central Station and arrived at Saranac in
only four hours—and it was a pleasant trip, too. All the women
and children would take carriages down to the siding to meet
the trains. In those days they built sprawling eight-hundred-
room hotels to accommodate a summer crowd that would come
back year after year. One of the great things about the Saranac

Lake Hotel was that in many cases it was still drawing the same
loyal clients who had stayed during the summers before World
War One. He thought it was marvelous that they kept coming
back.

Only in the summer, of course. The hotel was closed after
Labor Day. Strictly seasonal. He would be the first to admit that
the rooms upstairs, and yes, the hallways—especially the carpet-
ing—were threadbare. Yes, he agreed, they needed paint, too, but
Suzanne must realize that Saranac was still a really first-class
plant. It had its own steam boilers, its own generators, its own
waterworks—entirely self-sufficient. That's how costs were kept
low. All built at the turn of the century and still working just
fine. Mr. Merz would give them a tour in the morning.

Mr. Merz's tour the next morning was thorough, covering
every example of low-cost self-sufficiency spread over thirty
acres. Suzanne was walked to see steam being made, and then
electricity being generated. She was introduced to the meat
lockers and watched beef being butchered. Chickens were raised
in a chicken house, of course; and Mr. Merz allowed that
chicken pot pie was indeed a great favorite with the guests and
on the menu at least once a week. In the cellars below the giant
dining room they inspected kitchen ranges fueled by coal, warm-
ing ovens from which 400 dinners could be sent up at once
through the dumbwaiters, mountains of crockery and china and
glassware, a bit worn, to be sure, but still finer than anything
that could be bought to replace it. The wine cellar contained
racks to store 49,000 bottles of the world's most famous vintages.
Unfortunately their present guests did not often call for wine.
They were particularly fond of Saratoga Vichy water, said Mr.
Merz, and he trucked in 280 cases a week. Very healthful, he
supposed.

For the benefit of his client John Putnam put one searching
question after another to Mr. Merz—about occupancy rates, advertising budgets, per diem food costs. Between the machinery
and the cash flow, it was impossible for them to get away until
well past two o'clock. As soon as Suzanne's Buick was brought
up to the door she insisted the top be put down again: "Maybe
the smell will go away."

Driving south, John Putnam at first attempted to summarize

the significance of the figures he had extracted from Mr. Merz. Continuing the lessons he saw as his duty to impart, he emphasized that Suzanne must understand that Mr. Merz was Swiss, and the Swiss were the very best managers in the world at running that kind of place.

"Bullshit, John." Suzanne had curled herself up into a corner of the front seat, up against the door. From time to time she put her head out into the airstream beyond the windshield, letting it cool her closed eyes. The memory of that smell would never fade. God, the average age in that place must have been eighty. It stank of old piss, of the ammonia they used to cover it up. Was that what death smelled like? Stale urine?

Before breakfast that morning, she had come bouncing out to the porch, entranced by the bright sunlight shimmering on the lake before her and by the reflections upon the lake of the old green soft-shouldered mountains. She hadn't realized at first that a long row of eyes was watching her, but she felt them, and a shiver ran through her before she turned. They were lined up in wicker rocking chairs—across the whole length of the veranda. Someone must have propped them there like rag dolls. They were not talking to one another. They were staring at her with a strange intensity, and she realized that she was an offense, an outrage, an interruption in the long wait to which they were committed. They hated to be disturbed. They cherished the smell they had accumulated around them. They had abandoned foolish hopes and saw no excuse for new tolerances. They knew their own minds, they would have said; and they could think of no reason to be charitable about energies they had long since put aside. They hated intrusions upon the day's orderly schedule, especially before it was time for lunch. Suzanne felt she could not move until she had swept her own eyes down the length of their file. There were about fifteen men still surviving among one hundred and forty or fifty women. Most of the rag dolls looked as if they had lost their stuffing. "To hell with them."

But the memory of their gaze and the odor of that place lingered. As John Putnam drove along the shores of Lake George, pine resins and clear mountain air still would not dispel it. She guessed she needed time to think, but she sensed she might as well gamble.

"Tell me again, John, what we have in that place."

He kept his eyes on the road ahead, but reviewed the details of a second mortgage, fifteen years at fourteen per cent.

"I want you to sell it, get rid of it—whatever it is you have to do to get us out."

"Your mother and I and the Corn Exchange Bank all agree, Suzanne, that the Saranac Lake Hotel mortgage was a sound investment."

"It's nearly half of all we have left. And as soon as all those loyal guests croak, which is practically tomorrow, that place will be empty."

John Putnam drove on, shaking his head, depending upon the authority conferred by years of experience in dealing with excitable young wards. He was unaware, it appeared, that Suzanne was studying him. She was rehearsing once again how he kept his money in a flat wallet in his breast pocket. She had watched him pay bills at the restaurant in New York and again at the Saranac Lake Hotel. He was a meticulous man, reaching into his jacket with his left hand, then laying the wallet flat in his left hand while he peeled back with the middle finger of his right the corners of the bills he planned to extract. They were always crisp new bills, and he must have arranged them in the sequence of their denominations—with the dollars on top. He was meticulous and secretive. He had probably collected fees for placing the mortgage from the bank, or from the sellers, or from her trust account, or perhaps from everyone simultaneously. As long as he could continue to collect his fees he would probably be useful. Fees, she concluded, were probably unavoidable. "How far are we," she wanted to know, "from the city?"

He thought the best thing would be to stop at Saratoga for dinner; the Gideon Putnam Hotel was not at all bad. Then they would still have about five hours to drive before they hit the George Washington Bridge.

"I'm exhausted," she said. "We won't finish dinner until nine at this rate, and then you'll be much too tired to drive on and on like this. Couldn't we stay overnight at the Gideon Putnam—just the place for you, wouldn't it be, John?"

He was ready with what he thought would be an amusing explanation that unfortunately, although the names were the same, he was not related, but she interrupted him.

"Good. Then we can play a game to keep us from being bored while you drive."

"What game would that be, young lady?"

"It's called available unavailable. You are busy driving so you are available to me, but I'm unavailable to you." As she spoke she moved up against him and put her hand into his lap, searching with her fingers until she found what she wanted.

He pulled the car over to the side of the road. He huffed and puffed about what was out of the question, and certain standards that had to be maintained, and proprieties. He put Suzanne's hand away firmly the first time, but as she explained to him her rules, she could feel that each time she returned to the source of her powers she was gaining. "It's really very simple, John. As far as I am concerned, we can sit here by the side of this goddamn road all night long. As soon as you want to get started again, you are going to be available. I am going to play with you and tell you dirty stories until we get to the Gideon Putnam. Then we shall have dinner. After dinner we shall take separate rooms. You can come to my room if you like—if you want to find out at that point whether I'm available. In the meantime, I'm not; but you are. Drive on when you're ready."

On the Tuesday after Labor Day 1948, the Benson Family Trust sold its share of the Saranac Lake Hotel second mortgage, fifteen-year term at fourteen per cent. It was sold back to the Corn Exchange Bank, holder of the primary mortgages upon the property.

7

Campaign Contribution

1948

"MEI MEI WILSON and I were both accepted at Wellesley," Suzanne said, "but at the last moment—just after Labor Day—I changed my mind. I thought it might be more interesting to look for a job. Mother was furious."

Her mother had assumed Suzanne would be in Boston and Mimi away as a junior at Miss Porter's School in Farmington, Connecticut. With both daughters away more or less permanently, she wouldn't need the big apartment at 655 Park Avenue any more. A small apartment at the Sulgrave Hotel would do nicely. On vacations Mimi and Suzanne could share the extra bedroom. Besides, the Sulgrave had a nice little restaurant downstairs, and if Mary Benson had to entertain she could have supper sent up. "She hated to cook," in Suzanne's opinion, "because she didn't know the first thing about it. She'd never done it, you see."

From the summer house on Centre Island, Mary Benson planned one last social campaign for the sake of Mimi. To carry it off she would need Cleo, the cook at Oyster Bay, the last member of the Benson household staff remaining from the golden days of the thirties. After Mimi's debut, Cleo could be let

go. Fortunately, Mrs. Benson's cook revealed that she had saved
enough money to open a restaurant in Fort Lauderdale. Since
business in Florida was seasonal, Cleo was more than willing to
return to Centre Island for the next few summers.

Late on an August afternoon in the summer of 1948 Suzanne
wandered into the kitchen of the Oyster Bay house: "The two of
them—mother and Cleo—had been sitting there at the pantry
table for hours, sipping gin, telling each other stories. They were
both drunk. You've never heard such maudlin baloney. The good
old days, over and over; about how quickly James Moriarity
used to change his uniform to keep up with Daddy; about the
Irish maids who came and went; about Mademoiselle Rose who
cared for Mimi and me as if we were her own daughters. All that
stuff."

In September, because of Suzanne's new plans, the apartment
in the Sulgrave turned out to be too small for Mary Benson and
her daughter to inhabit simultaneously. Suzanne was gone most
of the day at the job for which she had volunteered at the Metropolitan Museum of Art—working in the museum's book-and-
card shop, just beyond the main entrance. She was out every
night, but her path inevitably crossed her mother's.

"Exactly when did you get in last night, Suzanne?"

"Late."

"God knows where you've been, or with whom," said Mary
Benson.

"True," was Suzanne's only answer before she disappeared. "I
have to wash my hair now."

They never saw each other for more than five minutes in any
day, yet they both felt they were constantly in each other's way
or had to suppress a minor opinion that otherwise might grow
into a major fight. The Sulgrave was a residential hotel, and
Mary Benson thought she might brighten up their apartment by
hanging what she imagined were some rather lovely curtains.
"Ghastly," said Suzanne.

Mary Benson yearned to get the advice of her old friend John
Putnam on the entire situation, but for reasons she could not
quite fathom she failed to hold his attention as she once had. He
continued to escort her to the theater every so often, or they still
met with old friends for an evening of supper and bridge, but he

would rarely sit alone with her through an evening dinner as he used to, and he stopped by for cocktails less and less often. His excuse was that his wife expected him at home.

"Mother was convinced," Suzanne said, "that his wife had nothing to do with it. She was sure her faithful beau had fallen in love with a younger woman. Especially when she got sauced, she would terrify herself by imagining that she would read in the newspapers the very next day the announcement of John Putnam's marriage to whoever this woman was. Then she'd suffer over being abandoned. She'd say she could bear it as long as John didn't marry the little witch. One night I was finally bored by the whole thing. I pointed out to her that John Putnam was already married, and had been for years, to a wife who lived in Cold Spring Harbor."

Her mother said of course he was, but his wife didn't count. He never went anywhere with her. They had no friends in common. She stayed out in the country and did whatever it was she did out there. She was a bore. That was not what she was talking about.

"Maybe," Suzanne said, "he's fallen in love with his wife."

Her mother was enraged. She said Suzanne was being stupid, just stupid, deliberately provoking her. She refused to speak to her daughter for nearly a week. To combat the threat she faced, she had her hair redone in several successive styles, but John Putnam approved of them all equally, with the result that her fears increased.

Suzanne took her mother shopping: "We did it in three days flat, and at the end of it she was equipped with an entire wardrobe of Dior's 'New Look.' She didn't think Mr. Dior would ever be accepted in Boston, but she had to admit she rather liked the effect just the same. On the last afternoon, we were on the main floor at Saks. I told her that at forty-one she was still a very attractive woman. She burst into tears and wept all the way home to the Sulgrave."

Before Suzanne could get out of the apartment that night, her mother was on her fifth martini. Yet what Mary Benson claimed was "Boston's gumption" still ran in her blood, and so she signed herself up for a rigorous program every Tuesday of health and beauty at Elizabeth Arden. She continued the exercises she was mastering for the rest of each week. One Tuesday, the young Spaniard who set her hair guessed her age to be thirty. Over cocktails she told John Putnam about it: "When I said I had two grown daughters, he just wouldn't believe me!"

"It is difficult to believe, Mary."

"You really think so?"

"I really do."

"John, now that the girls are practically married, or will be within a few years in any event, I think I've earned the right to a whole new approach to life. Don't you think so?"

"I think you've carried out your responsibilities for those two girls as well as anyone could have."

"They'll be gone soon, John. Then we could travel again. Relax a bit. We've earned it, haven't we?"

"I should say you have, Mary. You certainly have."

According to Suzanne's careful notations in her diaries, the move from 655 Park Avenue to the Sulgrave added a daily average of two martinis to her mother's previous quota. As Suzanne made her way to bed from her headquarters at La Rue, or returned from an evening's command post set up temporarily with Sam Harper at the Madison, the Stanhope, the Volney, the Alrae, or the Savoy Plaza, she could examine at 4 or 5 A.M. the litter in the sitting room at the Sulgrave. Judging by the abandoned bottles among the overflowing ashtrays and the stained demitasse cups, her mother's tastes were gradually shifting from martinis to straight gin. Since neither woman emerged from the privacy of her room before eleven in the morning, there were no grounds during most weekdays to present indictments. Weekends might, however, provide dangerous hours. Consequently Suzanne tried to be away "visiting friends" for the weekends, but one Friday afternoon in October she faced an empty weekend calendar.

She had arrived at La Rue for an early dinner with Sam Harper after a marvelous cocktail hour spent on the twenty-third floor of the Savoy Plaza. They had watched a glorious October sunset from a suite looking out over Central Park. Sam had continued to describe the advantages Suzanne would have if only she would get her own apartment. He offered to pay for it; an apartment would be a hell of a lot cheaper for him than the hotel-of-the-week. He hated living alone at the University Club, and he was on his way that very night to Greenwich, and this time for sure he would straighten out some kind of separation from Babette. Until he had a separation agreement, they would have to be careful. If Babs ever nailed him on a New York State adultery, there'd be hell to pay. But if Suzanne would take the apartment in her own name, everything would be much easier. He would call her first thing Monday and tell her how it went with Babette.

As Sam was leaving for Greenwich, Suzanne thought it was the best luck in the world that John David Garraty had come in and was at the bar. Sam said he wouldn't mind at all if Suzanne stayed and had a drink with Garraty before she had to go home. "Take care of my girl, John David; she's a rare prize."

She danced a few sets with Garraty. Then he had to leave her at the bar for a few moments to take a phone call. When he returned, he ordered up a double scotch, and had turned silent and mysterious. He would only say, "That, pal, was a very important phone call. History might hang in the balance. That's really something. Really something."

He appeared to be unable to make up his mind. Nor would he let her in on it. He would not say what he couldn't decide. He ordered up another double scotch before he would launch it. Even then he set out tacking back and forth.

She understood there was a national election going on, didn't she? Yeah; well, Dewey would probably win and the Republicans were due to have their turn. But there were guys in town who were betting on Harry Truman anyway, even if it looked like he was a new record in long shots. Even Minnesota wouldn't cover any more Truman money at working odds. Anyone wanted to get down on the Truman line was buying the little bastard at a discount.

But there were guys who needed Truman, guys who wouldn't get the time of day if the Republicans got hold of the White House, guys whose business depended upon having a Democrat administration. That's the way it worked: if there was nobody sitting in the White House they could have a little talk with, make a few phone calls for them, then no contracts, a lot of trouble with the union, worse with the tax man, and nothing but grief from the judges. So it was Truman or nothing. It had to be Truman, or down to Palm Beach for four years and hope it blows over. That's the way it worked.

Well, the point was that President Truman was off in the middle of the country somewhere, giving speeches off the back of a train. Just like the old days. The train pulled into town, stopped right in the yards, and a mob of people came walking across the tracks and stood there to listen to him. Truman was telling them what they wanted to hear, telling them that the special interests have been taking the bread off the table, and that if they elected Dewey they're going to be screwed. "Special interests" meant Republicans, and those people knew it.

The New York *Herald Tribune* hadn't caught on yet, but there were guys in this town who had seen those crowds in Indiana and Illinois and Kansas and Nebraska—places like that—and they were coming back saying little Harry's got a sporting chance. And these guys were no dummies. They could smell it, if it was there. Anyway, they were betting to keep Truman's train going.

Yeah, but the railroad biggies had handed the Democratic National Committee a bill for that train. It was over fifty thousand bucks so far. All the railroad guys were Republicans. They said the Democrats had to pay up the bill for the train, and put down another thirty grand in advance, or no more train. They wanted eighty thousand tonight, by midnight, or else they pulled the engineer off. Wherever that train was—some Godforsaken Iowa town—it went no farther unless the Democrats came up with a check. The railroad bastards probably figured to save the overtime for the weekend.

No, the Democratic National Committee was broke. They were always broke until after the election. If they won, then the money came in. Before an election, only Republicans had money. He was trying to explain it. He wanted her to understand the whole thing—the background. The Democratic National Committee had come up with the money. They'd found themselves a source, only there was a hitch.

That was the crazy part, and he hoped she wouldn't be pissed off at him. He was only bringing it up because he promised he would: "Mr. Joseph F. X. O'Connell will deliver a certified check for eighty thousand to the Waldorf as soon as you are delivered to him at the Carlyle for the weekend. That's it. That's the deal. I said I'd ask you. It's up to you."

Suzanne threw her head back and laughed. "Eighty thousand for a weekend?"

"It goes to the Democratic National Committee. For the train."

"Are you sure there's no mistake? Mr. O'Connell would pay eighty thousand for a weekend? For me?"

"He said the debutante. He wasn't interested in any substitutes. He could provide those for himself."

"The whole weekend?"

Garraty shrugged. "Yes."

"Who is he?"

Garraty said he thought O'Connell was about fifty. He had seen Suzanne at La Rue, and obviously remembered her. He was in the construction business in Boston and Philly; in shipbuilding in Fall River, Massachusetts; owned a piece of the Framingham race track and ran some horses, but basically construction. He didn't have too good a reputation. There were stories. He might be a little rough.

"Like what?"

Garraty said he really didn't know. He'd just heard stories, that's all. There was no reason for her to get involved in the whole thing. The Democratic party would survive. He had promised them he would ask, and he was asking, and if she said no, it was O.K. with him. He looked miserable.

Suzanne's reaction surprised him. She reached out and put her hand on his arm as if she were soothing away a little boy's fears on the first day of school. Then she made them both laugh at how silly he was: "It's all right, John David. I've always wanted to play my part in history."

She asked him to order her a double scotch too. She was going to the ladies' room and would be back in a minute. Her attitude seemed to be that she was off on some kind of lark. When she returned, Garraty checked his watch nervously, but Suzanne thought they should finish their drinks. There was plenty of time before midnight. Let what's-his-name wait. The Carlyle was no more than ten minutes away. If John David wanted, he could give the son-of-a-bitch a call and assure him he had a deal.

Garraty came back to the bar to report that he had spoken to O'Connell and everything was set: O'Connell was sending a certified check over to the Waldorf for Harry Truman's train.

"What else did he say?"

"He's had his car standing outside waiting for you since eight-thirty."

"Terrific." If Mr. O'Connell was going to be the kind of man who always got what he wanted, the weekend might not be too boring. "Listen, John David, don't worry. Just like a girl scout, I'm prepared for anything." She took her panties from her purse and began stuffing them into the breast pocket of his jacket. "I've put in my diaphragm, and since I won't be needing these, you can keep them as a receipt of our campaign contribution." She rearranged them as if she were setting his pocket handkerchief. "They're historic documents now."

Then she stood, keeping her hands on his shoulders so that he could not rise from his barstool. She planted a kiss on his cheek and said, "Good night, John David, and may the angels visit you in your dreams."

She left a dollar for Reni at the hatcheck stand. As she pulled on her coat, she said to her little blond ally, "How's your mother?" She did not wait to hear Reni's reply. The moment she stepped outside on Fifty-eighth Street, a chauffeur moved toward her from the curb: "Mr. O'Connell's car?" As he held the door of the Cadillac limousine open for her, he handed her an envelope. Going up Park, she opened it and counted ten new one-hundred-dollar bills. She put them away in her purse and tried to concentrate on a list of things she would buy. She thought she would call Miss Freddy and ask her to come up for the weekend. They could go to the opera, and shop.

She could see she was not being taken to the Carlyle. They went past it, and the driver turned east on Eighty-fourth Street, pulling up in a block of brownstones between Lexington and Third. The block was gloomy, and almost all the houses were dark, except the one the driver indicated. "Just ring, ma'am." There were lights still on behind the curtains on the parlor floor. The front door had a brass knocker, which she tried first. When there was no response after a minute or two, she searched for the doorbell. October at midnight could be cold. As soon as she had found it at last and pressed it, the door opened by itself, swinging back silently. Some kind of electric device. She closed it carefully behind her, at which the inner door of the foyer opened in the same way. A woman's voice spoke to her over an intercom. "Go to the third floor rear, please. You will see the door is open."

Spooky bitch, but Suzanne did as she was told. On her way past the landing on the second, or parlor floor, she could hear a man on the phone, asking questions in rapid fire, then there would be a pause, and twice she heard him say, "Then, do it." She went as slowly as she could, but decided against being caught eavesdropping and arrived at the third floor's open door sooner than she would have liked. The room was brilliantly lit by an enormous crystal chandelier hung from the center of its high ceiling. Its furniture consisted of a white-canopied bed, much like the one Miss Freddy had, a Récamier covered in white silk and set next to a fireplace in which a wood fire was burning, and a Louis XV chair, also in white, with an occasional table next to it; on the table was a black phone with buttons for six lines. One of the buttons was lit, so she still had time to explore. The walls and ceiling were completely covered with squares of antiqued mirror; there were no windows. She had the peculiar sense that the room was soundproofed in some way. She turned to look back at the door through which she had entered. It was closed.

All right. She took off her coat, dropped it on the Récamier, saw that there was another door, tried it, and found that she was in a rather elegant bathroom: all white in every fixture and cabinet, but mirrored and as brightly lit as the bedroom. On a small table next to the tub there was another phone with six buttons, and line one was still lit. There was a silver-handled brush, and she decided to go ahead and unpin her hair while she waited. She was almost bored with waiting when an intercom in the bathroom spoke to her. She could see where it was, above the mirror. This time, the woman's voice said: "Please take off all your clothes, everything, including your shoes, and wipe off any makeup. Put your clothes and shoes in the laundry chute beside the toilet. They will be replaced Monday morning. In the cabinet on your right you will find a bottle of Joy perfume. Cover yourself with it. Everywhere."

Suzanne would have answered the intercom, said something back to it, but after giving her its orders it had clicked off. God-damn thing just assumed she would do everything it said. She undressed and dropped her things in the chute. She listened as the shoes dropped, and guessed it went down to the basement. She soaked a washcloth in Joy and used it as if she were bathing in it. Altogether, she calculated, that should make a total of eighty-one thousand and seventy-five dollars. The light on the telephone extension went out, and since she supposed she was ready, she returned to the bedroom and stretched herself out on the Récamier. She had time to rearrange her long hair forward so that it covered her breasts, and she could bring its tips around her hips and disguise modestly the tops of her legs. But it was hot in that brilliant room, and she was sweating, and she didn't know what to do with her hands. When the door opened, what she saw surprised her completely. She involuntarily gave up the pose that she thought was seductive and stood in a single bound.

He was dressed in a Superman costume but masked like Captain Marvel.

She blurted out without thinking: "That's ridiculous."

He drew what looked like a real pistol from a holster strapped around his waist, leveled it at her, and paf! she was stung by what she realized must have been a BB. It sobered her. She was wary of him. She didn't need any more of that. It had hit her just above her right breast, and she rubbed at it, trying to get the sting to fade. She would have cried right away, but she bit her lip. Not yet, anyway.

"No talking unless spoken to," he said. "You may address me as Your Lordship."

"Yes, Your Lordship."

"Good. What's your name?"

"Snow White."

Paf! The BB pistol stung her again. This time just below the navel, in the soft, rounded white of her belly. She fell to her knees, doubled over, hugging herself. She couldn't help it: she began to cry.

During the next fifty-four hours, she never left the mirrored room. The brilliant lights were never dimmed. The contributor to the President's campaign came and went as he pleased, although there were no more costumes after the first session. When Suzanne was left alone, she slept—a restless, stupid sleep. She never had any idea of how long she had slept, nor any sense of how much time she had left to serve. Her white silk and mirrored cell was not equipped with any clocks or watches. She guessed that sometimes she was left alone for as little as two hours, but she thought there was one stretch of ten hours when she had a chance to sleep undisturbed. Each time she woke up, there was a tray of fresh food on the little table by the Récamier, and it seemed to her that at least one button on the phone was always lit. On what was at last Monday morning, a gray-haired matronly woman appeared, whom Suzanne recognized: she was, Suzanne was almost sure, at one time the buyer for the custom department at a Fifth Avenue store. She was the same woman, Suzanne was positive, who supplied the dresses for a hundred debutantes each year. In any case, the gray-haired woman pretended she did this sort of thing every day; she arrived with boxes of things: lingerie, stockings and a Balenciaga shirtwaist day dress. Everything fit perfectly. The dress was navy-blue faille lined in soft silk crepe, belted at the waist and trimmed at the collar, at the sleeves and on its double row of buttons with flat navy silk braid. There was a navy kid purse to match. Her things and the envelope were in it.

From Delman's there was a pair of navy kid pumps, but Delman's shoes had always been too narrow for her and these pinched across her arch just as they always had. Suzanne regretted her comfy I. Miller alligator pumps that had disappeared into the laundry chute. Once dressed and let out the front door to the sidewalk of Eighty-fourth Street, Suzanne took off the Delman shoes and carried them in her hand as she walked barefoot toward Lexington for a taxi. October's morning sun was much too bright. At first it made her squint.

8

Mrs. Richard A. Lyle, Jr.

1949–52

I SAVED the announcement in the Sunday New York *Times,* June 26, 1949, which certified for history the wisdom of the investment Mary Benson had made in her daughter's education:

> Suzanne Stewart Benson, daughter of the late Porter C. L. Benson and Mrs. Benson of New York and Oyster Bay, was married yesterday afternoon to Richard A. Lyle, Jr., son of Mr. and Mrs. Richard A. Lyle of New York and East Hampton.
>
> The Reverend Carleton Lorimer performed the ceremony in St. John's of Lattingtown Episcopal Church in Locust Valley, L.I. A small reception was held after the ceremony at the Piping Rock Club in Locust Valley. Mary Hadley Benson was her sister's maid of honor. The bridesmaids were Miss Mei Mei Wilson, Miss Marianne Shipman, Miss Leslie Bond, Miss Pamela Brooks, Miss Edith Lynch, and Miss Helene Whitney. Stephen Lyle was his brother's best man.
>
> The bride attended the Clearbrook Country Day School, the Spence School, and was graduated from Wavertree Hall in Wainscott, Va., in 1948. She was presented in 1947 at the Grosvenor Ball and the Junior Assemblies in New York. Her father, the late Mr. Porter C. L. Benson, was managing partner of Benson, Salas and de Sales, investment bankers of New York

and Paris. She is the granddaughter of the late Franklin P.
Stewart of Dedham, Mass., and the great-granddaughter of the
late Captain Cecil S. Hadley of Boston.

Mr. Lyle is vice-president and a project manager for Technical Managers, Inc., New York and Washington, D.C., management consultants to business and to foreign governments.
He is an alumnus of Phillips Academy, Andover, Mass., Harvard College, and the Amos Tuck School of Business Administration at Dartmouth. He is a grandson of the late Mr. Mahlon
Lyle, a partner of Lee Higginson & Co., investment bankers,
and of Mrs. Mahlon Lyle of Tuxedo Park, N.Y. After a brief
trip, Mr. and Mrs. Lyle will live in Falls Church, Va., a suburb
of Washington, D.C.

For the wedding, Suzanne's mother took from the vaults of the
Corn Exchange Bank a box of rose-point lace that had been
repacked in blue tissue paper by five generations of Hadley
brides. Her daughter's wedding dress was by Balenciaga, and
the rose-point lace was appliquéd over ivory peau de soie. The
dress was fitted at the waist, then flared from an inverted pleat
at the back to form the narrow triangle of a short train. The lace,
aged by time and only a few days of light to a candle color, was
embroidered with seed pearls and edged the skirt's hem and the
bride's sweetheart neckline. From a Juliet cap a fingertip illusion
veil fell to the tips of Suzanne's loosened deep-red hair. She
carried a bouquet of stephanotis and field daisies, and John Putnam walked her up the aisle to give her away. The bride's
mother cried, as convention permitted.

At the reception afterward at Piping Rock, Mimi caught her
sister's bouquet—still another hopeful sign to Mary Benson, who
was cheerful and happy in the early part of the evening. She was
charming, according to Dick Lyle's ushers, who took their du-
tiful turns dancing with her. When the bride and groom had
driven away, and only stragglers remained scattered among the
tables, Mary Benson looked as if she had been a witness to some
frightful battle. The field over which it had been fought was littered by scattered flower petals, half-eaten shards of cake, broken cookies, pink linen napkins dropped in the seats of pushed-
back chairs, a champagne bottle rolling on its side.

Mary Benson scoured the empty tables for just one more

drink, insisting at the same time to John Putnam that she did not
want to sit down at all. Too much champagne. Too much. Too
bad. Have to drive her home to Centre Island. Never make it
otherwise. Too bad. "Can't leave me now, John. Part of your job.
Have to drive me home. Not safe otherwise."

Even when he had delivered her to the house on Centre Island
she would not let him escape. She made him support her, half
carry her, up the stairs to her bedroom. She made him wait until
she was ready for bed, and then, propped up against the pillows
in a bed jacket, she sent him, as a child would, for a glass of
water. She demanded he sit with her for just a little while. Only
fair. All alone now. Too much champagne. Sleep after a while,
then he could go. Meantime he had to stay with her, talk a little
while. Mother of the bride. Certain rights. She had done all she
could, didn't he think so?

She had always done all she could. Everything. She hoped
Suzanne would be happy with Dick. Good family. Right background. No one knew what was best these days. When she had
married Suzanne's father, everything was different. Background
mattered. Not now. Chinese bandits accepted in Boston. Only
thing that counted was money. Family didn't matter any more.
Just money. Thank God Suzanne had finally settled down.

Not beautiful any more. Ugly! The war made everything ugly.
No one knew what was best. When she was a girl she could believe in something. Accidents happened, but just the same, had
to carry on. "Porter died in Paris, and that was an accident, don't
you see, but it didn't make any difference. I knew what I had to
do for my daughters." It wasn't just a matter of money and business and politics—they had all those things before the war too.
There were other values, other things young women had to believe in. Otherwise the whole thing would come to an end.
They'd see soon enough. The whole system would crash again,
like 1929, only much, much worse. Terrible. Too bad. No background.

As John Putnam listened patiently, the mother of the bride
drifted toward sleep. Eventually he was able to pull the covers
up around her shoulders and tiptoe to the bedroom door. She
groaned as if she would start up again, but in a moment her
mouth went slack, then dropped open. Still half sitting, propped

against her pillows, she began to snore. He could pull the door closed behind him.

Curiously, what Mary Benson had desired for the sake of her daughter was, more or less, exactly what Suzanne had chosen from the opportunities provided. In choosing to marry Richard A. Lyle, Jr., Suzanne had done all that her mother could have asked: Dick Lyle had the right "background." Not only was he rich, but the comforts to which he was accustomed came to him legitimately—by inheritance. Consequently no cunning scheme, or scandal, or sudden good fortune tainted the solid confidence his money represented. His family had long since been under the *L's* in the Social Register. He was a member of those clubs in the city convenient to his needs. He had attended the right schools, of course. He had also served honorably in the United States Army Corps of Engineers in France during the war, adding a touch of romance to the certain success his inheritance promised. After the war, he had studied at a business school to prepare for the responsibilities his education recommended—a mixture of diplomacy and finance, not unlike the occupation the late Porter C. L. Benson had followed. He was, in fact, an heir to all that Suzanne's mother held dear: Dick Lyle dressed conservatively, his speech was diffident, his manners were polished, and he danced beautifully.

Suzanne met him at La Rue, to be sure, but in many ways that might have been expected. By Christmas of 1948 she was seeing a great deal of Dick Lyle, and Sam Harper answered fewer phone calls from small hotels; Sam was still entangled by Babette anyway. Dick Lyle was taller than Sam—Dick was six feet two—and devoted to sports. Not those spectator sports followed so closely by John David Garraty, but squash, tennis, duck shooting, sailing, skiing. Sports never reported in the newspapers, but which were the continuing extracurricular fascinations of former athletes graduated from Andover.

If Dick Lyle was a snob about his sports, and much else, he was outrageous in a way Suzanne rather liked—he was amusing about it. At the bar at La Rue one night when a social butterfly advanced the claim that his family had "come over on the *Mayflower,*" Dick Lyle put him away by asserting that the Lyles had "come over on their own boat." It was more or less true. In any case, no one would have challenged him. He was the kind of man who liked to drink standing up to the bar, and there was always a space around Dick Lyle, as if those who hung about and waited for this prince to speak understood they ought not to press in on him.

In February 1949 Dick could get away from his business for two weeks to ski at Mont Tremblant, and Suzanne agreed to go with him. They took separate rooms, because his sense of the proprieties required it. The first morning they went skiing, he caught an edge on a patch of ice on the upper slopes of Ryan's Run and twisted his right knee badly. He had to be brought down in the toboggan. Instead of returning to New York, they sat by the fire in the main lodge for the next thirteen days, with Dick's knee propped up on a chair and wrapped in Ace bandages. They played backgammon for hours at a time, drank scotch and soda steadily, and Suzanne extracted from him explanations of his business, war stories from his days in France, and descriptions of the summers he spent on the beach at East Hampton as a boy. As she drove them back to New York, he proposed and they promised each other to go skiing every February until they were very, very old. They were married June 25, 1949.

Their honeymoon was spent at Cambridge Beaches, in Bermuda. Except for the many hours they spent in the late afternoons making love, Bermuda was an idyl similar to Mont Tremblant. They played backgammon again for hours on end—Suzanne came away six thousand dollars ahead—and they took their board with them to the beach, along with two Thermos bottles of rum swizzles. Once again Suzanne encouraged her husband to tell her every detail of the life he had passed. It was in many ways unfortunate that when they returned from Bermuda, they had less and less time to talk.

Dick's business required them to live in Washington, D.C. Because it could be so awfully hot—almost unbearable in August—they rented a small house out in Falls Church, Virginia, just off Route 50 beyond Seven Corners. Although it was a small house—just two bedrooms—it was all they needed. Behind their house, red clay Virginia farms and green woods and rolling meadows stretched west toward Middleburg. The house was cool and pleasant, or at least cooler than Georgetown would have been. In

about two months, Suzanne had "redone it": she had hung
bright new curtains, had new slipcovers made, rebuilt new cabi-
nets into the kitchen, and started her own flower garden. By September 1949 Suzanne could look around her nest and see not another thing worth changing. When Dick asked her what she
wanted for her birthday on the twenty-first, she said she wanted
flying lessons. There was a small landing strip and flying school
on the other side of Route 50, and she would like to get a pilot's
license. He was somewhat surprised; he didn't see where she
would fly to. She said that wasn't the point. Maybe she would fly
down to Charlottesville and back; maybe over to the Eastern
Shore of Maryland. She just wanted to learn how. They rented
Piper Cubs over there for fifteen dollars an hour. Then if Dick
wanted to fly somewhere on weekends, go to interesting places,
see someplace new, she would be his pilot. The point was she
didn't have much to do all day. In the end he relented, and she
started flying lessons. "Anything to keep my little bride happy,"
he said.

He bought her a car so she could drive into Washington
whenever she wanted, "and see some of your old friends for
lunch." She used the car to enroll in a course in French cooking,
because Dick said he loved the way the French cooked. Her
menus were increasingly complex and covered a wider and
wider variety of exotic delicacies—all of them requiring hours of
shopping and repeated trips across the Key Bridge. By Christmas Dick weighed over two hundred pounds, because he fell in
with her new hobby with such gusto. Returning in the evenings
from his office, he often stopped on the Georgetown side of the
Key Bridge to buy a new bottle or two of wine, on the theory
that they were educating their tastes. Before dinner they had one
or two martinis, then wine with dinner, and brandy afterward.
They often fell into bed drunk.

Unfortunately they could not have dinner at home as much as
they liked, but had to go out in the evening, driving to Georgetown for dinner to meet other couples much like themselves. For
each dinner of six or eight they attended, they returned the invitation. Suzanne entertained six, or eight, or as many as a dozen,
casually and without much fuss, but it was time-consuming. The
men were dedicated to the foreign affairs of America, the conse-

quences of victory at war, and the responsibilities of their new empire. They were almost all young men—contemporaries of Dick's—and at the beginning of their careers as foreign service officers, as analysts at the Tariff Commission, as junior officers at the Export-Import Bank, or at the growing number of agencies concerned with foreign aid, technical-assistance programs and such problems as trade and exchange treaties.

Suzanne listened patiently to the obsessions of junior proconsuls. They talked of food yields and population curves and rebuilding Europe. They always looked far into the future to assess the programs they were designing. They showed one another slides from their excursions to Africa, China, the upper Nile, and the interior of Brazil. They argued with each other easily over French parliamentary prospects, English constitutional law, and dams to be built across the waters of faraway rivers. While the men reviewed their plans for a stable world order, the women stayed quiet, sat up straight, smiled, and nodded.

At first Suzanne sought out the wives of some of Dick's friends for lunch because she expected that, given a chance, the women would have things of their own to say. Instead they said almost the same things their husbands had been so positive about only two nights before. Upon hearing the wife's version of Egyptian population growth, for example, Suzanne noticed that she explained her husband's solution as an ambassador would—smiling a great deal while advancing a hypothetical theory which could be withdrawn if necessary or if her husband was transferred to an even better post. Suzanne soon realized she was not in any different situation herself.

Dick's company had its offices just off Pennsylvania Avenue in one of the new buildings. A staff of accountants and engineers considered each week the plans and programs that might be developed to meet the desperate needs of other nations. The city of São Paulo, Brazil, for example, lacked enough electricity. Plans were drawn and studied for a tunnel that would run down from the lakes behind the city, be cut through the mountains, and then fall down to the sea at Santos. Turboelectric generators would be installed in the tunnels. As consultants, Dick's company decided whether the plan was "feasible," who should be contracted to build the tunnels, then whether the financing should be guaranteed by the Export-Import Bank or "qualified" for the loans or guarantees of other agencies. It was all very technical. It particularly depended upon careful business diplomacy. When Suzanne went with Dick to receptions at the embassies, or at the big houses along Foxhall Road, she wore simple dresses and smiled, nodded and said nothing. Dick said she was "doing a great job."

It gradually dawned on her she not only had nothing to do, but she would never have anything to add to what Dick was doing. From Technical Managers the Bahamas received the rules and regulations to establish a free port—a zone without tariffs. The Republic Steel Company paid for a study, both technical and financial, of a railroad to bring iron ore through the jungles to the coast of Liberia. A potential competitor to American Nickel looked into the profits that might be expected from mines in Cuba. In each case, the technical and management plans were drawn up in Washington, but of course the financing could only be arranged in New York. With increasing frequency, Dick had to "go up to the city."

Sometimes Suzanne flew from Washington to New York with him. They would stay in the guest room of his parents' apartment at 1088 Park. They saw *South Pacific* and *Kiss Me, Kate*. They had dinner at the Colony, went dancing at the Stork Club. Frequently Dick would say something to the effect that it couldn't be that kind of trip—not a holiday, too many people to see, he'd be back for supper the next day, only one night, he'd be staying at the University Club. When he was absent, as a channel to contain the flood of her resentment Suzanne would spend the day cooking a meal for his return that would outdo anything he could have ordered wherever it was that he ate when he was in New York.

Sometime in April of 1950, she took her flying lesson in the morning. She practiced touch-and-gos in the Piper Cub for less than an hour so that she would have time the rest of the day to prepare carbonade de boeuf. She drove an extra trip across the Key Bridge and back for two special bottles of Nuits-Saint-Georges. When she had everything ready, she took a bath in Sardo and washed her hair. At exactly six-thirty she put the casserole in the oven and set it at 275 degrees; then she drove to

Washington to meet Dick on the seven-thirty Eastern flight. At National Airport she went up to the observation deck, where she was sure that he would spot her as he came down the steps from the plane. It was a warm spring day, but breezy, and she was not distressed that the wind was blowing her skirt across her thighs and outlining her body to everyone on the tarmac down below. A man in the ground crew waved up at her, and she sent him a happy wave back. In return he doffed his baseball cap and swept the ground with it, bowing to her from the waist. They had to give up their mime just then, because the Eastern seven-thirty was on time, turning from its taxiway toward its gate. She waited until the last passenger had come down the steps before she would believe that Dick wasn't on it.

She realized that if he had tried to call her in Falls Church he'd have gotten no answer. She tried calling his Washington office to see if he had left a message, but it was closed. The New York office wouldn't answer either. She knew the logical thing to do was to drive back to Falls Church and wait for a message there, but by then it was eight o'clock. If she left and he arrived on Eastern's eight-thirty, it would be ten before she could turn around and drive back from Falls Church to National again. She bought a copy of the *Saturday Evening Post* and settled down to wait at the Eastern gate. Except for the cartoons, it was the world's most boring magazine. She gave up after the ten-thirty.

Driving back to Falls Church, she swore that if the telephone rang she wouldn't answer it. The carbonade de boeuf she pulled out of the oven was a sunken, charred, dried-up mess. Standing up at the sink, she picked at one or two pieces of what was left of the meat, then scraped the rest away into the garbage. On the way to bed she weighed herself for the first time in months. She realized that if Dick had put on fifty pounds since they were married, she had gained ten pounds herself. Starting in the morning, she swore it was coming off. That night the phone never rang and Suzanne slept soundly; in fact, so peacefully it was almost as if she were a child again.

Dick called the next morning to say he'd be on the Eastern seven-thirty, just as he had promised. Suzanne said no more than that she would meet him. In the car driving away from the airport he complained that he had called her the night before, called repeatedly, and there was never any answer. There was a note of accusation in his voice: "Where the hell were you?" She said she'd been to see *Sunset Boulevard* on F Street, and that seemed to settle it.

Thereafter, oddly enough, the unavoidable weekends and holiday visits with Dick's parents no longer fazed her. The week she had spent during the previous August at their house in East Hampton had infuriated her. While Dick and his father played golf at Maidstone every day, she and Dick's mother waited at the beach cabanas. It was an excruciating experience, an overwhelming boredom from which her only escape was to swim endless laps in the pool. She sensed she was an object of curiosity to her in-laws, something they had acquired, like a delicate Chinese vase which they dusted every day before dinner. If anything, the week she had spent in Tuxedo Park, at the house of Dick's grandmother, Mrs. Mahlon Lyle, was worse. From Christmas Eve until the day after New Year's, Suzanne took long walks through Tuxedo's trails, but inevitably she would have to return at teatime. Thereafter, every month or so, Dick seemed to think it would be a fine idea to visit Tuxedo and his grandmother. Suzanne could devise no alternative but to pack for the weekend and go along—until Dick missed the Eastern seventhirty in April 1950.

The worst trials were Mrs. Mahlon Lyle's Sunday lunches. The family all dressed as if they had just returned from High Church or a funeral. They never actually attended the Episcopal services, but at exactly noon they were required to appear in the library, just as if it were a private chapel, and a butler passed sherry. Then, at exactly one o'clock, they were marched in a column of twos to the dining room, where a long polished Sheraton table was set as if for a dinner of state. After the place plates were cleared, the legatees of Mrs. Mahlon Lyle proceeded through a clear soup, a fish, roast beef and Yorkshire pudding, string beans and mashed potatoes, a green salad dressed only with lemon and oil, orange sherbet and mixed nuts. The silver bowls of cashews and almonds were passed by the butler with as solemn an air as all the rest. Each course had its designated wines, each of them sniffed and sipped with nodding approvals.

The usual seating for these invariable ceremonies put eighty-year-old Mrs. Mahlon Lyle, looking like a shriveled cardinal robed in black, at the head of the table, facing the pantry door, with her table bell at her right hand as the only necessary symbol of her office. This meant that opposite her sat her sixty-year-old son, Richard A. Lyle, as the living male head of family, representing the secular interests. Mrs. Mahlon Lyle could therefore place her favorite grandson, the hope of the future, Richard A. Lyle, Jr., upon her right, and he spoke with her familiarly throughout lunch, addressing her as "Granny." The wives—Hope Lyle and Suzanne Lyle—could take their places wherever they pleased, which meant that Hope sat between her husband and her son on one side of the table, and Suzanne alone on the other. They both addressed the old woman at the head of the table as "Mrs. Lyle," and if for some reason it was necessary for the maid or the butler to address one of the Lyle wives directly, Hope was known as "Mrs. Richard," and regardless of the wedding band she also wore, Suzanne was designated as "Miss Suzanne." It was the most sensible solution.

Suzanne knew that no lunch ever lasted more than one hour and forty-five or forty-six minutes, but whatever stratagem she formed to relieve the tedium was turned by the Lyles into a blind alley. Religion, politics and sex were, of course, forbidden topics. As far as the Lyles were concerned, there was no need to discuss any topic related to money, or anyone who had made or lost money, because as Dick's father explained with absolute finality, "Either you have it, or you don't."

Suzanne was under the impression at first that the Lyles might be amused by details from the world of ideas. Hope Lyle, however, quickly set her daughter-in-law straight. "The trouble with all those people," said Hope, "is that they have unpronounceable foreign names, write mostly in German anyway—an absolutely idiotic language, impossible really—and it all just leads to trouble in the end."

Dick's father quite agreed, quite right. The trouble these days, in his opinion, was that education was at fault. The children were not being taught to read. Since the government was attempting to educate absolutely everyone, it was bound to fail. The solution, as far as he could see, was to get back to basics.

Suzanne inquired politely about what the basics might be.

Her father-in-law specified the classics, Latin and Greek, and that no one should be allowed to graduate from high school without having read all of Sir Walter Scott's Waverley Novels, particularly *Ivanhoe*.

At the mention of *Ivanhoe* Mrs. Mahlon Lyle always sighed with delight. It was never clear to Suzanne whether Granny went soft at the plot, or because of some adventure of her own that had taken place long ago, a secret drama played out across the romantic landscape of England.

At every lunch after October, Hope Lyle would list the schedule for next summer's plans. She would say they planned to be in London in May. Granny would answer, "For the season, of course."

Suzanne noticed that the litany of summer itineraries had a peculiar quality to it. No matter how many times it was repeated, every detail in the schedule was greeted as new. Hope Lyle would say, "Ascot." Granny would inquire with a sigh, "And the Derby?"

Then Hope Lyle would list a route meandering back and forth across the English countryside at houses always described as "great" and stopping at castles invariably inhabited by "good friends." For each one Granny added the appropriate sigh. The summer tour ended at a castle in Ireland, and Granny would say, "A first-rate stable." When Scotland was passed, Granny said, "Fine salmon." Finally Suzanne's mother-in-law would bring the duet to a close by saying they would be back in East Hampton for August. Mrs. Mahlon Lyle would exhale one last time: "England is lovely at that time of year. So green."

When these luncheons finally came to their appointed ends, Mrs. Mahlon stood first, set down her napkin, then marched at the head of the file either to the drawing room or, if the weather was fine, to the perfect lawn behind her English Tudor house where a croquet match was to be played. At first Suzanne thought the old woman carried the scene to excess. Suzanne was timid about whacking croquet balls through wickets, supposing that she ought to continue to conduct herself with the same ladylike manners, the same vapid, banal restraints that had obtained at the long luncheon table. After Dick missed the seven-thirty Eastern at Washington's National Airport, however, it happened that in May Suzanne and Dick were summoned to Tuxedo Park for Saturday night and Sunday lunch, and it also happened that on the lawn after lunch Mrs. Mahlon Lyle's ball fetched up touching Suzanne's near the middle wicket.

It was Suzanne's turn. She clamped her left foot down on her own red-and-white stripe, and swung her mallet with every ounce of strength she could summon, driving the old lady's ball in a forty-yard bouncing arc into the roots of a boxwood hedge. Suzanne thought it was Dick who cleared his throat behind her, but she turned to the grandmother anyway and said: "How do you like them apples, Granny?"

Granny returned the grin. If she had viewed Suzanne through suspicious eyes and with evident distaste until then, she apparently changed her mind on the spot. To the amazement of Mr. and Mrs. Richard, and to the embarrassment of Dick, Mrs. Mahlon Lyle and her grandson's wife played vicious croquet with each other, with obvious delight. On the few occasions they would meet again, given the opportunity, they smacked each other's balls into impossible situations and skipped their way to their next shot like little girls. Each concentrated only on her opponent. The other players might as well have not been there. Granny tucked her long skirts into her belt, and her black high-button shoes almost danced across the lawn. She whistled through her teeth when she concentrated over a nice shot.

In June 1950, Suzanne and Dick drove up from New York to Farmington, Connecticut, for Mimi's graduation. On the way back they stopped in Tuxedo to pay a call on Granny. After lunch the croquet mallets had to be fetched, even though it was beginning to drizzle. Afterward, on the way to La Guardia, Dick said he thought the two of them were quite a sight: "I've never seen anything or anyone before that could get Granny skipping."

Since the moment was convenient, Suzanne asked him directly: "Where does all the money come from?"

"It's in bonds, mostly. A few stocks."

"What kind of bonds?"

"Originally it was railroad bonds."

"Who made it?"

"Actually, it was Granny's father who made most of it, originally in the Kansas Pacific."

"Where did that railroad go?"

"It never went anywhere, but it made a lot of money for some people. My grandfather—Granny's husband—did well enough with what he married, and father hasn't done badly either. None of it is in railroads now, but it's been kept in the basics: oil, coal, steel and copper. Anaconda Copper did particularly nicely for everyone during the war."

"How much is there altogether?"

"Why do you want to know, Suzanne? There's plenty."

"How much is plenty?"

"You'll never have to worry. No one's going to starve, if they're sensible about it."

"How sensible do we have to be? Couldn't we travel if we wanted to? Why couldn't we go to London for the season the way your father does?"

"That's part of his business. Many of his accounts are English. Their taxes over there are impossible. He invests for them here."

"But we could still go, couldn't we, if you wanted to?"

"No, we couldn't, because Technical Managers is just getting started and all the action is in Washington."

"If there's so much money, Dick, I don't see why you work so hard. We didn't go skiing this year. You promised we always would."

"I like to work. I want to work. There's much to be done to keep peace in the world, and I'm part of that."

"What happens when sweet old Granny dies?"

"That has nothing to do with it. It's not likely to happen very soon anyway—as you surely know, the way you have her skipping across the playing fields of Tuxedo Park."

"She has to die someday."

"Suzanne, that's not going to make any difference."

"All right, suppose it doesn't. I don't understand why everything has to be such a secret. I'll bet your mother knows how much there is, and to the penny, too. Summer plans, my eye. Is there one million? Ten million? How much? Twenty million?"

"At least," Dick said with a finality that made clear he considered the discussion to have ended.

No more than three weeks later, the peace—about which Dick Lyle and the other bright young men with whom Dick and Suzanne exchanged so many dinners had talked so earnestly —had ended. At the end of June President Harry S. Truman committed United States Army divisions to the defense of South Korea. The consequences of that exciting little war included a frantic demand for the kind of technical, management and financial assistance that Dick Lyle's company could provide. The need quadrupled for Oliver tractors, turboelectric generators, small cranes, power shovels, diesel engines, irrigation pipe, freight cars, steel beams, copper windings, barbed wire, Johnson outboard motors and Portland cement. Yet the most important element in this sudden expansion was financing, especially the complex guarantees that could be earned in Washington by the approval of "feasible plans." Consequently Dick shuttled back and forth between Washington National Airport and New York's La Guardia week after week. When he did find time to rest, he was exhausted upon his arrival in Falls Church, drank too many martinis before dinner, tasted little of what was put before him, and fell asleep as soon as he could.

Suzanne began to keep track of the martinis, using the same code in her diaries she had once used for her mother—nothing more than X's with circles drawn around them. What seemed odd to her was that as success poured in on her husband's company, the number of martinis poured before dinner increased step by step. On the other hand, her records had many gaps, and the gaps grew longer—periods for which she had no reliable evidence, because Dick was away.

On her birthday, in September, she went up to New York with him, and they stayed at his parents' apartment as usual. They planned to meet at the Palm Court of the Plaza at six for drinks, and then have dinner. To occupy herself for the day, Suzanne had made a lunch date with Marianne Shipman. After lunch she would visit Tiffany, Steuben Glass, Abercrombie, and Georg Jensen, presenting each store with a short list of wedding gifts that she proposed to return for credit to her account.

Lunch with Marianne was great fun, as it turned out, and lasted longer than either of them expected. Perhaps they had more wine than they meant to—their reunion was so full of fascinating gossip. Since Georg Jensen was only a block away, Suzanne and Marianne parted at its doors, promising to see each other as soon as possible. Suzanne went into Jensen's in a mood of tender nostalgia.

To the clerk who approached her she announced herself as Mrs. Richard A. Lyle, Jr., and explained the purpose of her visit. As soon as Jensen's agreed, she would have the wedding gifts she wanted to return shipped directly to them. Although the clerk could not have been more respectful of "Mrs. Richard A. Lyle, Jr.," he was intransigent when it came to accepting the wedding gifts as returns. He was smooth and polite, even servile, but smug. It just couldn't be done; it had been more than a year.

Suzanne would have stamped her foot and shouted at him if she hadn't realized that he hoped that was exactly what she would do. He said he would check the policy about returns for her once again, but he was really quite sure that he had expressed it correctly. He didn't say so in so many words, but he wanted her to understand that because she was Mrs. Richard A. Lyle Junior, and because Mrs. Lyle Senior had been a customer of his for oh, so many years, he would make an extra effort. He would speak with the manager, who was, he indicated, in an office on another floor, if she didn't mind waiting. Suzanne said she wouldn't mind at all. She would like to speak to the manager herself. She would wait for the manager. She would wait all afternoon if necessary.

She sat on a stool next to a glass counter illuminated to display a collection of eggs. They were rounded and polished semiprecious stones, and the grains and swirls of their patterns were fascinating. There were aquamarines as small as a robin's egg, pink chalcedony hen's eggs, and goose eggs of brown carnelian. In addition to those displayed beneath the glass, about a dozen had been cleverly arranged in a wicker basket atop the counter as if they had been gathered in a farmyard. The price tags ranged from sixty to six hundred dollars. Suzanne picked up a pale yellow aragonite, feeling its weight and smooth surface in the palm of her hand. She put it back. An offbeat peach-color aventurine caught her eye—$340—it was cool to her touch. She opened her purse and dropped it in.

The clerk and the manager arrived together shortly thereafter, explaining as best they could that Georg Jensen's policy could not be any other than it was. After a year or more, wedding gifts could not be returned, not even for credit. Surely she could understand that Georg Jensen would never be able to maintain sensible controls over inventory by any other policy. They wanted her to know how exceedingly sorry they were, but they could not make an exception. It was impossible.

Instead of anger, the emotion that surged up in her was very similar to the excitement she felt when she was bringing a Piper Cub down to the strips for a landing. There was always an instant, just a fraction of a second, when the nose had to come up and the horizon would be all blue sky, and she would catch her breath until the flare ended and the wheels had touched, and the plane was in control again on the roll-out down the runway. Suzanne took a brown topaz egg from the wicker basket, plopped it into the palm of the manager, and directed him to mail it to her immediately at her Virginia address. Yes, that would be a charge. It was the manager who reached the door first. He held it open for the formidable Mrs. Lyle Junior as she swept out to Fifth Avenue.

She walked north and kept walking. Her first objective was the zoo, at Sixty-fourth Street, but the energies pouring through her were such that she thought she might as well go on to the pond, past Seventy-second. At the pond there was still more than an hour to kill before she was due to meet Dick at the Plaza, so she walked on to the reservoir entrance at Ninetieth. By the time she had walked all the way back to Fifty-ninth, her feet were swollen and aching, but she was still exhilarated. For once, Dick was on time, and it turned out to be a grand evening: they had dinner at "21," then went over to the Stork Club and danced until two in the morning. When they finally tiptoed into his mother's apartment, Dick may have thought he was going to roll over and go to sleep, but she said: "I'm not through with you yet, Dickie boy."

In October Dick was named executive vice-president of Technical Managers, Inc. He was away the last three weeks of the month on a trip to London and Paris. Suzanne used the time to solo, and by the end of the month she had her pilot's license. During the first week of November, Dick went up to New York and refused again to take Suzanne along. He would be gone only three days, he said, and there was no point in making an expedi-

tion of it. Suzanne used her empty days to fly down to Charlottesville and visit Miss Freddy. They had dinner together and
talked far into the night like sisters. They promised each other
something more. "But not until," said Miss Freddy, "you are
ready again."

Flying back alone the next morning, Suzanne encountered bad
weather all along the Shenandoahs. She was forced to turn north
of Fredericksburg, landing at a little field near Richmond. She
parked the little Cessna she had rented in front of the shed that
served as a control tower, hung about drinking coffee until three
that afternoon, waiting for the weather to clear, then decided it
was worth another try. If she couldn't make Falls Church, Baltimore was reported open. The low-pressure system was moving
northeast, breaking up along the coast. Might as well drink
coffee in Baltimore.

Once she was in the air again, it was worse than she had expected. She flew scared at five hundred feet over Virginia farms
and beneath black rain squalls. Her radio reported everything
west of her closed again. She was not as sure as she should have
been about her navigation; besides, it was almost impossible to
concentrate on flying the Cessna and balance her chart and the
radio book on her lap at the same time. If she looked down to
read the columns of radio frequencies, when she looked up again
the nose was elevated or she was over a landscape that was entirely unfamiliar. Because her instructor had often taken her out
over the Chesapeake for her lessons, she decided it would be familiar territory. She changed her heading to sixty degrees.

It seemed like forever, but it was really only about twelve
minutes before she spotted the lighthouse at Point Lookout below
her. She then stayed low along the western shore of the bay to
Fairhaven before leaving it to bank west for Washington, but
she had no alternative as she neared the capital except to climb
into dense clouds until her altimeter showed 6,500 feet. It was almost too dark to read the frequencies, but National Airport
tower finally acknowledged they had her on radar. She was trying to think of a way to explain that she had only a vague idea
where they might be.

Then, as if by magic, she was flying through broken nimbus
under a low but bright sun. And there was the Washington Mon-

ument shining like Excalibur, still wet from the departing rains, and glistening. She threw a salute to it, and she hummed a medley of dance tunes all the way to Falls Church. When she was safely on the ground, she promised herself she would always fly like a man—perhaps speculative about the dangers of bad weather, and never taking any stupid chances if she could help it, but master of her emotions nonetheless.

Dick was away again on the morning of November 16, 1950, when John Putnam called her from New York to say that her mother had died the night before in the apartment at the Sulgrave. Putnam would not be clear about whether she had died of a heart attack, or whether cirrhosis of the liver was the cause. She'd been going to New York Hospital about the liver and probably should have been hospitalized, but had refused to accept what the doctors had been telling her. Yes, it could have been the booze, but it really didn't make any difference now. In New York, Suzanne looked down at her father's wife in a silk-lined coffin and realized that John Putnam was right: it didn't matter any more; there was nothing to say now; it was finally over.

Suzanne would remember the entire sequence of funeral arrangements as a horror show. Instead of being any kind of practical help, John Putnam badgered her to decide the most idiotic questions. What did she want done about the Sulgrave lease? Would she want to keep the apartment for a while? Well, then, where should the furniture be stored? How soon would she be ready to go over the details of the estate? He kept assuring her that he wanted everything done exactly the way she thought best. He exasperated her, and he would only be satisfied if she snapped back answers at him. All right. If what John Putnam wanted was orders, by God he'd get 'em.

Her husband was no one to lean on, either. He had a string of excuses that made it possible for him to arrive late for the service at St. James on Madison. Dr. Lorimer came in from Locust Valley and insisted upon a dreary eulogy he said he'd prepared but which could just as easily have been said over the body of any dead woman. No more than twenty of what Dr. Lorimer identified as "her many friends" bothered to show up at the church. Exactly six people dropped by the Sulgrave apartment afterward, including the doctor from New York Hospital and the Reverend Lorimer and his wife. Suzanne estimated the good doctors came as a polite way to guarantee their fees—probably always did it.

The next morning, Suzanne, Mimi and John Putnam were the only ones to take the Merchants Limited to Boston. For five hours on the train Mimi alternated between bouts of silent weeping and tedious explanations about the importance of art to everyone's life—the immediate result of her freshman survey course at Radcliffe. It was such a shame, in Mimi's opinion, that their mother had never really appreciated art. It might have been the one source of pleasure in her life. Suzanne started to argue that their mother had been shrewd enough to know what art was worth, but Mimi answered that money had nothing to do with it, and Suzanne dropped it. As usual, the Merchants Limited arrived in Boston late.

The burial had been arranged in the Hadley family plot in Dedham. In the graveyard it was blowing thirty knots northeast, and they had to stand with their backs against a driving rain. By the time Suzanne could throw the traditional handful of dirt into the pit, they were soaked to the skin and chilled. Back in Boston, Suzanne shut herself in the room she had reserved at the Copley. She refused to join Mimi and John Putnam for dinner. The next morning she left the shoes she had worn to the graveyard in a wastebasket. They were ruined. She had also started a magnificent cold, which would take until mid-December to shake off.

By December, John Putnam had gotten the figures on the estate together, and he said he was ready to go over them with her. Suzanne met him at his office at 40 Wall Street. He said they really didn't have that many choices—not in his opinion, not if they were going to be realistic about it. She could see that he had a fine view of the East River. In the distance there were tow barges plowing upriver against an ebb tide.

John Putnam, expert on estates, went about his business. As Suzanne already knew, the only thing her mother had to her name was the house and its effects—some of the furniture was quite good—at Oyster Bay. The fact was that the Internal Revenue Service would assess the house, including the value of its contents, and take half of it. Whether or not the house was sold.

Those were the rules. No, there were no alternatives. They could be held off for a period of time, but in the end the tax men had to be paid in cash. They would probably collect sixty thousand dollars or so. It was his recommendation that the house be put on the market immediately with one or two real estate agents he could suggest. It was up to her. She didn't have to decide right away, but she would have to decide sooner or later.

Where Mimi would live when she was not at college was indeed a problem. The cost of Mimi's education at Radcliffe would run about five thousand, maybe six thousand a year altogether. It was just unfortunate that this was Mimi's debutante year, and that all the commitments were already made: the Grosvenor Ball and the Junior Assemblies and all that. Too late to cancel everything, and in any case Mimi ought to go right on with it because it was always a good investment. John Putnam thought it had turned out remarkably well for Suzanne. Brought down expenses, didn't it? The son-of-a-bitch winked at her.

Well, the totals came to an estate of one hundred seventy-six thousand—assuming the Oyster Bay house would bring about one hundred twenty thousand, of which sixty went to the tax men. Only the house was taxable, not the trusts their father had set up for them. Suzanne must understand that it would only be practical to budget forty thousand dollars for the next four years for Mimi. That would include her college. But she had to live somewhere too, and perhaps travel a little. If they were lucky, Mimi would find a husband too. He did not try the familiar wink again.

The point was simply this: after taking everything into account, and the taxes, and the costs of administering the estate, Suzanne and Mimi would have between them one hundred thirty-six thousand dollars. That should provide an income of about six thousand a year, after taxes. Yes, as he had pointed out before, after tax was the only practical way to calculate. "Just the same," John Putnam insisted, "that's a substantial sum of money. There's no reason to make faces at a nice little income of your own—above and beyond what your husband provides."

Suzanne stood and went to the window. She could see much of Brooklyn, spread out under a haze from smokestacks, and the cranes by the river there—that must be the navy yard. She turned, half sitting, using the hot-air register below the window sill as a perch. Putnam would remember that she was smiling, she was happy, and if anything her eyes were shining. "I want a divorce, John. Start getting it for me."

He didn't think she was making any sense. She was just upset. They shouldn't have been going over all this so soon after the funeral. She should take some time to let things settle down. She had a fine husband who could give her anything she wanted.

"I have already thought about it, thank you." She seemed to think it was a marvelous joke. "I want ten thousand a month from Dick Lyle. You're my lawyer. What do we have to do?"

Well, for one thing, in New York State there had to be grounds, and the only grounds were adultery.

"Nope. He works too hard for adultery. When he's not working, he's drinking. As many martinis as my mother, and then some."

Ten thousand a month was too high, in John Putnam's opinion. It would be different if there were a child to support, but he doubted any New York judge would award ten thousand to a healthy twenty-one-year-old woman. Two thousand, maybe.

"But if there were a child?"

Well, yes. It would all depend, of course. He would have to show that ten thousand meant nothing to Dick Lyle, and he was sure that the lawyers who handled the Lyle family affairs weren't going to be easy. The way these things were done was that first a separation agreement had to be worked out, and the agreement was the basis later for a divorce in Idaho. There would still have to be some sort of grounds.

"Abandonment. He's always away."

"Lots of husbands are always away, Suzanne."

"What if I were caught in adultery?"

He didn't think that was a good idea.

"You didn't think it was a bad idea in Saratoga."

The best John Putnam could do with that was to clear his throat, then resume his litany: If she was involved in any scandal at all, she would be likely to get nothing. Not too practical. She would have to be innocent, entirely clean. Mustn't provide the other side with any ammunition. In his opinion, she should go back to Virginia and think this all over carefully. Marriages, in his experience, were almost always worth preserving despite everything.

"Dick Lyle is worth at least twenty million. How much are your fees going to be?"

He thought she was making a great mistake. She was upset by her mother's death, that's all there was to it. Had she discussed this with her husband?

"Not yet."

She was still so young. She must understand that marriage was more than puppy love. It was serious business. It often took hard work. It usually made economic sense too. As Mrs. Richard A. Lyle, Jr., she already had all the privileges that twenty million or whatever it was could buy. Why not give it some time? Why not see if she could talk over the problems, whatever they might be, with her husband?

Well, divorces could be costly. His firm would require fifteen thousand in advance. Yes, on the barrelhead. There was nothing he could do about that; that was the policy of the partnership and he must abide by the rules. Webster, White, Moore and White would bill her with a monthly statement as they went along, against the fifteen, until it was used up. Then the firm would require a deposit of another fifteen thousand. That was their policy, simply stated. In his opinion, a case like this could be extremely difficult. Especially since there were no grounds. "New York State besides. Extremely difficult."

Suzanne had twisted sideways on the window sill. Using it as a counter, she was already bent over her checkbook, filling out a draft on her Corn Exchange account, just as if she had found something in Bonwit's she had to have. When she was done, she looked at it again to make sure she had the zeros right. Then she started toward his desk.

He, too, stood up, because it seemed the right thing to do. She held the check up at him between her thumb and forefinger so that she could look over its top edge into his eyes, and as a coquette would, she grinned. "Don't you think it might be a good investment, John?"

She put her check into his hands. As he looked down at its amount, she reached up and pinched his cheek as if she were dealing with a naughty little boy of whom she had always been extremely fond. "There's your fee, lawyer. I'll want you to do your part. I'll do mine. Ten thousand a month, after tax. Only realistic way to figure it, right? After tax?"

Perhaps—he cleared his throat again—she would like to have dinner. He would call his wife in Cold Spring Harbor and say he'd been delayed. He'd like to talk over "strategy."

But she was already gathering up her purse and pulling on her coat. "There's a Mrs. Putnam, is there? Hope it makes economic sense for you, John. How nice." She was in boisterous high spirits. "Do give your wife my regards. Someday I hope I can meet her. I've got to get back to Washington. I'll call you when I'm ready."

Instead she stayed an extra night in New York in the Sulgrave apartment, but it was too depressing. Early the next morning, she was at the offices of Douglas Elliman. She took the first apartment she was shown, at 3 East Seventy-seventh Street. It was a bit dark, and needed paint, but it would do. It had two bedrooms, so there would be a place for Mimi on vacations. She called Putnam at his office, instructed him to get out of the Sulgrave lease and to buy the co-op at Seventy-seventh Street. He pointed out she was already complicating things by establishing a separate residence, but he agreed that if they put it in Mimi's name that would solve the problem.

Once she was back in Falls Church, however, Suzanne had to go slow. She would wait until the right moment presented itself. Dick was away at least one night each week, but it didn't matter any more. When the weather was fine, she flew short hops to Winchester, Richmond, anywhere at all, and back, but flying hardly interested her, and she was just logging hours on her license. She began to read again, and read seriously. She went through Gordon Childe's *Prehistoric Migrations in Europe* in a week.

Mr. and Mrs. Richard A. Lyle, Jr., spent Christmas and New Year's at Granny Lyle's, in Tuxedo Park. Dick went into the city every day, yet Suzanne felt as if she were sailing downwind in the trades. Despite the musty, dark and grim interiors of the Tuxedo house, what was belowdecks only served as a contrast to the rolling whitecaps and blue skies and fresh breezes that Suzanne was breathing. She gladly played backgammon and gin with Granny in the library by the hour for a penny a point. If Dick was half sloshed every evening, that was just fine.

Then she discovered she had been lucky. She had assumed that she missed her period on December 5 because of the whole funeral thing and the cold she had caught in the Dedham grave-yard. She'd missed a period like that before, and there had been some spotting, so she couldn't be sure. She was due again on New Year's Day, which came and went, and her hopes began to climb. Still she waited, because she would have to be absolutely positive. During the first week of February, she was finally sure.

But the baby growing inside her almost made her change her plans. She was no longer as full of resolves as she had been. Her objectives didn't seem to matter as much. Each morning, she was mildly nauseated, but no more, and after she had gotten some breakfast down, the day that followed always seemed so pleasant. She was in a dreamy mood, and when Miss Freddy called, suggesting that Suzanne fly down to Charlottesville, she put Miss Freddy off, indicating that the flight was really only a distant possibility. She was just as vague to John Putnam. He called from time to time to ask if she wanted him to do anything, and she would say, "Not yet." She was wavering, and if not wavering, at least going through a strange lull she could not quite explain. On the weekend just before Valentine's Day, she almost confessed to Dick he would be a father, but before she could, he announced he was leaving Monday for a three-week tour of Technical Managers projects in Europe, with a week in Leb-anon. Had to be done. Great potentials. Europe was coming back. Atlantic community. France would take the lead. He was so proud of his patient little wife. She really understood. "She was a great help."

Once Dick was gone, Suzanne got back to work. What she wanted to know was confirmed by a gynecologist at George Washington Hospital. She furnished the apartment at 3 East Seventy-seventh Street partly with things from the Sulgrave, partly with furniture from Oyster Bay. She bought herself a new double bed at W. & J. Sloane. John Putnam found a stockbroker who had just remarried who would rent the Centre Island house from Suzanne for the summer. Putnam thought they had a good chance to sell it after Labor Day. In Falls Church she packed up what she would need, and she made four round trips to New York to make sure everything was ready. She had to be prepared for a long siege. When there was nothing more to be done, she wrote a note upon the Tiffany stationery that had "SBL" engraved in blue at the top. It read: "Dear Dick, We're getting divorced. Love, Suzanne." She propped it up on the liquor cabinet for his return and closed the front door of the Falls Church house behind her with great satisfaction. If she had regrets, they were the kind she supposed the pioneer women must have felt when they pulled closed the door of a Connecticut Valley farmhouse and then got up on the wagon seat to go west to the promised land.

Actually, the first stages of her journey were not as difficult as she had feared. It was easy to "stay out of trouble," as John Putnam constantly reminded her, because she was pregnant. She lived like a recluse, but it was a busy self-containment. She used the time for a passionate study of American history, and on many days walked the entire distance back and forth to the New York Public Library, where she became such a regular she was recognized with smiles at the main desk. She loved being alone so much that she dreaded the arrival of Mimi from Radcliffe. Fortunately Mimi signed herself into a tour of Europe's great museums for the summer. She stayed only five days in the new apartment, and then off she went and Suzanne was alone again.

As soon as Wavertree Hall closed for the summer, Miss Freddy moved in as companion, cook, and eventually nurse. Although they remembered fondly the voluptuous days of their love affair, it would be more or less accurate to describe their new relationship as one of understanding, like the sweet scent of lemon rinds, and of overwhelming tenderness. They spent a fortune on cab fares to lower Third Avenue to shop for fresh vegetables, and the constancy of their new arrangement had more to do with spinach, green beans, tomatoes, radishes and green peppers than anything Dick Lyle might have assumed, even if he had known something about their past.

Of course, Dick was outraged, hurt and then bitter. His lawyers took their time about getting around to the facts of the matter, but Suzanne was absolutely obedient to John Putnam's instructions and refused to talk to Dick about anything. The result was that Dick's lawyers didn't even know about the baby until July. Then they began to soften up, offering two thousand a month on a separation agreement, just as Putnam had predicted.

Angelique Lyle was born in Harkness Pavilion in the early-morning hours of August 22, 1951. Within a month, Dick's lawyers had caved in. In return for visitation rights and the right to choose the schools, they came across with ten thousand dollars a month. Suzanne and Miss Freddy tried to guess whether old Granny Lyle had her hand in it. Since another feature of the deal was that there would be a separate trust for Angelique administered solely by the National Community Trust Company, and the trust was set up so that Suzanne would never have any access to it, they guessed that Mrs. Mahlon Lyle was moving somewhere behind the screen of her grandson's lawyers. In any case, Putnam urged Suzanne to accept ten thousand dollars a month, even if it was pretax. As long as Dick lived, Suzanne would be depositing his checks without any distinction between alimony and support for the child. If John Putnam had to take the matter before a judge, there was no telling what might happen. Once the agreement was signed, Suzanne would be free to go to Idaho, establish six months' residence and get her divorce. Dick would not contest it.

Sun Valley already had two feet of snow by the fifteenth of October. To the extent that Suzanne had been scholarly in New York, she went to the opposite extreme in Idaho. She played with her baby by the hour. She found Gisela, an Austrian girl, to mind Angelique while she skied. She took as a lover a ski instructor, a Canadian boy of her own age, and they made love in Suzanne's chalet with all the force and stamina of youth.

Suzanne stored up health. While she waited for her divorce to be final, her energies rose week by week, like a reservoir filling up behind a new dam. By April she looked as supple and quick as all the ski instructors who were by then her friends. Particularly with her baby daughter in her arms, Suzanne appeared to be no more than sixteen: her waist-length hair plaited in two flying braids, her skin tanned across the high ridges of her cheekbones, the whites of her eyes and her white teeth flashing all-American outdoor enthusiasm.

After skiing every afternoon, she spent an hour in a hot tub, luxuriously soaking her muscles and caring for her skin with soaps and oils and lotions. In the back of an antique shop in town she had found an old photograph, nearly three feet long and about a foot high, that nobody wanted. It had cost her only fifty cents to carry it away, but it had cost twelve dollars to get framed. She hung the photograph on the wall right beside her tub, so that she could "study it" every afternoon.

It must have been a secret joke of her own, of course, but the photograph was in its way amusing. It was one of those composite pictures, in which sections had been pasted together to give the effect of a panorama. In the lower right, a legend had been penned in with white ink: "Annual Dinner, New York City Chamber of Commerce, Waldorf-Astoria, March 4, 1927." The panorama showed something like eight hundred men in tuxedos peering up from their tables of ten, waiting for the official photographer's flash. The effect was of a sea of white faces, barely distinguishable and each face just like the next, on a field of black tuxedos. Her young ski instructor asked her if she had hung it because there was someone in it that she knew. Suzanne said no, she liked it because she thought it was so funny.

He was a sweet young man, and by spring he was explaining awkwardly that he would offer to marry her, but he didn't think he was ready for marriage yet. He would have to save up some money first. She thanked him over and over. She kissed his eyes, and his nose, and his ears, and his shoulders, and told him that it was all right, it wasn't necessary, she would be going back to New York soon, and she would always remember how strong and young and full of life he was. The last night they were together, they made love incessantly. Much of the time, they were laughing at each other, but there was no bitterness in it.

In May 1952 Suzanne brought Gisela back to New York with her, because she was going to need steady care for Angelique. She was still unpacking when John Putnam called, late in the afternoon. He said he had some bad news: Dick Lyle had been killed in an automobile accident in Rome two days before.

"So what, John?"

Well, if she had been the widow, she would have inherited the twenty million; as it was, the trust fund for Angelique still stood, but the ten thousand a month was off. "It looks like you mis-played that hand, young lady."

She could hear satisfaction in his voice. He was continuing with more authority than he deserved: "I've talked to the Lyle lawyers, and they've agreed there will be one more check—June. But that's going to be it. The only thing I can think of is that you might want to see if you can patch things up with old Mrs. Mahlon Lyle. Get to the funeral, anyway."

"Never," was her reply. There was so much steel in her reaction that John Putnam stopped being so smug. "It's not going to make any difference, John."

"It seems to me it's made a hell of a difference. You've just dropped back from one hundred twenty thousand a year to six thousand. And now you're paying your own rent to boot."

"You'll see." And she hung up.

ACT II

Snow White

9

Tableaux Vivants

1952–60

SUZANNE never looked back. She never gave way to remorse or regret, because she saw no need for them. They were extravagances, luxuries, useless debilities. At the foundation of her success was a granite realism, and upon this unshakable base she built a house designed with an unwavering logic. There would be moralists who sniffed at her behavior, and others who said she was destructive. Perhaps she sometimes was. Yet in her view these silly critics were nothing but sentimentalists, and she would sweep them away with a wave of her hand: "Fiddlesticks!"

She was only rendering to Caesar. By 1952 everyone agreed that the main business of America was business. General Eisenhower was elected President, and businessmen were said to have the answers. Before the inauguration thirty businessmen went down to Sea Island, Georgia, played golf for ten days and agreed there were important tasks ahead: if America was to maintain its leadership, business would have to grow. Those who wailed or gnashed their teeth at the advent of a fat, stupid Republican administration were unrealistic, in Suzanne's view, and not being practical. Instead of wringing her hands, she took up the study of business mechanics, its principles and its philosophy.

In 1952 she registered for courses at New York University's School of Commerce. She applied herself to the basics of accounting and commercial law, then monetary theory, money and banking, the operations of the Federal Reserve system, techniques in international trade, the complexities of tax law, and the metaphysics of mortgage-money markets. Altogether, it would take her eight years of late-afternoon classes before she finally earned her master's degree in finance. While she studied theory she practiced applications.

It never occurred to her that her determination was unique; there were many others in her classes who were equally devoted to their studies. She was unusual in that she was never converted to the theology to which she was exposed. Like all the others, she meditated upon the lessons provided every morning in *The Wall Street Journal*. She accepted these mysteries as useful, but she never believed a word of it—like a priest who continued to walk with his breviary, and admire its truths, long after he had lost his faith. On the one hand, she admired with all her heart the ceremonies of money; on the other hand, she was never seduced by their sentimentalities. She thought possession of large amounts of money was a logical necessity; that it would never be possible to act whimsically without substantial capital—"individualism," it was called by President Eisenhower. Yet experience had taught her that money was an unreliable standard. Since the society through which she moved chose to adore money, Suzanne adopted its manners in much the same way that she shortened her hems to be in style.

In addition to her theological studies, she took her first job in the summer of 1952—the result of a long lunch with Mr. Peter Dickerson, age fifty-six. After allowing the pontifical Mr. Dickerson to lay out the ground rules for what he imagined might be a long and dangerous flirtation with a woman far too young, Suzanne also accepted a job to sell real estate from the offices of Dickerson, Rolfe and Streitfeld, on Forty-ninth Street between Madison and Fifth. Suzanne understood precisely that as long as Peter Dickerson was never required to consummate the affair that was within his power, he would be generous.

Dickerson's generosity consisted of allowing her to take the elevator to the second floor of his company's offices every morning and to occupy an empty desk equipped with no more than a plain black telephone. Her desk was in the last row of six identical rows; four other "agents" occupied identical metal desks and answered black phones in each row. Dickerson, Rolfe and Streitfeld advertised in the *Times* and the *Trib* weekdays and Sundays, listing apartments that might be rented or bought. In return the black phones rang—sometimes all at once, but usually as a digression from the office gossip that occupied long, restless days. When prospects were secured, the agents of DR&S fanned out through the city's "silk stocking district" to show apartments that "should be just perfect." One apartment was indistinguishable from the next, but it was, Mr. Dickerson reminded everyone, a highly skilled effort in matching tastes. The pay was a 5 per cent commission, split fifty-fifty with Mr. Dickerson's company to cover "advertising and overhead." Most of Suzanne's co-workers competed with each other, sometimes viciously, for the juicier listings, such as the chance to sell a big co-operative duplex along Park or on Fifth to a successful wife who planned to bring in her decorator. When there were droughts between big listings, the other agents sipped coffee from paper cups and bitched about the money they were making.

Suzanne, on the contrary, was delighted by the whole scheme. She was planning ahead. She made less money than any other agent, but she was learning for the first time the geography of the city in which she was going to campaign. She made no effort at all to secure the juicier listings, and instead concentrated upon a category her co-workers did their best to ignore: men who had just been divorced and needed only one bedroom; executives from out-of-town companies who were looking for six-month furnished sublets; those graying men in their fifties who would look at only one or two apartments before they made up their minds, who gave a deposit to cover three months' rent, and who would then produce a nervous young woman of no previous address to sign the lease where the X appeared. Since money was not Suzanne's main concern—as if she were working at real estate merely to fill up her days—her co-workers happily tossed her these less remunerative commissions, like tossing a bone: "Let Mrs. Lyle handle that one."

Consequently, by 1953 Mrs. Lyle had built a constituency of her own. She kept records of every address and telephone number, man and woman alike. She had no difficulty in picking up her customer's birth date: "I'm a Virgo," she would say. He would then hear that his own birth sign had special qualities that he had never realized before. In due time, he would receive a card on his birthday that reminded him of his more interesting qualities. The card would be unsigned, but unquestionably scented with Calèche, and there were few who could not recall who had remembered them. Some addressees telephoned Dickerson, Rolfe and Streitfeld in an attempt to locate her. After 1953 she was gone, finished with playing agent. Yet she continued her system of birthday cards faithfully, and added to her list the names she picked out of *Fortune, Business Week* and *Dun's Review*.

Simultaneously with her research in real estate, and as a laboratory experiment for the theories she was learning at New York University, Mrs. Richard A. Lyle, Jr., would call the offices of presidents of corporations. She would say she was a stockholder —which was often true by then—and explain to the secretary that she had a minor question about the annual report. If it would not be too much trouble, would the president be kind enough to call her back? Nine out of ten returned the call, answered the inquiry she derived from the footnotes, and then discovered that their birth sign was one of the explanations for their company's success. Even if it wasn't true, there couldn't be any harm in it.

Beginning in 1953, the rumors about Suzanne multiplied. When she appeared at La Baroque for lunch, or at the Colony for dinner, or was seen dancing on Sundays at the Stork Club, there were those who were absolutely sure she was the birthday-card woman. There were others who had not received any cards, and perhaps felt left out. There were rumors passed among men who stood at the bars or met for drinks at the Racquet Club. The stories just grew on their own after a while. Only in the very beginning did Suzanne start any of these stories herself, but with the help of her old pal John David Garraty, the results of her public relations campaign spread into every corner of the city's consciousness. Like her direct-mail campaign, it had an effect of its own—once it had been given a start.

Garraty didn't have to do much more than what he loved best. He told improbable truths around the tables at which he stopped. With a wink, a nod, a smile, a pause, he implied to those he fascinated that he was on the inside; that there was even more to tell than even he was at liberty to reveal; that she was a debutante, to be sure; that she had married one of the richest guys in America. She was widowed in some versions, and divorced in others, but she could be had, for five thousand dollars. An improbable sum.

Garraty's audiences were made to drag the story out of him. He could be reluctant to share what he knew. Only to those in whom he placed absolute faith—because of their sophistication, of course—would Garraty explain: The deal was one of those crazy things, pal. Five thousand dollars and she was yours for the weekend. Nope; no weekdays, no discounts, no afternooners —the whole weekend, reserved in advance and paid in advance. She would go anywhere, and anything goes, but she didn't play around with guys who couldn't get away from the wife for the weekend. She didn't spend any time with guys who didn't have the scratch, either. Hell, she didn't need the money; that was the point.

The john had to be willing to play ball in her park. Anyway, the line was a mile long. The word was she was booked up until the end of the year. She turned them away. No reservation, no chance. Threw back the little ones to let 'em grow. One guy came on with her and said he'd go ten thousand for a Wednesday or a Thursday. She said no thanks. When he figured he had to wait his turn, and caved in, and like a good little boy asked which weekend she'd give him, she said she'd call him someday. Poor bastard. He's afraid somebody would find out he couldn't get it for ten thousand. Unbelievable. He offers ten grand, but no Snow White.

There was a story about the guy who waited two months for his weekend. Finally it's D day. He had it all set up in a suite in the Stanhope. She arrived, says hi, I'm Snow White, and he couldn't wait two minutes. Off come the clothes, bang-bang, and it's like the end of the world, and he falls asleep. While he's snor-

ing, she calls up room service, and they send up the drinks—the
mixers, the bucket of ice, the whole rig. The next thing he
knows, she's stuffed an ice cube up his ass, and he's so wide
awake he can't believe it. She told him he'd paid his money, and
whether he liked it or not, he was going to get what he paid for.
Monday morning came around, he was so wrung out he had to
spend the day in the steam baths at the New York A. C.

"She handles her own bookings, for all I know," John David
Garraty would allow. "Under her own name, in the phone book,
Mrs. Richard A. Lyle, Jr., Three East Seventy-seventh Street."

There were men who could not resist putting in the call, just
to see. Even if they had believed they were going to avoid it,
they were soon being interviewed and the questions came to
them with such charm that they were soon flattering themselves.
Whether or not they were able to "make a reservation," they
were never allowed to believe they had been refused absolutely.
In fact, once they took the first step of placing the call, they
were justified in the impression they held that they had somehow
already joined the blessed inner circle. With the fear of exclusion
relieved, there were those who pretended they had already made
the list and paid the exorbitant price of fame, with the result
that Mrs. Lyle's popularity was somewhat exaggerated. In any
case, every man who called provided the oracle on Seventy-
seventh Street with his date of birth, and sooner or later he received a birthday card that suggested marvelous sexual idiosyn-
crasies that perhaps he never before had fully understood. These
cards were in themselves great prizes. "She's a lay analyst," John
David Garraty would say to his audiences. It always brought
him admiring laughter.

Garraty had the good sense to confirm every rumor brought to
his attention, whether it was true or not. He nodded, smiled and
winked, saying something like, "Could be." There was a story
that Snow White, or Mrs. Richard A. Lyle, Jr., or Suzanne, or
whoever it was that she was supposed to be, went to Las Vegas
for the weekend with the president of a plywood company. Five
minutes after they had their bags unpacked, Snow White took
the check for five thousand, cashed it, and tried to play it over
the hump at the blackjack table. On her first pair of cards, the
dealer had to pay her. She left ten thousand on the table. She

won again, and left twenty thousand for the next deal. "The third time, she's busted."

Meanwhile, her lover was winning at the craps table. He couldn't believe the luck he was having. Every time he got ahead ten thousand, he split it with her. She would take her five grand back to the blackjack table and lose it again as fast as he was making it. Three days and two nights went by. They flew back to New York even. He made sixty thousand dollars, and was happy as a lark. She'd lost every cent of it. "They never wasted a minute between the sheets with each other."

Another story, possibly true, described Snow White's limousine trip with a man who'd made a fortune in Wall Street over and over but kept losing big chunks of it to the wives who divorced him. The way Garraty told it, the wizard of over-the-counter stocks was weird for shopping. His thing was to have his chauffeur pick Snow White up at about ten on Saturday morning. The chauffeur drove his boss and Snow White around Central Park three times, trying to keep his eye on the traffic and the rear-view mirror at the same time. As soon as Snow White satisfied the boss in the back of the limousine, the chauffeur was told to drive them to Bonwit Teller. He parked the Cadillac in the bus zone and waited, along with his boss, while Snow White went shopping for a ten-dollar scarf, or something like that, wearing her fur coat but with nothing underneath. Half an hour later, she got back in the car, and off they went again, for a drive on the West Side Highway. All the chauffeur could see was the back of her head most of the afternoon, but he had to wait while she went shopping at Bonwit Teller, Bergdorf Goodman, Henri Bendel and Saks. By the end of the day, according to Garraty, the chauffeur was worn out from driving in Saturday traffic around Central Park, up and down the West Side Highway and the East River Drive, across the Brooklyn Bridge and back. "And that's all there was to it," said John David Garraty. "One hundred and fifty miles of road and four stores."

Garraty would neither confirm nor deny: that Snow White joined the harem of Marshal Sarit of Thailand when the Marshal arrived in New York to speak before the United Nations Assembly; or that two old geezers, retired from the garment business and both living in the Waldorf Towers, played gin for her; or that a guy who lived in the Dakota bought her as a birthday present for a weekend with his wife. All these stories had about them a consistent quality; they were mysterious, but simultaneously appealed to the pride of men who wanted to certify their own success and the credo by which they lived—money could buy anything. One year to the day after Suzanne returned from her Idaho divorce, she sat down once again in John Putnam's paneled office at 40 Wall Street to talk business.

When they had cleared away the small talk, he composed a church and steeple of his fingers, rocked back in his chair, and brought up the subject with the utmost gravity. He said he'd been hearing stories.

"Where?"

He'd heard a story about her at the Union League Club. In the past month, as a matter of fact. He had assured the fellow who had passed it on that it was a libel.

"Union League Club?"

Yes. Suzanne must understand that once that type of story started around, it was extremely difficult to stop. Very grave matter. He paused, because the effect of his sermon seemed to require her to do some searching of her conscience.

"I don't think I have too many Union League Club types, John. I can't think of one. Not one."

His point, she must realize, was that whatever it was she had been up to was creating a scandal—a quiet scandal, but a scandal just the same. It might not be as amusing as she appeared to think. She'd better give some thought to whatever she was doing that had caused this kind of malicious talk.

"I have been pursuing life, liberty and property, John. Nothing more."

But she was doing it in such a way that incredible stories were being told about her.

"They're all true, John dear. And I expect you to do your best to pass them on, in a discreet way, of course. Especially at the Union League Club."

She was not being serious.

"Twenty-four weekends at five thousand each," she pointed out, "makes a total of one hundred twenty thousand a year. That's all cash. After tax."

For the record he said he was shocked. She was only twenty-three years old.

"I am twenty-two, as a matter of fact. Twenty-three in September. It seems to me that it is not a business that has many prospects after the age of thirty. So we are going to make the best of it. And I hope you will continue to handle my legal affairs."

He huffed and puffed, just as she expected, until she too had to be as upset as he appeared to be. She pretended she was especially disheartened at the prospect that she would be without his advice, without his wisdom, and among strangers at another law firm. His high-minded moralities, she regretted, had put her in the most awkward, and embarrassing, and distressed state. He was just not being fair.

All right. She had selected two brownstones that were available on East Ninety-third Street, between Third and Lexington, south side of the street. Quiet block. Gardens out back. Both twenty-four feet wide, sixty deep, side by side. Listed on the cards at Dickerson, Rolfe and Streitfeld at eighty thousand. She wanted Putnam to offer fifty, but he was authorized to go as high as sixty thousand for both. Total. She wanted two separate mortgages of fifteen thousand on each house. She estimated it would cost her twenty thousand each to fix them up. She was going to expand.

She needed a place "for the overflow." It would take her six months to get them ready, and another six months to get rolling —a year altogether, but then her basic cash flow would run about ten thousand a week. Yes, a half million a year, for starts.

No, there were not going to be any problems with the New York City Police Department. She'd already taken care of that. She'd had a little chat with Judge Gordon and they'd come to an agreement.

"Ephraim Gordon?" John Putnam was not necessarily shocked, but obviously uncomfortable. "Suzanne, now I know you're in over your head. Ephraim Gordon is the lawyer for all kinds of . . . Well, for one thing, he represents Amedeo Scutari. These are not the kind of people you know anything about. You have never moved in those kinds of circles."

"Judge Gordon embarrasses you, John?"

"We've never had any dealing with that kind of fellow."

"That's because you are all Republicans."

"We do a great deal of legal work with Democratic administrations too, Suzanne. Republican has nothing whatever to do with it. Ephraim Gordon's clients have a government of their own."

"Exactly," was her answer. "And I am to be their ambassador." As if she were examining its possibilities for the first time, she held her invention up to the light. "Ambassadress," she concluded.

John Putnam, Esq., always wore such an honest face. She would see if she could make him grimace. She launched into a lecture on the responsibilities of an ambassadress to the Democratic party. She would not be doing anything different from what Webster, White, Moore and White did for their Republican clients. If, for example, an American airline needed to pass along some money to a congressman, was it John Putnam's position that only his partners should be allowed to handle it? Not democratic. That was small *d*. Or suppose the same congressman needed to borrow a small sum to finance his re-election. Investment opportunity. Own a share in America. Certainly Webster, White, Moore and White had arranged that kind of service for Republicans now and again, had they not? She would only be doing the same kind of thing. In return for her services to the Democratic party, and to those corporations whose interests were broader than those of the clients of John Putnam's partners, Judge Gordon had promised her what amounted to diplomatic immunity. Her brownstones would be places in which "things could be talked over," without any trouble from the precinct house at 103rd Street. It was all arranged.

Of course, she'd have to contribute to the pad at the precinct. And the Christmas fund too. Put that down to operating expenses. Peanuts. She figured her brownstones should still turn somewhere in the neighborhood of a half million a year, and that's why she wanted John Putnam's advice. He was so clever at tax shelters. All right, two separate corporations, one for each house, and each in turn controlled by a holding company, if that's what he thought was best. If it was available, Brownstone Holding Corporation was as good a name as any. By late May

1953, John Putnam had incorporated Suzanne's activities in the state of Delaware.

By the time Suzanne had finished her redecoration of the two brownstones she purchased side by side on East Ninety-third Street, somewhat more than six months had passed. The delays were unavoidable. She also spent more than twice the forty thousand she had budgeted to create what she believed was necessary. On the other hand, from the day she opened officially, March 19, 1954, her cash flow also exceeded her expectations. By March 1955 she was doing a predictable seven hundred and fifty thousand a year. In retrospect, she was pleased she had taken the time and the money to do it right. The principles she followed rigorously combined to make "Snow White's place" an extraordinary success.

First, as she explained it, she insisted upon "not leaving a trace." She created an aura of secrecy because she understood how secrecy would be one of her major appeals. If she was to open her club to only a favored few, then logically she would have to turn some away. There were mysterious passwords, invitations and introductions necessary before entry was possible. Besides avoiding notoriety, and in addition to giving the "members" the impression that they were safe from scandal, the principle of not leaving a trace avoided jealousies, bad publicity, raids and blackmail. She carried the logic of a secret club to such lengths that she would not allow even the members to arrive except by appointment; no one was permitted to park his car on Ninety-third Street, or to have a limousine waiting, or in any manner to call attention to the two brownstones. Her members respected her discretion. From the outside there was not one sign of what was offered at her address. There were neighbors who lived for ten years directly across the street from Snow White's but had never heard of her.

Secondly, secrecy contributed to the fantasy she had created of the Mrs. Richard A. Lyle, Jr., society matron, divorcee, who was really "Snow White" to those who knew. She added mysterious details to these two characters by always behaving in a ladylike and modest way. She never gave in to riotous pride in her success. She never allowed herself to be boisterous, or to call attention to her business, except by indirection. Even when a member arrived in her parlor for an appointment that was bound to result in a raucous evening, he was met with a pleasant rectitude and offered an arm's-length handshake of the kind practiced only in the strictest old Boston neighborhoods. If a member arrived early enough, he might even be subjected to a polite cup of tea, poured from a silver service, to watercress sandwiches, and to delicate inquiries about his health and the weather, before he was allowed to meet the woman Snow White had chosen as just right for him. By making her members "behave themselves," she convinced them that their club was even more naughty than they had imagined it could be.

Third, from the first night she made it plain that she was not available. She might go away with a man on certain weekends, but the price was said to be ten thousand dollars, and even then she could say how unfortunate it was that on the date proposed she "already planned to be away." Few of her members ever questioned her independence, accepting it as part of the manners of their club. When Suzanne was actually absent, Miss Freddy was accepted as her adjutant—just as unavailable as Snow White herself, and just as cool and gracious a hostess.

Suzanne's reputation was somehow known almost as soon as she had signed the deeds for her brownstones. Word spread through the city. Secretaries were probably the ones who heard first and then passed on the connections. As a result, Suzanne was inundated by inquiries and applications. At first scores and then hundreds of young women thought they might like to practice at Snow White's new address. The telephone in Mrs. Lyle's apartment rang out of control.

To solve the problem, Suzanne changed the number and canceled the "Mrs. Richard A. Lyle, Jr." listing. Snow White sublet an unused portion of an advertising agency's new floor at 585 Madison. She incorporated still another business, listed in the phone book as Public Relations and Research, Inc. She expected that her new location and telephone number would need some explanation, perhaps a mailing to her birthday-card list, but to her amazement her audience made the transition without skipping a beat. The offices on Madison made her even more accessible, and she used them to conduct interviews of the cast who would play their parts in the theaters she owned on Ninety-third Street.

It was her good fortune to have tapped by accident a great underground river of discontent. She immediately heard from the city's professionals, and from their pimps, but she turned them away. Instead she interviewed applicants who were college students, secretaries, airline stewardesses, type designers, accomplished actresses, artists, book publicists, fashion designers, dancers, musicians—a great pool of undeveloped or unused talents; an endless parade of pretty and plain, exotic and ordinary, witty and accomplished young women. They were apparently relieved that someone was finally offering them something interesting.

Suzanne interviewed the wife of an Air Force captain on duty in Korea; the daughter of a bank vice-president; the niece of an ambassador from Britain's empire to the United Nations; two Brearley girls who arrived dressed in the blue skirts of their school uniforms; an extraordinary number of suburban housewives; and both sisters of a psychiatrist who practiced at New York Hospital. A tricky finesse was necessary to introduce the sisters to each other, and then explain to them their common ambitions, but happily they reacted to the news with a roar of laughter and mutual recognition. They embraced each other. They themselves were the ones who suggested that they play "twins."

The twins not only made a great reputation for themselves but increased Snow White's. In the brownstones the twins were famous for the scenes they played of depraved abandon. Within less than a year, however, they were reported in the society columns to be cruising together off the southern coast of France on the gigantic yacht of a Greek shipping tycoon. The tycoon married off one sister to the agent who handled his real estate in London, and he married the other sister himself. He had a call upon the services of either sister, or both, whenever he pleased. Snow White was sorry to lose the twins. Not every career she sponsored prospered so neatly, but the celebrity of the twins' success did Snow White no harm. Typically, what would have been a perfectly ordinary housewife from suburban Great Neck was transformed, as the result of her insatiable desires, into the constant companion of one of the world's greatest art collectors. In another case, a pretty little brunette graduated from Sarah Lawrence as an English major with two years of incredible experiences behind her, and immediately converted her combined education into a best-selling book. Such miracles as these, once reported, brought converts by the score.

With so much talent available, Snow White could maintain a Rolodex listing hundreds of names and telephone numbers. The cast at Ninety-third Street never had to be the same two nights in a row. Besides a constant freshness, Snow White was able to increase the impression that the members of her club were attending a salon like those that had flourished in Paris under the bourgeois empire of Louis Napoleon. Although arriving by appointment, members could not choose favorites for themselves. If what the member desired was to be familiar, Snow White would supply the phone number after obtaining the favorite's permission. "Good habits end up boring," she said. Instead, upon his arrival each member was introduced to a woman whose gaiety and natural shyness and excitement at discovering the man's qualifications were unfeigned. The women could flirt without pretending, and the men could boast without embarrassment, because the situation called upon both to do their best.

In selecting the cast for her productions, Snow White looked first for an ability to talk and the instinct for when to remain silent. With an exception from time to time for an exotic decoration—like the girl who was six feet three in her stocking feet— the qualities Snow White sought above all were intelligence and imagination. For a while she required all applicants to be rated by a commercial psychological testing service, but the results were inadequate. After Suzanne took the trouble to take the tests herself, she realized they were stupid tests, and she canceled them. Thereafter she wanted her applicants to be employed at some regular job, and she examined their résumés exactly as if she were hiring at the level of vice-president for, say, a large cosmetics company. After all, she said, if the pay was the same, the qualifications also ought to be equal. In Suzanne's opinion, any of her choices could have replaced most corporate vice-presidents in a twinkling. In any event, she pointed out, she had to be certain that her members would not find anything at Ninety-third Street less attractive than what was available to them at home for far less.

Assisted by Miss Freddy, Snow White saw to it that the natural talents of her stars were sharpened by education, by training, by rehearsals, and then by exquisite presentation. Every woman was costumed for her part at the expense of the company. The costumes were not only seductive, they fit. Above all, not one detail could be said to be either coarse or vulgar. If a schoolgirl was to be the part, then her uniform was the real thing: she had books on a strap, buckled shoes, pigtails with ribbons, a pressed dirndl skirt, a white blouse, her nails were clean, and her cheeks as rosy as apples. If a cast was to be assembled for a small intimate dinner for twelve, then the dinner dresses on Snow White's ladies were as good as those any man present would have seen if he had been seated at a benefit for the Metropolitan Museum of Art. Moreover, the table talk would be of art. What happened after the doors upstairs were closed was to contrast with what the members had seen or heard up until the very last moment. Unveilings were to be dramatic, possibly shocking, and as Snow White constantly reminded her staff, "No one is going to pay these prices for what they can get free."

She split fifty-fifty with her actresses. Depending upon what *tableaux vivants* were scheduled, Snow White's players might take home anywhere from five hundred to twenty-five hundred for a single evening's performance. Yet, as in Suzanne's own case, it was rarely ever the money that was at stake; much of Snow White's success with her talent must be attributed to her understanding of her casts' motivations. For one thing, she provided an alternative to just waiting for something to happen. For another, at Snow White's they were somebody.

They were as delighted as she was with the opportunities she provided. Both brownstones were the kind that were entered by descending three steps from street level. Ninety-third Street went uphill from Third to Lexington. The "Uphill House," as it came to be called, had ivy growing up its walls from boxes beside the front door. Once inside the door of Uphill House, and then through the inside door of its double entry, the visitor would be seated in a small foyer on the first floor or escorted directly up a flight of stairs to Snow White's parlor office, which was on the

second floor at the front. It was a circular library, completely
lined to the ceiling with shelves of books. At its center was a
campaign desk from which Snow White would rise to extend
her hand to her visitor, then guide him to an overlength couch
along the east wall, where they could "chat."

On a late-November afternoon a typical visitor would be escorted into her library and see that a wood fire was burning in
the fireplace. After the commonplaces of introductions, he would
be asked if he would like tea. The scotch and soda he preferred
would arrive in a moment. While he waited, Snow White's ami-
cable chitchat on the Dow Jones for the day made him feel comfortable. The atmosphere created by soft green curtains and a
deep green rug and the magnificent crystal chandelier overhead
all contributed to his impression that their discussion would be
businesslike yet feminine.

Invariably the new member was shy. Suppose, for example,
she discovered that he was one of those men trapped by inheritance into the duties and responsibilities of a partnership in a
middle-sized Wall Street investment house. He commuted to
work every day in the summer from Rumson, New Jersey. In the
winter, he attended dinners organized by his wife at their Park
Avenue apartment. At his club, he could cite to his fellow
members the names of a great number of relations—cousins or
uncles or someone they had married—whose names would be
recorded in history, even if only in a footnote. For his own account, Snow White would guess, there would not be much that
could be said. At exactly the appropriate moment she would rise
and pull closed the library's double doors because she wanted to
be sure he understood their discussion demanded absolute privacy. She would reseat herself closer to him on the couch, as if
now confidences could be exchanged. "Don't you have to travel
a great deal?"

"Not really," her new member would answer.

"Wouldn't it be better for your investment house if you had a
firsthand look at the companies you are recommending?"

"We do that. We meet the managers eye-ball to eye-ball."

"Do *you* do that?"

"No; we have people to do that. They make very thorough

studies for us. Go over the ground, analyze it, then our partners meet on their recommendations."

"Why don't you do that yourself?"

"I suppose I could." His eye wandered to Suzanne's collection of precious eggs in a basket upon the coffee table in front of the couch. She followed his glance, then caught his eyes as they returned to her. "How old are you?" she asked, and her question was tough, almost clinical.

"Fifty," he confessed.

"Good," she said. "Perfect, in fact. I have an American Airlines stewardess, twenty-seven years of age, who adores Holiday Inns."

"Holiday Inns?"

"You can meet her in any city in the country, and in the Caribbean, I believe. And for 10 per cent of the air fare anywhere in the world. *She* has a free pass. It's called an F-20. She would meet you wherever you like, as long as it's a Holiday Inn."

There was no doubt in Snow White's mind that he had never spent a night in his life in a Holiday Inn, but she could afford to wait while he considered it. Eventually he asked, "What's she like?"

"Does it matter, darling?"

"Well, if she . . . Twenty-seven?"

"Yes. There are certain conditions, however."

"What conditions?"

"She works. She will meet you in any city your investment business takes you to, but she will only meet you on her schedules, not yours."

"I'm not sure I can do that," he said, keeping to himself those prerogatives to which he thought he was entitled.

"That would be a shame, darling, because you don't expect her to give up her job, do you?"

"No, I wouldn't expect that."

"Well, there you are. Can you be at the Holiday Inn in Tulsa next Tuesday night at seven?"

He was not entirely sure. He would have to check his schedules. He would call her the next morning to confirm. As soon as he did, however, Snow White delivered him over as a package to American Airlines, age twenty-seven. Actually, the stewardess

was as baffled by Snow White as the new member had been.
"Why Holiday Inns?" was her incredulous question. The answer
was that he would be good for an extra thousand per trip, provided he never knew more than a week in advance where he
would have to be and when.

"Look," said Snow White, "it makes it easier for you. There's
bound to be a Holiday Inn on your schedule wherever you need
one. One more thing: don't ever let this pigeon keep his balance.
If for any reason you are too tired, or not up to it, let me know
what room he's in and I'll get someone there to take your place
and surprise him."

"Are you telling me he's going to be a tough assignment?"

"No," said Suzanne. "You'll like him. He's sweet and gentle. A
pussycat, as a matter of fact."

Across from the library from which Snow White managed
these negotiations was what could have been a living room. It
was light and airy and had a wood-burning fireplace with a fine
marble mantel, and above the fireplace a mirror rose to the
moldings of an eighteen-foot ceiling. French doors opened to a
small ironwork balcony overlooking a handsome garden. The
walls were covered with a red Boussac fabric in a repeating
floral design. The living room was an opulent setting for cocktails, receptions or other public business. Two facing couches
were set on either side of the fireplace. There was a baby Stein-
way—Snow White believed no party should be without music—
and two backgammon tables beneath the windows. The backgammon tables were occupied nearly every afternoon from the
moment the stock market closed. There were regular members
who preferred Snow White's to their other clubs. They came almost every day to while away two or three hours before dinner.
They gambled at backgammon while the piano soothed, and
rarely went upstairs.

All the public functions on the second floor—in the library and
the living room—were serviced from the kitchen and pantry on
the first floor. No glass was ever allowed to stand empty; there
was always something to nibble. A butler, two maids, a crack
chef and two assistants were constantly on duty. From the
kitchen a dumbwaiter rose behind the living-room wall into the
apartments on the third and fourth stories, where there were

four apartments altogether, front and back on each floor. If the rules were followed, and proper notice was given over the inter-com telephone, visitors could be guided up the stairs to these apartments and could close the door safely behind them. They would never be seen either coming or going, if that was their preference.

These four apartments in Uphill House were always booked far in advance. They were in demand not only for evenings with Snow White's actresses but also as a place of assignation for married lovers, and unmarried lovers, and on two occasions they were reserved by couples for their wedding anniversaries. The habitual lessees, however, were corporations, "persons" to whom the expense was next to nothing. Despite a flat fee of five hundred dollars for the use of an apartment for an evening, and a five-to-one markup on the drinks and food sent up by dumb-waiter, the expense was deductible anyway, collected by Public Relations and Research, Inc., 585 Madison, for "outside counsel," or "promotional services," or some such device. The bill went to a corporation whose officers instructed the company's treasurer to pay it. It was a company-to-company deal, lessor and lessee, and Snow White's logic was impeccable: whatever purposes the corporation had in mind for the use of an apartment was not re-ally her affair. If five executives wanted to play poker all night, or if six wanted to watch the Giants play football on TV on Sun-day afternoon, the affairs of her lessees were not her business. She offered extras, of course. If dinner was sent up from her kitchens by dumbwaiter, or served at the company's tables, what she provided was no more than room service in a brownstone on Ninety-third Street, like a hotel. She often referred to these bookings as "my convention business." Everything in Uphill House was managed in a quiet, orderly way, with great restraint and rectitude. To ensure privacy and security, all four "uphill" apartments were totally soundproofed, and their doors could be locked or unlocked electronically from a console situated behind Snow White's library desk. Her lessees appreciated her sense of discretion.

Downhill House was also entirely soundproofed. It had an ad-ditional advantage in that the next house to the east was a school, and always vacant after six in the evening. Consequently,

Downhill House was securely positioned between two barriers against any disturbance. Moreover, the windows it showed in front were false: its walls were filled in completely, and it had to be air-conditioned from top to bottom. No natural light ever entered. Except for deliveries from the moving vans that were frequently at its address, its front door was perpetually locked.

The only way to enter Downhill House was to go through the sitting room behind the kitchen and pantry on the ground floor of Uphill House. The sitting room opened to the garden behind both houses, and to a patio sheltered by a yellow-and-white-striped awning. Even on the hottest days of a city summer, the garden was a pleasant setting for a sunset cocktail party. Under the patio awning, the garden door opened into Downhill House, where on the ground floor, corresponding to the sitting room of Uphill House, there was a room Snow White's casts referred to as "Backstage."

Costumes hung along both walls on pipe racks. Between the rows of costumes two professional makeup stands, as in a theater, with light bulbs lining the circumference of their mirrors, were littered with debris from forgotten performances—scattered tissues, jars of creams, the dusts of fine powders, hairpins, a broken clasp, one high-heeled black sandal upon its side. Past this abandoned battlefield, a narrow hallway led to the stairwell. On both sides the passageway was crowded with light boards, coils of ropes hung on pegs, extension cords, ladders, what appeared to be the control panel for the air conditioning, another pipe rack of costumes, covered by a sheet, a gymnast's horse, and a rowing machine set on its end and balanced up against the wall.

Up the stairs to the second floor, the character of Downhill House began to change. Seen empty, it was gloomy, giving the impression that it contained one joyless chamber after another, but its interior lighting had been designed and installed by Dexter Horace, Jr., three-time winner of Broadway Tony awards for lights and staging. When Snow White gave the order, Downhill House could be plugged in, and blazed with whatever lights were necessary.

"Main Stage" was on the second floor, a room that could have been a ballet company's rehearsal hall, running the length of the house from front to back—about sixty feet—with practice rails along both walls. On an afternoon before a performance, Snow White stood at the head of the landing, directing her stage crews where to place the furniture and props. Main Stage was permanently carpeted in gray and mirrored along both walls and on the entire ceiling, exaggerating its length. At one end of the room, the gray carpet came up over a low riser to create the effect of a small stage. Once the gilded chairs and the long tables she rented were in place, however, the double doors on the landing of the second floor could be thrown open to reveal an intimate French restaurant; or the devil's hideaway could be represented, or even, with some extra effort, a sylvan picnic setting from Shakespeare's *As You Like It*. No furniture or props stayed permanently on Main Stage; they were lugged up the stairs as necessary for the dramas Snow White designed.

Similarly, the decorations of the four small apartments on the third and fourth floors, front and back, of Downhill House could be changed easily if need be. At one time or another Snow White re-created: the interior of a Pullman sleeper, complete with an alleyway of curtained upper and lower berths; a rustic attic of abandoned furniture and dusty trunks, with a hammock hung from its rafters; an Art Deco room accented with steel and glass and Bauhaus leather chairs; and a Victorian bedroom filled with overstuffed furniture, lace antimacassars, mahogany wardrobes and a magnificent sleigh bed. In all these rearrangements she had the good sense to consult with the women who would play the starring roles.

"Take sheets, for example," she said. "It would be a rare man who knew where his knees were. Patterns, colors, designs, stripes —none of that makes any difference to men. There's not a woman ever born who wouldn't notice."

The Roman baths and the Greek symposium on the third floor exchanged places easily with the health club, if Snow White's members went in for that kind of thing. She consented to an igloo against her own better judgment, and had the thing constructed of styrofoam. It was not very popular, just as she had expected, and its presence was short-lived. A more or less permanent feature on the third floor rear was the dungeon and jail, equipped with stocks, a rack, an appalling display of whips and straps, and manacles set into chains bolted to the walls.

"You'd be surprised," was her explanation. "The longer the
entry in Who's Who in America the more likely the request for
the dungeon."

She needed specialists for those scenes—it was not the kind of
thing that could be handled properly by some teen-ager. The
fact was there were a half dozen men she'd come across who
made very exciting jailers, and dozens of women who'd happily
play a part not much different from that she herself had played
with Joseph F. X. O'Connell for the sake of Harry Truman's
campaign train. Those were the facts of life. It took an intelligent and experienced woman to play dungeon with one of the
Who's Who types, but if she was good at it they'd be back again
and again.

On the top, or fourth, floor, there was a special wall between
the two apartments. On one side it appeared to be a black mirror. From the other apartment, the wall turned out to be one-
way glass. From the rear apartment—what Snow White called the
"observation deck"—the lights in the mirrored apartment could
be controlled by dimmers. Hence it was possible for a small
party to sit unobserved in a candlelit eighteenth-century drawing
room, sipping sherry and pretending to quote from Gibbon's lessons on history, while at the same time looking through the glass
at a brightly lit re-creation of one of Messalina's Roman orgies.
Sound between the two apartments could be transferred by intercom or shut off by a switch. Although the history of Rome
may have seemed a peculiar fascination for twentieth-century
corporate executives, Snow White's staff had so many requests
that it became known as "doing a Ben Hur."

According to Snow White, the most "amusing" use of the one-
way mirror occurred after a wife caught her husband *in
flagrante delicto* with a weekend guest. She came upon them in
the pool house at their home in White Plains. The angry wife
was about thirty, and the offending husband in his fifties. It was
Snow White's impression that the wife had some hold over her
husband that was special—maybe it was her money.

The wife paid a formal call upon Snow White. They had tea
in the library while the wife described what she wanted. Snow
White knew the husband as one of her "Racquet Club regulars,"
mostly as an afternoon backgammon player, but she said nothing

about his being a member. She agreed she would help the wife
to have her revenge. They were allies as soon as the wife explained that she would prefer not to pay by check but would instead offer a diamond lavaliere her husband had presented to
her as a peace offering. It was, the wife said, her way of returning it to him. She did not say so specifically; it was only the
wife's manner that had suggested to Snow White that the marriage was funded by her money.

Two weeks later, the wife arrived towing her husband. She delivered him over to Snow White and disappeared. He was
escorted by Snow White through Backstage, then up to the
fourth-floor "observation deck," where the oak chair from the
dungeon had been set up. "You'll be sitting here," she indicated.

He was going to be stuffy about it, perhaps difficult, and not
as subject to Snow White's authority as he was to his wife's.
Once she had him seated, she began to rope his wrists to the
arms of the oak chair. "What the hell is this?" was the way he
thought he'd resist.

"These are your wife's orders. Want to agree, or want to quit
now?"

He said he was prepared to go through with it.

"Then, I'm going to accord you the privilege of being as comfortable as possible. She and I agree, though, that you are a son
of a bitch."

She finished roping his wrists to the arms of the chair, making
sure the ropes would not interfere with his circulation. As she
pulled the knots tight, she made it plain they could have been tied
not quite as loosely. She turned off the lights so he would be sitting in the dark, then turned up the illumination in the room he
was facing and would be watching through the one-way glass.
Before she left him, she asked whether he preferred the sound on
or off.

He chose off. The brightly lit room he watched was furnished
with a low king-size bed, covered by chocolate-colored sheets
and pillowcases. A small table was set for four. There were fresh
daisies in a vase at its center. He did not yet believe his wife
would actually carry out what she had threatened. He assumed
she'd call it off when she had made her point. Then three young
men dressed in the summer uniforms of the French Navy en-

tered, joking with each other and delivering mock punches to one another's arms. Eventually they tossed their caps into the corner and settled down at the table to try the wine in the ice bucket. His wife was making them wait too.

When she finally entered the room, they stood up for her like schoolboys and fell all over each other for the honor of holding her chair as she sat down to supper with them. She wore tailored pajamas of crepe de Chine covered by a loose-fitting robe of beige silk with a damask stripe, which hung to the floor. Throughout supper she sat with her back to the mirror, and her husband could only see the faces of the boys she would take as her lovers. He could not hear a word of their increasingly boisterous talk, but it was accompanied by wild gestures, much waving of the hands, and fond smiles.

Supper was taking forever. The husband began to feel uncomfortable upon the seat of the oak chair in which he was imprisoned. He was compelled to shift constantly in his seat. His mouth was dry, his tongue thick. At the moment he was ready to cry out for water, Snow White reappeared, dressed exactly as his wife was, and brought him a glass of water. "I am going to stay with you," she explained, "and bring you whatever you like— brandy, water, coffee; and to light your cigarettes for you; and to make sure you stay awake."

She drew up a chair behind him where he could not see her. She would not be engaged in any talk. He had to give up his bids for attention before long, because his wife stood up from the table and brought her stallions to their feet with her. As each stripped off his blouse, she went from one to the next, admiring with the palms of her hands their chests and the muscles of strong young arms. Then she came around the table until she was facing directly into the mirror. She stripped off her robe, and then the pajamas, slowly. Her eyes probably never left the image she saw of her own body, but the effect was as if she were looking through the mirror directly at her sweating husband. Their eyes were no more than three feet apart. When she was ready, she turned to her lovers. To each one in turn, with her arms high over their shoulders, she surrendered a kiss. They were ready too. She took the biggest one first.

Before she could exhaust all three, it was nearly dawn. Her

husband was stiff and sore from his penance upon the oak chair. Both his feet had constantly gone to sleep, but Snow White had rubbed them back into circulation, again and again. She would never speak to him. He had cut into his own palms with his fingernails, and in the morning she had dabbed iodine into his wounds against any chance of infection.

According to Snow White, "They've lived happily ever after."

What was marvelous, in her opinion, was that the three men were *real* French sailors. She had been able to get them only at the last moment, but there they were on Broadway. Sometimes she had difficulty finding men who would play the games she designed. She always had an enormous surplus of women who would chance anything, or were at least intrigued; but men, despite all their talk, were stingy with themselves. Yet there were exceptions. At the instigation of a group of attractive men, Snow White produced for six years a monthly dinner on the Main Stage—the ballet practice room on the second floor of Downhill House. The dinner was always at eight on the last Thursday of the month, was always a seated affair, black tie and long dress. Six men and six women would have cocktails at one end of the long room, then move to the other end to a table set with crystal. A dozen was really the perfect number for a supper party, in Snow White's opinion. She was particularly fond of the "Last Thursdays."

The rules of the game appealed to her, and she attended herself almost every month, even if the rest of the cast she supplied varied. The long dresses had to be strapless, because the moment each woman arrived at the door and handed over her wrap, the master of ceremonies for the evening gave her the most formal bow, kissing the back of her hand as if she were a queen, then fastened her hands behind her in mink handcuffs. The result, said Snow White, was most entertaining: if she was to have a drink, she had only her eyes or her teeth with which to flash for it; if she wanted to eat, she had to be fed; if she was to conquer, she had to provoke; if she could be outrageous enough, she was guaranteed surrender.

Snow White had applicants to attend the Last Thursdays that exceeded demand by ten to one—from women. Most of the men who attended were regulars. Her principal client for banquets was the president of the General Television System, and Snow White always defended Frank Grey against his detractors. He was a courtly and imaginative man, she said, and that distinguished Frank Grey from the rest of the crowd. He was eventually cashiered from the presidency of General Television because GTS wanted an image, as the major stockholder explained it, of "flaming noncontroversy." Although Frank Grey produced shows and profits for General Television beyond his board of directors' wildest dreams, they dumped him as dangerous. Snow White admitted he probably was—to them. He was packed off to the never-never land of independent production in Hollywood, and replaced by a smooth-faced lawyer whose chief skill was an uncanny ability to bribe, extort or blackmail politicians to favor General Television's franchise as a network, regardless of how dull it might be.

Snow White got to know General Television's new president as a regular too, but David Kaufman's idea of an evening's entertainment was to bring along some judge who could have been bought for a lousy five hundred bucks, or some alcoholic member of the House Ways and Means Committee who could be convinced of anything with two drinks, and then spend two thousand dollars of General Television's public relations budget to "get 'em laid." David Kaufman's manners were such, said Snow White, that if he had produced *Peter Pan*, "the audience would fold its arms rather than clap for Tinker Bell."

When David Kaufman replaced Frank Grey, the Last Thursdays came to an end. Snow White continued to stage productions celebrating the ancient medieval rights of *droit du seigneur,* and she set up a pirate's den again and again, even if as far as she was concerned it always flopped. She had several Irish contractors who were big for the voluptuous-nun number. The scene in which Hollywood moguls, the producer-director-agent crowd, got themselves suited up as Arabs and bid for slave girls on an auction block never failed to work, because "that was where those types were coming from every day."

Curiously, it was not the big productions that required most of her energies; nor were the little bread-and-butter scenes *deux à deux* in the apartments difficult. It was really no effort at all, as Suzanne put it, to supply "Grand Hotel for the obsessions of the day. Anyone could have done that." Almost all her energies were required, however, to maintain the double illusion of Snow White, notorious madam who left no trace; and, simultaneously, Mrs. Richard A. Lyle, Jr., widow—or was it divorcee?—with a passionate interest and inexhaustible funds to contribute to worthy causes, the good of the community, and the hopes of the Democratic National Committee.

Suzanne attended every April in Paris Ball, bought tickets by the table for the Irvington House benefits, contributed generously to the Hobie Baker Boys Club in Locust Valley. She had to be constantly visible, yet always modest. She was careful to attract as an ally every woman she could in the city. In several cases she was said to have patched up husbands and sent them back where they belonged. She meticulously returned phone calls, wrote thank-you notes, sent flowers, and invented small favors that might not have any return for decades.

Without complaint she attended meetings at Gracie Mansion of the Mayor's Committee on Youth and Delinquency. She solicited the members of her Brownstone Club to arrange summer jobs for the underprivileged young people the Mayor's Committee designated. She was a regular Democrat in the most faithful sense of the word, and never demurred, no matter how preposterous the organization's candidate might be. It was said of her that she always had the city's interests at heart.

After 1956, when she moved to the big penthouse at 30 Central Park South, Mrs. Richard A. Lyle, Jr., never refused a single request of any kind to give a benefit cocktail party for Democratic primary candidates, or for the American Crafts Council, or the Business Committee for The Arts, or the Association for Aid to Crippled Children, or United Cerebral Palsy, or the Red Cross.

This consistent effort upon Suzanne's part had a curious effect, and very nearly the result she intended. There were enough rumors about her as Snow White to make her the object of much curiosity; yet her demeanor as Mrs. Richard A. Lyle, Jr., was so simple, so plain, so charming, that the stories circulating about Snow White added piquancy to the reputation of Mrs. Lyle; and the good works of Mrs. Lyle lent celebrity to the brownstones occupied by Snow White—whoever Suzanne actually might be.

By 1960, in Suzanne's cool assessment, the national mood was desperate for heroes or heroines. As a result, the community of New York—society in the broadest meaning of that peculiar word—accepted both her characters almost without cavil. As evidence, Suzanne cited the Piping Rock Club dinner dance in Locust Valley in August 1960 for the benefit of the Accobonac Summer Camp for Girls.

When Suzanne's party walked in to occupy its table, there was a noticeable hush. Heads turned to whisper secrets into ears. There were shrugs and eyes cast up to the heavens. Despite the legitimacy of her background on Long Island's north shore—a golden girl who had danced as a debutante and married under green-and-white-striped tents—Mrs. Lyle's appearance at Piping Rock had triggered furtive whispers about Snow White.

Suzanne knew only too well the benefit's chairman. He was a stupid old fool, "a whirlpool of pretensions," she said. He had solicited a contribution to the Girls Camp from her in the library at Ninety-third Street, panhandling for tax-deductible causes. Now that she had actually dared to join the dinner dance for which she had paid, the old fool was embarrassed—and to make matters worse, as he stood he knocked silverware off his table. Leaving the clatter behind, he marched, blushing, to the bandstand and ordered Lanin's orchestra to play. They were only half unpacked, but did their best and struck up anyway: Cole Porter's "Just One of Those Things." Titters. No one took the floor.

There were eight at Suzanne's table. They exchanged animated talk with each other, like missionaries doing their best to ignore the stares of the hostile tribe that surrounded them. Then from the corner of her eye, Suzanne saw that Frank Grey was on his feet at the far corner of the ballroom, making his way through the maze of tables. Suzanne kept her table guests in focus, but every other head followed Frank Grey's progress, wondering what he proposed to do. When he had made his way to her chair, she had no alternative but to turn her face up at him. Gallantly he bent his long frame low over her hand, exactly as if he were the master of ceremonies meeting her at the door for the monthly Last Thursdays. When he had kissed the back of her hand, he asked her to dance.

They took the floor alone. They two-stepped toward the bandstand. He asked Lanin's orchestra to switch to a Vienna waltz, gathered her up in the most confident embrace, and swept her through turns along the very edge of the dance floor. As they passed the tables of their audience, her skirts brushed the backs of the nearest chairs. Frank Grey was a particularly handsome man, and without any question a gorgeous waltzer.

On their second time around the edge of the floor a light applause began. It began to gather, partly in time to the music but then out of control, more and more of it, until finally men and women alike had put down their napkins and found themselves upon their feet, applauding wildly. For reasons they later were never able to explain, most of the men were cheering and several women had given in to barely disguised tears.

10

Earned Income

1956–64

I WAS among those who stood and cheered for her. Although the forces that determined the trajectories of Suzanne's life and my own were different, there were times when our paths crossed. By 1960 I had landed a job as an associate editor at the newsweekly where I still work. If I no longer moved in the same social circles as Suzanne did, I caught sight of her at a distance from time to time. I could always inquire of the city's many sources on the progress of her career. Long before she demonstrated the waltz at the Girl's Camp benefit, I knew that Frank Grey, president of GTS, and Suzanne were seen frequently in each other's company. Frank Grey was a suitable escort for Suzanne, and at the civic ceremonies they both were required to attend Mrs. Richard A. Lyle, Jr., young widow, made a lovely ornament for the president's arm.

Frank Grey was a bachelor, married once, but divorced. On public occasions it would have been awkward for all concerned if he came alone and left alone; and even more so at the intimate dinners staged in the city's private apartments. Although hostesses claimed they searched for extra men, they preferred bachelors who would not present any sexual dangers to the la-

dies seated among the powerful. Most small dinners had as their
purpose a reassurance to all those at the table that their seats
were held securely; that their places were reserved. Hostesses
preferred, therefore, to add extra men from a small list of *New
Yorker* cartoonists, Washington *Post* columnists and famous nov-
elists who would mind their own business. Extra men should be
safe, "fit in" and compliment the others at the table on their success. Because Frank Grey was himself powerful, and the kind of
man who would frankly inspect a woman's throat, it was easier if
he arrived with a companion of his own choosing and left with
her, and never threatened to disturb the security of the table's
order.

He was in his mid forties, but because he was tall and slim
and always at his ease, he looked younger. His neatly clipped
gray hair added to the impression he gave of coiled energies. His
languid confidence, his fastidious manners, his ability to smooth
away difficulties, his quick rise to the top, his guile, his reputation for ruthlessness combined with generosity, all contributed to
the assessment that Frank Grey was "charming."

As president of GTS, his civic duties included attending private screenings of potentially successful films, then spending an
hour at the reception afterward to assure the movie's director, its
producer and its bankers that he had just seen a sure thing. As
president of GTS he was also expected to attend Saturday
lunches at "21" for the benefit of the corporate campaign division of the American Red Cross or other similar organized expressions of good will. Typically, once each year all three presidents of the great national networks took seats in the second row
on the dais at a massive dinner hosted by the Archdiocese of
New York. For several hours in the Grand Ballroom of the Waldorf-Astoria, one hundred tables of ten each could see that the
barons of television entertainment smiled at the thought of an
improved moral climate. The president of GTS listened attentively while the bishop at his left whispered suggestions.

Frank Grey's affair with Suzanne was based, therefore, upon
what amounted to an alliance of common defense. The duties of
Mrs. Richard A. Lyle, Jr., included attending many of the same
affairs, displaying much the same sense of good citizenship, and
coping during the winter season with as many small and in-

timate dinners among the community of the city's women whose good opinion was necessary. In the summertime, both Frank Grey and Suzanne passed long weekends at country houses in Virginia, in the Hamptons, in Newport, or in the northwest corner of Connecticut—the Berkshire region. The president of GTS and the society widow smiled secretly at the irony that the demand for their company increased measure for measure with the gains made in the Nielsen ratings of GTS and the rumors passed about the entertainments produced at the two brown-stones on Ninety-third Street. They marveled at how hostesses defined "interesting people who did interesting things."

Nevertheless, discounting the ironies of their celebrity, they indicated that they traveled together. They arrived in East Hampton in a GTS limousine, adding charm for a weekend to the household of a man who had made fifty million in agricul-tural chemicals, and of his wife who dabbled in Broadway shows. Despite a record of one musical that lasted thirty-seven weeks and subsequent investments in seven straight flops, the wife hoped eventually to have her husband appointed ambassador to Paris. If not Paris, at least Brussels. If not Brussels, then Luxem-bourg. Since Oslo would not be acceptable, it was the wife's duty, as she saw it, to continue her campaign and widen her hus-band's acquaintance. She added color to her patient efforts to locate the right connections when she put Frank Grey and Su-zanne Lyle on the list.

Similarly, the easy smile and the stunning beauty went to-gether by chartered Cessna to be guests at the magnificent Con-necticut house of a couple whose interest in art had steadily ex-panded. Both husband and wife believed correctly, as it turned out, that forty million dollars acquired suddenly in rental cars might be baptized—blessed by the grace that could forgive even original sin—if only their collection of modern painters might someday be accepted by the Museum of Modern Art. If not the Modern, then the Whitney. If not the Whitney, then at least Chicago. The guests who assembled in Connecticut for a long weekend to admire the nuances of modern art were delighted by the beauty and wit contributed by Frank Grey and Suzanne Lyle.

Among the first to recognize their attractions was Mrs. Ellen

Burns, who maintained a fairyland castle on sixty manicured acres thirty miles from Saratoga, near Bennington. Mrs. Burns was particularly fond of Suzanne, perhaps because she took pride in having spotted Suzanne's talents early—she remembered seeing her at La Rue when she was still a debutante; or, perhaps because Suzanne's vivacity impressed her; and because Suzanne was one of the few young women "Aunt Nellie" had ever come across who apparently wanted nothing from her.

In any case, the two women admired each other and accepted each other's celebrity as fascinating without quibbling over its truths. Besides, Suzanne was democratic—in the broadest meaning of that debased word—in her attitudes, while Aunt Nellie was catholic in her associations, which added up to nearly the same thing. Aunt Nellie could afford to tolerate democratic ethics because she had inherited every cent of her immense fortune and could not think of a single reason why she should be ashamed of the accidents of birth.

Inevitably there would be those who insisted that Aunt Nellie was peculiar because the rich were different from everyone else; that among the rich money somehow created its own fraternities and equalities; that the freedoms established by money created their own paradise. Yet Aunt Nellie was an exquisite example of the very opposite: a demonstration of the great chasm between old money and new; between ennui and hope; between an established order and mere ambitions; between the structures of an accumulated past and nothing more than a lucky rise of four hundred points in the Dow Jones. Precisely because Aunt Nellie was an heiress of the fourth generation, she could not be charged with any crime, nor be subjected to any indictment brought against the American Syrup Corporation, any of its subsidiaries domestic or foreign or its officers past or present. Aunt Nellie was immune to all the petty hazards of the law—a significant distinction that Suzanne could not help but admire.

Aunt Nellie was born Ellen Tomlinson, great-granddaughter of Hamilton Tomlinson, legendary dry-goods and notions traveler of Hartford, Connecticut. The genealogical connection was not a choice made by Ellen Tomlinson. She was only asked to accept it, and she always did her best to understand what was expected of her. As a matter of fact, nothing much was expected of her: that she was born rich was an accident; she could just as easily have been born poor. She remembered her mother as sweet and beautiful and always smelling of flowers. Her mother delivered over to her daughter the care of a baby brother; then, two years later, her mother inexplicably died. Ellen Tomlinson was only six, yet she could see how great wealth granted immunities of some kinds but not others.

After Ellen Tomlinson's mother died, her father lived on for another twenty years. He could not disguise that he was a sorrowing man. If he was ineffectual as well, his daughter defended him against any such allegation. He wore grief for his lost wife like a topcoat, pulling it on with a sigh every morning as he went to his office to make sure "everything was shipshape," checking it at the desk of his club when he stopped on his way home for a drink or two with his friends at the round oak table. He claimed he was never bored, because he had the responsibility to look after things, but he was probably relieved, his daughter admitted, when his heart quit at last. His great wealth provided him with many privileges, but he never used them.

His example was a major lesson in the education of Ellen Tomlinson and her younger brother. Financial matters ought always to be kept in good order; as to the rest, they should do their best to enjoy the few pleasures they might devise. Yet, unlike those who represented "new money" and might have been delighted by a variety of pleasures, the Tomlinson children were too experienced to expect their enthusiasms to relieve the pattern of their circumstances.

Ellen Tomlinson's younger brother eventually took his inheritance in a lump sum—a negotiated settlement by the estate of approximately one hundred and fifty million dollars. His share was unquestionably far more, but at the time he saw no point in disputing it. Meanwhile Ellen Tomlinson married in succession four men with good names, clean fingernails and strong bodies. Then she settled upon a burly Irish squire nearly twice her age. Mr. John Patrick Burns was a caricature, a daguerreotype, of the tweedy Irish landed gentry west of Dublin who hunted foxes across rolling meadows. She picked him out at Saratoga. He exported bloodstock for the good of Ireland and anyone else who cared. The breeding in his Irish barns tended to produce massive animals with great stamina, although they might be a bit slow to start. When an animal resisted its schooling, John Patrick Burns was at his best. There was not a stallion or a mare that played hard at the bit that John Patrick Burns could not cure. He spent his days mucking about his stables from early dawn, was perfectly happy to stand by the hour with his elbows upon the top rail of his training ring, drank to excess in terrifying bouts no more than three times a year, and chased down any pretty skirt that caught his fancy—including his wife's when she could provoke him.

Ellen loved Squire Burns with all her heart, partly because he paid so little attention to her demands and so much to his own; and partly because her money made no difference at all to him. He would have gotten along just as well without it. Certainly her contributions to his breeding expenses improved the quality of his stock, but he accepted what she offered, spent it with an open hand, asked for more without embarrassment. Unfortunately, as he cantered one of his hunters into the woods after a running fox one morning, a tree branch was a mite too low. When they found him, his skull was dented in an even line from the outside edge of one eyebrow to the far edge of the other. She had loved him, and the son-of-a-bitch had gotten himself killed. In his honor, Mrs. Ellen Burns swore that she would never remarry. Consequently the final box score was known by the time she was forty-five: five husbands, no children, no regrets.

Unlike her brother, who was perhaps better known, Aunt Nellie was said to have an iron will. Some estimated that she would have been a modern replica of her great-grandfather, founder of the American Syrup Corporation, but she was a woman and therefore limited in her ability to affect directly the continuing success of the company. Everything Aunt Nellie accomplished had to be done by indirection, with great patience and the circumspection expected of her sex. She could get what she wanted only through the cooperation of the lawyers and managers employed by American Syrup.

To her credit it was said that she never gave a direct order. She maintained the fiction that she was merely assenting to the proposals American Syrup's executives brought to her attention. Even then she usually encouraged her servants to "do what seems best." She kept her distance from the operating executives of American Syrup, just as she would not interfere in her own kitchen—familiarity with too many details might encourage servants to forget their place. Although she owned only 6 per cent of American Syrup's common stock—traded upon the New York Stock Exchange—she controlled the directors of four foundations whose total holdings in American Syrup equities represented another 40 per cent. Moreover, an examination of the annual report of American Syrup would reveal echelons of preferred stocks, A and B, voting and nonvoting, warrants, convertible bonds and other fiscal instruments—securities arranged like flights of migrating geese, with the common stock representing only the leading and lowest wings. The total value of Aunt Nellie's holdings in American Syrup was therefore difficult to count accurately, but an experienced eye could make a general estimate of the flying numbers by round figures: say, something like three billion, give or take five hundred million. The company's board of directors could not fail to see what their duties were.

On one occasion a deluded braggart who prowled Wall Street attempted a raid by offering to pay five dollars per share more than the New York Stock Exchange listed trading price. Aunt Nellie's directors turned away the difficulty within two weeks. Although the case was given two or three days of surprising publicity, probably because the very idea amused so many floor traders in an otherwise lackluster month, the challenger soon found that his own insurance company had been bought out from under him, that the funds from which he had based his tender offer were no longer his to deploy, that he was retired permanently to Arizona, and that American Syrup had gotten control of a nice little insurance subsidary in the bargain. Aunt Nellie's board did not even meet to handle the situation. It was all managed by phone. If the question had come up in midwinter, they might have called meetings for the sheer entertainment of it all, but the challenge was presented in August and everyone was away.

Yet no one had any basis to assert that Aunt Nellie's supervision of American Syrup was lackadaisical. Of the many toys she could have played with, her great-grandfather's company was by far the most interesting, and she imagined that he could have found little to criticize. Just as he had done, she hired the best men, paid them wages no competitor would have dared to meet, and saw to it that the managers of American Syrup would remain faithful to its future. If any of her executives failed to meet the standards expected, she nevertheless rewarded "every member of the team." She even recommended them for jobs as good as the ones in which they had failed, and used the co-operation of the banks and insurance companies and institutional investors who were her quartermasters to promote the careers of her worst failures. There was no reason, in her opinion, "to create enemies or jealousies unnecessarily."

"Cooperation" had always been the policy at American Syrup; "Good Citizenship Is Keeping Up With Progress in America." Before the turn of the century, the tariff—a much misunderstood topic—had assured American Syrup a profit of one half cent on every single pound of sugar consumed by the American family. If American consumers had thought about it for a moment, they might have objected to paying a half-cent tax for the sole benefit of Mr. Hamilton Tomlinson of Hartford. But no one did object, or pause over breakfast at the magnificent cheek of American Syrup's private tax.

After the turn of the century, tariffs were not as important as they had once been, because supplies were guaranteed and technological advances facilitated great savings in the expense for labor. American Syrup moved with the times, taking the lead in packaging sugar. They dispensed with the old method of weighing out the sugar upon a scale in front of the housewife, and substituted instead packages on which the price was already marked, the weight guaranteed, the quality of the sugar uniform, standard and assured; and above all, they saved invaluable time and guaranteed a fixed margin of profit. It was unjust to charge American Syrup with attempts to restrain trade, or divide the market with one or two others, because in fact American Syrup did no such thing. It was never necessary. In any case, sugar was a commodity traded worldwide. Its price varied according to the laws of supply and demand, like oil. Allegations that American Syrup's business practices in foreign lands were not in conformance with American ethics at home were beside the point. Business practices in foreign countries were not the same as those at home. Besides, the laws of the United States had no effect, nor did any United States regulations have jurisdiction, beyond the water's edge.

Domestically, American Syrup was recognized as one of the most progressive of companies, contributing to both great political parties equally—completely bipartisan support on both the national and state levels. Neither party could expect favor over the other. In addition, American Syrup supported the National Council for Court Reform; a variety of revisionist and reform attempts to make the tax laws fair; two major programs of medical research; five ongoing programs in social studies at major universities; the best in opera, not only at the Metropolitan in New York, but at experimental companies distributed geographically in other states; a ballet company in San Francisco; and a highly respected series of television programs of public education. In sum, the company was a model citizen. Aunt Nellie had every right to be proud of what American Syrup accomplished.

On the other hand, it was unlikely that anything exciting would ever happen at her corporation. Because American Syrup was so secure a property, Aunt Nellie had not only everything she wanted, but more than she wanted. She could have been whimsical with her money. Unfortunately she could not find any fantasies to absorb her. Except for the stable of race horses she had inherited by accident from her Irish squire, and the fairyland castle she had bought near Saratoga to be near her horses when they ran, there were no illusions capable of holding her attention for long.

The castle was her happiest distraction. Built in the gargantuan proportions admired at the turn of the century, it was a folly designed by Stanford White. Four stories floated up from a park of green lawns and were capped by minarets and towers like those in the illustrated versions of *Grimm's Fairy Tales*. Blue Vermont granite for the castle walls had been quarried sixty miles away and hauled to the site by a private narrow-gauge railway. A small section of the railway remained across one corner of the wooded, sixty-acre park, where a working steam engine, coal car and two open passenger coaches were available in the summer to carry Aunt Nellie's guests to a picnic.

In the main entrance hall the brass pipes of a three-story

organ rose sixty feet to a vaulted ceiling. Tapestries from France, suits of armor picked up at auction in London, and yards of Italian landscapes in ornate gold frames were examples of the plunder taken from Europe. As weekend guests pulled up their cars in the driveway and allowed their bags to be unloaded by the butler, Aunt Nellie's companion and very good friend, Adam Shepherd, would play on the organ the dinner march from *Norma*, followed by the "Colonel Bogey March." They were the only two pieces he knew, but since he was in charge of entertainment, his welcome could not be stopped.

Inside, the castle was not the mausoleum it at first appeared to be. The guest suites upstairs were cozy. The library, dining room and living room downstairs were bright and comfortable. The weekend's schedule was always posted on blue cards left upon the bedside table or propped up on a bureau, so that Aunt Nellie's guests might know when to expect dinner, how to dress, and what entertainments were planned. The blue cards were headed by the Tomlinson family crest, and the instructions typed below were much like those that were once supplied to the first-class passengers of transatlantic liners: charades after dinner in the main lounge, horse racing with cardboard horses upon a linen field, the playing of cards, perhaps a musicale. These diversions were staged by Adam Shepherd, Aunt Nellie's consort, a fifty-year-old Englishman who was, according to his own description, a "serious artist" but who in addition knew perfect country-house manners, how to light the cigarettes of the women he was near, and how to place and answer Aunt Nellie's phone calls for her. He also played gin with her if she was alone for any great period of time.

Adam Shepherd was at Aunt Nellie's side when she took her seat in her box at Saratoga's race track. He sat at her dinner table in the place of host. He marched at the head of each weekend's parade—and these campaigns followed an invariable route. They began in the library for cocktails promptly at seven. They stayed in the dining room until dessert was finished. They crossed into the living room for coffee and brandy or Calvados or crème de menthe. Although Aunt Nellie insisted that "in the country I like to live the simple life," the men were dressed in dinner jackets and the women in long dresses. Aunt Nellie's own

choice might be a gypsy dress designed for her by a Paris couturier and executed in flowered silk taffeta, or perhaps a fine
white linen bodice with hand-stitched embroidery and a bouffant
moiré silk skirt, joined at the waist by a wide black velvet band.
Simple peasant costumes helped her disguise a waist and hips
that were thicker than they had been when she was younger.
As a courtesy, the ladies who kept her company dressed as she
did. Dinner at Aunt Nellie's was a display of six or eight gentlemen in dinner jackets seated between six or eight gypsies
wearing diamonds and emeralds.

During August, Aunt Nellie's collection of guests was heavily
represented with those involved in horse racing at Saratoga.
During the rest of the year her gatherings were more varied:
doctors whose work in medical research was said to be at the
frontiers of knowledge; retired actors who had made fifty motion
pictures; senators who had run for the presidency; bankers,
brokers, remittance men, generals, strategic thinkers, analysts of
third-world potentials, and Hollywood press agents. She liked,
she said, "a good mix, but no ministers. No men of the cloth."

In the winter, what she called "the young people," who included Suzanne and Frank Grey, used Aunt Nellie's castle as a
base to ski Bromley or Stratton. Beginning in February 1956,
Suzanne became something of a regular visitor, because she admired Aunt Nellie and would have emulated her if she could
have. In return, Aunt Nellie was fascinated by Suzanne. There
existed, therefore, a mutual frontier between the two women, an
understanding at the border where the paraphernalia of their
boundaries—the toll gates, and customs men, and inspectors of
passports and visas—could not be dismantled unilaterally. The
geography of one depended upon the history of the other. They
were like neighbors who exchanged ambassadors to reassure
each other of their peaceful intentions.

One winter night, Suzanne and Frank Grey returned after
dark from skiing Bromley. Cocktails and dinner for twelve were
as pretty as ever. After dinner Adam Shepherd announced that
he would read the tarot cards and tell the future of each guest in
turn. He soon had ten of the company seated upon the floor of
the living room around him. Since he was expert at the necessary
patter, the mysteries he revealed brought sighs and groans and

polite hurrahs from his audience for each victim's fate. The senator's wife had the Emperor reversed: immaturity, lack of control, subservience. The eminent Boston banker was ruled by the Hermit; thus his forecast included a meeting with a wise counselor who should be heeded. The Wall Street lawyer's wife who wrote mystery stories was warned that she was subject to unseen influences reached only by divinatory powers. The voices of the company on the floor rose and fell like those of children astonished at each new wonder. A brisk fire in the hearth flared up on its own cycles.

On either side of the hearth, Suzanne and Aunt Nellie sat facing each other. Aunt Nellie had taken the master's chair on the left. It had its reading lamp, which she had switched off; its side table, upon which she had placed her own bottle of brandy; its humidor, from which she had selected and cut her small cigar. Between swallows from her snifter, Aunt Nellie watched the fire in the hearth. Suzanne had agreed to join the children on the floor when her turn came for her fortune to be told. Meanwhile she was content to keep Aunt Nellie company, and share the moment of reverie.

It was characteristic of Aunt Nellie that the more brandy she consumed the more her brow darkened, something like low clouds scudding across a tropical island, heavy with rain that soon would be falling somewhere downwind. Even so, there would be moments when the sun could still break through and her eyes would brighten with all the dewy freshness and sparkling innocence of a ten-year-old girl. Then another swallow of brandy, the stormy horizon would close in again, and the whitecaps under the patch of sun that had been out there a moment before would be gone. Giggling from the distinguished children upon her living-room floor interrupted her. She spoke to Suzanne as if she had come to the conclusion of the thought they had both been watching in the fire.

"Well, there's one thing I believe in."

Suzanne was diplomatic: "What might that be?"

"God," said Aunt Nellie. She punctuated her deduction with another big swallow of brandy. "No question about that."

If it had been within Suzanne's powers to agree with Aunt Nellie, she would have. Indeed, Suzanne's emulation of Mrs. Ellen

Burns included purchasing in 1964 a country house of her own near Saratoga and drawing up schedules of guests to be invited for simple country weekends. In time the two hostesses had almost interchangeable guest lists: famous men, chic women, decorative couples, accomplished citizens, and those indispensable characters who made every list because it was said they were amusing. Suzanne no longer needed to juggle invitations from others or provide escorts like Frank Grey for herself but could supervise a court of her own. The formidable Mrs. Burns was flattered by young Mrs. Lyle's imitation, and through an unstated alliance the two women improved the variety of their entertainments by exchanging luncheons, dinners, picnics and outings. If by chance some malicious gossip indicated to Aunt Nellie that the sources of Suzanne's income were not—how should it be said?—as legitimate as those earned by American Syrup, Aunt Nellie dismissed such envy with a wave of her hand. Among neighbors, as a matter of principle, it was live and let live. "As far as I am concerned," said Aunt Nellie, "Suzanne is almost like a daughter to me."

In any case, moralisms upon the sources of money were inappropriate. Suppose Suzanne did create savings by the surplus value of her labor; if she invented and entertained, why should anyone sniff at the sources of her income? Suzanne's earnings, whatever their source, were, in Aunt Nellie's traditional view, no different from anyone else's. No one was compelled to pay the outrageous prices Suzanne was said to demand. Aunt Nellie could not have cared less that money was accumulating in Suzanne's accounts like magic: Suzanne's story was no more than a variation of a common story of American success. Suzanne was talented, and talent should be rewarded. "This is a free country," Aunt Nellie said, "and you get what you pay for."

Aunt Nellie's defense of Suzanne's reputation was something Suzanne never actually had the opportunity to hear, but she would have been honored by it, grateful for it, appreciative that the baroness of American Syrup would defend the owner of two brownstones on Ninety-third Street against common malice. It seemed obvious to Suzanne that the money her brownstones earned was valuable because, put simply, it was the only law that worked. The comforts Aunt Nellie had inherited along with American Syrup were rather nice examples of how the law of the land was designed: practically speaking, nothing was barred to a whacking amount of capital.

Suzanne's brownstones generated cash—what the catechism of capitalism described as "earned income." To the extent that Suzanne reported the amounts she received for the lease of her personal services, it would be confiscated in whole or in part by taxes. As even the dullest lawyer could explain, lust was worth money, but only if it could be laundered. Yet Suzanne needed opportunities beyond lust. The first investment opportunity Suzanne found that would qualify as a "capital gain" was brought to her attention by what could only be described as good luck.

When she had first started to work at the real estate offices of Peter Dickerson and was in the earliest stages of her direct-mail campaign, she had fallen into the habit of walking to work if the morning was fair. The distance was twenty-eight blocks, a little over a mile and a quarter. Along the way, she passed a small flower shop, hardly more than a stall, on Madison near Sixty-first Street. The proprietor was usually busy opening his shop at about the same time that Suzanne passed its door. It cheered her to stop and buy a sprig of lilac as a modest corsage for her dress, or a spray of blue bachelor buttons for the lapel of her suit, or perhaps fresh daisies for a vase in an attempt to brighten the cold gray metal desks of Dickerson, Rolfe and Streitfeld. It became a tradition for Suzanne to interrupt her walk for a few moments to enter the shop of the old Greek florist.

Mr. Hermes Antoniadis was then somewhere in his seventies. What was left of him was too small for the clothes he wore: his sweater hung in folds around where his biceps had once swelled; his pants drooped because the muscles of his buttocks and thighs no longer strained them. His gray hair was coarse and thick but cropped as short as a monk's. His mustache was a handlebar that he must have spent a fair amount of time twisting and turning to keep it flying from his cheeks. Above this remaining example of his youth were black eyes—shrewd and mischievous. Suzanne stopped each morning for Mr. Antoniadis' flowers and a word or two. The understanding between them was that if it was raining she would go to work by taxi; but if it was not, Antoniadis could expect her.

If the beautiful American missed a day, Antoniadis met her arrival the next time by pretending at first to be too busy. He would make her wait, which she would do with evident pleasure while he bustled about, preparing his shop for the day. He would give a benjamin tree water, talking all the while to it, explaining that the princess had many others to visit in her great kingdom; that there was no cause for alarm, or reason to shed leaves in sorrow; that the princess had returned—she was there now, as she had promised. "She's returned, you can see for yourself, hyacinths. Stand up straight there, Mr. Gladiolus; she may have use for your sort before this day is out."

One morning, Suzanne entered absorbed in a world of her own thoughts. She was distracted, late for the office, and not really paying attention. Without thinking, she took from her purse a quarter, handed it to Antoniadis and ordered a sprig of lilac that she would pin upon her dress.

Antoniadis brought her back to the real world: "Not today."

"What's that?" Suzanne pointed at the lilacs waiting in their vase. "From those, right there. And a pin, please."

"No."

"What, Mr. Antoniadis, is the difficulty?"

"Princess. You are once again the first customer of the day for my flowers. They adore you. They have waited for you since early morning. Even at the market on Ninth Avenue I have promised them that on this beautiful day you would be here. I have here hyacinths who would bend over your desk with joy all day. And here daffodils, jealous of little hyacinths, because daffodils can stand as straight as grenadiers. But none for a quarter, just like that. None for a dollar, with a snap of the fingers, so. None for a thousand dollars, a million dollars, without a glance. You have insulted them. You will bring bad luck. For their sake, and my own, I will have to spit where you have stood if you take them away from me for nothing but money."

She lowered her eyes from his. "What is it that I must do, old man?"

"I have lived seventy-two years, princess. Now I sell flowers from a shop. But not for twenty-five cents with a snap of the fingers. Not from my first customer. Later in the day, when it is busy, it is another matter. Then it makes no difference. Now first you must look at my flowers. Then you must choose among

them, and look upon me, and do me the small honor of bargaining for a little while."

He was right, she knew. That day they bartered with each
other for more than twenty minutes before she carried away a
dozen daffodils for one dollar and fifty cents. Thereafter, their
collaboration continued. When the brownstones were opened on
Ninety-third Street, they were always filled with flowers. Although Snow White would not allow flowers to be ordered except through one source, not a month went by without an argument about the bills Antoniadis rendered. When the day came
that the brownstones were accumulating cash in amounts impossible to disguise, Antoniadis was her first partner, and by the
time he was eighty she had made him a millionaire in his own
right.

Actually, the idea was Sam Harper's. Just as Suzanne gave
Antoniadis the respect he deserved, she found ways to use
Sam Harper's intricate scholarship. Handling the extraordinary
amount of cash that flowed through Snow White's brownstone
corporations was exactly the kind of problem Sam Harper loved
to solve. His divorce from Babette had left him alone in New
York with a growing law practice, and he was bored. He went to
the fights with John David Garraty, took his vacations to coin-
cide with the New York Yacht Club cruise or the race to Bermuda, where he sailed as a welcome crew aboard the yachts of
friends. Yet there were many long evenings, especially in winter,
when he liked to hide himself away in his apartment with his
shoes off, his feet propped up on an ottoman and a legal note
pad at his side, sucking a pencil and reading the forty thousand
pages of the Internal Revenue Code. Every year thousands of
rulings were issued by the Treasury Department, hundreds of
them referring to hundreds of others. For the sake of Suzanne,
and through his own Talmudic turn of mind, Sam Harper, Jr.,
was probably one of the few men who bothered to study the
contradictions of the law. "Some people," Sam Harper explained,
"like to do crossword puzzles. I just happen to think the tax code
is more interesting."

One of the curious facts he turned up was that a ruling had
been made that allowed corporations to depreciate the value of
any green plants used to decorate their offices. It was the atti-

tude of the United States Treasury Department that living plants, trees, bushes, used inside an office could be "written off" in a period of six months. It was even possible to interpret the rules for shorter periods: cut flowers, for example, were a deductible expense. Hence the trick would be to form a company whose business was to lease plants and flowers to corporate offices.

The flower company would provide the greenhouse plants, care for them and replace them for an annual fee. The corporate customers who subscribed to these horticultural services would not have to bother with the difficulties of indoor gardening, and moreover could write off the cost of the lease as an entirely deductible expense. If the Internal Revenue Service should ever audit the flower company's books, who would ever be able to say what the proportions were between tropical plants and cut flowers? Any cut flowers would long since be gone to the city's dumps. The rhododendron in a bank's lobby might be the original one, or a replacement for the original, and the replacement could by then be sold again. The geraniums that spent their first six months at the reception desk on the thirty-second floor of 666 Fifth Avenue might spend their next six months in an oil-company president's office.

For accounting purposes, a flower-leasing company had two advantages. First, the fast depreciation in plants and flowers allowed capital to accumulate at low tax rates; some taxes should be paid, but only enough to keep the business out of trouble. Second, cash from the brownstones could be poured into the flower company for both tropical plants and cut flowers, and the amount invested in "inventory" was an untraceable illusion limited only by the bookkeeper's imagination. Imaginary flowers could be bought at wholesale, sold at retail, or leased for the year, at whatever rate the houses on Ninety-third Street needed. Sam Harper doodled for weeks upon scratch pads in an attempt to estimate how many greenhouses would be necessary to hide all the brownstone cash. "All we need," Sam finally told Suzanne, "is a florist we can talk to."

Suzanne explained to Mr. Antoniadis how it would work. At first he did not understand: no tropical plant that he cared for would ever die in less than six months. As he gradually realized that his green plants would be dead only to the tax collector, the sweetness of the idea grew. Suzanne would supply him with the corporate customers. He would have to forgive them if they took no interest in what he grew and tended for them. They were not that kind of men. It couldn't be helped.

She would share ownership in the flower and tropical plant leasing company with Mr. Antoniadis. They would operate their own greenhouses. After several weeks of bargaining they agreed on a fifty-fifty split. Mr. Harper would supervise all the legal work and decide how much to mark up certain bills that would cover the cash Suzanne put into the company each month. Antoniadis objected to Branches, Inc., as a name for the company until Suzanne and Sam Harper agreed that the name would apply only to the holding company registered in Delaware, and that each local franchised store could carry any name Antoniadis chose. In less than three years there were outlets not only in New York but in Chicago, Minneapolis, Miami, Los Angeles, Phoenix and Washington. Every outlet was managed by a different cousin in Mr. Antoniadis' inexhaustible Greek family.

The roster of clients read like a sample taken from the list of *Fortune*'s 500 industrial companies. Yet, from the beginning, banks and insurance companies were always their biggest customers. By 1964 the Antoniadis operation had a cash flow of 3.5 million per year. Then Suzanne was able to arrange the leasing contract she savored more than any other. Through a specially formed greenhouse subsidiary, she was the sole bidder to supply green plants east of the Mississippi to every IRS district office, regional office and service center. The taste of the Treasury Department was for rubber trees, or other tropical specimens that were typically flat, or dull—in other words, nothing that would ever bear a flower. On the other hand, as Suzanne loved to point out, "according to IRS regulations, all the green plants in IRS offices are theoretically dead anyway."

11

A.k.a. Tony Scott

1956–64

THE capital gain created from dead flowers was only one of Suzanne's successes. Like her other adventures, it depended upon the strategic position she occupied and a realistic assessment of the needs of her society. Just as Aunt Nellie's American Syrup had once bought legislators, controlled the tariff and then forever after controlled the distribution of sugar, so also did Suzanne supply what society desperately wanted. "The more a woman makes love," Suzanne pointed out, "the more happiness she spreads, don't you think?"

In the brownstones of Snow White, Suzanne provided energies for which there was an unending demand. Having leased out happiness, Suzanne bought the penthouse at 30 Central Park South, where, as Mrs. Richard A. Lyle, Jr., she entertained in the more conventional style—with the blessings of Aunt Nellie and the consent of leading women like her.

"Dinners at the penthouse at 30 Central Park South, and weekends at Saratoga," said Suzanne, "were just a way to get people together who had things in common." The men who attended were absorbed by the acquisition, management and disposition of money and power. They wanted these pleasures without interference from the Internal Revenue Service or difficulty from any other constitutional authority. To get money and power, any means that could be invented was defended by the men as legal and natural. The women reacted to these arbitrary authorities with charms of their own, releasing gaiety and laughter. "By 1960 it should have been clear," in Suzanne's view, "that what had passed for the social contract was in reality every man for himself.

"Then why not the women too?" she continued. "After a certain point, you know, adultery is the only decent sport."

Few arrived at Suzanne's dinners or spent the weekend at Saratoga without leaving with a connection to the services they wanted. To ensure that her clients found what they were looking for, Suzanne created a superb intelligence system. The brownstones were part of her system, but as the 1950s were ending, she gave them less and less attention. The illusions fostered by conventional entertainments at her Central Park South address took so much of Suzanne's attention that she delegated the management of sexual fantasies at Ninety-third Street to Miss Freddy. The pleasures Miss Freddy had to abandon—initiating schoolgirls in the rites of spring—were replaced by responsibility for more adult ecstasies. Miss Freddy agreed at last to leave Wavertree Hall forever to become, in effect, the headmistress of a more practical school. Her management of the brownstones differed only slightly from the pattern Snow White had established, but under Miss Freddy's administration a far greater proportion of the regulars were women.

"Actually," said Suzanne, "Miss Freddy was a genius at it." For one thing, Miss Freddy started the club called The Sevens. They were seven women who met once each month for lunch seven months each year. They skipped the months from June through September, when vacations might interfere, and omitted the month of December because of the Christmas season, children and other encumbrances. Their long afternoon lunch was staged in Downhill House.

The group included a famous actress, the second wife of a United States senator from a western state, the very young wife of an old investment banker, an editor of a paperback publishing house, and the tiny Dresden doll who had married a famous but boring historian. At lunch these leading ladies would talk of what interested them, and the gossip was blunt. The men they invited had to listen to them attentively, respectfully, asking questions with wide-eyed innocence, flattering their hostesses, just as these same women were ordinarily required to ornament the men next to whom they were capriciously seated at more official tables. The point was to reverse the usual roles, since every woman in The Sevens did in fact have a legitimate right to have her intelligence and power respected. After lunch the men performed whatever sexual services their ladies demanded.

"The blow for freedom struck by Miss Freddy," according to Suzanne, "was the recognition that women are more direct about the sexual fantasies they want to act out, far less timid about their pleasures, and never impatient for what men think are results. One of those luncheons could give a woman a bigger boost than spending all day at Elizabeth Arden."

The guests these women invited were men who in fact danced attendance upon the women's individual courts anyway. They could be compared to the magicians and jugglers, jesters and troubadours in the age of chivalry—or any other civilized age in which feminine energies were spent to brighten life between wars. The men chosen to attend a lunch of The Sevens were actors, musicians, painters, art dealers, stockbrokers, lawyers and bank officials. "It did them a world of good," said Suzanne, "to learn they would have to do exactly what their mistresses for the day wished. If only once each month, everyone got the chance to play out the realities. If it did nothing else, it taught the men a lesson in manners."

The Sevens were also useful. The club added to Suzanne's formidable information network. Miss Freddy's connection to some of the city's leading women could be combined with data collected in the brownstones or at Suzanne's formal penthouse dinners. As a result of Suzanne's education at New York University's School of Commerce, she knew how to use the New York *Times* Index, *The Wall Street Journal* and Dun and Bradstreet reports. To these obvious sources of business information, she added reports from private detective agencies, studies commissioned at universities, investigations paid for by tax-exempt foundations, and staff studies collected by the special committees of the

House and Senate. She frequently advanced monies to journalists for magazine articles that might, or might not, be published. The advantage to using journalists, said Suzanne, was that "they're quick, accurate and cheap."

In any event, Suzanne had at her fingertips more "intelligence" than she could use. She applied what she gathered at the dinners staged at 30 Central Park South, and brokered what she knew. Dinner was always black-tie and included pretty women in long dresses. But at the penthouse dinners, as opposed to the brownstone dramas, the women appeared only as catalysts, not as principals. They were decorations before dinner while the drinks came fast. They were seated between men at dinner to reflect with their beauty the business of the evening. Suzanne's menus were deliberately so simple that no man would be distracted from the conceits of his own ambitions, or the details of his competitors' affairs.

"There may be men who really are gourmands," said Suzanne, "but if you watch them carefully you'll see what they really like is steak. Or better yet, creamed chicken hash—so they don't even have to pick up their knives."

Peas were out, because few men could bother to chase them across the plate. String beans were ideal. The wines ought to be heavy, and Suzanne's instructions to her staff were that an empty wineglass would be a major offense. In all the ways that a woman could use the preparation, tastes, odors and decorations of food as a weapon, Suzanne did so.

She also made sure these miniature civic banquets never ended late. Despite the quantities of scotch, wine and brandy the men consumed, there were few who did not glance down at their watches around eleven o'clock. Suzanne honored the pretense that her heroes had a busy schedule to meet the next day. In fact, the underlying purpose for the penthouse dinners was to celebrate the major issues the men were going to dispose. By eleven, most men would usually have accomplished the goals for which they had attended. Thanks to Suzanne's network of intelligence, the place cards at her dinner table were carefully thought-out arrangements. They allowed, for example, the publisher of many newspapers to meet an editor dissatisfied with his present assignment. Typically, a contractor whose inherited family business supplied the asphalt for the city's streets shared an evening with a Manhattan judge. Contractor and magistrate talked of sports and the future of the Democratic party and avoided sedulously the annual indictment brought against the asphalt company for short weights, but once they'd met, there was no reason for anything explicit to be said. Similarly, the investment banker who syndicated tax shelters might meet the Broadway producer about to bring a show into town; or the environmentalist reformer might meet the party contributor who would one day be the source of a federal appointment. By the early 1960s Suzanne was scheduling two dinners each week. She did not charge fees for her services. She was collecting influence.

Since Suzanne's banquets were for the good of the community as a whole, the women who attended were unavoidably the wives, or officially recognized mistresses, of the men present. These official pairings tended to be dull. On the other hand, sometimes single men were included by chance—because they were up from Washington for just one evening or in from London for the week. These arrivals were opportunities for Suzanne to provide women for the table who were finely crafted objects, like diamond bracelets set in worked gold by Italian craftsmen— similar, that is, to the jewel Suzanne had once made of herself. The extra women present had to be accomplished in their own right, or recognized mistresses of still other famous men. Their presence in the penthouse was ceremonial, not erotic. But they too were activists in the city's social and civic affairs, and so the women on display at the penthouse dinners were often the same women identically, or interchangeably, as those offered in Suzanne's notorious "Green Book."

Actually, there were many Green Books, not just one. They were similar to a set of encyclopedia, except that they were ordinary three-ring binders with green plastic covers, available at any stationery store. Each book consisted of glassine sheets, the facing, or right-hand, pages of which constituted a scrapbook of press clippings collected from "Suzy's" society column in the *Daily News*, the women's page of the New York *Times*, or articles from *Town & Country*, or *Harper's Bazaar*, or *Vogue*. Leafing through one of the Green Books allowed the interested reader to follow the high points of the well-publicized career of

one of the city's leading matrons. A catalogue was provided of
the well-known Mrs. So-and-so making the rounds of her civic
duties for the benefit of the Junior League, French-American
amity, the blind, those afflicted with diseased hearts and any
number of other medical conditions. The Green Books were dic-
tionaries of good will: women working at charities, heading committees for banquets and balls for the sick, the poor, the underprivileged.

It was the reverse, or left-hand, pages of the Green Books that
were the cause of their celebrity. In the library of Uphill House
either Miss Freddy or Suzanne could take down from the shelves
the Green Books, one by one. Either of them would turn the
pages with a leisurely hand, as though there was all the time in
the world, while she described each woman's contribution to
civic affairs. What the man unavoidably saw, however, were extraordinary photographs of, presumably, the same women of
good will in poses that were suggestive, particularly since their
faces were turned away from the camera, or obscured by an object in the foreground, or hidden by a veil, or disguised by a fall
of hair. The backgrounds of these photographs were opulent,
timeless, strange—offering a paradise of desires where no practical details would ever interfere.

Suzanne would pause over one such display: "Wouldn't she
be marvelous?"

What the man saw in the photograph was a woman reclining
against the pillows of a single bed, and he might guess that she
was pictured in the Plaza, or the Carlyle. His eye would travel to
her breasts, half hidden by the folds of her black peignoir. Her
hands were folded behind her head. Her hair, loosened, was
spread out against the pillows. She was wearing a sleep shade
that disguised her identity; or perhaps suggested that she did not
choose to know who her lover would be; or perhaps did not care.
The single bed beside her was vacant, but its sheets were neatly
turned down. If the man chose to accept the invitation, he might
arrive to find himself in exactly the place the picture had suggested, with every detail included, even the other bed turned
down.

There was nothing new in a catalogue of women posed as if
they were available—Suzanne was only imitating what Holly-

wood producers had for years offered either their investors or each other. Suzanne's exquisite variation on this old theme, however, was that her Green Books showed women as objects of art, erotic but never vulgar. Beneath each photograph there was a caption, neatly written in what surely was each woman's own hand, suggesting variations she might like to practice, or offering a quote from the verses she loved best and leaving the rest to her lover's imagination. The prices for a weekend with these famous offerings ranged from five to ten thousand dollars, depending upon how exotic the buyer wanted it to be. The effect was to imitate the very same trick Suzanne had played: here were the city's leading jewels, displayed upon velvet cushions, wanting mere money to appropriate their energies. Although the Green Books allowed the unsophisticated to moralize, Suzanne started these advertisements because there were women who wanted for just one night to taste what they had heard of Suzanne's career. Suzanne provided it for the women, just as she provided brilliant dinners in her penthouse for their husbands' ambitions, without collecting fees or commissions of any kind. She was collecting power.

In some cases Suzanne was supplying voluptuous memories. In other instances she offered revenge or relief. Whatever the Green Books may have meant to the men, they enrolled female energies in Suzanne's cause. Among her allies there existed an inner circle Suzanne called her Escadron Volant—"Flying Squadron." Its membership was not fixed to any number, but it was an association of women who, like Suzanne, were meeting the threats of the city with their wits and leashing the men by those special powers sophisticated women could improvise.

The ladies of the Green Book and the favorites known as the Escadron Volant were not presenting themselves as sex objects; nor were they comparable to any inexperienced, guileless, empty-headed girl next door. One Green Book photograph featured a woman examining her body in a mirror, noting for herself the flaws that age was bringing to her beauty. Any man who chose to accept what she knew had better be prepared to share her sadness. Another member of the Escadron had six lovers on a string at one time. She appealed to Suzanne for help, saying that she was exhausted by the whole lot of them and the demands they were making upon her patience. Suzanne's answer was to telephone several allies, who delivered over a seventh lover, known to them all as "Kick Me." Whenever the six lovers exhausted the patience of their heroine, she demanded that Kick Me take her out to dinner. As soon as she had satisfactorily aroused his passions, she dismissed him peremptorily. Everyone was satisfied.

It would be inexact to describe the combination of the brownstones, Miss Freddy's club of The Sevens, the Green Book and the Escadron Volant as Suzanne's organization. "Men organize," Suzanne pointed out, "whereas women create associations."

Taken together, however, all these activities were a force of Suzanne's own, communicating by telephone to effectively swap husbands, wreck marriages, nominate candidates for political offices, or have men named to posts such as assistant Secretary of the Treasury. During one Christmas season, while Suzanne stayed on the beach at Lyford Cay in Nassau, a mixed group from the Escadron ran up the stock of a worthless Texas conglomerate, then dumped it. They made money both long and short. The subsequent investigations by the Securities and Exchange Commission discovered next to nothing. As a matter of fact, Suzanne's allies had not bankrupted the Texas company for the money they made from it, but for the fun of it. A few dinners, several lunches, and thirty phone calls were all it took.

Suzanne used the telephone to round up, at the last moment, companions for the leading officers of an international corporation who were flying to London in the company plane. The men were to attend to the company's sales and financial meetings. The women who went along had a chance to do some shopping in London and return in less than two days. In another instance Suzanne used the overseas circuits to supply five Green Book volunteers for a corporate Boeing 707 that circled over Paris for six hours. By happenstance, her volunteers were already in Paris to attend the fall fashion showings.

Suzanne's association flouted convention constantly, but since the women were always discreet they got away with excesses habitually, and deliberately undermined any possibility of ever feeling bad. "Chastity, obedience, all those stupid virtues," Suzanne said, "enslave a woman's powers. Making love always increases them."

One of Suzanne's Escadron was being courted by a financial wizard who bored her to death about modern art. Since Nan Kaufman was deeply involved with the city's leading artists, her lover constantly badgered her to provide a "happening" for him. He'd pay for everything, he said.

"Make him wait," Suzanne advised.

Nan told her lover a famous artist would stage a happening just for him in February, but then it was postponed. In March, Suzanne advised Nan to keep postponing it. All summer long, Suzanne and Nan would think up tidbits from Krafft-Ebing. Nan would pass them on to her lover, and Suzanne would ask the artist if he could approximate them. In October the financial wizard was told everything was finally ready. When he arrived in a studio loft near Houston street, he was asked what parts he would like to play. Just as they expected, he said he only wanted to watch.

"All right," said Nan, "we'll let you watch."

For the sake of art, the financial wizard was hoisted up the side of the studio wall in a parachute harness the artist had ready for him. There the poor fool hung for nine hours while the artist, his gang of assistants, and Nan, who had managed it all, enjoyed every variation they could devise upon the studio's floor. Suzanne passed along clinical descriptions of his distress to every member of the Escadron the next day. After a week a giddy lunch was given at Le Magistral in Nan's honor.

Suzanne's part in most of these delectations was to be an ambassador. Or, as she once had said, "an ambassadress," surely one of history's most honored and oldest occupations. Her embassy was superbly organized. She rearranged the evidence presented to her, examined its premises in a geometric way, and deduced elegant solutions. From the topography that was her specialty, she surveyed curved surfaces and delegated responsibility to those who would enjoy them best. For example, Miss Freddy's management of the brownstones was a more honest occupation, and a more rewarding one, than attempting to educate rich girls who rode after foxes at Wavertree Hall. Similarly, Mr. Antoniadis was a millionaire Greek immigrant; but more important, his cousins all had businesses of their own in sixteen major cities.

Sam Harper, Jr., divorced from his wife, was encouraged by Suzanne not only to leave behind the vapid eccentricities of Greenwich, Connecticut, but to live as a free man and to pursue his two hobbies—the things he truly loved. One of these was his collection of glass paperweights, which he bought at inordinate, but never foolish, expense. He delighted in owning them, feeling their smoothness in the palm of his hand, turning them under a light, testing the refractions of the figures fixed in their gravitational centers, holding a magnifying glass to each interior design. He was rewarded in a magnificent way when Suzanne confessed to him that she collected precious eggs by stealing them from Georg Jensen.

The bond between Suzanne and Sam Harper, therefore, was only partially based upon the fact that they had been lovers, or still visited happily with each other but without passion. Sam Harper's second hobby was the study of Suzanne's intricate financial affairs, but in an abstract way—like his paperweights, the pure, cool pleasures of scholarship without end. He took no pleasure at all in the actual operations, only in the theory of them.

Operations were given over to John C. Putnam, as chief of staff. As an executive, he was relieved from the polite manners required of a trust lawyer and could at last glory in the opportunity to be the last word, or at least the next to last word. Since Suzanne needed a bully—every organization must have at least one—John Putnam could not recall a single occasion when she had ever contradicted or countermanded any order he had given. That he grew rich with her in his own right was also important. It allowed him to afford a seventy-two-foot Sparkman & Stephens racing yawl. At the wheel of his ship, he was captain and master; yet the authority he played at while racing to Bermuda was nothing compared to the power he exercised as Suzanne's chief of staff. He could breed money from money without restraint. Sam Harper designed the schemes, and John Putnam saw to it that they worked. He no longer needed his sad and honest face, and he could abandon the shining hypocrisy that had weighted his previous life like lead. Thanks to Suzanne, he could give vent to his wrath if the need arose and engage in whatever treachery the situation demanded.

John David Garraty prospered equally. Everywhere he went he was recognized. His opinion was sought in even the most delicate matters of public relations. He came to the bargaining tables between unions and management, genial, with a kind word for all, but respected. Thanks to Suzanne, Garraty's name was added to the list of trustees of one of the city's major universities. In return, he conducted a fund-raising campaign for the expansion of the university's medical facilities that was considered a model for others to imitate. Everyone agreed that his Washington legislative staff was the best; they could use the Speaker's office as their own. Yet none of these accomplishments compared to the thrill it gave Garraty to carry his scotch and soda in a paper cup from the Directors Club in Madison Square Garden to his own box seats. Anytime during the season, he could watch the Rangers skate and the Knicks play. He'd invite a pal or two to the game, get down a bet of a thousand one way or another, and tell his guests the parables they loved to hear, then sum it all up for them from the vast perspective of his experience. "That's it, pal," he'd often say. "That's what makes the world go round—booze and cooze!"

The trouble with Garraty, in Sam Harper's opinion, was that he never had a plan; he just blew this way and that. John Putnam agreed, but for different reasons. At the end of each year, Garraty's public relations operation never showed any improvement in profits. Garraty was all clamor and tilting at windmills. For his clients he would run some stock up fifty points on the American Exchange, or win some stinking primary in Brooklyn, or spend a year on a corporate takeover, including vicious full-page ads in *The Wall Street Journal* to let blood out of some dim-witted management, but at the end of the year Garraty's fees barely covered his expenses. Sam Harper and John Putnam complained to Suzanne, then spent precious days anyway with Garraty, going over his income and expenses.

In contrast, they found Billy G. Fenn an absolute pleasure to work with. Suzanne spotted him when he was working as an assistant trust officer at Chase Manhattan—a young man stymied in a pointless job. He was not yet thirty then, barely out of Duke's law school, a husky country boy who had played guard for Tennessee. At first he was not what either Putnam or Harper would have thought was needed. But Suzanne insisted, so they hired him. He was appointed president of the National Bank of Corinth, in the village of Corinth in upstate New York on Lake Luzerne, twenty miles north of Saratoga. Billy G. Fenn would make a superb banking executive, Suzanne guessed. He was mean and sly. "Good ol' country boys like Billy G. understand addition, subtraction and silence."

"The county bank operation" was another of Sam Harper's designs. After the first year, John Putnam had to admit Suzanne had been right again. He let Billy G. Fenn run the county banks virtually on his own, because he was satisfied that "Billy G. knows where the bottom line is."

The first of their county banks had been prosperous in its modest way when the paper company situated at the dam on Lake Luzerne had been locally owned. The National Bank of Corinth used the deposits from the paper mill to make loans to local farmers for seed and machinery. Then the local paper mill was absorbed as a division of a giant paper conglomerate with headquarters in New York City. Simultaneously the local bank's deposits evaporated. Suzanne's team bought up its shares for next to nothing. Once they owned the upstate bank, it was relatively easy to obtain a charter for a similar operation in Suffolk County, in the town of Riverhead, on Long Island. With two banks, Suzanne's team could move funds from one to the other with facility. The combined profits were spectacular.

County banks had a number of advantages over the kind of banks more closely supervised by Federal Reserve auditors. The cash deposits from the multiplying Brownstone Holding Corporation subsidiaries, such as the flower business, could be washed through a state bank without anyone knowing. Bills in large denominations could be exchanged for hundreds and twenties without reports. Big banks made loans to little banks, which in turn could make them to still other ventures. As long as the transactions had at their base some connection with agriculture, banking and tax authorities beamed with approval, just as the regulations required them to do. With Suzanne's connections it was possible to get friendly administrators in Albany, or at the county seats, to deposit state or county funds until the accounts of the political jurisdictions involved were consolidated at the end of a quarter, and sometimes after the end of an entire year. Meanwhile the funds collected by taxes and fees from the public at large slept like the dead in the county bank's assets, without costing the bank a penny in interest.

What delighted Suzanne when Sam Harper explained the purposes of banks to her was that these elegant thefts were mandated by the federal and state banking laws. Deposits, of course, never earned profits for a bank, but Suzanne's team had an endless list of proposals brought to their attention that deserved loans. The interest collected on mortgages and loans earned income and accumulated capital. Besides, when Suzanne's banks made loans they had a right, by law, under the provisions of the Banking Fraud Laws, to obtain credit information from FBI reports, and even from tax returns, about anyone at all. It was a privilege that could not be abused, but there were times when Suzanne found it convenient to know absolutely everything about a new acquaintance, his credit, or his taxes.

It was the kind of intelligence Judge Ephraim Gordon also found useful, either for himself or for his client Mr. Amedeo Scutari, also known as Mr. Tony Scott. As Judge Gordon explained to Suzanne: "Mr. Scott's business interests have covered a considerable range over many years. Mr. Scott is a highly respected man in certain circles."

From the beginning, these certain circles had guaranteed immunity to Snow White's brownstones. It was Mr. Scott's associates who saw to it that there was no harassment from the Police Department of the City of New York. They were also helpful in other small difficulties. For example, a shopping-center promoter deposited stocks and bonds as collateral for mortgage loans from Suzanne's county banks. Unfortunately it developed that the paper securing the loans was stolen. It looked as if even Billy G. Fenn had been stung. Suzanne telephoned Judge Gordon: what did he advise?

"How long ago," Judge Gordon inquired, "did this happen?"

Suzanne explained the circumstances, told Judge Gordon all that her people knew about the swindler, and said that a month had already passed. Judge Gordon would only say that he would make the appropriate inquiries. Within a week the hot stock was redeemed in cash by a messenger at the Saratoga bank. Suzanne expressed her thanks to Judge Gordon, and asked what had changed the promoter's mind so quickly.

"He wanted to take a vacation," said Judge Gordon. "You won't see him around any more."

Suzanne laughed. "Where will he be going?"

"Away."

Any further inquiries about exactly what had happened would have been undiplomatic. Similarly, Judge Gordon and Mr. Scott never inquired or interfered in any way in how Snow White ran her brownstones, or who was entertained at Mrs. Lyle's penthouse. By consistently acting as a hostess and fund-raiser for Democratic party hopes, regardless of merit and without any promise of reward, Suzanne was eventually understood to have paid her dues to the party of Jefferson, Jackson and Roosevelt. When the spoils of victory were distributed, she was awarded bones; but these modest appointments to committees on court reform, education, prisons and world's fairs had their uses. The committees never did more than meet, compile reports and congratulate themselves, but Suzanne sat through their deliberations without cavil. The Internal Revenue Service, for example, met twice each year to assess the value of artists' work. Suzanne could not think of a more fatuous waste of time. On the other hand, in return for her advice a red dot appeared in the upper-right-hand corner of her tax returns during the years when the Democrats held power. In addition, because Suzanne's circle of acquaintance in New York and Washington was so wide, every so often Mr. Scott could telephone.

With Suzanne, Mr. Scott was always the gentleman, always polite, and he never asked her for anything more than to act as an emissary: "Suzanne, I need to have a private talk with this fellow."

Mr. Scott and Suzanne kept their internal affairs separate. During political campaigns they might act in concert when Suzanne, or a jointly approved designate, would hand two envelopes of cash simultaneously to the candidate's representative, indicating as they were passed which one was from Mr. Scott. Other business affairs were conducted in somewhat the same, "common market" way. Mr. Scott's corporations were growing, and he needed directors, executives, managers, accountants, lawyers and whatnot who were "clean down to the tips of their shoes." He needed respected members of the community; men with inherited memberships in the Racquet Club and the Union League Club; men with impeccable credentials and good connections. He needed Republicans, who could be supplied from Snow White's brownstones; he needed Democrats, who were supplied from the active life led at 30 Central Park South by Mrs. Richard A. Lyle, Jr. Generally speaking, Mr. Scott could supply judges, district attorneys and police officers without any assistance, but Suzanne was sympathetic to his situation when he said: "You can understand that at a certain level there are some people who do not wish to do business with Italian immigrants. In the meantime we will look out for each other."

Thanks to Mr. Tony Scott, Suzanne's team won control of two nicely run insurance companies in Dallas, Texas. He was a partner with them in their sixteen suburban shopping centers. They shared between them "good connections" with twice that many mayors, and they paid particular attention to the real estate assessors they wanted to be sure they could reach for reduced valuations.

Judge Gordon and John Putnam co-operated with each other, although it disturbed Putnam, as he pointed out to Suzanne, "that Mr. Scott always knows more about what we do than we know about what he does." The difficulty was that Mr. Scott's "various interests" left fewer traces than Suzanne's. Only an estimation of their extent was possible. Even that had to be based upon the career of Judge Gordon, Mr. Scott's lawyer and therefore inferentially representative of the Scutari empire.

Ephraim Gordon was elected judge of a Surrogate's Court in the City of New York without opposition, endorsed by the Republican, Democratic and Liberal party organizations. The administration of trusts and estates in a Surrogate's Court was said to be worth three and a half million dollars a year in lawyers' fees. No judge distributed these legal fees without suitable contributions in return to the future of the democratic process. For Judge Gordon to have retired from so lucrative a bench, Mr. Tony Scott must have made it worthwhile. Judge Gordon was known as an astute business adviser to major corporations, a multimillionaire who had once specialized in labor law, a successful mediator in some of the city's most delicate labor negotiations, a frequent contributor to law-association journals on the common objectives of labor and management.

Judge and Mrs. Gordon entertained at their own apartment frequently, were invited to Suzanne's, and were included on many other lists. Among the Gordons' friends were stars of Broadway and Hollywood, the owners of leading talent agencies, and many journalists. The Justice Department, or its Federal Bureau of Investigation, periodically alleged that Judge Gordon was an intermediary between "criminal elements in union affairs and the leisure and entertainment industries."

Occasionally Mrs. Gordon would be away in Arizona or Florida, "taking the sun." When such opportunities occurred, Judge Gordon would invite eight or ten of his friends for dinner at the Colony. With a great deal of wine and a fine meal behind them, they could enjoy with good talk the sense they shared of life's foolish mysteries. Since quick banter and juicy gossip were the medium of exchange at Judge Gordon's suppers, he always invited Suzanne. For his sake, she did her best to star. On one such night at the Colony, Suzanne pretended she was a reporter interviewing him.

"I understand, Your Honor, that you are an influential figure in the entertainment industry."

"Only in a very modest way; not at all on a scale comparable to your own."

"Isn't it a fact, Judge, that you are a major connection to the underworld?"

"And who," asked Ephraim Gordon, "makes these allegations?"

"Well . . . informed sources," answered Suzanne, with a brow as solemn as that of any New York *Times* reporter.

"Do they have names?"

"They are highly placed government sources."

"Do they have titles?"

"They allege that you are engaged in bribery, kickbacks, extortion, fraud, loan-sharking, drug deals and the concomitant underworld methods of enforcement and violence."

If the others at the table shifted uneasily at Suzanne's daring, it did not faze Judge Gordon. "These allegations," he answered smoothly, "will be used to wrap tomorrow's fish."

"But they have been made," Suzanne insisted with a twinkling eye.

"Libelous," he answered. He wanted the game to continue.

"You have taken part in a conspiracy"—Suzanne was wagging her finger at him—"to bribe a United States senator."

"Ask the senator."

"You have suborned members of the House of Representatives."

"Ask the members."

"Representing both yourself and associates, and by reason of your connections with organized labor, you have influenced elections."

"Ask the governor."

"Do you deny these charges?" Suzanne was smiling broadly for him now, and even his other guests agreed to play along with her comedy.

"Is there a bill of particulars?" Judge Gordon loved debate.

"No," she admitted.

"Has any prosecutor, state or federal, brought forward an indictment?"

"No, Your Honor."

"Then, these charges are no more than trial by press release."

"They are in the newspapers."

"Who are the federal officials slandering me from coast to coast?"

"They have not been named, Your Honor."

"Who are these well-informed Justice Department accusers?"

"I'd have to ask the Washington *Post*, sir."

"All right, Brenda Starr." Judge Gordon brought his case to a close with great satisfaction. "I will predict for you that as soon as the FBI gets its budget approved, these lies will be forgotten. Those guys will go back to chasing communists."

Suzanne led applause for Judge Gordon from his table. Toasts to His Honor's health and continued success were proposed from his other guests, particularly those who had been most uncomfortable only a moment before. In answer to the sentiments offered him, Ephraim Gordon toasted his opponent. "It takes," he said, "a beautiful woman to make a man proud."

As to the substance of the charges in Suzanne's mock interview, Judge Gordon was entirely correct. As the Vietnam protests spread, the FBI was busy on other matters. In early 1964, sometime in January, as Suzanne recalled it, Judge Gordon asked if Suzanne and John Putnam would find it convenient to meet at lunch with Mr. Scott. They had a plan they wished to discuss privately. Mr. Scott would be honored if they would join him at Jack and Charlie's "21" on Saturday at one o'clock.

At lunch, Amedeo Scutari did not open the subject of the plan until coffee was on the table. Regardless of the actualities of his career, he was always at his ease, always had plenty of time. His exaggerated courtesy, the thoughtful manners, the calm dignity, were in the antique style of landed nobility from long ago. He discussed the weather quite seriously. He listened attentively to John Putnam's analysis of the stock market. He was gray-haired, sixty-two years old, and solemn. Above all, he was patient. Somehow it had been impressed upon him that this year's crop would be followed by next year's; that summer always gave way to fall, then fall to winter. When spring came again it would be time to plow, just as generations had done before. His patience was especially attractive because it was expressed as an habitual modesty. He conveyed to everyone he met the need for time to improve today's crisis, and delay to quiet tomorrow's fears. Typically, he disposed of difficulties by saying: "Take it easy. Something can be worked out. Something can always be worked out."

His plan, when he began to reveal it, was addressed to Suzanne. Although she was a woman, she was exceptional. "We need some Republicans. I am glad you have your *consigliere* with you, because we have something special for him."

"Amedeo, you are marvelous. No one but you would describe John as a *consigliere*."

"Have I offended you, Mr. Putnam?"

"Not at all, Mr. Scott. I am proud to be Mrs. Lyle's *consigliere*, as you put it."

"Good. It seems to me, and Judge Gordon agrees, that this man who was Vice-President for General Eisenhower, and who has lost his campaign to be governor of California, might be useful to us."

"It would be hard to imagine how," said John Putnam with considerable authority. "He is a born loser."

"It is sometimes true, Mr. Putnam, that a horse who loses by twenty lengths at Santa Anita can be rested, perhaps trained in a different way, and brought back to run here at Belmont with entirely different results. In such a case, the odds on the California horse would be very good."

John Putnam announced that his sources from within the Republican party indicated that Governor Rockefeller and Senator Goldwater were going to fight it out. The winner of the California primary would be the candidate.

"And he'll lose," said Judge Gordon. "Which gives us some time to think ahead."

"Yes," Amedeo Scutari said. "And our California horse will need time and money behind him before he runs again. I think he is worth a small bet, say five million dollars, to get him to the track in 1968. Then maybe fifty, sixty million for the entry fee. Usually the way it works—once the horse is at the track and entered on the day's program—everyone is willing to bet, for or against. It makes no difference, but the money is put down, and the odds are totaled and posted. It is before that when it is difficult. Five million for a horse that is not running at all is a long shot."

"I'll say it is," said John Putnam. "Especially for that one."

"Ah, Mr. Putnam, you are not a betting man, I can see. But I can see from your smile, my dear Suzanne, that you have understood me."

"I have, Amedeo. I certainly have. What do you want us to do?"

"I think we sell shares in the California horse. I am prepared to buy two shares for myself and my friends. Each share at five hundred thousand dollars. It is difficult, however, for me and my friends to go about selling these shares without causing what we might say would be jealousy. Judge Gordon here is a betting man too, but his friends are all Democrats. Unfortunately, in this case we must have Republicans. I have always voted Democrat

myself, but a Republican dark horse brings the better odds, don't
you think, Suzanne?"

"I think we ought to sell thirty shares of five hundred thousand each. I can sell them with a few dinners. Let's call it the
Thirty Club. Sounds right. Original members get first choice
from the winnings if the horse goes the distance. Thirty shares
makes a total of fifteen million, covers any extra expenses that
might come up. What's the legal way to handle this?"

"It's not very difficult." Judge Gordon turned to John Putnam.
"As soon as Suzanne has recruited a new member for her club,
that man instructs his corporation to hire your law firm as a con-
sultant on taxes, or antitrust, or whatever suits your partners.
Each member of the club gives us an indication of what he will
want if we win. Meanwhile you've made the California horse a
partner. He's set up in your stable. You pay for his oats and hay
and the boys you will need to walk and groom him."

John Putnam felt he should indicate he did not need any lessons from Judge Gordon. "We have some experience at this kind
of thing too, Your Honor. Not all Republicans are totally helpless. But my partners are going to have a problem with the governor. He represents a fair share of our business, and his people
are not going to be pleased if we get involved with the California man."

"Do as you please, Mr. Putnam. But you will have to find us a
Republican law firm, here in New York."

"I believe," said Mr. Scott, "you gentlemen will find no problem after November. The Texan wins, easy, going away. Then
the governor's people will want to cover their bets. They always
do. Mrs. Lyle can sell them a share along with the others."

"I'll sell two shares to the governor's friends," said Suzanne.
"Maybe three." The idea had her grinning.

"Listen, sweetheart," said Mr. Scott, who was laughing too.
"In this kind of setup, it's best to take it easy. Keep it spread
around. Only one share to a customer."

Her smile was still mischievous. "Not even for the governor's
friends, Amedeo?"

He spread his hands, palms up. "Who are they to have two,
when my friends can only buy one?"

"You have two already."

"One for myself, one for certain associates."

"And what will be on your shopping list, Mr. Scott?" John Putnam was all business.

Judge Gordon fielded the question: "We have a pension fund for which we want no indictments. We can take investigations up to a certain point, but no indictments."

"And for the other share?"

"A federal judge, to be named later."

"Let me indicate," said Mr. Scott, "that the candidate does not need to know, any more than the horse knows what's up on the tote board. So the shopping list we keep to ourselves: the trainer gets a copy, we get a copy, and Suzanne keeps the original of the book as the bets are entered. If your law firm, Mr. Putnam, does not care to have this horse in its barns, and you find some other firm to handle the entry, then even you don't get to see the book. Is that clear?"

Tony Scott's gaze was leveled across the table into John Putnam's eyes. Suzanne interrupted the scene: "I'm sure Mr. Putnam already agrees with you, Amedeo. Tell me, what are the odds on our horse today?"

"Minnesota would give you maybe sixty to one."

"What's nice," said Judge Gordon to the table at large, "is that if we lose, it's deductible, right?"

"He's going to be a pain in the ass," was John Putnam's gloomy assessment.

"If we win," said Mr. Scott, "we got someone we can talk to in the White House."

"We'll have points, Amedeo." Suzanne was delighted. "Points in the American Way."

12

Paradise Island
1960-68

DURING the months from October 1970 to May 1971, when I served as Suzanne's biographer, I considered it a part of my duties to check—insofar as possible—the facts of her assertions, particularly in instances such as her Thirty Club. After all, it was disturbing to hear that major corporations were buying shares in a presidential candidate and doing it much as if they were betting on a racehorse. After reading the transcript of my interview, I checked our Washington and Los Angeles bureaus. They had nothing on the story. No references to anything of the sort were available in our morgue, nor in the files of any other publication. The following Saturday, when we met again in her library, I followed up with more questions on the Thirty Club.

I sat at the library desk as usual with my tape machine and notebooks. I remember that soon after we began she kicked off her slippers, stretched out full length, and with her ankles crossed, propped her heels up on the arm of the blue velvet couch. She was wearing a long blue velvet lounging robe, and the effect was blue upon blue, except where the robe fell away from her calves. Staring at the ceiling above her, she answered my questions with an amused tolerance. I pointed out that it was difficult for me to verify stories like her Thirty Club.

"That's because you are a journalist. You have no idea how things work."

I thought we did the best we could—and not a bad job at that —to report each week's news.

"Fiddlesticks," she said. "You write fiction."

"We check every fact we print. Double check and triple check."

"Don't be silly. You only check the facts you have. You can't possibly check the facts you don't have. In any case, fiction has as many facts as you do."

I thought we'd better get to work. I asked how difficult it had been to sign up members to buy a share in a presidential dark horse.

"I could have signed up fifty more, even at five hundred thousand each."

I wondered about difficulties either she or Amedeo Scutari may have had with the election law, and whether five hundred thousand dollars didn't seem to be a substantial sum of money.

"Poof!" She waved any doubts away. "In the first place, those who bought shares in the California horse were spending their corporations' money, and for legal fees at that—representing a minute fraction of what they spend every year for good will of some kind or another. Doesn't your newsweekly carry advertisements from the same corporations for the same purpose?"

I pointed out that there was a law restricting the ads—that if they attempted to influence legislation directly, they would not be considered tax-deductible.

"Hypocrisy! What you are saying is that as long as it can be shown that the ads you sell to your advertisers don't work, they will be allowed. Doesn't your publisher tell your advertisers that his editors can sway public opinion?"

I admitted he probably did, but more or less in the long run.

"Then, the only difference between us is that I have the means to deliver on my promises and you do not."

I insisted that it was not entirely the same thing.

"Perhaps not, Mr. Editor, but be careful: there is no crime worse than innocence. The next time you ponder the future of the nation, remember that I have changed some significant opinions in less than twenty minutes."

We agreed again to proceed on the materials of her biography. I needed to know how much difference it made to her operations when her long shot eventually won the national sweepstakes.

"Not much," was her conclusion. "The curious thing about the whole adventure," she said, was that "it turned out to be a waste of time." As soon as she had sold out the thirty shares, but long before the horse was running, she had a shopping list itemizing what each of her subscribers wanted in the event of victory. With the list in hand, she had lunch again with Amedeo Scutari, just the two of them, and she summarized for him how the members proposed to divide the winning stake.

At first he would not believe her. From her purse she pulled out three single-spaced pages, folded in half. He took his spectacles from the pocket of his jacket, set them on his nose, and went down through the shopping list, line by line, with his index finger. When he got to the end, he started over again at the beginning. He could not believe what he was reading. He questioned Suzanne. "All this guy wants is no antitrust case?"

Suzanne confirmed it.

"Just one? Just this one case?"

Suzanne was sure that was all he wanted.

"And this guy here." He was pointing to a member listed on the second page. "He wants the price of oil to seek its natural level?"

Suzanne said that was correct.

"What the hell does that mean?"

The best she could do was shrug.

"And this one: he wants the routes for his airline to include Pago-Pago? Where is that?"

"It is the capital of American Samoa, in the Pacific," Suzanne explained, adding diplomatically that it was her impression—although she was not entirely sure—that the name on the list they were reading should be pronounced "Pango-Pango."

Tony Scott nodded. He understood. "The *n* is silent. These guys are boyscouts. They are crazy."

"No," Suzanne attempted to explain, "they're just silly."

"I'll say. No judges? Not one of them wants a federal judge?"

"Not one."

"Who is the woman, this Mrs. Burns? She is the only one with any sense. Commissioner of banks—there's something I could use myself someday."

Suzanne identified her friend Mrs. Burns as the American Syrup Corporation, which Mr. Scott understood immediately. "They're into a lot of things now besides sugar, right?"

She agreed.

He folded the list in half and returned it to her. "Crazy," he said, shaking his head. He said nothing for a moment or two, staring off into space as if all that he had struggled for, all that he had waited for, was in the end going to be an inexplicable joke. Then he put the mystery aside and returned to more practical matters: "Mrs. Burns is a friend of yours, right?"

Suzanne explained that they saw a good deal of each other, both in the city and at Saratoga.

Mr. Scott's conclusion was that Suzanne was lucky: it was good to have a friend like that.

Lunches like the one they shared to review the shopping list of Republican ambitions were rare between Mr. Scott and Suzanne. They each had a share—"points"—in a number of the other's enterprises, but for the most part everything could be handled by their lawyers. One of the reasons the election results in 1968 made so little difference was that by then they had both found, in effect, countries of their own.

Mr. Tony Scott's "certain interests" bought control of a casino on Providence Island, in Nassau, the Bahamas. The former crown colony of the British Empire removed itself from the jurisdiction of the Queen's ministers, simultaneously keeping clear of any United States authorities. The local government, known affectionately as the "Bay Street Boys," took less than two years to unseat. After a new government was installed, the gambling franchise was moved across the narrow harbor to a strip of sand and jungle that had once been called Hog Island.

The government replaced the leaking old ferry and built a bridge with toll booths. When the cruise ships docked at Nassau, thousands of bored tourists disembarked, bought themselves straw hats and baskets, and then were carried by taxis across the new bridge to a complex of high-rise hotels and casinos bigger than those in Las Vegas. Thousands more each week were unloaded from Boeing 727s scheduled in from New York, Boston and the continental cities of the near Midwest. They, too, poured through the Tollgate Bridge and into the casinos to lose as quickly as they could every cent of cash they had inherited, earned or borrowed. Since a tourist trade so constituted might have thought twice about gambling all they had on an island called Hog, it was renamed Paradise Island.

What was most delightful about this speck in the Caribbean Sea was that from the point of view of Mr. Scott's friends it had, insofar as any practical application was concerned, no government at all. When Mr. Scott's organization arrived, the entire police force of the Bahamas Government consisted of five men. Mr. Scott needed that many to work a single shift at one craps table. Within a few months, it was apparent that Mr. Scott's army was considerably larger and better equipped than any volunteer force that might be raised locally. As the spokesmen of the government repeated frequently: "The economy of the Bahamas is dependent above all upon tourism, and gambling is one of our pleasant attractions." The law of the Bahamas was backed by the moral forces of necessity.

Yet there were even more significant consequences to Paradise. Any banking procedure that seemed practical could be invented to fit the immediate requirements of the moment. Money could be deposited or withdrawn or created or collapsed or counterfeited as Money went along. Mr. Scott and his associates carried cash from their casino in satchels on aircraft from the Bahamas to London, in whatever quantities they pleased, and bought up all the casinos in Great Britain they thought attractive. For the price of an airplane ticket, and sometimes for the cost of a radiogram, they could create credit in cotton futures and cocaine, or options on movie-company stocks. The banking traditions of the Bahamas were backed by the moral force of chaos.

The freedoms granted money by the government of the Bahamas soon attracted other practical men. American corporations by the hundreds had their names tacked up on the doors of the leading Bahamian law firms. With no more than a brass plate, a domicile for a corporation could be relocated. A New York bank opened a branch on Paradise Island, and presto, every transaction concluded at the address was exempt from confession. Several immense mutual funds saw advantages in so happy a place, where at last actions suited words: "The greatest good for the greatest number." These funds did no more than open the doors of the houses they established in Paradise, whereupon money rushed to them, emptying the accounts of New York brokers, and fleeing from European and Latin American banks as well. Those who lost control of these funds to the new Bahamian bankers complained to all who would listen that the islands were a haven for "black-market money." To which the Bahamians replied, with some justice, that the color of money was always green. "There will come a day," a prime minister of the Bahamas predicted, "when every major financial institution in the Western world will see the advantages of transacting the better share of its business upon our sunny shores, surrounded by the protection we can provide—mile upon mile of clear blue water."

He was soon enough right. Along with many others, Suzanne took advantage of Mr. Scott's offer of a share—"points"—in a big casino on Paradise Island. She, too, incorporated a bank, much like those Billy G. Fenn managed for her in Saratoga and Suffolk counties, New York. Yet the Paradise Bank had no tellers, no windows, no vaults, no customers hanging about, no audits and no reports to make, except those approved for legal reasons by John Putnam. It was a magic bank, with nothing up its sleeve, from which Suzanne could withdraw real money like handkerchiefs knotted end to end.

The technical mysteries of a Paradise for money amused Suzanne if ever she dwelt upon it. By 1968, however, she was absorbed by the intricacies of a paradise of her own, centered, of all places, upon Manhattan Island. By then Mrs. Richard A. Lyle, Jr., was identifiable as one of the "beautiful people." She moved in company with those blessed few who were cited constantly in *Women's Wear Daily* and other sacred texts. They were described as pacesetters, leaders in this and that, glamorous, trendmakers.

Suzanne was by then one of the elect who set the style. Simultaneously, although she was nearly forty, she could not resist taking as one of her lovers a jewel thief. She was fully aware of the dangers she risked from lithe, strong young men, but he'd picked her up at Raffles one night, just as if she were twenty again. He telephoned her every day for a week, until she consented to have a drink with him at the Palm Court of the Plaza. Over drinks he revealed he was going to pull a job within an hour, but he'd be finished at ten. Afterward he'd like to take her to dinner at Elaine's. He'd have the rented car he was using downstairs at her apartment canopy at exactly ten.

Just as he had promised, he was there. On the way up Third Avenue, Suzanne asked how the job had gone. She still didn't quite believe him. She had not yet made up her mind. He drove with his eyes straight ahead, watching the traffic and avoiding the cabs that cut across their path. "There's a bag on the seat there between us. Take a look."

She opened the drawstrings of a large leather satchel. Inside she could feel some ten or fifteen pounds of stones. She took a handful out and held them up against the windshield to catch what light the streetlamps provided. "Diamonds?"

"No," said her lover, and he began to laugh at himself. "The son-of-a-bitch stuffed his safe with zircons. I've been had."

Suzanne began to laugh along with him. When they stopped at a red light, he rolled down the window on his side and directed her to open the bag's top wide, then hand it to him. He upended the bag in the middle of Third Avenue as they pulled away from the light. They described to each other variations of the scene they imagined for the next morning as the commuters went to work and saw the streets of New York paved with what they believed to be diamonds.

Dinner at Elaine's was marvelous. Thereafter, Suzanne often went to bed with her jewel thief, but by an unspoken agreement they met only on the afternoons or evenings immediately after he had pulled off a job—when his heart was still pounding with excitement.

Then they not only made love for hours on end; they talked like happy children. They both moved constantly in the company of the beautiful people, if for slightly different reasons. They exchanged confidences, and secrets, and estimations. They both paid close attention to the gossip columns, where the beautiful people were always "just in from London," gone off to

Paris, or only stopping for a few days in New York, as if always in midflight.

Suzanne's jewel thief also followed the circuit that had something to do with the sun. She met him furtively in Saratoga in August. He'd just hit four dinner parties, one after another. While everyone was in the dining room, he went through the upstairs bedrooms and cleaned them out. "They leave the stuff there on their bureaus," he explained. "It's there for the asking. So I take it and leave, in my socks. I come and go dressed in a tuxedo, just like they are. The servants couldn't care less. I wear shoes one size too big, so they'll slip back on again easily."

He sent her a postcard from Los Angeles in the fall, but he was back in New York after Thanksgiving. They met again in the Bahamas in January. His pigeons, as he called them, were at Las Brisas in February. He sent her a postcard inscribed: "Nice ruby ring, wish you were here."

When March arrived he had his choice between Palm Beach, Antigua and Jamaica. He hit Newport in June and the Hamptons for the fifth straight year in July. Suzanne could not always match his schedule, but when he was in New York they made love after every job until she had absorbed from his skin all the fear he brought with him. When they were resting one night, she trailed her fingers along his chest and his young, flat, hard stomach, and asked him his definition of "beautiful people."

He said it was simple: "Rich is very beautiful. Middle rich, somewhat beautiful, especially if the husband is guilty about something and paying off his old lady with rocks. Ordinary income is downright ugly. Nobody buys what I want on an American Express card."

He was pleased with himself that night, because he had just collected about a million in jewels, cash and securities from the town house of the mistress of the chairman of a large conglomerate. He'd been in and out in thirty minutes without a problem. "They had the place wired," he said, "with one of those protective agencies. I got the code and answered them. Sweet and easy."

Suzanne quoted one of the goddesses of the beautiful people as having said a woman cannot be too rich or too thin. Did he agree with that?

He said he did, but noted the difficulty he sometimes had sizing up his prospects. "Some of them have nothing but celebrity. I have to make sure they are loaded with the real thing."

Suzanne wanted to know: "Am I beautiful?"

He said she was.

"Am I famous?"

He agreed she probably was.

"Am I too thin?"

He pretended he was feeling her flesh before he'd come to any conclusion. "You're just right."

"Am I witty?"

"Yes."

"Am I talented?"

"Sweetheart, you are the most talented woman I have ever come across."

"Am I rich?"

He said he guessed she probably was.

"Would you rob me?"

Perhaps he hesitated too long before he took a clean shot at it. "Sure," he admitted. "I would, if you gave me the chance."

He never got the chance, because only a month later he made a miscalculation in Fort Lauderdale. After pleading guilty to a reduced charge of breaking and entering, he was sentenced to six years anyway.

Suzanne's analysis of the sudden celebrity given to the beautiful people differed slightly from the summary made by her jewel thief. Her conclusions were perhaps informed by the education she had been given at Wavertree Hall twenty years before, but whatever her sources may have been, she was as practical as ever: "Public life no longer had any traditional meaning. When everyone looked out for number one, civic life was reduced to nothing more than a series of private contracts. So in place of the villains, the beautiful people appeared, posing for the responsibilities of honor." Suzanne shrugged at her own assessment. "That was all there was to it. The newspapers needed to have someone to stand up and take a bow, never mind for what."

Like other beautiful people, Suzanne took pleasure in herself, and consequently others did too. By honoring herself, she adapted to the reigning orthodoxy of the day. Any woman could enter the gates of paradise, all the magazines agreed, if only she would look upon the calm inner beauty with which she had been equipped since birth. If she would only understand her needs, and consent to them, beauty could be consecrated by its self-acceptance, and then accompanied by good works as the occasion arose. Like so many other beautiful people, Suzanne drew the tithes necessary to a clear conscience from her checking accounts on Paradise Island.

She did not insist upon any particular order to the luxuries she enjoyed, except that they had to be examples of her impeccable taste. She bought her important clothes in Paris, but she had no objection to a Mädler calf handbag for one hundred and forty-five dollars she found in New York, nor to an Yves St. Laurent belt for thirty pounds she discovered in London. She had mink coats of varying lengths, and a leopard, a rather handsome black seal, and a black lamb that would never go out of style. She could change her fate as often as she pleased: Gucci walking shoes might take her one way; a Mark Cross bag another. A South Sea pearl-and-diamond ring cost only nine thousand five hundred dollars at Harry Winston's. Bulgari provided a platinum chain with diamonds as accents for seventy thousand; a bit high perhaps, Suzanne thought, but then, why not? She could do as she pleased.

Tiffany & Company, at Fifty-seventh Street, exhibited rare watches from the archives of Patek Philippe. A round solitaire diamond of 2.45 carats set in a ring cost only eighteen thousand dollars. Italian craftsmen worked gold with fantastic skill for Buccellati, at Fifty-fifth Street; a bracelet of gold links cost only ten thousand. Halston opened a boutique at Bergdorf Goodman, where Suzanne found evening pajamas in tree-bark textured silk, a flowing cape with diagonal neckline over loose trousers. Oscar de la Renta had a variation in tricolor silk tunic, pants and side-wrapped shirt. "A vibrant contrast of red/green/purple that can change your destination, and destiny, with surprising agility," said the ad she clipped from *Town & Country*.

By the most fortunate series of coincidences, she discovered her mother's old chauffeur, James Moriarity, running a limousine service in Queens, of all places. She hired him immediately as chauffeur and bodyguard combined, and was ecstatic that she could afford their reunion. She let him choose the dark-green stretch Mercedes she would use on formal occasions, but she liked at times to drive herself upstate. For those blazing trips through space she bought a bright-red Mercedes roadster. Her pace, and the car, earned her one speeding ticket after another, which she turned over to Judge Gordon to fix.

One night in London she had dinner at Annabel's, too many drinks with a stupid English lord, went upstairs to the Clare-mont Club and to relieve her boredom sat down at the baccarat table. She had "the shoe" as banker for one hand at eighty thousand pounds. Betting against her was an Arab sheik with a stack of chips a foot high, but the eight fell. She walked away from the table one hundred and sixty thousand dollars richer. John Aspinall paid her by check, and in dollars. The check lay in the bottom of her gold mesh purse for three months, forgotten, she said. "Beyond a certain point, it didn't mean anything."

After 1968 she could afford to keep Enrique Cardinale by her side to perform many of the same tasks Adam Shepherd carried out for Aunt Nellie: master of ceremonies, decorator, architect, chief of games and entertainments, escort when the occasion arose. On her fortieth birthday, September 21, 1970, she commissioned Enrique to begin work on a temple centered in the lake she would build on her summer place near Saratoga. Not long afterward she decided she deserved a biography. "The point is," she told me, "money never had anything whatever to do with it."

13

The Countess de Montreuil

1968–72

PERHAPS Suzanne never understood the extent to which money actually did "have something to do with it." Then again, perhaps what she said was another one of her deceptions.

"When people talk about money," she once remarked, "they have nothing left to talk about. Even the weather is more interesting."

Yet from 1968 to 1972 Suzanne was apparently concerned with nothing but money, and therefore there may appear to be contradictions to her biography. My interviews confirmed beyond any shadow of reasonable doubt how proud she was of her success. I could confirm how pleased she was that she could buy any necessity she fancied. She thoroughly enjoyed all the considerable privileges of being rich. She had earned the means, she thought, to behave with abandon. And she believed with all her heart that if the appropriate moment should arrive, she could act, if necessary, with a ruthless immunity. She obviously loved all of money's uses, and she apparently understood her bank balances to be prizes—mementoes—of her many victories.

Yet, fatefully, she was at the same time an agnostic of money's mysteries. Perhaps the central element of her achievement was that she had never bowed her head, nor struck her breast over her heart, nor tugged at her forelock when the pieties of the national faith were mentioned. After all, she had created her successes by her own efforts, and her fortune by her own wits—not by good will nor by inheritance, not by magic or luck, nor by the intervention of some benevolent Majesty on High. What she had done, she had earned.

Worse, she had no illusions about the securities that money might buy. She had been born and raised in the cardboard landscape of money's assurances. There were no invitations issued to her later celebrity that she had not accepted long before. Consequently, when people talked of money in hushed tones, they were—as far as Suzanne could see—talking metaphysics. "Rubbish," Suzanne said, "it's just a matter of dollars and cents."

All money, in Suzanne's agnostic view, was measured in the same Arabic numbers, and the digits and zeroes were manipulated according to the accepted rules of positional notation. The arithmetic of money applied equally to dollars, francs and yen without regard to race, color, creed or sex. The power of money was a function of its quantity: more money equaled more power; less money inherently meant less power; and it must be obvious, therefore, that a stated amount of money represented a proportional amount of power regardless of any claims of legitimacy. Unfortunately, these axioms seemed so logical to Suzanne that she also assumed that every other abbess anointed in money's faith surely occupied herself with more substantive problems than slicing theological differences about money's legitimacy in this instance or that. Suzanne knew as well as anyone else the histories of American money's early saints, and she delighted in their dramas. Yet she took from these stories the details that amused her best: how Standard Oil used dynamite on the competition, how Ryans and Whitneys sold subway bonds to the City of New York again and again, and how one day Jay Cooke's bank cornered all of America's gold.

"Rich is better," Suzanne could say without embarrassment. It probably never occurred to Suzanne that anyone would assert that some money sinned, while other money blessed. Suzanne was just as bullish on America as everyone else, but she couldn't see any difference between gambling on the stock market and playing roulette in one of Tony Scott's casinos. How could there be any moral difference between what was called a "capital gain" and two to one on red or black? In both examples, the best percentage was always the bank's—whose commissions were paid even on losses and who collected on the green numbers designated zero. What Suzanne meant, therefore, when she said, "Money had nothing to do with it," was that she enjoyed singing the hymns in money's temples as much as everyone else apparently did—but that she sang because she rather enjoyed money's melodies, just as when she was a girl at Clearbrook Country Day School she had once enjoyed singing, "Holy, Holy, Holy," because it was such a lusty song.

Perhaps it never occurred to her that anyone would ever insist upon the sentimental dogma of some money's legitimacy. On the other hand, perhaps it was precisely money's hypocrisy which fueled her rebellion. To compound the confusion, if Suzanne was an agnostic of money's dogmas, she had to be described as an atheist of love's guaranteed truths. "Love and marriage," she could say, "have nothing in common."

The history of her affair and her marriage to Count André de Montreuil contains, therefore, a number of ambivalencies—and their interpretation may depend upon the faith of the observer. The difficulty in accounting for the miracle of Suzanne's marriage is complicated because Suzanne abandoned our collaboration on her biography in the spring of 1971—at approximately the same time she began her affair with André de Montreuil. Thereafter, I had to rely upon third-party witnesses to reconstruct what happened. Some would later explain that the alliance of Suzanne and André was a marriage of convenience—of money and ambition and greed. These exegeses may have elements of truth in them. Others claimed that the Count André de Montreuil was just another of Suzanne's crazy adventures—an interpretation also possibly true. Then there were those determined sentimentalists who insisted that in André, Suzanne had met her fate, and at last had found true love.

After her funeral I had to search for clues in my notebooks and through the tapes of our interviews. One tape fragment showed that as we talked in her library on a Saturday afternoon, we had wandered from the principal events of her life into a discussion of love. On the tape, I could hear her extraordinary voice, enunciating clearly, precise but never earnest, and always charming, because laughter bubbled along just beneath the surface of everything she said: "Love is the most dangerous of all crimes."

On the tape, I could hear my own voice pursuing Suzanne with questions in what I would have to admit was a style of eerie stupidity.

"Because in love," she answered, "someone must be robbed of their illusions. A love affair can begin in a second, but then it has no alternative but to go on. The clock never stops ticking. The moment arrives, sooner or later, when one lover or the other wakes up. The first one to get their feet back on the ground survives.

"Ah, yes, marriage—but that's an entirely different matter," she continued. "That's a business—like a shop, in which the partners open the doors each morning, and roll down the awnings, and at the end of the day divide the profits earned from customers. At night, marriage partners go to bed, but the next day they expect to do more or less the same thing as they did the day before. Marriage lacks passion, terror, violence, risk. It is consistent. Love, on the contrary, is a gamble."

I advanced the cliché that the greatest crimes were always done in the name of love. Suzanne tossed it away as if she were getting rid of the tissue paper that wrapped the gift. "No, no, silly. Love itself is the ultimate crime. That is its marvelous danger. Someone's going to have to give themselves up. Someone's going to get caught."

There again was my voice on the tape, proposing that many dangerous activities were not crimes.

"Sports," was her answer in a flash.

Love, I offered as my next banality, was said to be the greatest of sports.

"When played as a sport, it's not dangerous. Might as well play checkers. When played for high stakes, that is something else again."

Because love was dangerous, or a gamble, did not necessarily make it a crime. I thought an argument could be made that risks were the means by which societies advanced, and therefore love affairs did not have to be considered the moral equivalents of war, and so forth.

"And so forth," she said. She was getting impatient. "Look here. Someday, just once, wouldn't you like to rob a bank?"

"No?" I remembered how she had raised one eyebrow. "Wouldn't you be more alive for those few moments than at any other time in your life? Not for the money, silly, for what it would feel like! There you would be, telling everyone to get those hands up high—way up! Then you'd have to move fast, scooping up the cash into your bag, and then backing away carefully to the door."

She had embarrassed me—and for reasons I did not entirely want to understand. I explained that robbing a bank seemed foolish to me; that I would have nothing to gain from it; that it might well cost me more than I could afford; that I could see no reason to take such a gamble; that I thought the consequences of being caught at it were too awful.

"Exactly!" Suzanne said. "You don't object to the crime. You only are afraid to take the risk."

There was a long pause, a silence between us. She was apparently imagining for herself the drama of my capture, or perhaps she was thinking of her own.

"There is a difference," she picked up again, "between love for schoolgirls and love for a grown woman. A schoolgirl falls in love innocently. She says something like 'I can't believe this is happening to me, to me!' She must fight back the desire to tell everyone. She wants to leap up and scream, 'I'm in love, I'm in love, I'm in love!' She does things like ripping petals from daisies."

I could see no crime in innocent love, but Suzanne had no use for any footnotes.

"Nothing much ever comes of all that, usually, except tears and regrets. It's like young punks who stick up bank tellers, and set off all the alarms for something like one hundred and sixty-two dollars, and get caught. Schoolgirls always pretend how indignant they are about their lost love, or innocence, or whatever it is that schoolgirls are always losing."

It was a scene, I thought, often reconstructed in sonnets—particularly by young men, who longed for their love or claimed they were victims of indifferent beauty.

"Yes," Suzanne said, "I suppose so. Appalling! I mean something different: love without all that stupid innocence.

"A love affair when conducted by a grown woman should be deliberately guilty—or what's the point? It takes planning, and experience, and there must be dangers. You check it out, and you'll see: no experienced bank robber goes after the bank for just the money. They do it because that's when they are alive again."

Yet the professionals get caught too.

"And when a woman gets caught for being in love"—Suzanne was sure of herself—"she should know by then enough maneuvers and loopholes and legal rights to get away with it . . . the way bank robbers usually do. She has the right to remain silent, the right to counsel of her choice, all that. She can usually plead guilty to some lesser charge, take the rap for a year, and get paroled for good behavior!"

I wanted to prolong the discussion and searched about for some handy means. I cited to her that bank robbery was considered a crime of violence, whereas love between consenting adults was usually considered, at the very worst, a victimless crime.

Suzanne's response was a happy laugh: "Nonsense!"

My tape recording was dated Saturday, April 17, 1971. By then, according to Aunt Nellie, Suzanne's adventure with André de Montreuil had already been underway for more than two months. "Of course I'm sure," Aunt Nellie said. "I remember quite distinctly how they met. I introduced them in February 1971."

After Suzanne's funeral, in 1976, Mrs. Ellen Burns was not anxious to be interviewed, and she put me off for the first ten months of 1977. At first her response was, in summary, that I was wasting my time and ought to find some more rewarding topic. "One of the things you'll have to learn about Suzanne," she said, "is that she didn't leave a trace."

When Aunt Nellie finally understood that Suzanne had originally commissioned a biography and that I had in my possession something like seventy-six hours of tapes, she consented, partly, I think, out of her own curiosity. "You mean," she asked, "it is Suzanne's voice on those tapes?"

Aunt Nellie finally agreed to be interviewed in November 1977 on a Wednesday at four o'clock at the University Club. At the door, I explained I expected to meet Mrs. Burns. I was then directed to an anteroom of the "ladies' dining room," where I could cool my heels until Mrs. Burns arrived to secure a table for tea. The situation for a visitor—a non-member—to the University Club's facilities for "ladies" was awkward. The anteroom is in fact no more than a narrow hallway, where a pink brocaded couch is situated exactly opposite the ladies' room door. I waited on that pink couch for nearly an hour, inspecting the entrances and exits of several dozen members' wives, while "the ladies" freshened up after matinee performances on Broadway or shopping expeditions to Bendel's. I had the opportunity to reflect that of all the privileges of power perhaps the most significant was the ability to make everyone else wait.

When Aunt Nellie did finally arrive, she was dressed in a style best described as handsome—a black gabardine tailored suit, a crepe shirt, and black pumps. She gave the impression by both costume and manners that she was as much an executive as any other member of the University Club—despite the listing as an "associate" because she was merely a widow. She let the maitre d' lead us to our table, and she followed. She then ordered, as if I had already agreed, "Just tea, Paul, and some of those little sandwiches, please."

That was it: no apologies for the hour's wait. She didn't waste time with her first questions, either: "At what point," she wanted to know, "did you quit on Suzanne's biography?"

I explained that I hadn't stopped at all, and was unlikely to quit now.

"How many others have you talked to?"

I considered where I might draw the line: I said I had talked to a great many of Suzanne's associates and friends.

Aunt Nellie countered: "There's really no trace of her, you know. People will say you're just making it up. How are you going to handle that?"

As far as I was concerned, there were enough "traces," as she had put it, to satisfy me. As to how I would handle it, I wasn't

sure yet, but I thought it would be as fiction—a novel. Aunt
Nellie busied herself with her tea, adjusting by small spoonfuls
the amount of sugar she deemed to be just right. Then, as if reas-
suring herself one more time, she asked again when my tapes
with Suzanne had stopped. I answered truthfully that I had no
tapes after April 1971.

She relaxed. And she began to explain that she had invited
Count André de Montreuil to her house in Saratoga for the weekend. She had invited a number of other "interesting people
who did interesting things—for the second weekend in February,
1971."

She could recall the weekend exactly, because it started to
snow Friday night, it snowed all day Saturday, "and it was still
snowing right through Sunday morning, as a matter of fact."

Adam Shepherd had sent out the invitations for her, she said.
"Adam always handled all those details for me quite nicely. The
telephone calls and all the arrangements." The guests were old
friends of hers, but actually she had known André de Montreuil
for a number of years too. "No, not well, just seen him from time
to time at charity dinners, or the Nine O'Clocks—they're dinner dances, you know. André made a very handsome dancing
partner."

She insisted that there had been no special point to her asking
André de Montreuil to join her winter weekend group—he was
no more than an available extra man to her.

"André?" Aunt Nellie was being evasive. "Well, I would describe him as not being physically attractive in the same way as
my Adam. André is"—she searched for the right words—"he is
exact, very precise, neat. Everything about him is quiet,
dignified, well ordered. He was always so sure of himself, self-
contained. Dignified, I guess, is the word I have been looking
for. That's it, dignified." Then she wanted me to understand how
important it was to remember that "André stood up straight. A
gentleman, in that sense."

As opposed, I put it, to Adam Shepherd, who was not a gentleman? And there was a moment when I feared the subject would
be closed. But Aunt Nellie apparently regained her composure
enough to continue. She agreed that André was about sixty,
much closer to her own age than Adam Shepherd. She was quite

sure that André's title had meant nothing to her. "It is a legitimate French title," she pointed out. "Prerevolution, and quite a
famous old French family, in fact. The de Montreuils served as
Ministers of Finance for Louis XV and Louis XVI, but titles
mean nothing to me."

Her conclusion about titles was that they were only useful to
get appointments at the hairdresser. They no longer had any
meaning. "Continental flair" had nothing to do with it either.
"That is the kind of trash," Aunt Nellie said firmly, "only shop-
girls believe. A man's a man, no matter which fork he picks up."

Yet she would admit that because André was French, it might
have made some difference to her. It was often true, she agreed,
that otherwise sensible women can be foolish about a man who
is a foreigner. "I suppose," she sighed, "it could happen to anyone. Although by the time a woman is sixty, wouldn't you think
she would be immune to all the childhood diseases?

"Oh, yes, you could say that I have always been particularly
fond about the French, especially the French nobility," said the
heiress of American Syrup. "It's because they have lost all their
wars. Gives them a different attitude, entirely different than
Americans have. They've had to deal with the most awful cruel-
ties in some practical way, and then go about their business."

She paused to examine the plain gold wedding band she still
wore on the third finger of her left hand as the widow of John
Patrick Burns. She used her thumb and forefinger to twist it
thoughtfully. "Look," she said, "if what I wanted was André de
Montreuil I wouldn't have to give you or anyone else any explanation of why."

There was in her voice the resigned tone of a fatalist, and
since I thought that a confession of some sort was being delivered over to me, I waited. But when she resumed, it was with
philosophy.

"You'll see." She was playing with Squire Burns's ring as if she
could not let go. "Age has nothing to do with it. I can tell you
what it is like. The blood pulses. You are warmed by a growing
enthusiasm. You suffer what can only be described as bursts of
real pain. You are helpless. You revel in the inability to control
the outcome. You would agree to anything at all to relieve the
tension. That's what love is like. And for a woman, at any age,

one act of love is worth more than a lifetime of conscientious devotion. What if that is just philosophy, as you put it? In the end so is everything else.

"All right," she agreed, "what happened began perfectly sensibly. André was one of a dozen guests for the weekend. I had planned dinner for twelve Saturday night, but by noon, because of the snow, it was obvious that the photographer woman—I can't recall her name for the moment—would not be able to fly into Albany Airport. And even if she had, I couldn't have sent the car to pick her up. So I was short one woman for dinner and I asked Suzanne to join us. She was nearby, and I thought of her almost as a daughter."

That weekend, Suzanne was also upstate, because she was supervising a skiing party of Angelique's young friends—Angelique was about nineteen, and the young people were skiing at Bromley. After dark, Suzanne drove over to Aunt Nellie's place with Enrique Cardinale as her escort. Which made thirteen for dinner —not that Aunt Nellie was superstitious, but thirteen was always awkward to seat. She had two round tables set, one for six and the other for seven.

Suzanne arrived late, and Aunt Nellie had no alternative except to hold up dinner until Suzanne could have one drink. Suzanne was blooming with excitement, telling stories of what a devil of a time she had driving over through the blizzard. The roads were being plowed—they were always very good about plowing the roads upstate—but the wind was blowing drifts right back across them. According to Aunt Nellie, Suzanne made it sound "as if she had just returned from the North Pole with Admiral Byrd."

Before dinner was announced, Aunt Nellie noticed that Suzanne's eyes were especially brilliant and her cheeks were flushed as if with fever. "I assumed it was from the snowstorm," Aunt Nellie recalled. "They were going to be seated next to each other at dinner, but I did not have either the time, or the sense, to rearrange the place cards."

Aunt Nellie would not admit that women fall in love arbitrarily. Nor would she agree that Suzanne and André had caught sight of each other's secret desires in some mysterious flash of recognition. "That's middle-class psychiatric pap," she said, and dismissed it. She had read all that "junk" in the magazines for years, and she had heard it a thousand times at cocktail parties. "It only matches the facts for bourgeoisie women from Bronxville. Suzanne knew better than that.

"The point was," Aunt Nellie said, "that by the time Suzanne and André had sat next to each other for twenty minutes at dinner it was perfectly obvious Suzanne no longer gave a damn."

Aunt Nellie agreed that perhaps Suzanne was bored. God knows, Aunt Nellie could understand that: all those lawyers Suzanne employed did whatever they were told to do; and all those managers of her businesses were probably no different from the ones Aunt Nellie employed; fat, obsequious and dull. God knows, Suzanne had tamed everything around her, "and believe me," Aunt Nellie said, "I know the feeling.

"But the instant I signaled dinner was over and suggested that we would have coffee in the living room, Suzanne challenged André to a game of backgammon, and openly used the excuse of the match to separate him from the others."

Mindful of his responsibilities as Aunt Nellie's consort, Adam Shepherd took up her cause, insisting a bit too loudly that everyone was expected in the living room. Suzanne ignored Adam's protests. By then, in Aunt Nellie's opinion, it was too late to stop it without an awkward and indignant scene. Suzanne's own aide-de-camp, Enrique Cardinale, was confused at first about which mistress he was to obey, but eventually Enrique could not stay away, and joined Suzanne in the library. She would allow Enrique to fix drinks for her and her opponent, but it was clear Suzanne was going to have André for herself.

In Aunt Nellie's library Suzanne and André took seats opposite each other across the backgammon table. They must have been able to hear the talk and laughter drifting in from the living room, but they were quiet, and deadly serious, and Enrique had enough sense to be quiet himself. They began putting the pieces between them into their assigned places. André could see what she was after. He was cool and distant, and even more confident of his powers. She flushed, then brought herself under control: she would see about that. "What do you suggest the stakes should be, *mon ami?*"

He knew few women who could use their eyes so effectively.

"I will play," André replied in precise French, "for any stake you choose."

He had used to her the familiar *tu,* which only children, servants and lovers should expect to hear. He had said it with a thin smile, almost pure challenge. She sent it back to him: "I see that you are an excellent fencer. I hope you play backgammon as well."

"One must be fortunate to succeed at love and dice."

She proposed they each name his or her own stake, play an eleven-point match; "winner take all" was the phrase she emphasized. She would collect from him a check for ten thousand dollars on the spot if she won. She watched his smile expand. Some of his smile was due to a slight overbite, like a shark's. If that was excessive, she was in a mood to exaggerate. "It is up to you to name what stake you choose, *mon seigneur.*"

She lowered her lashes as if she had already surrendered. He was thrilled that he had assessed the situation correctly. He began to lay out his rules. He would collect her in person. It seemed to him, he explained, that it would be exceedingly dangerous for anyone to drive home in the midst of a blizzard. Therefore, to ensure her safety, he would harbor her against the winter's night in his suite. If he won.

Enrique would say later: "I thought I would die."

Suzanne roared with laughter, her head thrown back and her teeth flashing with joy. "Then, you must guard yourself well," she said. "For I intend to win. I have no choice, if I am to protect my innocence."

"Nothing," he said with a courtier's nod of the head, "leaves so little mark as the passing of a woman's virtue."

"You are heartless."

"I am your devoted servant, madame."

"I shall show you no mercy."

"I ask for none."

"Play, monster; you are boasting."

They began to play with an intensity so grim that it looked as if death hovered over the table. Suzanne won the first two games. Then André settled down and ran off six points in a row. They exchanged games until the score stood at nine apiece. As if drawn by the mysterious silence, the other members of the dinner party slipped one by one into the library to watch. Nothing Aunt Nellie could offer, nor anything Adam Shepherd could invent, could keep them away. They stood in a rough circle around the table between the two players. Someone asked, almost embarrassed to interrupt: "What's the stake?"

"Ten thousand dollars," said Enrique without looking up.

After the second roll of the next game, Suzanne doubled.

For the first time since they began, André spoke. "You are too daring," he pointed out. "No matter what happens now, you have made this the last game. You might have saved your double for still one more. You take risks you don't need."

"Don't try to teach your grandmother how to suck eggs," she said.

"*Comment?*"

"It's an American expression." Suzanne was impatient with him. "Do you accept my double or not?"

He accepted. As soon as they resumed play, his dice began to accumulate what appeared to be an insurmountable lead. With what could have been smugness, he was punishing her for having failed to calculate correctly the mathematics of the game. The spectators around them had to agree with him. They were hushed, waiting for justice to be done.

Then Suzanne started the most miraculous series of rolls. She needed double fours to enter a piece sent up to the bar. They appeared for her. She rattled her cup again, and blew curses into it, and double sixes answered.

"So," he was finally moved to say, "is that how they play in America?"

Her eyes blazed an answer at him. She was furious. Without letting him look away, she said: "Double sixes again." Then she rolled them. She let him look down at the dice first. When he looked up at her, she was smiling. She saw the astonishment in his eyes. She dropped her lashes again, as if she had just curtsied for a king.

Someone among those standing about the table whistled through his teeth. André played from his roll. Suzanne called, "Double sixes," once more, as if she wanted to be sure that he got the point. Again she rolled them. With an unfeigned admiration, one of the other women could be heard saying to her companion: "My God, what luck!"

They ran the rest of the game out, but André had lost. Without standing up, he drew his wallet from his breast pocket, tore out a check, and wrote the sum of ten thousand dollars to Mrs. Richard A. Lyle, Jr. As he handed it across the table to her, the others applauded him.

Suzanne folded his check in half, lengthwise, and without looking, handed it up over her shoulder to Enrique. Then she stood. As André rose, she went to him and put her arm through his, inquiring at the same time of Aunt Nellie if she preferred to have everyone in the living room now. Since Aunt Nellie also thought the living room would be more comfortable, Suzanne and André led the way arm in arm.

By then the dinner party had no more than an hour to go. Aunt Nellie's guests had their nightcaps. Gradually the talk fluttered down from its peaks of excitement. There was the usual discussion of summer plans, the latest movies and novels, the gossip about others they had seen or heard from. During this wrap-up hour Aunt Nellie had no alternative but to suggest to Suzanne and Enrique how foolhardy it would be to attempt to drive home through the snow. Beyond the windows it was continuing to fall. Aunt Nellie said she had two extra suites for them. Suzanne and Enrique would have to stay; that was settled, then.

Meanwhile Suzanne never left André's side. She had nestled in next to him upon the couch, as wives often do with their husbands after dinner, demonstrating by proximity, by familiar fingers upon his arm, the proprietary interest she held in the property at hand. Suzanne and André looked as if they were a couple accustomed to each other by a marriage of many years. They never looked at each other as young lovers do. Instead their heads turned together toward whatever attracted their common attention. Enrique was fascinated, and happy for her.

At last the time came for all to make their good nights and go to the suites Aunt Nellie had assigned. With Aunt Nellie hovering to give directions and Enrique following as if in the baggage train, Suzanne walked arm in arm with André to the foot of the grand staircase, where she stopped.

She turned toward him, placing her hand against his chest with her fingers spread out against his silk dinner shirt. It looked almost as if she were about to push him away, but her touch was light and tender. She searched with her fingertips for his heartbeat. Perhaps André saw it coming, because his eyes turned sad.

She was gentle, but firm: "It is such a shame that your luck turned."

"Luck is a fickle mistress."

"Yes," Suzanne agreed. "So she is."

There was without any doubt a tenderness in the look they exchanged then, but Suzanne continued: "Nevertheless, you may call me in the city next week. In the meantime I want to be sure you do not sleep a wink tonight, not until dawn. In the morning Enrique and I will sneak out of here like thieves so that there will be nothing to help you forget tonight. I swear that I will be thinking of no one but you, but you have lost, and so instead I shall take Enrique for tonight. It's a pity, because he always does exactly what he is told. Do you understand?"

Enrique did not see why it was a pity at all. He spent a night in paradise. He did the very best he could to satisfy every whim Suzanne invented.

Within a week, however, he was reduced once again to Suzanne's architect, and nothing more. Count André de Montreuil and Mrs. Richard A. Lyle, Jr., were instantly admitted as a working pair in all the comings and goings of the beautiful people. It was said they were a handsome couple, just right for each other, such a pleasure to be about. There was no question that they complemented each other's presence. Accordingly, since he was free to do so, André de Montreuil presented a formal proposal of marriage in May 1971.

Suzanne refused him at first. Their negotiations continued for over five months. Only one fragment of these was preserved, and so not all of Suzanne's objections can ever be known. The only surviving evidence was kept by Michael Hassett, an artist then only twenty-six years of age and not an entirely reliable source. During the summers, he occupied the studio cottage on the far side of the lake at Suzanne's Saratoga place. In the studio he worked all week at his canvases, keeping to himself. On the weekends, if he was lonely, he walked across the dam then under construction to the big house. He would join the groups assembled there. He liked to spend time in the company of Angelique.

One Saturday in August, after a luncheon given on the esplanade behind the house, Michael Hassett listened as André de Montreuil proposed once again.

"If we get married," Suzanne argued, "we cannot be lovers."

"It would still be possible," André said.

"It is never possible."

"There are married couples who remain lovers."

"Never. It is not the same thing."

André would not give up: "Marriage has its advantages too. It is forever. We could grow old together."

"That's an ugly argument."

"There are beauties to old age, and it comes in any case." He was getting angry but was still precise.

"With a lover a woman always has the privilege of dismissing him. She can *assassiner* a lover at will. With a husband it is not possible. She has no choice but to keep him, so he loses interest and goes away after other women."

"What you fear," he said, "is that I would *trompe* you?"

"If you were free, you would. As long as I can *assassiner* you, you are not free. As soon as we were married, off you would go. That is how men are. I know."

"But husbands must fear cuckoldry too."

"They should, but they don't. It is a great convenience to them. It gives them a license. They make a great deal of fuss, but they are always pleased, if they have any sense."

"Suzanne, you are impossible. In France we say that if two couples get into a Citroën to have dinner together, they drive away according to their class. If they are poor, the two husbands sit together in the front and the two wives in the rear. The husbands talk about football, and the wives about fish. They are happy. If they are bourgeois, one couple sits in front and the other couple sits in back. It makes the bourgeoisie happy to talk about the stocks on the bourse, and clothes. If they are aristocrats, one wife goes with the other's husband to the front seat, and so in the back of the Citroën they have also exchanged. They sit close to each other and talk about nothing at all."

"I don't see the point of that story, André."

"There's no point to the story. There's no logic to marriage either, Suzanne."

"Then, why do you keep insisting upon it?"

"Because I am afraid to die alone."

Her answer was: "Poof!"

That appeared to end it, according to Michael Hassett. Whether his recollection of that one conversation is accurate or not, the New York *Times* recorded that Mrs. Richard A. Lyle, Jr., was married by a judge to Count André de Montreuil on Election Day, November 2, 1971. They were married in front of the windows of her penthouse at 30 Central Park South, with a view of Central Park behind them. "Miss Angelique Lyle was her mother's maid of honor."

Because André's business interests required it, the new Countess de Montreuil bought, redecorated and opened still another house on "Q" Street in Georgetown, Washington, D.C. The household she managed for her husband included entertaining two or three nights each week. Their activity was an ambassadorial effort equal to those of many great nations, but Suzanne was accustomed to what she was expected to accomplish, having held the same kind of dinners and fetes in New York.

They did not cut their ties to New York, but flew up when they could. Suzanne's place at Saratoga became more important to them as the only place they could get away to. The differences between André's activities and Suzanne's field of action were that André's were international, while Suzanne's continued to be continental. Yet a merging of their interests had advantages: they could combine their intelligence activities, even if they often had to bribe different sets of bureaucrats. In the legislature, they were often bribing the same representatives, but for different reasons.

Suzanne thought Washington insufferably boring. It had not changed one whit since the days she had lived in Falls Church with Dick Lyle. She had James Moriarity drive her out to the airport where she had learned to fly, but Seven Corners was gone, buried under a cloverleaf interchange, and the airport strip itself had been replaced by another gigantic shopping center. "The trouble with Washington," she had said, "was that it was populated by men and women who believed they juggled the fate of the world. They insisted they were powerful. But it was like watching a clown in the circus toss the same orange—and only one—and catch it again, and then take a bow as if he deserved applause for his miserable trick." She had been in Washington during the Eisenhower administration, but the Nixon years were even more banal—"if such a thing could be possible."

Since their California dark horse was now President, she lunched with Amedeo Scutari from time to time over small matters that might be improved by her attention. "Just be sure," he reminded her, "that you do not lose touch with the smells and sounds of your own village." She assured him that she would not. She had a first-class staff in New York. She was sure that John Putnam, Sam Harper, Billy G. Fenn, Miss Freddy and John David Garraty could handle anything that came up. She was keeping in close touch with them every day. "It's not what they do, it's how they smell," said Amedeo Scutari. "And what you can smell, that they will never learn."

Yet André's activities and her own were increasingly intertwined. His calling card listed him as president of an investment banking partnership in Geneva: it was not so very different from the card her father had once carried. Actually, most of his partners' interests were in the United States, or managed through the banks on Paradise Island. At the end of the 1960s, mutual funds and insurance companies capitalized with Eurodollars had collapsed one after another. André de Montreuil walked through the litter of these collapsed houses looking in the wreckage for those items that might be worth salvage. "It was a junk business," he explained. "But junk is a very good business, especially junk money."

A mere listing of one complex worth billions that had collapsed in the Bahamas gave the flavor of André's activities: International Bancorp, Ltd.; Bahamas Commonwealth Bank; Overseas Development Bank; Transglobal Financial Services; International Investors Trust Management Corp.; Venture Management Company. An interest in these international instruments of capital, along with interests in real estate ventures, rock-crushing machines at Chilean copper mines, diesel-operated cotton gins in Brazil, and construction loans for dormitories at the University of

Mexico were supervised by Count André de Montreuil and his associates through the Providence Holding Company. Its name was derived from the most ordinary circumstances: "Providence" happened to be the name of the island on which was the capital of the Bahamas archipelago.

The specialty of Providence Holding, and of Count André de Montreuil, was sometimes called "mergers and acquisitions," more frequently referred to as "debt management," and at other times tossed carelessly into a portmanteau described as "the bond business." Regardless of how the function was described, it was a branch of the science of capital as old and as honored as any other. From the beginning of the history of investment, each gamble ending in success was necessarily matched by another, ending in failure; for each Columbus there were scores of navigators whose discoveries and fame were lost at sea. Hence there always had to be someone to see to the debts that could never be paid. The family of André de Montreuil, through wars and revolutions, pestilence and famine, had survived into the twentieth century precisely because it concentrated upon the liabilities created by ambition.

It was no easy task. For every railroad completed across the American continent, there were dozens abandoned. For every Comstock lode mined in the high Sierras, there were hundreds whose shafts cut into beds of iron pyrites. Each time a well came gushing up in the Gulf of Mexico, ten others had sent their bits down into salt water. Someone had to take responsibility for the situation when things didn't quite work out.

Count André de Montreuil had inherited the ability, it could be said, to sense a struggling company at a distance of a thousand miles, just as sharks instinctively have always known when blood has spread beneath the surface. His corporation— Providence Holding—performed useful social functions by tearing the meat off the dead and dying assets of corporations that would otherwise pollute the environment of commerce, industry and banking. To carry out this ancient duty, however, it was necessary to avoid any sentimental distinctions about what property belonged to whom. After all, if the bonds could not be paid to the bondholders, then logically the legal instrument that had issued these monetary promises was dead. Nothing rightfully was owned by anyone. Nice distinctions about what might be "mine" and all that was "thine" no longer were applicable. Yet misconceptions lingered about the useful work performed by André de Montreuil and Providence Holding.

Fortunately, Count André de Montreuil never needed to explain the realities of his occupation to his wife. She was as practical as he was about the social landscape through which they were traveling. They could share with each other the quicksilver excitement of each new day. Their marriage was happy because it was based upon common understandings and devoted to joint objectives. The Count and Countess de Montreuil were the epitome of success in Washington and New York, representatives of all that was admired.

If they had been innocents, they might have felt helpless or put upon, or been on the defensive against some of the envious charges brought against them. Instead they could put all that aside, and turn any charges away as "without foundation." Suzanne could easily show that she had no connection whatever to a series of spectacular jewel robberies in Saratoga one summer; nor was she acquainted in any way with any member of the gang that purportedly had planned the escapades. To the libel that she had "fingered" the jobs, she could reply that she was nowhere near the scene of the crimes at the time. André could demonstrate that he was not connected in any demonstrable way with the buffoonery of Watergate. To the slander that his investment partners had obtained dispensation from prosecution under the antitrust laws in the case of two mergers, he could honestly answer that he had never held any discussions with either the attorney general or the White House on that topic. Neither the Count nor the Countess de Montreuil had any qualms about legal loopholes, maneuvers, investigations or machinations that passed for law. As a result of their practical education, André and Suzanne knew that few laws remained that were based upon any consideration except those imposed by conscience or taste.

14

Sam Harper's Lament
1972–76

"AFTER Suzanne married André," Sam Harper said, "she really
didn't need me any more."

Consequently Sam Harper, Jr., retired at the age of fifty-five
from daily participation in the law partnership of Fletcher, Mahoney, Browne, Adams and Harper. Although Suzanne continued to telephone from time to time to ask for Sam's advice, her
calls were never on any significant question. After the summer of
1973 John Putnam also ceased to consult Sam Harper on the
designs of new corporate plans. Thereafter there were few reasons to invite Sam Harper to the meetings conducted in Suzanne's administrative offices at 200 Park Avenue. Finally, by
1974 Billy G. Fenn had made the situation clear by failing to return Sam's phone calls even when complex tax questions were at
issue.

After Sam retired in 1972, he moved into a newly constructed,
high-rise apartment building at the corner of Ninety-first Street
and York Avenue. In January 1976 I stopped by Sam's apartment
late in the afternoon. The building might be described as a version of "Miami modern" built on Manhattan Island by mistake.
If all of Sam's tastes were taken into account, his choice seemed

somewhat out of character. He shrugged at the building's sterile tower and explained, "But I like the view."

His apartment was on the thirty-second floor, and glass window walls wrapped around its entire north side. From that height, he could see fifteen miles across Queens to Nassau County. He pointed out the Throgs Neck and Whitestone bridges in the northeast. He kept binoculars upon the window sill to inspect any river traffic that caught his attention as it moved through the tides under the Triborough Bridge at Hell Gate.

To the north his aerie looked out across the Bronx, and he pointed out the Bronx County Courthouse. He said that at night the span of the George Washington Bridge, in the northwest, looked as if it were strung with a pair of diamond necklaces. We stepped out on the miniature balcony hung on the west side of his living room, and we looked down upon uptown Manhattan: across the reservoir to the West Side, and as far south as the Essex House, the Park Lane, and the Plaza—lined up along Central Park South. I asked if he could identify Suzanne's building for me. "Yes," he admitted, "at night if I use my binoculars I can pick out the lights of her penthouse, next to the Park Lane."

Sam's apartment had a small kitchen and a large, L-shaped living room. He used one bedroom as his bachelor digs, but he had converted the second bedroom into a library. There was a service bar with a small refrigerator so that when he had visitors he would not need to interrupt the discussion to fill drinks. I settled into a comfortable leather armchair with a scotch and soda and Sam seated himself at his desk.

Along one wall were his shelves of law books, in long, orderly rows. On the opposite wall Sam had installed glass shelves to display his collection of glass paperweights. Five rows, each holding six perfect examples, sparkled with a marvelous brilliance under the cold fluorescent lights that shone down upon them. Each paperweight was set vertically upon a stand of its own. Without leaving his desk, Sam Harper could see the butterfly, or the Japanese pine, or any of the designs fixed in each crystal center. As I looked across these curiosities, Sam chuckled: "Garraty insists they look like rows of glass eyes. I suppose you could say they do.

"John David Garraty is the same as always," Sam mused. "He's lost almost all his hair—practically bald, and I've tried to tell him he is grossly overweight and courting a heart attack, sooner or later, but John David just waves it away with another cigar, as ebulliently as he ever did. He's still telling the latest stories going around town and laughing harder at his own punch lines than anyone else." Sam imitated his old friend: "How d'ya like that one, pal? Ain't that a pistol?"

Sam ran his fingers through his own coarse hair. He had kept it all, although it had turned completely white. He said he kept fit by swimming for an hour every afternoon at the University Club pool. "And as often as I can, I walk, rather than take a taxi, to those appointments when my legal advice is still sought."

He no longer played squash, but he had taken up golf. He had attempted to convince Garraty that golf was a fine game. "The only result of my sermons on the necessity of keeping fit and the pleasures of golf was that John David hired a Beechcraft and a pilot and we flew down to Augusta for the Masters Tournament. I walked the course with the gallery, but the clubhouse bar was as near as John David ever got to fairway or green."

Yet Suzanne's two oldest friends were grateful for each other's company. They went together to Madison Square Garden for important Knicks games. They used up a day here, or a night there, at Belmont playing the horses, or in Garraty's box at Yankee Stadium. In 1974 they bought, between them, a twenty-four-foot Chris-Craft sport fisherman, which they kept at Dick Sage's boatyard in East Hampton. "As long as there's plenty of beer," Sam said, "fishing is a sport John David can tolerate."

After Christmas 1974 they flew together to Las Vegas with a pair of charmers supplied by Miss Freddy. No matter how they passed the time, they talked about baseball, hockey, and sometimes politics, "but never about Suzanne and André."

To occupy his days, Sam had accepted a professorship of law at New York University. It was an appointment he could have obtained on his own merits, but he was grateful nevertheless for John David's intervention. Sam found that evenings were sometimes difficult to fill. He corrected exams and prepared his lectures, but when he was younger he had taken pleasure in the hours he spent reading the law. Now with accumulated experience behind him there were few decisions that could capture his imagination. "I look forward, therefore, to those occasions when visitors drop by and share a drink and some talk."

Sam rose from the chair at his desk, taking with him one of the precious eggs Suzanne had collected. He crossed to my chair, placed the egg in my palm, returned to his desk and sat down, saying: "Exhibit number one."

I hefted the egg. "I've got one like this too."

"That one is coral. Very difficult to get coral these days."

"Suzanne gave me one for Christmas about five years ago."

"Yes, she often gives them away for Christmas. The coral one in your hand comes from Tiffany. Costs about six hundred dollars. Most of the ones she gives away she steals from Georg Jensen."

"On Fifth Avenue?"

"No, Jensen moved to Madison in 1970."

"Do you think she boosted this one from Tiffany? That couldn't have been easy."

"She always steals them. You don't believe me?"

"What if I do believe you? She does a lot of crazy things. You know that. She always has."

Sam Harper seemed to find it awkward to be frank. Perhaps he felt what he had to say would be difficult to explain. "I think Suzanne is headed for trouble."

I put the egg on the side table next to my chair. Sam Harper was advancing his deductions cautiously, because I supposed, he wanted to make sure I would understand the complexities. "When she steals eggs," he continued, "she's not in any real danger. If she gets caught, they'll make a fuss but drop it. They'll settle up. She can afford it, and they'll just write it off as a quirk."

"By now," I said, "she could probably buy the store."

"But she steals something pointless from them, just the same."

"Sam, that happens all the time. The stores have procedures to deal with shoplifting. Especially at the better stores. It's always a woman who could easily afford what she has boosted. In many cases, she has enough in her purse to pay for whatever it is she's stolen. It's a standard psychiatric problem."

"Yes, of course it is," Sam said. "She steals the eggs because she hopes the store will catch her. There will be a rumpus."

"But then she'll get out of it."

Sam examined the cuticles of his fingernails before he continued. Then he said, "My information is that André and Suzanne are planning to grab control of one of the major New York City banks."

I said I didn't see the connection: "What does that have to do with stealing eggs?"

"Well, for one thing, she won't have the money in her purse if they catch her at it."

It seemed to me that Suzanne and André wouldn't be trying to rob a bank. If they had some sort of plan to acquire control—by buying stock or making a tender offer—that was the way the game was played. I asked if Sam knew which bank.

He appeared to be turning my question this way and that. He freshened my scotch and soda and refilled his own. Finally, he said he was not entirely positive about which bank. Even if he knew, he thought it would be a serious violation of confidence to name the bank to an editor at a news magazine. In any event, it didn't matter. The point was that Suzanne would soon be in great danger; couldn't I see that?

I didn't see.

"Whether you people in the media believe it or not, there is an establishment in this country. They are not going to sit still for one minute and let someone like Suzanne move in on their territory."

Perhaps I agreed with him, but instead of saying so, I asked whether the establishment which posed such a threat to Suzanne met secretly once a month, or flew to a hunting lodge hidden in the woods of Minnesota, or perhaps was called together only once each year at one of the Rockefeller resorts, where they donned black robes and chanted magic spells like sorcerers before subdividing Africa for its mineral rights.

Sam Harper decided he would have to try a different tack. He started off by explaining that for André and Suzanne there had existed from the day of their marriage a fateful place, an objective to their love, which they had agreed they would someday reach. In effect, it was a secret contract about when they could someday rest. In some marriages this contract would be fulfilled, the partners said, when the children have all grown up.

"In others," Sam continued, "husband and wife promise each other that when he retires they're going to travel. These days, thousands of marriages are held together because there is a quarter-acre lot on the west coast of Florida, all paid up in full. And that's where the marriage is headed, or at least that's what they tell each other."

I agreed that retirement villages had turned out to be lucrative investments.

"Yes," said Sam, "I suppose they are. The thing is, regardless of how far away from fulfillment a marriage contract really is, and irrespective of the distance yet to go, all happy marriages resemble each other in that the partners have always agreed at the start to arrive someday at a place where they can stop."

I thought Sam was quoting Tolstoy.

"Not quite." He smiled. "The ambition shared by André and Suzanne to seize control of a major New York City bank is an agreement that could be described as a result of natural causes."

"And if they are successful," I added, "they will live happily ever after."

Sam ignored me. "They don't see anything preposterous about it. They don't think they're overreaching. They don't see any reason to doubt their success."

"Maybe they can do it."

"It's grotesque."

"Between the two of them, Sam, maybe they have enough capital now to pull it off."

"Money has nothing to do with it. On that level it all equals out."

"The fact is," I said to him, "you *do* know which bank they're after."

"It isn't Georg Jensen, Mr. Editor. Nor Tiffany, either." He paused to see if he had made his point.

"You don't think they'll get away with it, is that it?"

Sam admitted the banks were in trouble. He agreed they had overrun their capital. He thought they had made a mistake when they created loopholes in the banking acts and then drawn legal devices such as real estate investment trusts through the loopholes. Everything they had done was authorized by Congress, but unfortunately the bubbles of these land booms burst, and the real estate divisions of the banks were unable to repay the mortgages issued, in effect, to themselves. The result of Congressional authorizations was that Federal Reserve examiners had to allow the banks to "write off" stunning losses. If it appeared that too many losses in one year would shake public confidence in any bank's liquidity, the comptroller of the currency allowed the disaster to be distributed over several years. I suggested that banking stupidity would clear the way for Suzanne's ambition.

His answer was: "Their stupidity is permanent."

But wouldn't their arrogance be Suzanne's opportunity? I cited how each manager of each division in every bank was required to compete against his own associates. Since there was competition not only between banks but within banks, loans had been made for an extraordinary list of adventures that paid marvelous interest rates to each bank's statement of profit but simultaneously increased the probability of the bank's eventual losses —exactly the kind of situation in which André de Montreuil reveled.

"No," said Sam. "The government of the United States is not going to allow a major bank to lose money."

Certainly someone had to pay. The banks had lost billions on oil-tanker loans. They had earned spectacular interest, to be sure, until the moment their tankers sank. Then the banks had suffered tremendous losses.

"Not at all," said Sam. "It's in the regulated price of the oil— except for the cost of the spills, which must be paid for from local taxes."

I cited the apartment buildings that had soared up in city after city. When they could not be rented and they defaulted on their mortgages, hundreds had to be taken over by the banks.

"On federal guarantees," Sam answered.

But in manufacturing and industry, if a company failed to meet its competition, the banks stood to lose all they had loaned.

"You mean like Lockheed."

I thought Lockheed was an exception.

Sam ignored my "exception." He pointed out that the major New York City banks had moved half of their transactions to the

Bahamas, just as Suzanne and André had done. In those islands of banking paradise and total secrecy, eighty-five per cent of all bank profits were being earned by making loans to dictators from poor and starving nations. The bank executives who arranged these loans in a babble of languages won promotions and raises, although the debts ran into the middle of the twenty-first century, and no one knew how defaulted notes would be collected without landing the United States Marines. Finally, Sam pointed out, the cities and municipalities of the United States itself, and particularly the City of New York, had issued bonds and notes and promises to pay in spiraling amounts for which there was no security at all except the full faith and credit of politicians. "A group notoriously inept at either keeping promises or desisting from making them."

Sam's library had grown gradually dimmer as the sun set and dusk faded away. Night filled the study where we sat in a gloom relieved only by the fluorescent lights shining down upon his shelves of paperweights.

"That's what banks really do," he said. "They issue paper, called money. Any mistakes they make are covered by our government. When they bought worthless paper from the City of New York, the United States Treasury guaranteed to take it off their hands at eighty per cent of its face value, no matter what it was really worth. Any notes or bonds they couldn't stuff into the trust accounts of the widows and orphans for whom they were responsible, they just gave back to the nation as a whole to pay. Keeps the system running, they say. Heads the banks win, tails everyone else loses."

I suggested that the banks must have considerable political influence to get along so well.

"Typical journalist's question. You are always looking for a conspiracy. Or ten thousand dollars in a paper bag left behind on some senator's desk. You refuse to recognize that at the heart of the American system is our banking system—isn't that so? All right, then: no one gets any bribes, it's just how things work."

"How does Suzanne's plan work?" I asked. "Explain that to me."

"Secrecy is important to her."

"I'm not giving away any secrets on Suzanne, Sam. You ought to know that by now."

He paused, but concluded, I suppose, that he could trust me. "Beginning last August, André and Suzanne started to buy shares in one of the big city banks."

"Which August?"

"This last August, 1975, five months ago."

"Which bank?"

He still wouldn't say. It didn't matter, he said. The scheme was mathematically simple: André had calculated the price of The Bank's shares, then multiplied the number of shares they needed for control to arrive at the total sum they had to raise. Actually, no more than forty per cent of The Bank's outstanding stock would be necessary to win control. André and Suzanne would not have to own all of it themselves. They needed only to get that many shares into friendly hands—shareholders who would vote with them to elect directors to The Bank's board.

I interrupted, because I didn't see how forty per cent of the voting shares would be enough to win a majority of the directors.

"It's the same thing as any election," Sam answered. "Usually a plurality is enough. Many shareholders don't vote. Others split their vote. The two major factions rarely need more than forty per cent, and sometimes less than that. Those are the rules of democracy, right? With a plurality of the votes, it's winner take all."

According to Sam, the amount necessary to buy control of The Bank was about four hundred million dollars. Some of this amount was being drawn from Suzanne's and André's own accounts. Some was being raised by André's associates in Providence Holding. Some stock in The Bank was being bought up by friends Suzanne could enlist, including Mr. Scott and his partners. The balance was being raised from two small insurance companies controlled through the Providence and Paradise Island holding companies. The total—four hundred million dollars —was a small sum to win a bank with listed assets of over nine billion.

It seemed to me the arithmetic did not make sense.

"That's because you want to believe that money is a mystery.

You genuflect before its tabernacle, but you never look inside for yourself. You just repeat the mumbo jumbo of its prayers, and hope to God it's all true."

I said that was all very well, but it didn't account for buying nine billion in assets with four hundred million dollars in stock.

Sam's explanation was that a combination of causes made the stock a bargain. The Bank's management was considered to be among the stupidest in the city—a reputation reflected in a low price for the stock but never commented upon by newspapers or magazines. Moreover, The Bank had suffered devastating losses in its real estate investments, and its foreign banking operations were managed by men chosen for the task as if ignorance were the primary requisite. They spoke no languages and knew no history, but no one dared comment—except that the price of the stock was low. Finally, no sensible observer believed The Bank's portfolio of municipal and state bonds should be rated anywhere near the value The Bank itself had put upon it. To question the value of governmental securities would be to doubt the solvency of the political system itself—and surely no responsible commentator would raise questions about American progress. Consequently the only symptom of The Bank's cumulative stupidities was the price of its stock. Despite assets listed at nine billion dollars, control of the board of directors could probably be purchased for less than four hundred million.

"As Suzanne buys The Bank's stock," I asked, "doesn't that have the effect of driving the cost of each share up?"

Sam agreed that it did, but Suzanne and André were prepared for that. The stock had already climbed from nine dollars per share to nearly fifteen dollars. Yet The Bank's executives were not yet alerted to any threat.

"Couldn't the price of the stock eventually rise beyond Suzanne's reach?"

There was some risk of that, Sam thought, but as Suzanne and André closed in upon their objective, the rising price of the stock was not entirely disadvantageous. Suzanne had been recruiting allies by making promises, just as political candidates do. The promises could not be fulfilled until after the election was won. Those who had bought stock in Suzanne's campaign might be tempted to desert, except that the paper profits they appeared to have made helped to quiet their fears. For example, Suzanne enlisted her friend Tony Scott early, and he agreed to put up forty million for the "buy pool." In addition, Tony Scott agreed to be subject to a "call" for another forty million. "As I understand it," Sam said, "he's also promised to deliver an equal amount from his associates—so Suzanne has a total for her pool from Mr. Scott amounting to one hundred and sixty million."

I had to interrupt again. I was quite positive that "pools" had been illegal since 1933. The Securities and Exchange Commission were sure to crack down on any "pool."

"Oh, yes," Sam agreed in a patient tone, "that is the law. Pools are illegal, just as you say. There are, however, no penalties assessed against victors, only against those who lose."

I wanted to know what kind of promises Suzanne had to make to enlist Tony Scott's support.

"Still looking for the bribe? Looking for the secret deal? Want the evidence of the smoking gun? It's just not done that way. Nothing shows."

I supposed it was all done with a wink and a nod.

"No," said Sam Harper. "You are still missing the point." He explained that neither Tony Scott nor his associates would appear as "owners of record," or in the case of any subpoena—if it ever came to that—as "beneficial owners." There would never be any evidence of Tony Scott's ownership of The Bank's shares. After Suzanne and André won control, there were favors they could do. For example, Mr. Scott and his associates were in trouble with the Internal Revenue Service about a number of pension funds. The Bank could agree to serve as trustee or designated manager of the disputed funds. The complaints of the Internal Revenue Service would cease, yet Mr. Scott could continue to do as he pleased. Similarly, branches of The Bank could be designated to launder the cash Mr. Scott's associates earned by the sale of cocaine and heroin. As soon as the money was exchanged at a teller's window, its source, in effect, evaporated. All perfectly legal.

In Sam Harper's opinion, the most fortunate aspect of Suzanne's timing was that just as she was advancing upon voting control of The Bank, the city of New York was finally admitting that it was bankrupt. Control of one of the city's major banks at the very moment of the city's default opened up the possibility of robbing not only The Bank itself but an entire population. "Once Suzanne controls The Bank," Sam concluded, "nothing can be denied to her."

"So you think she's got it?"

Sam got up from his desk, took my empty glass and filled it once again. He poured another for himself before he sat down again. While I waited, he sipped from his scotch, and his eyes wandered across his display of glass paperweights, as if at the center of his crystals the future was revealed.

"No," said Sam. "They'll kill her."

"Literally?"

He didn't mean it that way, he said.

I tried one last time: "Which bank is it?"

Sam Harper was going to fend me off again, but then he apparently changed his mind. "I guess it doesn't matter now," he said. "It's Aunt Nellie's bank."

I said I thought Aunt Nellie controlled American Syrup.

"Of course, of course." Sam was impatient.

But American Syrup in turn controlled The Bank?

Sam was already off again, like some ancient mariner spinning a tale of despair: Aunt Nellie's control of The Bank brought with it peculiar powers. Nine billion dollars of assets carried with them great weight, a kind of density. They made Aunt Nellie—in our society at least—a religious figure, something like a pope, whose authority on moral issues is simply not to be doubted. Once the mass of those assets, that holy authority, was set into motion, it had a momentum of its own. It could not be seized simply because Suzanne wanted it. It could not be bought with just money. Aunt Nellie's control of American Syrup and its bank created an entire army of people who were accustomed to its privileges—and they would not give up those privileges any more than bishops would give up going to Rome.

I thought describing Aunt Nellie as some kind of pope of bank shares was a bit odd.

"Suzanne," said Sam, "thinks it's another lark, but it's not."

"Maybe," I thought, "she can pull it off."

"Never. Aunt Nellie and her troops can't give it up, even if they wanted to. It's not going to be a matter of money, but of power—which has its own reasons."

"Not even," I asked, "if Suzanne and André actually own more shares than Aunt Nellie?"

"You'll see," said Sam. "It doesn't matter. You are Suzanne's biographer, and you will keep her secret so that you can certify the outcome—whichever way it goes—because you claim that history is your business. But you never approve or condemn, because you think no decision of history is ever final. You report with a vague tolerance everything you hear, while the system sways and staggers on. You believe you can always say, 'on the other hand.' And if a case comes along like Suzanne's, where you can learn how things really work, you pretend it's too complicated to understand."

I pointed out that it was nearly ten o'clock, that we had not eaten, that Elaine's was only a couple of blocks away, and that I was starving. Things couldn't really be as bad as Sam thought. Suzanne would survive, because she always had.

"Her marriage to André," he was sure, "has blinded her."

Even if it had, wasn't he hungry? "C'mon, then," I urged. "Turn off the lights on those goddamn eyeballs of yours, and let's get ourselves something to eat. John David Garraty is right. They do look like eyeballs."

We parted after dinner at Elaine's in January 1976, and I did not see Sam Harper again for nearly two years. In retrospect his analysis had elements of truth. If what happened when Suzanne attempted to grab control of Aunt Nellie's bank was to be understood, Sam Harper's lament had to be considered.

His indictment of journalists—the vague tolerance with which we report all that we witness—had its merits. To the extent we spice our stories with morsels of scandal, we enlist readers. We offer the fiction that they are participating while history is being made. Perhaps we hold their attention for only a few moments on the evening news. Perhaps we deceive for a day or two, even as long as a week. Yet there are so few ways still open for the majority of citizens to abandon themselves to experience. They have no alternative but to take the next-best thing: to listen to reports of distant events and pretend that they may somehow be involved. It is precisely this illusion of participation which provides the reason for fashionable crowds to rush first this way, then that—after whatever next catches their attention.

Some of Suzanne's recruits in her campaign to seize Aunt Nellie's bank joined Suzanne's crusade for no other reason than that "it was the latest thing." There were others who lusted to share in the distribution of spoils. Scavenging in the city's ruins might turn up something to relieve the helpless discomfort of their lives, and a connection to The Bank would provide the license they desired. Their motives would be similar to those of gluttons, except that the appetites of scavengers were limited while those of gluttons were unending. For these two related ambitions, Suzanne could promise the assets of a great bank as a support to indulge a range of tastes—from unlimited American Express card dinners at luxurious restaurants to Sparkman & Stephens cruising yawls seventy-two feet over all and summers spent sailing the Aegean islands.

With the assets of a great bank nearby, Suzanne could promise opportunities to squander without limit: modern houses built in the Hamptons, collections of Impressionist art, charge accounts at Henri Bendel, Rolls-Royces, Mercedes-Benzes, round diamonds and square emeralds, rare furs, mistresses taken and dismissed, lovers kept on short leashes. Yet all these pleasures for which money could be spent were no more than alternative expressions of why money must be saved. Both spendthrifts and penny savers could be promised the pleasure of holding between their thumbs and forefingers either money itself, or everything money could buy. Suzanne could promise, with The Bank's help, the opportunity to hoard, or to hear before any others that the city's notes would be paid after all, or promise that certificates of deposit at The Bank would earn favored rates of interest, accumulating money from money silently, as if by magic.

The dreams of some of Suzanne's friends took other, more potent shapes. What they craved was not so much possession of things in themselves, or the money that might represent anything at all, but the thrill of waging battle to obtain the power to spend and save. Suzanne could promise the clamor of combat as well as its prizes. With the assets of one of the city's major banks, she could guarantee to combine with, or against, gangs of opportunists in stock raids, tender offers, municipal elections, contests for seats upon the board of directors of industrial corporations, or seats among those designated to be a President's trusted advisers. By joining Suzanne's battle for control of Aunt Nellie's bank, some of the city's angriest men hoped to give vent to their taste for destruction either by active participation in rousing battles or, if they chose to forgo an active role, by sitting in judgment in a black sulkiness that would nevertheless command respect. Their wrath could be expressed—with The Bank's backing—in the snarling contests waged in political primary campaigns or, silently, by denying membership for unstated reasons to an applicant at one of the city's best clubs.

To others, Suzanne could promise to extend their influence, with The Bank's help, through dozens of major corporations. As opposed to the more singular delights of gluttony, hoarding, combat and wrath, corporations provided many means to pursue fraud. Wearing the smooth faces of just men, corporate executives could order up images by the thousands. Using the techniques of advertising, corporations could play upon desire, rummage up fears, abuse and corrupt language until the very grammar of meaning had evaporated. Benefits untold could be guaranteed, if only a face cream was applied without stint. Mouthwash might dispel germs. Drugs might assure sleep. Potions would surely deliver love. More of everything could be promised. On the other hand, if the corporation's officers preferred disaster, appropriate studies could be commissioned, and scarcities predicted, and the findings released, with the proper solemnities, as "crises."

In addition to these lies, wishes and dreams—supported by The Bank at the prime rate plus 2–3 per cent—there were still other services Suzanne could deliver. A bank would have a share, at interest or *pro bono publico*, in movies, theater, arts and dance. Symphonies would need its support. Museums would benefit from its kindly gaze. Schools, especially public schools, could not be funded without The Bank's purchase of their securities. Hospitals could not be expanded without mortgages, and if The Bank abandoned them, child-care centers, nursing homes, and psychiatric hospitals would have to close their doors. Even burial grounds needed their fundings, and gravesites were maintained—their grass cut and their flowers trimmed—with the cooperation of some bank.

Suzanne understood perfectly how every necessity of the city's life was intertwined in Aunt Nellie's central position: Her bank could breed money, regardless of how nature or skill had been applied. Yet it was not money that dissolved the ties of love and community; it was the powers, the energies, at Aunt Nellie's command. Particularly because in all these transactions The Bank could never do anything except what the society in which it was chartered would approve. Aunt Nellie would always be innocent.

Innocence was Aunt Nellie's most attractive power. Her bank could employ battalions of lawyers, and set them forth to harry like a pack of mad dogs any object of her displeasure. If the lawyers let the money paid to them stick to their fingers as they traded justice, that would be no concern of Aunt Nellie's. When trickery, hypocrisy, expediency, chicanery and the counseling of fraud crazed the citizens of the city, none of these activities could be either approved or disapproved by The Bank or its directors. They would be innocent—as long as adequate balances were maintained. When citizens took to the city's streets as thieves, or to foment rebellion, or to raise up civil strife, none of these violences would be Aunt Nellie's affair.

Nine billion dollars of assets represented to Suzanne the kind of erotic delights for which she had always searched. By August 1976 all that Sam Harper predicted was in motion. By then Suzanne and André were reviewing their plans for the final coup. They gathered every scrap of intelligence available on the disposition of their enemy. And by then they knew their purchases of The Bank's stock had finally alerted The Bank's officers. They were also aware that some of the promises that Suzanne had made—the shares of the spoils to be divided after the conquest— had been taken too literally in a few cases. Unavoidably, an enthusiasm to sack Aunt Nellie's assets had caused some members of Suzanne's expedition to break silence—although no major damage to the element of surprise appeared to have been suffered. Rowdy talk was probably unavoidable.

"Mr. Scott has suggested I give you a call," said Judge Gordon to Suzanne. "His information is that they know you are coming."

"Please thank Mr. Scott for me, and pay my respects. We think we have 30 per cent in friendly hands even now, and we shall be moving soon."

"Our advice," Judge Gordon continued, "would be not to delay too long. These people have quite a few friends of their own."

It was to Suzanne's credit that she did not dismiss carelessly anything she heard: "Like who?"

"We don't have information on that. When we get it, we'll pass it along."

"No one in particular?"

"Not at this point, but as you know, they have some heavy connections over there."

"Whatever you hear, we would appreciate it, Judge."

"Nothing serious at this point, Suzanne. We know they have you pegged as Snow White and The Shark—I thought you'd enjoy that. We are with you in this all the way. Mr. Scott personally has placed a substantial bet upon your success, and as you know, so have a number of his associates. So you can be assured of our cooperation for whatever you may need. Just ask, that's all. Just ask. And you got it."

15

Law an' Order

August 1976

Not one white piece of paper ever remained for more than a minute or two upon the polished surface of the desk that was the command post of Thomas G. Phelps, chairman of The Bank. Aunt Nellie described him as a man of decision: quick, abrupt, an admired administrator, a tough negotiator, who could alternately charm and persuade, or threaten with fearsome thunder, to get his way. He was compact and muscular, and to watch him was to observe a man in motion: leaving his own offices on the twenty-second floor of The Bank, traveling corridors, then through the doors of other executives, striding along midtown streets into restaurants or clubs, or into the headquarters of his principal customers. Doors opened ahead of him, held even by complete strangers, who sensed it would be a mistake to impede his progress by any delay. Although no scars showed, Tom Phelps had been through his share of corporate wars. When the rumors first began that Snow White and The Shark had their eyes upon The Bank itself, Tom Phelps was the first man to seriously consider the possibilities. After The Bank's annual report was out of the way in January 1976, he shifted the emphasis of his lunch schedules and went to work.

At first he said nothing about what was on his mind to his staff. Obviously there was no need to alarm Aunt Nellie unnecessarily, but by March he'd put a special team of The Bank's best lawyers to work. To the extent that anyone had to be specific about the problem he had identified, it was referred to in Tom Phelps's offices as "The Snow White Affair."

Although Tom Phelps was reasonably sure that Snow White was behind the purchases of the daily trades The Bank's specialists were now watching with a sharp eye, one difficulty he faced was that he could not be sure who else might be involved. Despite a considerable effort, it was almost impossible to identify all the actual owners of The Bank's common stocks. At most, any investigation would end at a post-office box number in Delaware, or at the address of a law firm in Manhattan or some strange place like Schenectady. If the shares were held in any foreign account—the Bahamas or Switzerland—they might as well be on the moon. Nothing could be discovered about their owners. It was Tom Phelps's guess that if Snow White was acting alone, the situation was manageable: give her a seat on the board, maybe two, and the thing would blow over. On the other hand, perhaps contingency plans should be drawn up, and then the board of directors informed.

The Bank's team made a list of moves Mr. Phelps and the board might want to consider. The Bank could split its stock, two to one, even three to one. With the number of shares increased, Snow White's share of The Bank's stock would remain at the same percentage, but The Bank would have the opportunity to get additional shares into friendly hands. Another possibility was to increase the dividend at the next quarter, because higher dividends would tend to push the price of the common stock up, making it expensive for Snow White to continue to buy. Moreover, the tendency would be for all those little old ladies and their trust accounts to hang on, rather than sell their stock. To maintain their control, the directors didn't need to worry about the big blocks of stock—they could hold those by various means; it was all those one-hundred-share lots held by the peasants in the countryside which were being bought up by the opposition.

But stock splits and dividends for the shareholders were not appealing alternatives to The Bank's directors or to Aunt Nellie.

She would be diluting her equity to some extent. More important, she would be distributing her control, creating problems for
the future. A more attractive alternative was to consider the possibility of a "defensive merger." That is, offer to Snow White a
swap: The Bank could afford to give generous premiums for everything Snow White owned, take over her businesses and run
them, pay her off, and tell her to go away.

It was an alternative Aunt Nellie said she found attractive.

To establish the cost of a swap, Tom Phelps's team investi-
gated every business they were sure Snow White controlled. The
price for absorbing them all was next to nothing compared to
what was at risk. The difficulty was that Tom Phelps just did not
see the virtues in owning half a flower business run by a bunch
of Greeks, two brownstones on Ninety-third Street where God-
knows-what was going on, a couple of two-bit county banks beyond the trading area allowed by state banking regulations,
points in a gambling casino, and the liabilities of a string of overseas mutual funds that were scandalous in every meaning of that
word. Tom Phelps thought Aunt Nellie would wrinkle her nose
at "the defensive-merger alternative," not to say what the bank
examiners would do when they started working through that
mess of "fringe stuff."

"Follow that up," Aunt Nellie ordered.

Thereafter Tom Phelps redoubled his team's efforts: never
mind the Bahamas funds or the brownstones uptown; Snow
White had been plowing money into other businesses besides
flowers. The other businesses were here in the United States
somewhere. "Find 'em, because to buy our stock she is borrow-
ing on what she owns somewhere else. Let's find a way to hit
her where she lives."

A memorandum outlining the essential elements of Tom
Phelps's plan of attack was forwarded to Aunt Nellie at her place
near Saratoga. It was returned by mail to Tom Phelps's headquarters at The Bank, with one word at the top: "Right! E.B."

The Bank's team found one of André's insurance companies almost immediately. They did not locate the second positively
until mid-August. Significantly, the second insurance company
had been under investigation for some time by the Internal Revenue Service and the Department of Justice in connection with

allegations of kickbacks from several pension funds. These trust funds were said to be controlled by Amedeo Scutari, a.k.a. Tony Scott; or by Tony Scott's representative, Judge Ephraim Gordon.

A two-page "private memorandum" on Judge Gordon and Tony Scott was forwarded from Tom Phelps to Mrs. Burns. No copies were distributed within The Bank. A summary of the relations between the insurance companies and the pension funds ended with a suggestion that perhaps there were "working relationships" between the pension funds and two IRS district offices "at the level of Regional Counsel." The summary was written in crisp, but careful managerial language—an opaque style in which nothing is quite clearly stated. The original of the memorandum was returned to Tom Phelps's desk by hand within two days. At the bottom of the second page, an unsigned handwritten note said: "I will call Detroit."

Upon the receipt of this news, Tom Phelps revised his lunch schedule once again, and canceled all but the most necessary of his other appointments. The case he brought to the friends of The Bank varied slightly from one instance to the next but fundamentally contained several substantial points. At lunch, on the phone, by personal call in Manhattan, taking the shuttle to Washington and back, he emphasized again and again that the friends of The Bank should "resist this thing with all the means available."

Tom Phelps emphasized how awkward it might be if someone not accustomed to The Bank's traditions were in a position to know everything about the financial affairs of The Bank's customers. Not only would corporate business transactions be placed in the hands of outsiders but personal trust and family affairs as well. Tom Phelps was extremely careful not to say where he believed the challenge to The Bank might be coming from, but he indicated—as it was his duty to do—that the challengers were "not at all the right kind of people." He never actually said that there was any danger to one of The Bank's old friends in having a daughter's trust account supervised by the likes of Snow White, or The Shark, or Mr. Tony Scott. In fact, he never named them at all. It was only necessary for Tom Phelps to shake his head sadly at the right moment to get the idea across.

The Bank was a money-market bank as well, a major dealer in the securities issued every day by the United States Treasury Department, and a buyer of the bonds and promissory notes issued by five hundred major U.S. corporations. The top executives of these institutions, public and private, did not need to be told twice of the implications inherent in letting any outsider be their partner in the daily efforts that were their duties. To a man, they responded handsomely to Tom Phelps's outline. Without exception, they offered: "Let me know what I can do to help."

Again without mentioning any names or any specifics at all, Tom Phelps called upon the regional officers of the Federal Reserve System, the comptroller of the currency, the director of internal revenue, an undersecretary in the Justice Department, a close friend of the governor, and made the final stops on his check list at the offices of the Securities and Exchange Commission, the Senate Committee on Banking and Currency, and the House of Representatives Committee on Banking. Everyone Tom Phelps called upon said much the same thing: "Hell, Tom, you just give us a call if you need anything."

On Wednesday afternoon, August 25, at exactly five o'clock, Tom Phelps placed two telephone calls in quick succession. He closed the door of his office and dialed the first call himself. Good general that he was, he wanted the consent of his commander in chief before he went ahead. Mrs. Burns probably said no more than "All right."

Tom Phelps placed his second call to the New York *Times*. The next morning, Thursday, the *Times* featured on its financial page a photograph of Count André de Montreuil. Next to it, the story began by asking a question: "Can a mysterious foreigner move in on the American establishment and knock off one of the biggest prizes in sight?" An explanation followed which indicated, as far as the *Times* was able to report, that the conglomerate of companies called Providence Holding and controlled by de Montreuil was said to be making a bid for the shares of one of New York City's leading banks. The bank's chairman, Mr. Thomas G. Phelps, was said to have replied: "We intend to resist this with all the means at our command, and these might turn out to be considerable."

Reached at his summer home near Saratoga, Count André de

Montreuil answered the *Times*'s queries by saying that he had no plans to acquire control of the bank in question; had not met with any of the bank's officers; and could not imagine a situation in which anyone would attempt to take over any company against the wishes of its operating management.

Despite de Montreuil's denials, the common shares of The Bank were up four, to nineteen and seven eighths, at the close of trading Thursday afternoon. It would subsequently be alleged that someone, not named, at the Securities and Exchange Commission had called Tom Phelps sometime Thursday, although the time was not specified, to inquire whether Mr. Phelps wished to have the bank's stock suspended temporarily, in view of the heavy trading. According to these reports, never confirmed, and probably without substance, Mr. Phelps was said to have replied: "No, let her ride!"

Because Suzanne spent that Thursday afternoon in her reserved box at the old Saratoga race track, Judge Gordon did not reach her until she returned to her summer home, at about seven o'clock. "Are you sure," he inquired, "that your sweetheart knows what he's doing?"

Suzanne said she was confident that André would manage, thank you.

"Any dumb mistakes at this point could be costly; do you understand me?"

Suzanne pointed out that the stock was up, no matter what happened. Judge Gordon's good friends should not have any complaints.

"Suzanne, I want you to know that Mr. Scott and I will always be your friends, whatever happens. We've been together, one way or another, too long. But some of Mr. Scott's associates would break a leg for only five hundred dollars, if you see what I mean."

16

The Bottom Line

Thursday, August 26

SUZANNE put the white phone by her bedside back into its cradle. The night-table clock said seven-fifteen. She was still in her dressing gown, and she and André were due down in Saratoga at eight o'clock. It was a half-hour drive. They would be late, but it wouldn't matter too much, because Aunt Nellie's annual dinner at The Spuyten Duyvil was always a madhouse anyway.

"Who was that?" André asked.

"Judge Gordon."

"What did he have to say?"

"He said the stock was up four today on heavy volume."

"Then they must be getting ready for us."

"Apparently," said Suzanne. Before she resumed her seat before the mirror of her dressing table, she stopped to gaze through the windows of their bedroom suite at the west end of her house. Just as Enrique Cardinale had designed it for her, her view from her second-floor bedroom looked out across the artificial lake—from the stream that filled it, if she looked to her left, to the road across the dam that contained it, to her far right. At that very moment, as she watched, the sun was setting: dropping behind the rounded mountains to the west, turning the mountain of pine forest across the way into a massive black shadow of its own. When she had first dreamed of how her lake might look someday, she had hoped that it would be a scene much like the perfect sight she watched at that instant. The day had been insufferably hot; not one zephyr had sneaked across the lake's surface; the heat accumulated during the day continued to rest exactly where the sun had deposited it. Out in the center of the lake, she could see her gazebo-temple on its island, the museum of her ambitions. She was sure that not a leaf rustled to relieve its silence.

André had often asked her at first what she and Enrique were "up to out there in the lake." She had successfully put him off by asserting that every woman needs some secrets of her own—some mystery, a place of privacy, at least one location forbidden to her husband. Otherwise he would get bored with her. Someday, she promised, she would tell him what was in her temple: when they were old; when it wouldn't matter any more. André eventually accepted her reasons, and the subject of her *musée*—as he called it—did not come up any more. Yet tonight she was within a hair's breadth of telling him everything, of taking him out on the lake and into the *musée* to show him how she had commemorated her life.

André interrupted her reverie: "Suzanne, we're going to be late."

She turned away from the last long yellow shafts of sunset upon her little temple, and sat down to finish her makeup and arrange her hair.

André was in an ebullient mood. He was nearly ready, closing the cufflinks of his dress shirt. "Tomorrow," he predicted, "is our day."

Suzanne was concentrating upon her eye shadow, but she could see him from time to time as he moved through the perspective of her mirror.

"We shall allow John Garraty to leak the story to the *Times*," he continued. "About how we are anxious to meet with management."

"André"—she was trying to stop him—"let's go away."

"The story appears in Saturday's papers, while all the markets are closed. Perhaps Sunday evening, or Monday morning at the latest, the phone rings and we have our little chat with Mr. Phelps and his people. Not bad, eh? Then we can go away—take two months off if you like."

"Let's go now. Tonight."

He finally heard her. He stopped his pacing. With his dinner jacket still in his right hand, he sat down upon the corner of their bed. He was gentle. "What are you talking about, my love?"

"We could go to Australia and start life all over again. We could raise sheep. We could go to Brazil. Anywhere. It doesn't matter, but let's leave right now. This minute."

He looked down at his watch, and then with half a smile pointed out that as a matter of fact they were expected at The Spuyten Duyvil for dinner with Aunt Nellie in five minutes, and it was at least a half-hour drive. Was she afraid? There was no reason to be afraid. No matter what happened, they had accumulated enough stock to force Aunt Nellie to give them at least two seats on the board of directors.

"Are we going to accept that?" she countered.

"Well, yes," he said. "Why not?" There would be no point in turning them down. With two seats on The Bank's board, they would have access to everything they wanted anyway.

She turned back to the arrangements she still had to complete at the mirror. "Then, we are only gambling for a slice of the cake."

"Exactly," he agreed.

"Why not gamble for the whole cake?"

"That's pointless, Suzanne; you know that well enough."

There were pins in her mouth as she put masses of her hair into their proper places. She had apparently thought of a new diversion. "I am thinking of joining a nunnery," she announced as if she had already decided. "I will enter a nunnery, and you can go to a monastery. Then we will write each other long letters, like Héloïse and Abélard. Would you like that, lover?"

Thinking he was on more familiar ground once again, André was happy to join in her little play. "I know you well enough, little wife; without any question, you would be appointed abbess in less than a year."

"Ah, yes," she said. "I would certainly have to arrange to be abbess. Then I would send for you to hear my confessions."

"And what terrible stories I would hear!" He rolled his eyes to heaven in mock horror.

"And I would confess to you the sin I love above all the others," she continued.

Taking the part she had assigned him, André made the sign of the cross over her, pretending he was about to hear her confession.

"Hear me, Father, for I have sinned."

"Speak, my child," he intoned, just as the priest would.

"I love to gamble."

"Do you seek the Lord's forgiveness, my child?"

"No."

At last he saw where she had been leading him. He did not choose to play the part of her confessor any longer. He stood up from the edge of the bed, starting to pull on his dinner jacket, saying something to the effect that he would wait for her downstairs when she was ready. But she was not finished yet.

"André, I am not satisfied by two seats on the board of The Bank. It seems to me they are not very interesting. I think we should ask for the whole cake."

"That's not practical, *chérie*."

"Only because you don't want to gamble."

"There's no gamble to it. Tomorrow we total up what we have and what they have, and then we sit down and cut up what you call the cake. That's the bottom line."

"I don't see why we can't use what we have to tell them to just go—leave—out!"

"Because we won't have an absolute majority. It is better in such cases to make a practical compromise."

"But we could bluff."

"Suzanne, the bluff might work and it might not."

"If it worked, we would have The Bank to ourselves."

"We get everything we might want from absolute control by having two seats on the board. Members of the board always extend—how shall we say—courtesies to each other."

"If our bluff doesn't work," Suzanne persisted, "we get those two seats you want anyway. So it pays to bluff."

"You want to gamble when there is no reason to take risks. That is foolish."

"The only reason to gamble is to take risks. I mean when the stakes are really high, and the fingers dig deep into the green cloth upon the playing table, and little bits of cotton come up under your fingernails while you wait for the card to be turned—don't you love that part?"

"No, Suzanne; not as you do."

"Aha!" She laughed at him. "You are just like every other man, when it comes right down to it. Men never have to gamble everything the way a woman does."

To make peace with her he bent over her shoulder and placed a kiss upon the nape of her neck. He said again that he would wait for her downstairs. He reminded her of how late they were. "There is no reason," he grinned, "to make Aunt Nellie angry by being late to her supper." As he turned to go, Angelique was knocking at the edge of her mother's open door. "Good heavens, Suzanne," said André, "look at this. Here is the beauty who will turn every head in the crowd tonight!"

He held Angelique at arm's length, his fingers at her elbows, turning her slightly this way and that, as if he could not believe the vision in his hands. "No doubt about it," he said, smiling from one to the other. "You are your mother's child."

"Out, out, out," was Suzanne's reaction. "Or we shall never be ready to go to Saratoga."

As soon as André was gone, Angelique pulled a chair up beside her mother's. She was, Suzanne had to admit, a devastating sight, with her golden hair, her scrubbed and shiny youth, and barely a touch of makeup. Her daughter even had the sense to wear a clear lipstick—a determined innocence played as her best foot forward. Her evening dress was one of Halston's clean, straight lines: skinny, strapless, in beige satin. Angelique wanted, it would have seemed, her mother's advice: "Should I wear big earrings?"

Suzanne studied the question for a decent interval, then concluded she should not.

"Some pin as an accent?"

"Nothing is needed." Suzanne rose to pull her own costume on —a variation of the new romance by Yves St. Laurent, a gypsy fantasy of a long double skirt in red silk faille, sashed in dark green, and worn with a red chiffon blouse trimmed with lamé. There was a lamé-and-green-chiffon fringed stole to be thrown around her shoulders. She would need accents of gold to finish the illusion: a twisted gold choker, big drop earrings, a jeweled cuff bracelet.

At her dressing table again, Suzanne searched through her jewel box—a clear plastic tray about two feet long and a foot wide, with a second tray fitted within it to divide it into two levels. It was like the boxes that were designed to hold a collection of fishing lures, or the clear plastic boxes divided into little compartments that a master carpenter would use to keep separate screws and bolts of various sizes. Tossed into these compartments were all kinds of jewelry—necklaces, earrings, rings, pendants, bracelets and pins, but no item was in its proper place. Instead all the different lures were mixed together haphazardly. There was fake stuff, and semiprecious materials too: lapis lazuli, onyx, malachite, rock crystal, rose quartz, tiger's-eye, amethyst, moonstone, and tangled strands of cultured pearls. Scrambled among these fakes were truly valuable jewels in worked gold, cut jade, rubies, diamonds, emeralds, a double strand of oriental pearls, and a big topaz ring. Suzanne tried the oversized loop earrings first, for effect.

Angelique asked: "Are those real?"

"Of course not. You should be able to recognize amethyst by now."

Suzanne took them off, and tried instead the ruby pendants: a circle of tiny rubies, set in gold rings nearly an inch across: "What do you think, *ma petite?*"

Angelique answered her as if she were a schoolgirl reciting a lesson: "Very gypsy. St. Laurent, about three hundred and fifty dollars, right?"

"Wrong. You are exasperating me. VanCleef & Arpels, about twenty-two thousand. Really! You know better than that. What are you up to with that young artist we have in the studio across the lake?"

"Nothing in particular. He's an amusing man, that's all. Michael Hassett's not so young as all that—he's thirty."

"He has a beautiful body."

"He has a fine mind, too, Mother."

"Fiddlesticks. Art is the last refuge of scoundrels."

"Well, I like him."

Suzanne stood, smoothed her skirt, took the ruby ring from the jewel box at the last moment, and tried it for her right hand. It would do nicely. She was ready.

Angelique stood too, continuing to measure her mother, then followed her downstairs, where André and Michael Hassett were waiting to drive the women they admired to Saratoga.

In retrospect, André said that he might have been more alert; that he should have suspected that Suzanne was "up to something"; that perhaps he could have headed off her ability to "create little dramas." On the other hand, he pointed out, she was never deterred by any practical notions: "That was the thing, don't you see? She didn't give a damn about how the world was made."

He remembered driving Suzanne to Saratoga in the green Jaguar; and that Michael Hassett followed them with Angelique in another car—Hassett's car. "During the summer, that fellow rented the studio on the far side of the lake, doing his paintings, or whatever artists do in their studios."

On the drive down Route 9N to Saratoga, André was in a mood to chatter. "I was on top of the world that night. The bank business would come to its logical conclusion over the next few days. We could have talked about that, about who would be at Aunt Nellie's dinner at The Spuyten Duyvil, about anything at all, but I could not draw Suzanne into it."

He had asked her if she was "somewhere else, far away."

"Yes," was all she would say.

He offered her a penny for her thoughts.

He recalled distinctly that his penny bid brightened her. She replied she thought a penny would not buy them, but seven seats on the board out of twelve—an absolute majority—would receive from her a fair hearing.

He tried another topic, which he hoped might be closer to the mark: Was she thinking about Angelique?

She admitted she was.

"She is a great beauty," he agreed. "Devastating."

"Yes," said Suzanne, "so she is."

André's impression—when he had time much later to review what it was they discussed that night—was that perhaps Suzanne was jealous of her daughter's youth. It would have been a perfectly natural explanation. In his experience it was only an assumption—a typically American sentimentality—that mothers and daughters should be friends. In Europe the opposite was understood to be true. The conflict between generations was in the end the only battle that mattered. In his opinion, American children had too little respect for the effort made by their parents. Suzanne, for example, had done all those things American mothers do for their daughters. There was always a good nurse until Angelique was sent away to school. The girl was sent to the best private schools, then allowed to study as she pleased at Bennington College. Suzanne took the trouble to go shopping with Angelique and to help her select the most becoming clothes. There was no question in his opinion that Suzanne had spoiled that girl. When Angelique wanted an apartment of her own, didn't Suzanne arrange everything for her? It was his conclusion that Angelique had no right to be sullen about her mother. Absolutely not. Suzanne had been a perfect mother.

What, if anything, in his opinion, did Suzanne's relations with her daughter have to do with the events that followed? André de Montreuil considered several possibilities, then concluded: "Probably nothing."

Was Angelique what he actually discussed with Suzanne on the way to Saratoga? André de Montreuil admitted that for the better part of the drive not much was said between them. Suzanne was "far away in another world," as he had already pointed out. "It was as if she was making up her mind about something."

Was she worried about the bank deal? André de Montreuil thought she might have been thinking about The Bank—it was certainly very much on everyone's mind that week. On the other hand, it didn't seem to worry her, or excite her particularly, one way or another. She was—he could not find the exact words he wanted to describe it—very calm. "What you have in English," was the way he put it, using his hands to demonstrate how it would be possible to cup water in the palms of his hands, "called the calm before the storm." He agreed that the trouble with clichés was that they were often true.

In any event, it was nearly nine o'clock by the time they reached Saratoga and drew near the Finney Pavilion of the Fasig-Tipton Company. Since the annual auction of yearling thoroughbred race horses had begun promptly at eight, getting the car through the streets leading to the pavilion was difficult. It was already dark, there were people walking across the street in whatever way they pleased, and André had to drive at a snail's pace. Near the pavilion itself the mob grew dense, waiting along the curbs or behind the barriers to catch a glimpse of the celebrities of horse racing, just the way crowds gather at the openings of movies.

To get through this mess, André took the Cartier cardboard invitations which admitted them to the sales, and waved them out the window of the car. A cooperative state trooper picked up one end of a sawhorse barrier, swung it back, and signaled them to drive directly to the canopy of the pavilion. For another five-dollar tip, André was able to get a black man at the door to jockey their car away.

André and Suzanne walked arm in arm up the red carpet to the glass doors of the modern, semicircular amphitheater. They had to wait until the security men at the door found their names on the list, and checked them off, and hung around their necks the blue badges on chains that were like those issued to delegates at political conventions. Once inside the Finney Pavilion, however, André and Suzanne declined the offer to be ushered to their seats in the amphitheater where the auction was in progress. Instead they walked around the semicircle of glass and concrete at the rear until they exited into the barn area at the pavilion's rear. They passed along a carpeted path running beside roped-off circles where the young horses were being walked on tethers by their grooms, and curried and calmed until it was time to go into the main arena as a "hip number" in the catalogue of the auction. The walking circles were floodlit and as jam-packed with spectators as the main entrance had been. In the dense air of a still August night, moths were fluttering up into the floodlights' arcs.

By crossing through the floodlit area behind the pavilion, past the walking circles, André and Suzanne finally reached the back entrance—the garden gate—of The Spuyten Duyvil. Because of the blue badges already hung upon the chains around their necks, and because they were dressed in formal evening clothes, the Count and Countess de Montreuil were admitted without delay.

Just inside the gate, a photographer asked them to pause, if they wouldn't mind, for just one picture. It was then, André remembered, that Suzanne's broad smile reappeared and she was her boisterous, happy self again. She put her arm through his, and with a big grin, looked up at him and made him laugh. "Do you suppose," was her impish question, "there will be anyone here tonight we know?"

ACT III

La Princesse Lointaine

17

The Spuyten Duyvil

Thursday Night

MOST of the year, The Spuyten Duyvil was closed, its doors shut and locked and its bar empty of customers. But, for a few nights each year—during the auctions of thoroughbreds in the Fasig-Tipton Pavilion at its rear—it always roared with excitement. Inside The Spuyten Duyvil, men and women stood jammed together so closely that a passage from the bar's front entrance through to the garden patio in the back might constitute a voyage of an hour or more. In the garden, beneath a green-and-white-striped tent, tables were set out with hurricane lamps upon pink linens, and the local girls who served as waitresses made their way from place to place with great difficulty.

Aunt Nellie's table was in The Spuyten Duyvil's garden; a table for sixteen, which André and Suzanne were to join; a party to which Aunt Nellie had also invited Angelique and what Aunt Nellie called "her nice young man"; a dinner that Aunt Nellie conducted annually at the same place and the same time during the auctions for a very simple reason—she'd always done it.

Because Aunt Nellie was always there, The Spuyten Duyvil never failed to hold a reservation for her. Theoretically, reservations for tables in The Spuyten Duyvil's garden might change hands, as long as there was no one who cared to inherit them. Over a period of years, a few new faces had been added from time to time. For the convenience of the regulars—both those at reserved tables in the garden and those packed into the main bar —the auction of horses at the pavilion next door was piped across fifty yards of grass by closed-circuit television. Hence it was possible to send agents to bid for a likely horse without leaving one's seat; or to cross over into the auction's amphitheater and bid in person for the item listed in the catalogue the auction company provided, and then return to The Spuyten Duyvil satisfied or frustrated by what money could or couldn't buy.

The auction conducted in the pavilion carried with it a mysterious, ancient excitement. The yearlings being sold were untrained, untried, unknown, and some were wobbly-kneed. On the many television screens placed strategically around The Spuyten Duyvil, or from the seats of the pavilion's orchestra and balcony, bidders could see colts and fillies brought into a center ring and stood for inspection. The auctioneer identified each one by the "hip number" in the catalogue. He reviewed with enthusiasm each yearling's forebears, suggested by tracing its lineage or by pointing to its conformation that the horse standing at sale was potentially a bargain, a winner, a delight, with all reasonable possibilities of success—for those who would take the chance and gamble.

The auctioneer would begin his patter. Placed at observation posts facing his audience were the auctioneer's spotters, dressed in tuxedos, ready to answer the bids signaled to them with a cry —a surprising exclamation—that sounded something like "Hup!" Bidders made their wishes known to the spotters by no more than a subtle blink of the eye, perhaps a nod, sometimes by scratching with two fingers along the right side of the nose. About two million dollars' worth of horses were hammered down in a single evening.

Each horse sold was listed in the catalogue. Page by page, the catalogue traced the genealogy of the animal standing patiently before the crowd. Beside each sire and grandsire and great-grandsire were the exact dollar totals won at stakes races; and beside the names of their well-known dams similar figures gave proof of speed, endurance and temperament. By choosing from

among many lines of "breeding," the bidders hoped to own winners of their own.

The excitement the auction generated had many sources. Perhaps the calm and serious eye of the horse standing in the amphitheater's ring would be the quiet eye of another Secretariat.
The result of a shrewd or lucky guess, combined with a successful bid, would bring to the bidder not only millions of dollars
but permanent fame. Moreover, the auction conducted in Saratoga each August could rightfully trace its history as a continuous ceremony practiced for thousands of years, going back
beyond the place where history's veils part, traceable to Asia
Minor before the days when Hittites rode down toward Baby-
lon's towers. Over all those years, the main elements of the ceremony had not varied substantially: if horses were to race—and
despite wars, revolutions, and regimes and governments of every
stripe, horses had always run—then horses would have to be
bred. Once sired and foaled, some would be stood at sale.

At the same time, any unprejudiced observer could not help
but notice that some of the excitement at an auction of young
horses was contributed by the women present. They, too, were
proofs that despite wars, revolutions, and regimes and governments of every stripe, the business of breeding had always been
superior to any other consideration as a guarantee of the future.
Economic and political theories were irrelevant if some prince
would bid half a million dollars or ingots of iron or whatever
princes at the moment happened to have at hand. When princes
bid for the qualities of speed, endurance and temperament, any
woman who failed to take notice of what celebrity was worth
was not a woman of any sensitivity.

Just as it must have been continuously true at all the auctions
of horses in all societies through all the aeons of recorded genealogy, the annual sale of yearling thoroughbreds at Saratoga
reeked with the perfume emanating from the women present.
When they smiled, their teeth dazzled. When they looked, their
eyes flashed. When their hands moved, or their backs arched,
there were few men who would not speak just a shade louder—to
be heard better against the cacophony of the crowd, of course.

The air of the pavilion itself and the nearby garden of The
Spuyten Duyvil was dense with maddening odors: the acrid

fumes from the glowering kerosene lamps; the food sent haphazardly to the tables; the liquor swilled around and around with
melting ice at the bottoms of glasses; the heavy effusions of rare
perfumes sent out from elbows and from behind sweating knees;
and the more ancient scents of ambition and hope. Besides,
every woman glittered with her best jewels; or wore herself as a
jewel that lacked only a setting. Consequently the noise, the talk,
the laughter at The Spuyten Duyvil's tables were quick and
heady, not unlike lovers' patter.

It also happened that on that Thursday night in 1976 the accumulated heat of the day had created a thunderstorm to add a
major chord, a rumbling *basso profundo,* to the light conversation around Aunt Nellie's garden table. The storm was still a
long way distant—somewhere deep in the Adirondacks—when
Suzanne and André arrived and took their places among Aunt
Nellie's guests.

Aunt Nellie would have been proud to describe every one of
those assembled at her court as "beautiful people." They might
have earned her approval by inheritance, or by right, or even by
achievement. She had arrived early with her companion, Adam
Shepherd, to lay out place cards. Once her guests were seated,
however, she didn't mind at all if they went table-hopping or
regrouped themselves as they saw fit, because that's what always
happened in The Spuyten Duyvil while the auction was going
on. It added to the pleasures of the evening.

She expected her guests to enjoy themselves, and she watched
with approval when they did. Adam Shepherd and Enrique Cardinale leaped to Suzanne's side almost as soon as she arrived
and hovered over her, teasing her. They said they had a surprise
for Suzanne. She would have to guess what it was. It was bigger
than a bread box. It was animal. It was not a horse. It was not a
dog. Cats were smaller than bread boxes. It was not a fish. Fish
weren't animals. No, they wouldn't tell her. Yes, Aunt Nellie
knew what it was. No, Aunt Nellie wouldn't tell either. They
would bring it over tomorrow night, when dinner was to be at
Suzanne's house. If they told, it wouldn't be a surprise. They had
stumped Suzanne; wasn't that marvelous? Yes, Aunt Nellie said,
that was just marvelous, but what she wanted was a brandy and
soda. It seemed to be impossible to catch the eye of a waitress,

so wouldn't Adam and Enrique be good boys and fetch drinks from the bar.

Enrique promised Aunt Nellie he'd deliver her brandy in only a moment. Adam gathered up the balance of the table's orders. Together, Adam and Enrique went off toward the bar mightily pleased with themselves. Of those at Aunt Nellie's table, it need only be said that there were a couple from the magic land of Hollywood, and a senator and his wife—who would also be at Suzanne's house the following night for dinner. There were those handsome men and beautiful women who passed like princes and princesses through the Excelsior Hotel on the Via Veneto in Rome, stayed in Las Brisas in Acapulco, stopped in New York at the Plaza and the Stanhope. Whatever their names or occupations or histories in actuality, they were those magic apparitions listed repeatedly in the gossip columns. Their first names were known not only to each other but to a million secretaries and working girls, who followed the adventures of these gods from week to week, while eating cottage cheese at lunchtime at their office desks and dreaming as shepherdesses must once have done that one of the gods would lose his way and dally for just a little while.

Mixed in with these beautiful people at Aunt Nellie's table, and commingling with the gods and goddesses supping at nearby tables, were men and women circulating through The Spuyten Duyvil's garden to conduct the business of trading horseflesh. Although the faces of these members of the annual thoroughbred convention were not as familiar to the correspondent from *Women's Wear Daily*, or to the dark-haired columnist from the *Daily News*, or to the baffled observer from *New York* magazine, as the faces of certified "jet-setters" would be, the horse traders constituted a minor aristocracy of their own: table-hopping Kentucky colonels, Irish breeders, English lords with exiled pounds, round-faced Japanese investment managers with blocked yen, slow-talkin' good ol' boys up North to buy for the King Ranch, the Aga Khan's men, the appropriate representatives of the clans Whitney, Vanderbilt, Woodward and Ryan—and Spanish-speaking jockeys strutting on high heels, the jockeys' eyes never higher than the breasts of the big-hipped Spanish women they'd decked out.

Even inside the garden of the gods there were hierarchies of occupations: veterinarians to inspect a horse before sale as sound; breeders who could guarantee its mating; trainers who could teach it the essentials of coming out of gates; handicappers, gambling men, bankers; promoters, cooks and maids, butlers and thieves, procurers and pimps, pretty girls with whom to while away the hours that an owner might feel settling too long upon his day. There were always one or two Foxcroft girls, or pretty young things from Wavertree Hall, who claimed their main interest was in "hunters" but whose eyes scanned The Spuyten Duyvil like radar, looking for the blips that might represent incoming husbands.

Since so many jewels were being displayed, security men mingled with the crowd. Of these, a long-time favorite of Aunt Nellie's was John Tallman, and when he came beside her chair at the head of the table she actually rose to meet him, to embrace him and plant a kiss upon his cheek. She introduced him to everyone at the table whose attention she could reach as "My annual FBI agent."

When he shook hands with Suzanne—who was seated down toward the middle of the table—she was flippant to his gallantry: "Ah, Mr. Tallman, are you guarding us from robbery tonight, or are you spying upon us?"

Tallman had no trouble with her at all: "Countess, I would take it to be not only a duty but a pleasure to do both." After Aunt Nellie completed her introductions, Agent Tallman went on to other tables, much like a ward leader making his rounds at a club's annual picnic.

Aunt Nellie meanwhile had taken Angelique and Michael Hassett "under her wing," and was explaining the meaning of the auction as it progressed on the closed-circuit TV screen they watched. Buying any horse was a great gamble, Aunt Nellie emphasized, but the important gambles were always made on fillies.

There was a roll of thunder to punctuate her idea. Michael Hassett remarked that it sounded as if they would be getting a summer squall. Angelique hoped it would pour, to relieve the heat.

Aunt Nellie wanted to be sure that Angelique understood why the female line of the horses being bid was so important. A successful colt was one that grew up to run his races and win. The winner of the Kentucky Derby, the Preakness, the Belmont or the Travers was more or less a known quantity. Then accountants and lawyers were brought in, and syndicates were formed, because the male could be mated with fifty to sixty females each year. By multiplying the number of successful matings per year times the number of years that a champion could be stood at stud, the syndicate could approximate the value of a champion. Secretariat and Riva Ridge, for example, were worth thirteen million dollars between them, because they would eventually get in foal so many mares. Stripped to its essentials, the value of a male champion was a matter of arithmetic and tax considerations. Bidding on fillies was far more interesting, because the genealogical line of champions could be improved only by the dams. "Smart breeders gamble on fillies," Aunt Nellie concluded, "at these auctions."

"Do the fillies bring higher prices?" Angelique asked.

"Yes, child, they do," said Aunt Nellie. "And you may think because you are still young that it is a man's world today. But tomorrow always belongs to the females."

Before Aunt Nellie could continue this lesson in philosophy, however, a flash of lightning cracked not far away. The thunder that followed rolled in under the tent flaps upon the crowd in The Spuyten Duyvil's garden. There was a hush of respect, then some few gathered up purses and cigarette cases from the tables, indicating that they would press in to the bar, in case the storm hit. They could wait it out until the wind and rain stopped, then go back to their tables when it had passed. As soon as the first few left for shelter, others began to follow them. A second and a third flash of lightning came down. Then another, still closer. As the cracks of thunder became sharper, the garden of The Spuyten Duyvil emptied.

Michael Hassett spoke for both Angelique and himself: "Would you like us to carry your drink inside for you, Aunt Nellie? It looks as if it's about to pour. I'm not sure how dry it will be under this tent. If it blows at all, as summer squalls sometimes do, the rain will drive right under its edges."

Aunt Nellie declined, saying that she would join them in a mo-

ment. She wanted to have just a brief private word with Angelique's mother.

Within a moment, no one remained under the garden's green-
and-white-striped tent except Suzanne and her old friend Aunt
Nellie. Just as Michael Hassett had guessed, it was soon pouring.
Water ran in sheets down the tent's draped canvas, then fell
along its edges in a continuous waterfall. The two women moved
to seats in the center of the tent.

Despite his fear of lightning, Enrique Cardinale went out into
the garden during the storm to attempt to get Suzanne and Aunt
Nellie to join the others inside. Upon his arrival they broke off
discussing whatever it was that kept them out there, and they
jointly dismissed him so harshly that he returned with his feel-
ings hurt. He waited in the safety of the doorway between the
garden and the bar inside. From that vantage point he could not
hear what they were saying to each other.

Moreover, the thunder was by then deafening. He was sure
that they were arguing. He saw Suzanne shake her head emphat-
ically *no* several times, but he never heard what it was that she
refused Aunt Nellie.

Finally he saw Aunt Nellie stand up. She was furious. She
held up two fingers almost underneath Suzanne's nose. Suzanne
stood up too, and she was laughing and shaking her head *no* all
at the same time. She held up the middle finger of her right hand
to Aunt Nellie. Enrique said Suzanne was wearing a ruby ring
on it.

18

John Putnam's Explanation
Friday

ACCORDING to John Putnam, he received a telephone call from Thomas Phelps at 9:01 A.M., Friday, August 27. The chairman of The Bank wondered if it would be convenient for Mr. Putnam to drop by The Bank's offices at about four that afternoon. By then, Mr. Phelps suggested, there might be one or two items mutually interesting to discuss.

John Putnam accepted Mr. Phelps's invitation. Then he authorized John David Garraty's public relations company to issue a press release stating that talks were under way between the management of The Bank and representatives of the Providence Holding Company, an investment company said to hold a substantial number of shares of The Bank's stock. Within ten minutes he called Suzanne in Saratoga to inform her that everything was going according to plan. He was completely surprised by her reaction.

"Get the release back," she said.

"I can't do that. By now it's probably already at the *Times*."

"Well, then, if they call you for comment, don't say another goddamn word."

"I wouldn't have anything to say until after I've met with Phelps and his people anyway."

"Don't go to that meeting."

"Suzanne, someone has to go to that meeting. Someone has to talk with those people, or at least begin talks. You can't expect American Syrup to sit still and twiddle its thumbs while you make a grab for control of its bank."

John Putnam would later be quite positive that Suzanne's reply sounded as if she thought they were discussing the grandest joke in the world. He insisted he had never heard her happier. "Don't worry," she said. "You can bet your ass she hasn't been sucking her thumb. Have a nice day, John."

As soon as Suzanne hung up, John Putnam began to get the reports. The call director at their offices in the Pan Am Building was lit up all day. As each new piece of news arrived, Putnam attempted to forward it item by item to Saratoga, but Suzanne would not come to the phone. She did not appear to be interested. She said André could make any decisions that were necessary just as well as she could. Around lunchtime Putnam insisted that André point out to Suzanne that they were in an increasingly awkward situation, that they would have to make some difficult decisions, that the matter was serious, and that time was running out for them. Putnam's advice was the time had come to make their deal with Aunt Nellie.

"I have already pointed out all of that to my wife," André replied. "She has gone off to have her hair done."

Putnam put the issue to André squarely: "Are you suggesting we make our deal with Mrs. Burns's people without Suzanne's approval?"

"I don't see that we have much choice," André answered. There was in his voice a husband's embarrassment, an apology for his wife's irrational behavior. "She's just not making any sense on this. She is pretending she doesn't give a damn."

"That's not really like her, André. Is there something else going on—I mean between Suzanne and Mrs. Burns?"

"No," André said. "Nothing. They appear to be the best of friends, just as they have always been. Aunt Nellie is coming to dinner tonight, as a matter of fact."

"I can't wait, goddammit. The meeting is scheduled for four this afternoon."

"Well then, John, do the best you can for us."

Later, in attempting to explain all the difficulties he had to meet that day, John Putnam wanted to make clear that the problems he faced did not necessarily come to him in any orderly or sequential fashion. For example, he said he had to handle fifteen phone calls from Hermes Antoniadis about the flower business—hardly their most important concern. All branches of Antoniadis' flower business were notified simultaneously that they were going to be audited by the IRS and to produce all their books and records for the past five—not three—years. "Mind you," John Putnam said, "the IRS district offices claimed that the audits of nineteen branches of one flower company had been selected at random. Nineteen simultaneous random audits!"

Around lunchtime, the FBI turned up in the precinct house at 103rd Street, demanding that the New York Police Department raid Miss Freddy's brownstones. The FBI explanation was that Miss Freddy was harboring a jewel thief whom they had a warrant to arrest as a fugitive. The city police told the FBI to cool it, they would work things out. They called Miss Freddy and said, "Look, be practical. Deliver the guy to the door and the FBI will go away."

Miss Freddy told them the truth: she didn't have the man they wanted; but the FBI agents were not going to take no for an answer. So all afternoon phone calls were going back and forth from Miss Freddy to the precinct house, from the precinct to Miss Freddy, from Miss Freddy to Judge Gordon, and between Judge Gordon and John Putnam. In the middle of everything else, John Putnam complained, he had to conduct a United Nations plenary session over the raid the FBI wanted on the brownstones. By five o'clock, Judge Gordon's advice was to let it happen. He'd have Miss Freddy out on bail in thirty minutes.

The poor cops from the precinct house had to surround the place as if they had the mad bomber trapped inside. The cops were embarrassed. Five smug FBI men stood across the street, making sure "New York's finest" did their duty. To watch this comedy, the FBI had invited the *Daily News* and all five local TV stations. They had even timed it so perfectly that there was

not only plenty of daylight left for the cameras but time enough
to get the film on the six o'clock news. The police stood around
in their riot helmets with shotguns and bullhorns. When everything was all set, and there was a big enough crowd on the
street, two FBI men walked up to the door, knocked politely,
showed their warrants, did the part where they read off the
"Miranda" rights. They made sure the cameras got it all. Out of
Suzanne's brownstones walked Miss Freddy, five pretty women
with their hands up, four guys from the Racquet Club, and a city
councilman. Miss Freddy, said John Putnam, gave the crowd a
big wave; "and I'm told," he added, "they gave her five minutes
of cheers." The result, however, was that the brownstones were
ruined property. "I don't think the Snow White thing was really
what upset them," said John Putnam. "They made use of it.
They probably talked about it. I am sure that Tom Phelps was
capable of saying something like . . . oh, something to the effect
that in the midst of the city's financial crisis it would be bad policy to have a madam in control of one of the major city banks.
He'd emphasize the image thing. Talk about bad public relations. But hell, he wouldn't really care one way or another."

Before he would continue, John Putnam told me he wanted to
go "off the record." Well, then, if what he said was not "off the
record," he wanted to be sure there would be no direct attribu-
tion. "Highly placed source" would satisfy him.

"The trouble with you journalists," he said, "is that you are always looking for some sneaky conspiracy. There are no conspira-
cies. There might be what muckrakers like to call a 'club,' with
all those overtones of exclusiveness; or what is constantly being
called the 'establishment,' but there really isn't any establishment either. It is only a matter of arithmetic. There are these
piles of assets, and somebody has to take responsibility for
watching over them. Otherwise there would be anarchy."

Having delivered his speech, he picked up the threads of his
story: By the time he walked into Tom Phelps's office at four
o'clock, he said, there were really no choices left about what was
the practical thing to do. "Just listen," he said, "to what The
Bank and their friends at American Syrup had accomplished by
Friday afternoon."

First of all, the stock of The Bank was up fifteen points by noon. There was no longer any way for André or Suzanne or Tony Scott or anyone else to buy in at any practical price. Simultaneously, the stocks of André's land companies were being sold off in such massive lots that by noon they had lost 80 per cent of their value, and the Securities and Exchange Commission stopped trading, pending an investigation. The investigation would turn up nothing, of course, but meanwhile Suzanne was locked in and her brokers and banks were calling for cash to cover her margins.

The shopping-center company, which was traded over the counter, dropped from fifty-five to four in two hours; same thing—trading suspended. The stocks of the two insurance companies were driven down in the same way. In addition, both insurance companies were given notice that their state departments of insurance wanted to audit their operations. There was nothing wrong, the auditors eventually agreed, but by then it was six months later. "Sure," John Putnam agreed. "They were running short pools.

"Against the law?" John Putnam laughed at the very idea. "Of course it was, if Aunt Nellie lost. But she didn't lose. The law comes down on the side of the victors—that should not be a shocking revelation to any educated citizen."

John Putnam ticked off a few laws American Syrup thought would be useful to maintain their control over a major New York City bank. In Albany, the governor discovered that in a similar case in 1969, the legislature had passed a law forbidding "takeovers" of major banks without a study by the governor's office of the possible effects. Such a study would take not less than six months to complete, if it ever was. In Washington, a comparable bill, introduced by the chairman of the Senate Banking and Currency Committee, included provisions instructing the comptroller of the currency to make a similar study "on any bank whose interstate interests might affect the welfare of the nation as a whole." Still another bill with identical purposes was introduced and assured passage in the House of Representatives. Both bills, said John Putnam, were actually drafted by American Syrup's law firm in Wall Street and flown down to Washington that morning. "What you must understand," he emphasized, "is that the language of the provisions in one bill contradicted the language of the articles in the other. There would be no possible way for anyone to straighten out the almost perfect confusion created by those two bills in anything less than five years. In the meantime, the comptroller of the currency had the clear duty, as expressed by Congress, to consider any change in the control of a major bank very carefully."

The Bank, he said, paid the legal fees to draft both congressional bills. One hundred thousand dollars for a work of genius "like those bills were" was, in his estimation, "one tenth of what they were worth."

Under the circumstances, said Putnam, the offer made at four that afternoon was generous and an offer he would advise Suzanne to accept. When he sat down with Tom Phelps and The Bank's team, "no one was baring any teeth. They were being perfectly reasonable. There was not going to be any element of revenge, they said. Nothing like that."

American Syrup offered to buy up all the companies whose stock they had spent all day wrecking. There was some discussion back and forth about whether the prices ought to be as of the closing on Thursday night at their highs, or Friday afternoon at their lows. The American Syrup people argued that if they paid the Thursday-afternoon price, they would end up paying twice for the stock they had sold off. Tom Phelps overruled them, saying that with The Bank's loan department behind them, the companies in question could probably earn back any losses for the stockholders, or be merged in such a way that no one had to be hurt.

The bank people, however, were extremely difficult about the Providence Holding Company equities in Nassau. Fortunately, the American Syrup people were willing to pay nearly the price André asked. He would be paid by transfers from their tax accounts: "The United States Government will pay for them." Once these major elements were worked out, both Tom Phelps and the American Syrup people agreed to withdraw the rash of lawsuits instituted that morning against everything and anyone identified with André or John Putnam. More than fifty suits were involved, but the bank's lawyers and those of American Syrup agreed they could all be settled amicably. In each case André or John Putnam or their nominees would be "held harmless," and the legal fees absorbed either by The Bank directly or by American Syrup, or if need be, by the subsidiaries acquired. As a guarantee of American Syrup's good faith, The Bank would offer two seats upon its board of directors: one for Count André de Montreuil, or any nominee he chose to name; and one for John Putnam, as representative of Suzanne's associated interests.

All these matters were settled in less than forty minutes. John Putnam was back in his office at the Pan Am Building before five o'clock. He telephoned Judge Gordon immediately afterward, and Ephraim Gordon stated unequivocally that he was sure Mr. Scott would be entirely satisfied.

Within five minutes, in fact, Judge Gordon called back to say that he had just spoken with Mr. Scott; that Mr. Scott approved everything Putnam had arranged; and that Mr. Scott wanted John Putnam to know that in Mr. Scott's opinion, "Putnam has handled the entire matter extremely well."

"Tell Mr. Scott I am honored by his comments."

"There's one more thing, John."

"What can I do to help, Judge?"

"Mr. Scott wishes you to tell Suzanne that his information is there is a contract out on her."

"Oh, Jesus. Are you sure?"

"John, we are sure. We want to make clear to both you and Suzanne that it is not our contract. These people are from Detroit, and we already have lines out to stop this thing, because there is no point in it, no point at all. These things just cause trouble and raise a lot of unnecessary questions. You will tell Suzanne we are working on it, won't you?"

"Well, whose contract is it, then?"

"That's not so easy. The Detroit people are crazy. We've had problems with them along these lines before. We'll do what we can."

"Can you give us a guess?"

"John, this is too much talk on the telephone already. But Mr. Scott told me to go ahead, because he says Suzanne has always been such a fine woman."

"Some kind of guess about where she should see it coming from?"

"The sugar lady, but that's only our guess."

"I've just settled with them."

"That's the point we'll be making with Detroit."

19

Public Relations Man

Friday Night

AT FIVE o'clock Friday afternoon, John Putnam telephoned Saratoga to relay the good news. André de Montreuil took Putnam's call, explaining that Suzanne had gone out to the island in the middle of her lake, that there was no practical way to reach her, that she would not be back for at least an hour. Yet André was anxious to hear the news.

"They've agreed to two seats," Putnam said.

"On the board of the sugar company or at The Bank?"

"At The Bank."

"Not so bad, John!"

"All we could have hoped for, André."

"What about the suits?"

"They will drop them all—with prejudice, André."

"Does 'with prejudice' mean the same thing as 'hold harmless,' John?"

"Yes, as a practical matter, as far as we are concerned, it will mean the same thing." Putnam chuckled as he continued: "They were not too pleased with the book values of some of those companies of yours, but they took them all anyway."

André wanted to be sure: "Did they buy them at Thursday's closing price or at today's lows?"

"There was a bit of haggling over that, my friend, but they finally accepted Thursday's highs. They will be merging all that junk of yours into the American Syrup Corporation. They will swallow the losses, take the tax write-offs, and then probably spin off anything of any value after a year or two."

André insisted that not everything in the portfolio of Providence Holding was, as John Putnam was describing it, junk. "There were some substantial values there."

"Sure," John Putnam said. "But just think of it this way, citizen of France: thanks to our tax laws, the government of the United States of America will be paying you for all the water in your offshore stocks by giving you shares in the domestic American sugar market. You're giving up very little to mix sugar with your water!"

"Ah, John. And Suzanne's interests?"

"They have not done quite as well, but she'll survive."

"And the two seats, John; who takes the two seats on the board of Mrs. Burns's bank?"

John Putnam spelled out the decision he had made. He enunciated just a bit more carefully: "I told Tom Phelps that you would be taking one and I would take the other." He waited on the line through no more than a two-second pause before he continued; "that seems about right, don't you agree?"

André de Montreuil had apparently understood. He answered just as carefully. "Yes, that seems about right. Together we should be able to watch out for Suzanne's interests."

"We see eye to eye, André." John Putnam could bring their exchange to a close. "There's one more thing. I still need to talk to Suzanne tonight anyway. The moment she returns, please have her call me. It's just a detail, but it might be urgent."

"Anything I can do, John?"

"Not a thing. It's probably nothing major, but I would rather speak to her directly."

"Any message I can pass along?"

"No, it's not really what we might agree to call a company matter. It's more or less personal. Just be sure she calls, all right?"

"Not to worry, John. I don't think you and I are going to have any difficulty agreeing on company matters. We'll all be on the same team. And I'll see to it that my wife calls. Let me say you've done a great job, John, under very difficult circumstances. A fine piece of negotiation for all of us."

"Thanks, partner. I try to do my best."

When André put down the telephone, John Putnam's call left him in a mood of proprietary satisfaction. The bank deal, after all, had worked out quite nicely; in many ways, far better than he had expected. Since he would probably be required to wait at least another half hour or so before Suzanne returned from her temple in the lake, he went to the pantry door, ordered the kitchen staff to deliver a drink to the porch behind the house, then stationed himself in a white wicker chair to await Suzanne's return. It would be a pleasure to announce to her the news of their victory.

With a gin and tonic in his hand, André surveyed Suzanne's lake as if he were a sentinel, or perhaps as the new lord of the manor. In the late-afternoon August sun, the lake glittered with light, and its centerpiece shone—the circular, columned white marble temple upon its little island—flashing bright, dazzling whites, almost as if it were itself a source of light.

Sipping his drink, André could savor the advantages of a traditional bank connection, and at the same time watch for Suzanne's appearance upon the island's shore, emerging from the interior of what he called her "*musée*."

André knew that when she did appear she would be in the company of Enrique Cardinale, the architect and designer of what André tolerated as his wife's "little hobby." Since Suzanne had not yet allowed him to enter her private temple, and Enrique was apparently free to know everything, André had to admit that his exclusion sometimes subjected him to small twinges of jealousy—perfectly foolish, of course, but incurable. Suzanne and Enrique spent hours over drawings and plans and sketches André was never allowed to see. On the other hand, as Suzanne was quick to point out, Enrique was perfectly harmless, and Suzanne unquestionably had a right to go over the plans with her decorator. After all, whom else should she consult? Suzanne always put André off when it came to seeing what had been done, saying that it was not ready yet, or when it was all finished, or some such.

Even if he did not yet know what it might contain, André assumed he would eventually. Besides, despite his uneasiness from time to time, as he watched Suzanne's project take shape he had gradually accumulated a certain pride of his own in her achievement, because it was—without doubt—a considerable engineering feat. He expressed his pride in his own wry way by telling his friends that his wife "was building her very own Panama Canal."

André had watched the progress of construction almost from its beginnings. The temple had been built first. A road was paved through the meadow and run to the wooded knoll that would become the island. A paved road was necessary to carry the weights of the equipment and the loaded trucks that hauled the steel, concrete and cut blocks of white marble to the building site. Nearly two years were spent on the construction of the temple itself, and then another year was devoted to its interior. Because upstate New York winters were severe, most of the work had to be accomplished each year during the short summer. André knew that inside the temple's circular façade there was some kind of labyrinth; and, from bits and pieces of information, he inferred that a great deal of plate glass was used somehow in the museum's interior.

In 1974 the temple itself was substantially complete. The next year was spent removing the road used to construct it, then building the earthwork dam, facing the earthwork with granite riprap, constructing the spillways, and building the gates that eventually contained the mountain stream, and thereby creating the lake. To do all this, gigantic machines were necessary: yellow cranes, bulldozers, bucket loaders, backing and filling at their task for a year. Finally, graders and crews of men smoothed away any signs of the effort. Grass was planted again and curried. Trees and bushes were restored along the lake's new shore, as if Nature herself had created the whole effect.

Yet André was told that the *musée* was still not ready. Suzanne and Enrique continued to work on the effects of its interior. There were substantial difficulties, because every scrap of material had to be ferried by barge to the temple's isolated site— across the shallow but considerable new lake. André watched these comings and goings with an overwhelming curiosity. Despite his worldly experience, he found himself spying like a child before Christmas, and still learned nothing. Cargoes ferried across the lake were always shrouded, or wrapped, or disguised in cartons. "In due time," his wife promised him, "I shall lead you through a guided tour. With a string, just as Ariadne did."

It was Suzanne's own reference to Ariadne which was one of André's surest clues: her temple must include some sort of labyrinth. Hence, having just won what he planned to describe to Suzanne as "quite a nice little victory," André stood guard in a white wicker chair on the back porch of his wife's house, sipping gin and tonic, and waited to tell her news of the bank—news that was freighted not only with all the perquisites of victory but perhaps at last intimacies long overdue as well. Whatever it was that Suzanne played with—the toys she shared in her secret dollhouse out on the lake with no one but Enrique—could hardly compare with the importance of the merger accomplished that August afternoon with Aunt Nellie's bank.

In that sense, then, the Count André de Montreuil viewed the landscape of Suzanne's beautiful lake almost with new eyes: the pine-covered mountain standing as a backdrop; the studio nestled at its base, providing scale; the stream emerging from the woods on the left and then cascading across the dam upon the right. It was indeed a very satisfactory picture; his wife was, he could conclude, a woman of great taste. It was just then that he could finally make out, across the lake, the figures of Suzanne and Enrique emerging from between the temple's encircling columns. He could see they had rowed to the island in the skiff instead of using the outboard-powered barge, which was still moored to the dock at the landing upon the near shore. The pleasure of André's mood was heightened when he saw that as the skiff left the temple and approached the shore, it was Suzanne who manned the oars and Enrique who sat in the stern, trailing his hand overboard just as romantic young women sometimes do when being rowed around the park. André stood to welcome their approach.

When Suzanne had made the skiff fast and finally came walking up the slope of the lawn toward her house, André was waiting for her at the top of the piazza's stairs, ready with all the good news.

"We've won two seats," he said. He was exultant.

"Marvelous," said Suzanne. She had been barefoot as she

walked up the lawn, but now she stopped to put on her shoes, using Enrique's shoulder as a support for her balance. She seemed almost uninterested.

"American Syrup bought us out, right down the line. They gave us prices that are just fine. Really, not bad at all." He smiled as he waited, as if expecting to be rewarded.

"Terrific," was all that Suzanne said as she started up the steps.

Perhaps she didn't understand the significance of what he was saying: "They've agreed to drop all the suits," André added.

"Couldn't be better, darling." She had reached him at the top of the stairs and bestowed upon his cheek the kiss he deserved for his victory.

"Aren't you pleased?" he asked.

"Of course I am," she said. "Everything that makes you happy makes me happy too." She appeared to be sincere.

"We're allies now. Partners, in effect, with Aunt Nellie."

"So it would seem, my pet." There was no irony in her voice.

"Which will be grand fun, don't you think?" There was a hint of petulance in André's query. "I mean, you have always been close friends anyway."

"So we have, André, so we have."

"Suzanne, you don't seem to understand. We took a bit of a gamble with all this, you know. But we've come out of it quite nicely. Two seats on the board of The Bank, and all the co-operation of American Syrup—why, that's worth its weight in gold—no, in diamonds!"

"My adorable husband: I'm just as pleased as you are, for heaven's sake. And we'll celebrate, just as you suggest. I am only a bit weary now, and we must get ready for dinner. I am truly glad it has turned out so well, just as well as you predicted all along. I am too old to do cartwheels, but I'll try if that's what would please you. Really!"

"No, no, Suzanne, this is no occasion for anger. Tonight's a night for celebration. Isn't it marvelous that Aunt Nellie is coming to dinner tonight anyway? I mean, now that we are all partners?"

"Aunt Nellie never discusses business on social visits."

"Of course not. Nevertheless, we know, and she knows, and we know that she knows. Delicious, don't you agree?"

"André, you are not at all The Shark everyone says you are. At bottom you are a romantic little boy. That's very sweet."

"Putnam asked that you call him just as soon as you came in. He's left the number where he is waiting for you. It's on the pad beside your bedside phone."

"If you will let me escape your endless crowing, I shall do exactly as you say. I shall go upstairs to my bedroom phone and call John right away like a good little girl. Did he say what it was about?"

"No, he said it was just a detail to be cleared up, but that it was urgent. Be sure," André called after her as she started for the screen door, "to tell John Putnam what a fine job he did. Difficult circumstances, too. According to John, Mr. Scott is as pleased as we are."

Suzanne had stopped momentarily with her hand poised on the screen door's handle. "Well, that's one good thing."

"The point is, Suzanne, that it is good to stay on the right side of fellows like Mr. Scott."

"I've always thought so, André."

When the screen door had banged closed behind her, André turned to Enrique, who had stood aside silently while husband and wife compared notes on their victory. "Well, it's a fact isn't it, Enrique? Women can certainly be baffling at times."

"Yes, I suppose you could say that," Enrique replied. Then without pausing, he explained that he had a few details he would like to see to in the kitchen—for tonight's dinner. "So that it will be fun," he said, as he too left the porch.

For another ten or fifteen minutes, André occupied the wicker chair on the back porch. He inspected the ice in his glass and watched the beauties of Suzanne's lake as August's sun lengthened its shafts toward evening. Then he left his drink behind to join his wife upstairs in their bedroom. He wanted to know what John Putnam had to say.

Suzanne answered that Putnam had told her much the same thing as he had told André: everything had worked out perfectly. "I agree," said Suzanne, "that with you and John on Aunt Nellie's board my interests will be well taken care of. Would you like to hear a rundown of our guests tonight?"

"Aunt Nellie, of course," said André.

"And," Suzanne added, "her very good friend, Adam Shepherd."

"Don't Enrique and Adam have some sort of surprise for you?"

Yes, Suzanne thought they did. No, she had not guessed what it was. In addition, she said, she had asked Michael Hassett to come across from his studio and join them—as an escort for Angelique. Then there would be Ms. Gail Fowler, the fashion editor—she was staying with the Russeks in Saratoga, and Suzanne had sent James Moriarity with the car to pick her up. Gail Fowler could be paired with Enrique for the evening.

Senator Lewis Reeves from Wyoming and his wife, Nadine, were spending the week with Aunt Nellie, and they would be coming over in Aunt Nellie's caravan. He is a bit of a bore on the subject of the environment, Suzanne remarked, and her advice to André was to avoid the topic if possible, or to simply agree with the senator if necessary until he ran out of steam. They would all be better off if they didn't have to hear long speeches on energy and all that. The senator's wife, on the other hand, was quite charming, in Suzanne's opinion. It was her money the senator used to get re-elected every six years. It was too bad Nadine Reeves didn't run herself, instead of using her husband as a stand-in.

To round the party out, Suzanne had invited Mr. and Mrs. Richard Gould, who were people André surely remembered—they were the couple with the box next to theirs at the track. "He's a bond dealer," André said. "I've known him for years."

"Twelve altogether," said Suzanne, "at eight o'clock in the bar."

Between eight and eight-thirty the guests of the Count and Countess de Montreuil gathered in the bar Suzanne had redecorated like a miniature Las Vegas casino. Along one wall was a row of slot machines, and they were machines that really worked. At the mahogany bar running along the opposite wall, saucers held quarters, half dollars and dollars for the guests who would like to play the slots. If any guest was discouraged by a long run without hitting a jackpot, Enrique would come out from behind the bar with a key, unlock the back of the machine, and resupply the saucers with coins. No guest could lose unless he chose to.

The cocktail tables were blackjack tables, cut down slightly so that the women could sit comfortably upon the six chairs around their circumference. But their felt covers were marked for the squares to contain the decks and the squares where each player's cards would be dealt. Either Suzanne or André sat in a dealer's chair, which they had found was an admirable way to keep conversation going before dinner. The bar was small, but the entire effect—the Las Vegas chrome and black Naugahyde imitation-leather stripping—made it a silly enough place to loosen everyone's tongue.

Aunt Nellie's group arrived at eight-thirty. Suzanne embraced her with the enthusiasm of a daughter who had not seen her mother for a year. The two principal women in the room were not only openly affectionate with each other but spread from their common bond a kind of generous joviality that soon infected everyone else. Not a word about the environment was heard from Senator Reeves. Not a sentence about inflation from Richard Gould. Instead everyone began to insist upon seeing the present that Adam and Enrique had kept a secret from Suzanne.

Adam Shepherd went back out to Aunt Nellie's car and returned with a birdcage covered with a white linen cloth. When Adam pulled off the cover, he unveiled a thick-billed parrot about eighteen inches long. The parrot was soft green, from Mexico, with a red cap and bright red markings at the shoulders of his wings and along the plumage down near his short legs. On the swing of his cage he gripped the bar with two toes in front and two behind.

Suzanne clapped her hands with delight.

"Does he say anything?"

"Only two words, as far as we know." Both Adam and Enrique were trying to explain at once: "'No comment.'"

With which the parrot dutifully squawked at them all, "No commen'," or something nearly like it.

Everyone laughed at the miserable bird. He surveyed them with his fierce and unforgiving eye, and repeated what he knew: "No commen'."

Suzanne asked, "Does he already have a name?"

"Of course he does," Aunt Nellie answered. "Tell her what you've named him, boys."

"You'll never guess," said Adam.

"We've had enough guessing games," said Aunt Nellie.

"We had to have something appropriate," said Enrique.

"We thought it was appropriate," said Adam.

"What is it, for heaven's sake?" Suzanne said.

"Public Relations Man," they said.

"Does he answer to that?"

"Try him."

Suzanne came close to the bird's cage, giving everyone the impression that she was going to meet the parrot eye-ball to eye-ball. When bird and woman had fixed their stares upon each other, everyone fell quiet. The parrot shifted its toes upon its bar.

Suzanne moved her face to within an inch of the cage between them. The parrot feinted with its beak toward Suzanne's eyes, but Suzanne would not flinch. Suzanne barely whispered at it: "Public Relations Man."

"No commen'."

No one broke the silence by laughter, or even a giggle. Suzanne moved her face even closer to the cage.

"Be careful, darling." André had spoken up behind her. "Those things can give you a really awful bite."

Suzanne ignored him. She had the parrot's eye now, and she was not going to give in to even a blink. She whispered this time so low that not everyone in the room behind her heard what she said clearly. Gail Fowler was near enough to the cage to swear that what she heard Suzanne say was, "Murder."

The parrot answered: "No commen'."

Suzanne turned around to her audience immediately afterward as a magician would, to take a bow for her performance, and quickly, before anyone saw how the trick was done. Everyone did as he was expected and applauded. "Thank you," said Suzanne. "That's a very intelligent parrot. Thank you, Adam, and thank you, Enrique."

James Moriarity coughed discreetly from the door of the bar. "Dinner is ready, madame."

At dinner Suzanne seated Michael Hassett upon her right, and she took Richard Gould at her left hand. For part of the time, she was able to get Michael Hassett talking about art, but when strawberries came around for dessert, there was no stopping Richard Gould: He had for some reason been prompted to remember the days in 1929 when the stock market was crashing.

Day by day he quoted the price of "Radio" as the stock fell from four hundred and something or other to thirty-five. He had the opening price, the closing price, and the number of shares traded permanently lodged in his head from Black Friday until sometime after the New Year in 1930. He was determined to make Michael Hassett appreciate the meaning of money in those days. Suzanne was relieved of Richard Gould's siege only when she could rise from the table and announce that they would take their coffee in the living room.

"Let's play hide-and-seek instead," said Adam Shepherd.

"Oh, yes, let's," said Enrique.

Rather than be trapped by another one of Richard Gould's histories of the stock market, Suzanne agreed. "What do you want us to do?"

Adam Shepherd must have planned it beforehand, because his explanation did not miss a beat. He said that everyone should go back to the bar. They could have coffee there, if Suzanne didn't mind. Aunt Nellie was wearing the Montevideo diamond, as they could all see. It came in a setting, he pointed out, that allowed it to be detached. It could be worn as a ring that way; or as Aunt Nellie was wearing it tonight, around her neck on a chain as a pendant. He would hide the diamond somewhere in the living room. When he was ready they could all come in and play "hot and cold." That was how the game worked. If someone was getting nearer to it, Adam would say he was getting warmer. If he was getting farther away, Adam would tell him colder. The first one to find the Montevideo would be the winner.

"Do we get the diamond?" said André.

"Don't be silly," said Aunt Nellie. She was already unlocking the latches that held the Montevideo in place. The diamond was egg-shaped, huge, about the size of one of Suzanne's Jensen eggs, and must have weighed in at forty carats. Aunt Nellie said, "You're putting up the prizes tonight, André my sweet."

"So I am, Aunt Nellie," he answered proudly. "Well, the winner gets a case of champagne—how's that?"

"Fabulous," said Adam. "Just fabulous!"

When they had all returned to the bar, Suzanne pulled Enrique aside and asked him to get the goddamn parrot out of there. "Take it into the living room. I've had enough public relations for today."

Enrique did as he was told, explaining to everyone that he was just getting the parrot ready for bed. "Parrots go to bed early; that's how they live to be a hundred." He thought the best place for P. R. Man to sleep would be on top of the piano, and he would be right back. Meanwhile the others waited, as guests after dinner do, for the last of the evening's entertainments to come and go so that it would be time to return home to their own beds.

After an interminable delay, time enough to empty a second after-dinner drink, Adam and Enrique appeared together. "Wait a minute," Angelique said. "You can't play, Enrique, because now you also know where the Montevideo is hidden."

Enrique agreed that he did, and that he would keep silent and give no more clues than those Adam gave. With that assurance, everyone trooped over to Suzanne's living room to begin the search. As they were leaving the bar, the last three people were Michael Hassett, Suzanne and André, in that order. "Wait, Michael." Suzanne stopped him and took a silver dollar from one of the saucers upon the bar. "Are you lucky?"

"Sometimes I am," he said.

"Play," she said, handing him the silver dollar and pointing at the slot machine.

Obediently he dropped the dollar in the slot and pulled down on the handle. The machine whirred, slowed to a stop and rang its bell. Silver dollars cascaded all over the bar floor—one of them rolling past André's monogrammed evening slippers and not stopping until it had disappeared under the radiator register on the far side of the room.

"You're lucky," said Suzanne, putting her arm through Michael Hassett's and walking away with him toward the shouts and cries in the living room. Behind them her husband stood still for a moment with his feet in a litter of silver dollars. As if rooted to the spot, he watched Suzanne disappear with Michael Hassett, then stepped over the dollars to follow them.

In the living room the game designed by Adam Shepherd had already turned into a disaster. "Warm," "hot" and "hotter" were in the area around the parrot's cage on top of the piano. "Cold," "colder," "coldest" were anywhere two feet away or farther. The game was pointless, no one was amused by it, and they would just as soon have had it end instantly. Without exception they all agreed that the Montevideo must be in the parrot's cage, and would Enrique please remove the night cover so they could see if they were right.

Somewhat downcast that their game had been such a failure, Enrique and Adam together pulled the cover up from the cage. The parrot fluttered his wings and puffed his chest and ruffled his feathers at them. He was blinking his eyes just as any old man would who had been robbed of his sleep. The Montevideo diamond, however, was not at the bottom of his cage. Adam Shepherd almost shrieked: "But I swear, that's where I put it."

In retrospect, what ensued perhaps made no sense. On the other hand, they were all tired, there had been plenty to drink at cocktails, and at dinner, and while they waited for the game to end. In any case, there was a great babble of confusion. There was bombast by Senator Reeves and Richard Gould, who seemed to be in a contest to outshout each other. There were pleadings, excuses, beggings for forgiveness from Aunt Nellie by Adam and Enrique. No one was listening to anyone else. Suggestions first made by Gail Fowler that perhaps they had been robbed by a cat burglar—which she would say later she assumed everyone would think was a joke—were then taken up as a cry to call the police, the state troopers, the FBI, immediately.

André did his best to calm everyone, to talk some sense, but no one cared to listen. Aunt Nellie had no objection at all to the police being called, and Suzanne aided and abetted her demand that André call the FBI immediately. Perhaps Suzanne had her own reasons, but the result of this silly scene was that Aunt Nellie ordered Adam Shepherd to telephone John Tallman of the FBI at the Albany office. Since Adam Shepherd was chagrined enough at the turn events had taken, he did as he was told.

Everyone then calmed down, taking a seat in the living room, waiting for the great detective to arrive, just as if they were assembled by Hercule Poirot in an Agatha Christie mystery—"and no one is to leave this room." André even played along with Aunt Nellie to the extent that he ordered the servants at the back of the house to remain in the kitchen until further orders, and to be prepared to be questioned along with everyone else. It would take John Tallman about forty minutes to get up from Saratoga, Tallman had said, but he was on the way.

While they waited, they mixed themselves a drink or two, and their hysteria began to subside. At first there was hardly a word spoken, because by then they were all too embarrassed to think of anything worth saying. Michael Hassett was the first to propose what was probably the solution: The parrot had swallowed the diamond.

Arguments against his conclusion were made, but they were desultory. If the parrot had swallowed the diamond, no one wanted to admit to being a fool without hearing it confirmed by proper authority. Angelique said, "Michael's right, and we'd better tell Mr. Tallman that as soon as he gets here."

When John Tallman did arrive and had listened attentively to the sequence of events laid out in an orderly form, he was diplomatic about his conclusions. He came to them thoroughly, but slowly, and he never laughed at even the silliest proposal he heard. He was cheery throughout, returned from the kitchen after having questioned the servants, and agreed readily with Suzanne when she suggested that the FBI "stake out" her place for the night "in case the robbers returned." He would stand guard himself, he said.

On the other hand, he thought that if they would all go on to bed and get a good night's rest, they would probably have a chance to find out in the morning "whether a parrot could pass a diamond."

"Yes." Suzanne picked up on his theme and the light style with which he was handling it. "Mr. Tallman will be guarding our doors all night. We'll be perfectly safe. Aunt Nellie and Adam, you can stay here with us, and so can the Goulds, and Gail, and Senator and Mrs. Reeves. The guest rooms are ready and made up. We'll have a grand breakfast in the morning; then we'll all go together to have a look at the bottom of the parrot's cage. André has to open the case of champagne for breakfast for us all."

She continued the theme she was developing. "Wouldn't you say that it would be best for everyone to stay right here, Mr. Tallman?"

"That would be a great help, Countess."

"You wouldn't object if Mr. Hassett walked back across the dam to his studio on the other side of the lake, would you?"

"I am clean, Mr. Tallman; you can search me," Michael Hassett chimed in.

John Tallman had already made his assessment of Michael Hassett, and he had no objections.

"I'd like to go with Michael, if no one minds," said Angelique.

Suzanne had been afraid that one was coming, and she had not thought of any way to handle it. To her surprise, it was Aunt Nellie who spoke up for her. "Just this one night, young lady, you should stay with your mother and keep her company."

There was in Aunt Nellie's suggestion an authority to which Angelique consented immediately. Within a half hour, Suzanne's overnight guests had been assigned and dispatched to the extra bedrooms. It happened that Angelique offered the second bed in her own bedroom to Gail Fowler, and while Gail occupied the bathroom, Angelique decided to return downstairs to help her mother turn out the lights.

At the top of the stairs, however, Angelique could see that the first-floor lights were already out. Only the stairwell lights were still on. In the semidarkness Angelique could hear the quiet voices of Aunt Nellie and her mother approaching the foot of the stairs. For reasons Angelique could not quite explain, instead of returning to her room she backed away from the banister railing above the stairwell into the shadows of the second-floor hallway. Although she could not see either her mother or Aunt Nellie, Angelique would later insist that she remembered exactly every word exchanged between them.

She heard Aunt Nellie say, "If my diamond shows up, I'd like to have it back if you don't mind. It has sentimental value."

Suzanne, laughing, answered, "But of course, darling. Thing is, as you know perfectly well, I don't have it."

"I mean in case you do."

"Well, I don't."

There were footsteps starting up the stairs. Angelique began to retreat toward the door of her bedroom, but she stopped as the footsteps stopped, and as Aunt Nellie demanded: "Wait, Suzanne, and listen. You and I must come to an understanding. I have given your men the two seats on my boards anyway, which is all they asked. I have no use for your Mr. Putnam, nor for André. I did it to make peace with you."

"How very generous of you, Aunt Nellie."

"You must understand, however, that I don't care much for some of your other friends, especially your Mr. Scott. I see no reason to do business with people like that."

"But I do, Mrs. Burns, because I am like that."

"Don't be silly, Suzanne. You come from a perfectly good family."

"I don't see how that makes any difference, do you?"

"Of course it makes a difference. Of course it does. It makes a difference in who we can trust."

"Fiddlesticks."

"Suzanne, what would it take to make peace between us?"

"I have no use for peace, Aunt Nellie. I want freedom, to do as I please, today and every day."

"You can't have that any more. It's too late for that. You have Angelique to think of. You must think about tomorrow, too. When you're my age, you'll see."

"Never."

"Suzanne, don't be impossible. I am trying to be reasonable, to talk to you as a mother would to her own daughter. You know how fond I have always been of you."

"Never."

"Suzanne, I beseech you. Try to understand. There is a great deal at stake. You simply cannot play with inheritances like yours and mine as if they were toys. Too many people depend upon us. Take my hand, give me a promise that you will stop. Let me believe we can trust each other."

Suzanne answered just as quietly: "You bought André off for nothing more than a seat on the board of your silly bank."

"He was for sale. You knew that."

"I know it now."

"It was in our mutual interest."

"I didn't agree."

Then, according to Angelique, Aunt Nellie said: "I'll send you back André anytime you want."

"As far as I'm concerned, you can keep him. I'll stick with the Tony Scotts."

"Suzanne, neither of us can afford the Tony Scotts. In the long run, we can't trust them."

"In the long run, Aunt Nellie, we are all dead."

"Suzanne!"

"It's a quote, Aunt Nellie, from Lord Keynes."

"I don't think I know him."

"He's dead. He was a famous economist."

"I don't know anything about that. You are not being serious, Suzanne."

"I am being perfectly serious. You want me to be solemn, like you are. Never."

"Suzanne, the point is that the Tony Scotts are criminals. We have every reason to be afraid of them. You should too."

"Tony Scott is a criminal only because he won't always play the game by your rules."

"A vicious criminal all the same."

"And not from a good family."

"All right, Suzanne. All right. What I am trying to explain to you is that we do everything we can to avoid playing by Tony Scott's rules. There's no point to it."

Angelique's impression was that her mother stepped down the two or three steps she had taken up the stairs. In the lull that occurred, Angelique used the pause to edge from the shadows of the second-floor hallway closer to the stairwell's banister. Yet she still could not see the duel, only hear her mother's voice resume.

"Are you threatening me, Aunt Nellie?"

"In a way, yes, because I must. It's for your own good. I have no alternative."

"If you were free, you would always have a choice."

"But that's what I am trying to explain: we are not free."

"In reality, Aunt Nellie, you're saying that you don't own your banks and your companies and all that sugar—it owns you."

"If you must put it that way, yes. If you want to say it that way, all right. And you are no different than I am now, because you have merged all that you earned into my companies, and whether we like it or not, willy-nilly, we have common responsibilities."

"Boring. What are you asking me to do?"

"Make peace. Separate our interests from Tony Scott's—and all
his friends. Work together."

"I can't do that."

"You must. We can work it out. You'll see."

"And if I refuse?"

"Please don't."

"All right, Aunt Nellie, I'll tell you what. I'll make you a
swap."

"At last! You're making sense. What can we do to join hands?"

"You keep André. He's got no sentimental value for me now,
and he would make a handsome pet. Very dignified. Fine bank
director. In exchange, I'll take your Montevideo."

"You can't be serious."

"Absolutely."

Aunt Nellie's answer came in a hiss: "I'll see you in hell first."

Then, because she could hear her mother starting up the stairs
once more, Angelique scurried down the hall, retreating behind
the door of her own room. According to Angelique, neither of
the two voices were ever raised. "It was all said—well, quite politely."

Within another hour, Suzanne's great house did at last settle
down. Every light went out, even the pair of lanterns that usually remained lit outside the front door. The plain green government Dodge parked in the driveway in front of the house
showed no lights either, except a flare from time to time when
John Tallman or his fellow FBI agent from the Albany office lit a
cigarette. They sat in the car's front seat waiting, pretending to
guard Suzanne's important guests from any further dangers—in
the aftermath of what later would be described with a smile by
some as "The Great Parrot Robbery."

Agent Tallman's companion was bored by the wait. "This is
bullshit, John, and you know it. It's time we got some sleep.
What the hell are we staked out here for? That parrot swallowed
the goddamn glass. Even crows will do that. They'll find it there
in the bottom of the cage in the morning. There hasn't been any
crime committed here, and you know it."

"Not yet," Senior Agent Tallman said, "but we'll wait just the
same."

20

Actes Gratuits

After Midnight

IN HER dark, silenced house, Suzanne lay awake beside André, listening to the sounds of night outside the windows of her bedroom. A whippoorwill advertised his position over and over, but finally gave up. Katydids sang choruses to each other. A night owl took the tenor's part for a while. When she was absolutely sure of the rhythm of her husband's breathing, she turned back her sheet and got up.

She pulled on her housecoat. She went to the bureau, slid back its top drawer carefully, searched with her fingers until she found the John Kloss Caprolan nightgown she wanted. She crossed the bedroom again, and had to drop to her knees to search the bottom of her closet with her hands until she could identify the lemon sandals by their straps. With the sandals and the nightgown in her left hand, she stood again, reviewing the checklist she had prepared, then crossed the bedroom once again in the dark, moving carefully as she neared her dressing table. As she moved the fingers of her right hand over the array of her pots and jars, she knocked the cover from the cold cream and it clinked. She froze and waited. The tempo of André's sleep continued. Then she found the bottle of perfume she wanted and her hairbrush, and her equipment was complete.

Getting downstairs was no problem at all. She went to the kitchen first, deposited her bundle on the kitchen table, but could not decide for a moment how to handle the problem of light. She was going to need some, there was no getting around that. She chose to use the light above the stove. Once she had pushed it on, she could see that it would be good enough for the sink, that it would shine through the windows on the lake side of the house, but because of the pantry it probably would not show at the front of the house where John Tallman's car was parked.

The next step went easily, although it was the one step in her plan she had feared the most. She turned the stove light out again. She walked through the pantry's swinging door, leaving it open for her return trip, walked through the dining room into the living room, picked up the parrot's cage from the piano, and returned to the kitchen, closing the pantry door behind her. She put the cage on top of the stove and turned on the stove light before she removed the night cover from the cage. Her theory was that the stove light would blind the parrot for the first minute or two. That would give her all the time she needed.

She had the shroud off the cage, the cage door opened, and her right hand around the parrot's neck before he could blink twice. With her left hand she clenched both his feet with all the strength she could summon. Once she had pulled him through the door of his cage, she held him upside down as high in the air as she could. Although his wings spread and flapped two or three times, in their upside-down position they could not stop her. She wrung his neck before he could make a sound.

She put a bread board next to the sink and placed Public Relations Man upon his back on the board. From the rack beside the stove she chose a carving knife, assuming that she would carve him just about the same way a chicken was carved. But the parrot's breast feathers were difficult to separate, and she lost some time trying to find where the knife should enter beneath the breastbone. When she finally gutted him, there was more blood than she'd expected. The stink from his guts was overpowering. Parrot shit and blood had splashed over the counter, and part of its explosion had stained her cotton dressing gown just above the belt. There was no alternative to searching in that mess with her fingers for the Montevideo. In a moment she had it.

She washed the stone clean under the tap, placed it on the kitchen table with her other supplies, then stripped off her cotton housecoat until she was nude. She left the parrot oozing from the bread board onto the counter, just as he was. By morning she supposed there would be parrot guts dripping to the kitchen floor. She put her housecoat into the laundry hamper with the linens from last night's dinner. Her kitchen staff would wash them all without thinking, if she was lucky.

She returned to the sink and washed her hands thoroughly, using detergent. Then she poured the perfume she'd brought along into her palms like water, rubbing it along her arms, on her breasts, and on the insides of her thighs. When she was done, the bottle was nearly empty. She recapped it and tossed it into the kitchen garbage pail, then slipped into her nightgown. She put the Montevideo into the toe of a sandal. Holding the sandals with their toes down, and the handle of her silver hairbrush in the same left hand, she turned off the light above the kitchen stove, took a deep breath, and with a smile of triumph over the scene that would come next, set out for the front door.

She opened the door with great care. It swung back soundlessly. As soon as she was ready, with the blue slate of the front doorsteps under her bare feet, she pulled the door closed behind her so that it slammed. As she had expected, the watchdogs of the FBI standing guard over her house pulled on the headlights of their car. She was outlined in their bright glare, spotlighted against the background of the front door.

What John Tallman and his sideman saw was Suzanne, in a sheer yellow full-length nightgown, bare at the center from the waist up, with shirred panels barely covering her breasts, tied together by drawstring bows and held up by slim straps. She held her hands back just behind her thighs. In the headlights of the car the men could see through the wispy yellow veil. They could see everything she expected them to see, and they did exactly what she expected them to do. As a courtesy to her beauty, the lights of the car were turned off again.

She waited for them. Tallman got out of the car and came toward her with a flashlight, but he held its circle toward the

ground and never pointed it directly at her. As if he, too, would
prefer not to wake anyone in the house by their conversation, his
questions were soft and quiet. "Where, may I ask, are you
headed?"

"I am on my way to keep an appointment with a lover."

"If I am not prying, ma'am, where will this tryst be conducted?"

"Do you want to know that for professional reasons, Mr. Tallman?"

"Yes, ma'am."

"If I tell you, does it become an official secret?"

"That would depend, ma'am."

"You mean that if there was a crime involved, you wouldn't be
able to keep it a secret; right, Mr. Tallman?"

"That's right, Countess."

"The crime is adultery. Does the FBI have interstate jurisdiction on adultery?"

"No, ma'am."

"Have you ever committed adultery, Mr. Tallman?"

"That would be a professional secret, Countess."

"Yes, of course it would. Well, I'm on my way across the dam
to the studio of Michael Hassett. I will pass this way again about
dawn, I should think. In the meantime, if there is anything you
need, you'll know where to find me."

"Yes, ma'am."

"There would be no reason to tell my husband, would there?"

"No, ma'am."

"Wish me well, then, Mr. Tallman."

She stepped off from the slate at the front door onto the gravel
driveway. She had made one mistake: the blue stone of the
driveway gravel cut fearfully into the tender soles of her feet,
and she winced through the necessary ten or twelve steps until
she could reach the cool, soft surface of the lawn. When she arrived at the corner of the house, she stopped and looked back.
John Tallman stood in the driveway exactly where she had left
him. He'd turned off his flashlight, but there was enough light
from the stars to enable her to see he had watched her departure. With her silver hairbrush and sandals still in her left

hand, she raised her right arm high, and waved at him. He waved back.

She turned the corner of the house and set out down the slope of the lawn for the road across the dam. The dew was so thick in the grass that she had to gather up the skirt of her nightgown or its hem would have been soaked. She could not let it down even when she reached the macadam surface of the dam road, because by then her bare feet and ankles were soaking—she might as well have been wading.

It was inevitable that Suzanne paused for a moment at the point where the road bridged the four sluice gates that contained her lake. Because the gates were lowered, the level of the lake on her left was perhaps twenty feet below the parapet of the bridge where she stopped. Because a hint of evening breeze rippled the surface of the lake, the pinpoints of bright stars reflected from a summer's night shifted their positions here and there—unfixed upon the water from permanent positions in heaven by the vagaries of imperceptible waves. Suzanne's perspective was such that she could identify her island in the lake's center, but her *musée* was no more than a vague shadow—an interruption of where stars should have reflected themselves, but an interpretation of her temple's position only possible because Suzanne knew exactly what was there.

On the downstream side of the bridge, at the parapet away from the lake, nothing could be seen at night, yet the invisible sounds of the cascade through the sluices in darkness was a more impressive rush than it would be by day. Suzanne loved the waterfall she had created, in part for its joyous froth and bubble, in part because folly could make so much pretty wash; but she loved it too for deeper, instinctive reasons. To the extent that the lake behind her held all its beauties in reserve, conserved its energies, stood still and quiet and sure, the cascade at the sluices was its complement—a tumbling, rushing, helter-skelter expense of energy, dispersing the old potentials by momentum, rearranging new patterns and associations with nothing but new possibilities ahead downstream. In the black hole forty feet or so below where she stood on the dam road, Suzanne could hear the frothing white sounds of chaos. They had always made her smile, and they did again as she turned away and resumed her journey toward Michael Hassett's studio.

When she finally arrived at his screen door, she had to knock repeatedly. From the loft bedroom toward the back she eventually heard a sleepy "Who's there?" She did not answer, but rapped again insistently. This time she knew he was up. She heard him moving there, and his answer: "Angelique?"

She spoke sharply and clearly: "No." Then she added precise instructions. "Don't turn on a single light, but get down here."

As soon as she was sure that he had started down the stairs from the loft, she let herself in. She then waited until he had crossed the studio floor and come up to her. Even in the dark she could make out that he wore long pajama bottoms in which to sleep, but no top. He stopped at arm's length from her, and folded his arms across his chest. She knew he had caught her scents, that he was shy, that he was embarrassed, and that he would listen.

"I want to tell you a story," was the way she began. "During the war, a pilot was shot down over France. The Germans saw his parachute coming down, and they knew approximately where he was. Before they could get to him, he ran and hid, and eventually arrived at the château of a woman who was, shall we say, just about my age.

"She took this pilot—this fugitive, who would then have been about your age—into her house. She learned from him immediately that the Germans were searching for him. She told him the truth: sooner or later they would come to her château, and she would have to give him up. There would be no place he could hide, or any place she could think of to hide him. In the meantime, she said, they should go to bed and make love. That's what they did."

Her voice came to him in the dark, along with her perfume, in such a way that he had no excuse to speak. He listened, just as he should have, for what would come next. When she had come to the conclusion of the fairy tale she spun for him about the pilot in France, she took a half step, to close the distance between them by just that much but no more. "Here," she said, reaching with her hand toward him in the dark. "Take this."

In his palm he felt the weight and the shape of the icy egg, and he realized instantly what it was.

"Don't speak yet," she said. "You are quite correct. You have in your hand the Montevideo diamond."

He spoke anyway: "But I don't want this. I have no use for it, and I don't want to get involved in a robbery. This is crazy."

"Listen first, then decide. I have no use for that diamond either, but I have delivered it to you as a present. You can do whatever you like with it. Give it back. Throw it away. Keep it. Anything you choose. But now that you have it in your hand, you will be more likely to listen, is that correct?"

Michael Hassett agreed that she was right.

"Like that pilot, my life is in great danger."

"Because you've stolen this diamond?"

"Be silent, for heaven's sake, and listen."

She moved the last half step she would need into the circle of his privacy. His arms were still crossed protectively against his chest, but because her voice would go lower, and because she would be speaking up toward his face, he would soon feel the whisper of her breath upon his shoulders.

"I am not going to tell you why my life is in danger. I am not going to give you a single reason to believe me, but I think you will believe me when I say that tonight might be the last night of my life. It is true that I could be wrong. It is true that I may find ways to escape. I shall certainly try. But if I fail, then I would not want to have spent my last night without making love. Can you understand that?"

Before he could answer, she had reached up and placed her fingers upon his mouth, gently but surely enough to remind him she expected him to stay quiet. Then she continued: "I want to make love to you until I have exhausted you. I have a thousand gifts I can deliver to you before morning. I do not want to hear a single word from you, except those groans and cries of pleasure that I can extract from the marrow of your soul."

Then she moved her body against the folded arms upon his chest, and they fell away. "The entire time that we are making love," she said, "I shall talk to you. There is nothing I want to hear in answer, any more than I want anything from the dia-

mond you are holding in your hand. Now put it down somewhere, and take me to that bed of yours up above."

He made a clumsy attempt at that point to kiss her, which she
ducked. "Not yet, *mon chou*. As an artist, surely you prefer to
work upon a canvas, not do your painting in midair—is that not
so? Well, I am an artist too, and I need a bed with sheets on it."

Upstairs, his bed was rumpled and king-sized, the kind of
workbench she knew how to use. "Take off those pajamas," she
said, "and lie back." She stripped her nightgown in the dark, but
he could see that she did it with her back toward him. Then she
knelt beside him upon the bed, and began to trail her long hair
across his belly and the tops of his thighs. "Will you be absolutely quiet?" she asked.

He answered, "Hmmm."

"Good," she continued. "Will you listen to what I have to
say?"

"Hmmm."

"To make love takes everything an artist can give," she said.
"Skill, practice, inspiration, persuasion, cunning, cruelty, persist-
ence." She accompanied each word with another fateful stroke of
her hair. "It takes courage too."

21

The Hopeful

Saturday Afternoon

THE tradition at Saratoga's grand old race track was to end the August race meeting on a Saturday with the running of the Hopeful Stakes—over a distance of six and one half furlongs for a purse of "$75,000 added." Listed on the program as the eighth race, a crop of two-year-olds raced in the Hopeful as the best of the juveniles. The significance of the race lay in the custom that most of the entries would be running for the last time before they turned adults and qualified as three-year-olds for the Kentucky Derby, the Preakness, and the Belmont Stakes. Saturday, August 28, 1976, was the seventy-second running of the Hopeful.

As expected, the stable of Mrs. Ellen Burns had an entry ready: Barbarella, listed in the program as the number six horse, OTB letter F; a dark-brown filly by Besomer-Barbara Mac, by Beaux Max. The overnight odds on Barbarella were long—sixteen to one, reflecting the understanding that fillies were unlikely winners in the Hopeful. Although her stable had entered a horse, Mrs. Burns saw no reason to arrive at the track until after the results of the third race were already posted.

When Aunt Nellie finally did arrive, however, she brought with her a group of good friends. They left a buffet lunch at her

house to be driven by chauffeurs in a caravan of cars to the clubhouse gates. Aunt Nellie herself was the first of her party to disembark, and it was obvious by her navy blue linen suit, matching blue straw hat, and blue pumps that if the odds on her filly
were long, she was nevertheless prepared to accept the prize in
the winner's circle. Marching at the head of her entourage on
her way to her season boxes, she could have been a *condottiere,*
stepping off upon the first leg of a successful campaign, sure that
the gates of cities would be opened for her rather than suffer the
consequences of siege. Spaces opened by magic in the crowd
ahead of her to make way for her passage.

Her troops trailed behind her. Marching one pace to her left
and two paces to her rear was her aide-de-camp, Adam Shepherd. For the Hopeful, he was fashionably turned out in a blue
blazer with gold buttons and piping on its lapels. The handkerchief in his breast pocket was neatly folded and displayed, ap-
propriately, Aunt Nellie's racing colors: gold and black. Adam
Shepherd moved in his commander's trail in such a way that he
too occupied the space she created in the midst of a jostling
crowd. The others in Aunt Nellie's party trailed behind her, making their own way through shoulders and elbows.

Her company included Senator Lewis Reeves and his wife,
Nadine, and Mr. and Mrs. Charles Montebanks, Jr. Her name
was Felicia, which few people knew, but everyone recognized
her husband, because he had starred in more than thirty motion
pictures. Once established in Aunt Nellie's two boxes, side by
side, boxes she had occupied for years, Charlie Montebanks
waved back across heads in the clubhouse crowd to those who
presumed they knew him. The fifth race was won by Hurry Marie,
the favorite, paying $3.40, but Felicia Montebanks had Next Place
to show, paying $22.20 for a two-dollar bet and providing the
opportunity for Felicia's husband to demonstrate his gallantry
once again by going to the two-dollar window to collect for her.

The seventh and eighth seats in Aunt Nellie's boxes were occupied by an odd couple: Enrique Cardinale and the daughter of
the Countess de Montreuil—Angelique Lyle. In answer to queries
as to what had brought her to Saratoga's track, Angelique replied with a shyness appropriate to her age that she had come because she wanted to see Aunt Nellie's horse win.

Among those who circulated between races, idling at this box or that, resting their elbows upon rails, exchanging salutations, invitations and gossip, Angelique's demure reply was repeated, sometimes with a wink, and in other instances with no more than a nod of the head in her direction, indicating that Angelique was the extremely pretty blond girl wearing the leghorn hat in Aunt Nellie's box. As often happens in a community as small as the oligarchy who owned and raced horses at Saratoga, stories had spread through the box seats even before the daily double closed about extraordinary "goings on" at the house of the Countess de Montreuil the night before.

The facts were reported to be that a robbery had occurred during dinner; that Aunt Nellie's Montevideo diamond had been stolen; that the FBI had been called in; that at first everyone assumed that a parrot had somehow swallowed the diamond, but in the morning the parrot was found dead and gutted, and no diamond discovered. These facts confirmed what many in the boxes already knew to be true: that Saratoga was constantly hearing news of new jewel robberies; that the FBI never seemed to be able to solve any crimes; that it was not worth it to take a decent jewel out of the safe-deposit box these days, it would just be stolen. On the other hand, the facts as they were circulated left open a number of intriguing questions: for example, how could a parrot have swallowed a diamond of that size anyway—it was a well-known egg-shaped stone of more than forty carats, and the bird would surely have choked.

But there was said to be even more to the story. A chauffeur was missing—he would be the one, of course. Wasn't it always the way—no one could be trusted these days. The report of the missing chauffeur eventually died out, because no one could substantiate it, and it was replaced by far juicier rumors. The Countess de Montreuil was said to have disappeared during the middle of the robbery, or after dinner. In any event, she reappeared as cool as you please walking up the lawn from her lake at eleven the next morning, dressed in nothing more than a shirt she had borrowed from the artist—what's his name—who lived in her studio across the lake. The affair was said to have been going on for some time. Her husband was standing there on the patio behind their house, waiting for her as she came walking up the lawn. A confrontation scene. A classic. Right out of a book. There were words exchanged, of course. Angry words. The outraged husband had ordered up his car and was driven away to the city, claiming he had pressing business there. On the last Saturday afternoon in August, mind you.

None of these stories traveled as far as the grandstand, of course, because they would have had no meaning there. Moreover, of all these circulating truths it should be noted that the outraged-husband version was the most popular in the aisles of the clubhouse boxes, perhaps because it was more comfortable than another variation also being told of what had occurred—a scene in which the angry words were exchanged between Suzanne and her daughter, Angelique, who was now sitting in Aunt Nellie's box. The story of a confrontation between mother and daughter over Michael Hassett was heard, curiously enough, with a distant, uneasy eye cast upon the willowy blond girl with the leghorn hat.

In any case, immediately after the finish of the seventh race, Aunt Nellie stood up to lead her company toward the paddock, where they would watch Barbarella being saddled. Angelique glanced at her mother's box, saw that it was still empty, and followed. Once again, Aunt Nellie marched ahead, up the short flight of stairs past the judges' boxes, down another flight to the bettors' plaza beneath the stands. Caught in the swirls and eddies, the crosscurrents of the crowd, Angelique struggled to keep up. Behind the clubhouse stands there was a macadam apron, but after passing the "spit barn," the macadam gave way to a gravel path. A light rain had fallen for about two hours that morning, an easy summer shower that had gone, but beyond the gravel path was wet grass, and inevitably, mud. Angelique had chosen to wear a green linen dress accented by a yellow Hermès scarf, and she wore green espadrilles—and so there was nothing Angelique could do about it, her rope soles were going to be dyed with mud and the green canvas of her shoes stained with water.

She caught up with Aunt Nellie's company in the paddock, where they had assembled under the oak marked with the red number 6. Aunt Nellie was putting sharp, businesslike questions to her trainer. He was a fat little man with an unlit cigar in the

side of his mouth. He squinted at Aunt Nellie's questions but answered her back with no sign of deference. Yes, indeed, the filly
could have been fitted with mud caulks, but he allowed that
"Them little things ain't going to make much difference in her
step." Besides, he added, the track was fast by now. He ordered
the groom to stop walking the horse around its circular path,
told him to hold her steady, and took his time cinching the
girth and setting the saddle. As a parting shot, he informed his
owner, "Fast horses get born that way, ma'am. Shoes ain't going
to change anything." Then, with a contrasting affection, he spoke
to the horse. "Time to run, little girl."

Angelique realized the paddock judge had signaled, and she
followed the saddled horses toward the walking ring. The white
leggings on Barbarella's hind legs were gathering brown mud
just as Angelique's espadrilles had done. A thin crowd lined the
walking ring's rails, held back by the presence of Pinkerton
guards but rating both the horses and their owners, now displayed inside the ring. A fat lady with a shiny raincoat recognized Senator Reeves, called to him, and demanded his autograph. He obliged her, signing his name across the top of her
racing form, folded in quarters, with his own ballpoint pen.
Others recognized Charles Montebanks, Jr., and called for him
to autograph their racing forms too, shouting "Charlie" at him,
"Hey, Charlie, how 'bout it?" He had the sense to send them a
friendly celebrity's wave, as if he were seeing old friends, but
he kept his distance. The ring judge called: "Riders up!"

The jockeys swung up into their saddles, settled their animals,
and the parade to the post began. Aunt Nellie's company
marched beside her entry, heading toward the tunnel that led
from the paddock, under the stands, then out to the track. Aunt
Nellie would not be parting from her filly until the tunnel, but
once again Angelique fell behind. She felt no need to keep up
with the palace guard walking beside Barbarella. She decided to
set her own course, chose as her landmark the red-and-white-
striped awning above the escalator she knew would bring her up
to the back of the clubhouse stands, and set off toward her own
objective.

The paddock area Angelique was leaving was like a quiet
copse, in which the concerns of each stable, its attendant party,

and its work force all concentrated upon just one horse: the owner's entry. In the paddock, mannered and intimate talk was absorbed in the leafy branches of overhanging oaks and maples. The area behind the grandstand, which Angelique was approaching was, in comparison to the orderly paddock, a more democratic zone, an open sunny plain—bright, boisterous and generally ill-mannered—in which discordant snatches of conversation could be heard buzzing about all the possibilities. From the paddock to the stands, Angelique passed through a geography of increasing energy.

The first clearing into which Angelique passed might be designated the zone of essential American services. There were stalls advertising DRAFT BEER, 60¢, PREMIUM 75¢; HOT DOGS, 50¢, TUNA FISH, 70¢, FRIDAY ONLY. The color scheme in which these necessities were offered was Saratoga's red and white: boxes of red geraniums hung from the eaves of the barns; red-and-white plantings were arranged around the turnstile gates; the girls working behind each counter were dressed in candy-striped smocks. Every sign was lettered in red upon a white background: ICE CREAM. BAR. GIFTS. SOUVENIRS. POST CARDS: YOU ADDRESS THEM, SARATOGA WILL BE GLAD TO MAIL THEM.

But these were merely services. Nearer the grandstand there were booths, garish signs, and raucous hawkers selling a system of support for the main business at the track: MORNING LINE CHANGES. LATE SCRATCHES. OVERWEIGHTS. EXACTA—LOWER LEVEL ONLY. DAILY DOUBLE CLOSES AT 12:40. Gambling, after all, was an art that required study, and calculation, and insight. At a kiosk beside the macadam apron leading to the escalator, a display encouraged those who would need specialized research: JACK'S GREEN CARD; LAWTON'S—75¢; and THE ORIGINAL NEW YORK HANDICAP—OUR 66TH YEAR!

Thanks to the education her mother had provided her, Angelique recognized the habitual loungers upon the green benches and in aluminum chairs. They were the nomads of racing, the regulars: touts, runners, bag men, the steady bettors who had started the season in Florida at Hialeah, then followed the sun north to Bowie and Delaware in the spring, moving on to Aqueduct and Belmont. They were about to leave Saratoga for the south again, because winter approached. Every one of these faithful wore some sign of catastrophe—an old hat, a torn pocket, a belt cinched too far around sharp-looking slacks that unfortunately now hung in pathetic folds. But they would, without exception, insist that no tragedy had occurred: *they would have another winner someday soon: it would be like the old days: they'd pick one, you'd see; maybe today, maybe tomorrow, but sooner or later, you'd see. Have to have faith. Have to stick with your own system, and not give up. The slacks would fill out again, 'cause of all the good eatin', Chinese maybe, and goin' to buy a new hat. A Cavanaugh.* For these students of the odds a white plastic board near the foot of the escalator noted in red crayon: WIND—SOUTHEAST, O.3. TODAY'S TRACK CONDITION—FAST.

The entire passage from the silent paddock to the top of the escalator took Angelique no more than three minutes. Over that short distance, the sound of the crowd continued to accumulate— from the whisper of a waterfall somewhere in the distance and as yet unseen, to the rushing, sighing, bubbling surge at the bank of a mountain torrent. When Angelique reached the alleyway at the top of the stairs behind the box seats, the crowd was waiting for the horses to be led into the gate, and there was buzzing anticipation in the air. Halfway down the stairs, Angelique saw a leghorn hat just like her own, alone in her mother's box. Angelique had planned to rejoin Aunt Nellie's group, but now she saw no alternative. She paused at her mother's side, and inquired first. "Mother, may I join you?"

"Of course. Yes, yes. Quick, please do. Angelique, you'll forgive me, won't you? You have always been the only pleasure I could ever count upon."

And then they made conversation with each other, as if nothing had happened; as if they had not been screaming at each other only an hour or two before. They talked about the race— about the Hopeful. Angelique wanted to know which horse her mother had picked.

Suzanne said she had chosen Banquet Table.

Angelique thought Aunt Nellie's Barbarella was a pretty horse.

"Never bet a filly," was Suzanne's advice, "against a field with stallions entered. Sometimes against geldings you can take a chance, but they are unreliable. Did you get your bet down?"

Angelique admitted she had not. Hers was a theoretical choice. She had only made an imaginary bet.

Suzanne was annoyed. "They are all imaginary, my pet." For a moment it looked as if she would scold Angelique, but she apparently thought better of it, merely adding that there was little sense in sitting at a track without making some kind of bet. "Here"—Suzanne brightened at a new thought—"hold my ticket for me, for luck. I have one hundred dollars down on Banquet Table. You hold our ticket for both of us."

Angelique said she couldn't; it wouldn't be fair.

Suzanne argued there was no time left before the race started. The horses were already being led into the gate. Angelique owed fifty dollars for half the ticket on Banquet Table, win or lose.

They laughed together like old friends. Angelique accepted the Banquet Table ticket from her mother, and together they turned their attention to the race just as the track announcer said, *"And they're off!"*

First Pretense takes an early lead, followed by Banquet Table, with Super Joy running third. The sound of the crowd had swelled up, the frenzy was accumulating, ecstasy near at hand, as if a wave were cresting. *At the quarter pole, it's Banquet Table by a head, First Pretense along the rail, Turn of the Coin a half a length behind.* Twenty thousand voices were gathering momentum, roaring now at the crest, and beginning to stand as the objects of their desire came around the turn into view. *At the half, it's Banquet Table by a head, Turn of the Coin on the outside, Barbarella moving up between horses, and Super Joy.* The crowd was now on its feet, and their voices blended, for the wave of their excitement was crashing at last, exploding, tumbling irrationally, crazily, idiotically to its end.

Angelique, with her mother's ticket crushed in her hand, was on her feet cheering for Banquet Table's every stride. *Coming to the finish, Banquet Table still holds the lead, Turn of the Coin within a length, and Barbarella coming fast on the outside!*

They finished in that order. Angelique was jumping with excitement. As the sound of the crowd began to recede, as the undertow sucked the old wave away to make place for the next one when it was ready, Angelique turned a happy face to her mother to say they'd won.

She had not realized Suzanne was gone. She had not seen Senior Agent John Tallman use the standing crowd to slip up beside Suzanne. Nor had she heard Tallman say in a matter-of-fact voice, "Countess, what you've got is a gunman we know as Little Jake from Detroit standing behind you at the rail up there behind these boxes."

Suzanne did not flinch, but replied, "Thank you, Mr. Tallman. I'll have to settle the diamond business with you later. It was really just a little joke."

"I figured," he said.

22

Museum

SUZANNE was lying again, of course. The little joke she concocted for Senior Agent John Tallman turned out to be another of her capers—an adventure, it might be argued, that in the end she eventually pulled off. Curiously, neither the police nor the FBI ever did find Aunt Nellie's Montevideo. All the efforts of Aunt Nellie's insurance investigators were also in vain. The Montevideo completely disappeared. Exactly why the agencies of law and order would fail was somewhat complex.

Although most of the facts were never in dispute, I was eventually in an equally embarrassed position—unable, as Suzanne's biographer, to explain all the mysteries of what happened next. There were no eyewitnesses at all to some events; other witnesses, who seemed cooperative in interviews, in my opinion were liars; and there were one or two others I would have judged to be habitual liars who may very well have told the truth. Yet the essential difficulty was that the most accomplished liar of all was Suzanne. She was extraordinary because she lied not only in what she said but, in a curious way, in what she did.

How this could be true was complicated, but necessary to understand. When I began her history, I assumed that as an experienced journalist I would be able to check and cross-check those facts necessary to approximate the truth. I believed that facts mattered. Then, as she and I had agreed, I would fictionalize her story—in effect, to protect the guilty. Nevertheless, it would be a biography more or less accurate. But Suzanne created her own life as she went along, and she was in many ways already a myth. Moreover, she enchanted me: having bitten into the apple she offered, I discovered how much I liked its taste, regardless of any ordinary consequences. I learned from her something I had always avoided before: just as there were hierarchies of truths, there might be hierarchies of lies.

Suzanne could lie in as many ways as Nature herself, using the same wonderful energies to invent variations of color, scent and feeling. She loved the appearances of ordinary lies, everyday lies, camouflaged lies, little white deceptions, friendly green disguises—and ugly gray-black lies emitted like ink from squid. She understood the eroticism of foolish lies, random lies, chance lies —and those that were distributed by self-perpetuating codes. She saw the beauty of an ascending lie, rising up like the branches of a tree, each twig reaching out upon a variation of its own but creating eventually one incredible theme. She took an exuberant joy in an associative lie, spreading like a hedge, each root searching for moisture along blind underground tunnels but pretending its progress was made above ground in a marvelous horizontal thicket. Yet of all the many kinds of lies Suzanne practiced, she loved best the transcendental lie—in which every specific detail could be certified as true, but taken together these facts actually established nothing more than a mystery. The verified empirical truths would go only so far, while cast over these guaranteed demonstrations there was still another truth—an invisible cloak of many colors, which, for reasons of economy, Suzanne would never confirm or deny. She was a genius—almost as if she had been touched by the finger of God—at the transcendental lies of economy.

Suzanne provided, for example, many versions of her pilgrimage. All of her parables were true, invariably, but each only as far as it went. Each of these economies reflected that event in Suzanne's life she guessed her faithful would love best, and therefore believe. Consequently, those who heard of her miracles adopted from among them the lesson they found most useful. The most popular story about Suzanne was the caper in which Suzanne was said to have fingered a jewel robbery—or, according to some accounts, a series of jewel robberies—in Saratoga for the sake of a lover. Whether there were contradictions between one version or another was no concern of Suzanne's. She treated her own reputation with a transcendental modesty for the sake of a higher truth, a central revelation of modern society, a matter of belief rarely stated in just so many words, but a matter of faith nevertheless: that wealth and robbery were complementary. For example, if jewels merely decorated a woman's throat, they might be no more than paste; but stolen jewels were value certified. Hence, Suzanne established through allegations of robbery—in her own peculiar way—a reputation for good works among her peers.

The parable of Suzanne as "Snow White" taught a similar lesson. The fantasy of the poor-little-rich-girl from Wavertree Hall who made a fortune running a brothel on the upper East Side was certainly true as far as it went, and in addition was spiced with the prurience the bourgeoisie loved. Yet the moral of her tale depended upon a mystery that could be accepted only as an article of bourgeois faith—that virtue was most piquant when stood naked at auction. Similarly, Suzanne's bank caper rendered to Caesar what was due, and precisely: it was steeped in sentimental facts, an earnest fairy tale of high finance in which it could be demonstrated by the righteous that Suzanne and André were thwarted by "quick action" by the "legitimate authorities." Whether Suzanne considered Aunt Nellie an example of "legitimate authority" missed the point, because Suzanne's "bank robbery" was an exact demonstration that if no one challenged the guardians of money, the rich would lack opportunities to prove their power. That is, Suzanne offered up to Aunt Nellie the transcendental fiction that Aunt Nellie had duties necessary to perform—as if the Devil at the end of the year spent his time reading annual reports from banks! What Suzanne did—what she had always done—was to hold up a mirror to those who loved her best.

Yet Suzanne's mirror never distorted, never exaggerated, was always reasonable. She never proposed a dream unless it was already the most important secret sleeping in her victim's heart. Suzanne's economy meant that she never extended her lies beyond the boundaries of her victim's hopes. To those, for example, who believed that meanings were always to be extracted from the myths of Greek drama, as modern psychotheorists insisted, Suzanne solemnly agreed that the death of her father was tragic, fateful, and central to the interpretation of her adult behavior. Suzanne would applaud such simple-minded interpretations while at the same time laughing behind her hand, because, in effect, she rather liked to hear the story again. To those, for example, who were sure that social history would provide the final judgments, Suzanne giggled and happily furnished one anecdote after another of her mother's irrelevant Boston manners, and then topped even those anomalies with perfect examples of New York's anarchy. To those who drew lessons from morals and law, Suzanne nodded her head with a matching piety, and then repeated what they had said, roaring with laughter, to whoever would listen—because Suzanne thought it must be obvious that any society that insisted that every man act in his own best interest was nothing more than a city of swine. "Hell," she would say, still laughing, "we turned an easy half million a year up at Ninety-third Street from lawyers alone!"

Suzanne laughed at all these idyllic truths because her own experience had taught her there was nothing to them. In fact, Suzanne guessed there would not be anything at all even at the epicenters of the universe itself. Perhaps there might be something comparable to charm, drifting wisps of chaos on aimless currents, but all the rest was a story made up for children. Obviously, if there were no awkward realities anywhere, what difference could a surrender to a few facts possibly make? Free from any ancient taboos, Suzanne could greet every new day as if she were not anyone in particular. She did not believe she had any real past, or any necessary future. She lived in the infinite present. She was no more than a story she happened to be spinning for her own sake. Hence, at the Saratoga race track, as fifteen horses came pounding across the finish line of the Hopeful, Suzanne undoubtedly heeded Agent Tallman's warning about Little Jake from Detroit and used the excitement of a "finish" to make her escape.

Why not? If she had no particular place to go, or no exact plan in the ordinary sense, she would be running through the landscape she loved best: the garden of chance, in which each place was as good as any other, and the probability of any single hope succeeding exactly equal to the odds on every other fate. Suzanne believed certain truths to be self-evident, among them that "Each toss of the dice has to be counted as a new game." Because the crowd at the Saratoga race track was up on its feet cheering the finish of the Hopeful, she had the opportunity to get up the stairs and past Little Jake before he could realize what had happened. Suzanne was merely starting another new game. Why Senior Agent Tallman also let her go at that moment remained a mystery. "She just went," was his explanation. "And I wasn't quick enough."

Tallman started up the box-seat stairs after her. There were too many people standing in the aisles. Before Tallman could elbow through the crowd to the head of the stairs, he saw Little Jake also realize that Suzanne was no longer in her box. Little Jake looked around for her. He was obviously furious. Then he, too, disappeared toward the back of the stands.

Tallman succeeded in picking up Little Jake's trail going down the escalator, and pursued Little Jake into the plaza under the stands as Little Jake presumably chased Suzanne. All three found it difficult to weave through the crowds—hide and seek through lines of bettors gathering at the two-dollar, five-dollar and ten-dollar payoff windows. At the clubhouse end of the track it was relatively easy to cut through a line with a smile and an apology. At the east end of the track, under the cheaper grandstand seats, the mob pressed closely upon itself and was not quick to forgive anyone with different purposes from its own— cutting in and out drew reprisals. There had to be some pushing and shoving. At first Little Jake may have used Suzanne's leghorn hat as a marker, but Tallman was sure he had seen her red hair for a moment—just the back of her head stopped in a line, as if waiting to cash a ticket. Tallman supposed she had ditched the hat by then. He had difficulty keeping up with Little Jake, because his quarry was short and disappeared into knots of the crowd from one moment to the next. "Thing is," Tallman admitted, "you could lose sight of Walt Frazier in a situation like that, and I lost them both."

Assuming the Hopeful finished at about five o'clock and assuming that Suzanne used up as much as a half hour dodging through the crowds beneath the stands attempting to shake off both Tallman and Little Jake, there was still no reasonable explanation of how she got to her car, or how she got the car through the usual traffic jam running from the clubhouse exits to the track's main gate on Union Avenue. Perhaps she talked her way out the exit to the barns and drove away down Lincoln Avenue. Whatever Suzanne did, there would be an unexplained gap between about five-thirty and seven-thirty that evening. Perhaps Suzanne led Little Jake a merry chase around the upstate country roads. She would have known the routes by heart, and he wouldn't.

While Suzanne raced along farm roads, Agent Tallman drove to Saratoga County Police Headquarters in Ballston Spa. He directed the county police to put out an all-points call for Suzanne's red Mercedes two-seat sports car. Unfortunately, Tallman had nothing with which to identify the car Little Jake was driving. But Tallman's theory was that if Suzanne was speeding, sooner or later either the Saratoga police, or the New York State police, would spot her. With the call that she was wanted, when they pulled her over she'd be safe. To make doubly sure, Tallman specified that she was dangerous and might be armed.

Meanwhile, Aunt Nellie had gathered her little group together at the track and issued them their marching orders. Her house guests were sent back to her castle in a caravan of cars, but she kept the blue Rolls-Royce for herself. Her guests were told she would catch up with them later, after she had done a small errand. She would be taking Adam Shepherd and Enrique Cardinale with her, she explained, "to keep me company."

When questioned later, Aunt Nellie would have a reasonable explanation for her drive to Suzanne's house.

"It was perfectly simple: I went there to confront Suzanne. She cut my stone out of that parrot's guts. There wasn't any question about that, was there?"

She would say she knew nothing about any gunmen from Detroit. She said she did not operate at that level: "That sort of thing would be no concern of mine."

She thought it was a bit precious for anyone to suppose that banks and major corporations went about hiring thugs. "It wouldn't be necessary."

In any event, it would not be the kind of thing in which "I would be involved."

She wasn't born yesterday, and she'd heard of isolated cases that might be similar, but as far as she was concerned, any implication that she, Aunt Nellie, would operate on the level of common thugs was, in her opinion, "just outrageous."

As to why she took Angelique along with her in the blue Rolls, Aunt Nellie's answer was "Again, perfectly obvious. The child was at loose ends at the track and needed a ride home. Really!"

According to Angelique, on the drive to Suzanne's house the only topic of conversation in Aunt Nellie's car was about how wonderful it was that Barbarella had finished third in the Hopeful. For Aunt Nellie's pleasure, Adam and Enrique did several replays of the race. Aunt Nellie sat in the back between the two of them, and Angelique sat up front with the chauffeur. Angelique said she did not mention that she had in her purse a winning ticket on Banquet Table, because "it might have seemed disloyal, in the circumstances."

As soon as the blue Rolls pulled up at Suzanne's door, Aunt Nellie suggested that Angelique might want to see Michael Hassett immediately. "You must not delay one second in paying a call on that nice young man of yours" was how Aunt Nellie had put it. "I'm sure you young people have a great deal to discuss."

Angelique would recall that she obeyed Aunt Nellie because "I thought I might as well." Angelique never entered the house, but walked down the lawn instead, along the road across the dam spillway, and then directly to Michael Hassett's studio. Thereafter, she said, neither she nor Michael Hassett saw or heard anything unusual. When asked later what she talked about with Michael Hassett, Angelique answered, "Nothing. Nothing in particular. The way lovers talk: about nothing."

According to Enrique, as soon as he arrived at Suzanne's house, Aunt Nellie and Adam Shepherd went upstairs to Suzanne's bedroom. "They knew exactly where they were going,"

Enrique recalled. "Aunt Nellie was giving the orders. No doubt about that. The first thing she told me to do was to go down to the kitchen and tell Suzanne's staff that she was not to be disturbed. She was acting like she owned the place.

"I was willing to follow orders," Enrique explained, "because I had no idea at all about what Aunt Nellie had in mind. Not a clue, really."

When Enrique returned to Suzanne's bedroom, Adam was already stationed at the window, scanning the landscape every so often with the binoculars he had brought from the track. "Well, he wasn't looking for submarines," Enrique said. "That's a stupid question. Yes, of course they were waiting for Suzanne."

Aunt Nellie had propped herself up on Suzanne's bed, rearranged the pillows as a backrest, kicked off her shoes, and while they waited, said nothing, but smoked one cigarette after another. She was obviously prepared for a long wait. "I have not the faintest idea why Aunt Nellie expected her.

"The only odd thing, it seems to me, is that Aunt Nellie was still wearing the blue straw hat she had worn at the track. Given the situation," Enrique said, "I'll never forget the hat. I mean, you can see that, can't you? She never took her hat off. It looked funny. Well, I thought it was odd."

Aunt Nellie had instructed Enrique to sit in the chair at Suzanne's desk and be quiet. It was the little desk, Enrique said, that Suzanne used to pay her bills, answer invitations, "write thank-you notes and things like that."

They waited in silence for a long time. Enrique couldn't say exactly how long, because he didn't wear a watch. "I never wear a watch. Well, if I had thought about it at the time, I would certainly have looked at the clock upon the night table, but I didn't think about it. Maybe it was eight o'clock or so. The sun was setting. How was I to know that it was the kind of situation where everyone was supposed to keep time sheets, or whatever?"

Enrique claimed he never left his seat at Suzanne's desk. He was told to sit still and be quiet, and that's all he did. While they waited, he admitted, Aunt Nellie brought up "the whole business" of the murder charge still open against him in Canada. She filled in enough details to frighten him. Whether the charges against him were true or not, he said, the point was that she

could have made trouble for him. "Those things can be just endless, you know, even if you're innocent. That's the point, really,
that Suzanne had always understood. It doesn't matter whether
you're innocent or guilty; they can keep you tied up forever."

Enrique said he had no idea how Aunt Nellie had come up
with "the Canada thing." He agreed that he was subject to
blackmail because of it. "But, when it comes right down to it, we
all have to make our own personal decisions on how we are
going to survive.

"The fact is"—he was adamant—"the Canada thing is neither
here nor there, because I didn't do anything, one way or another."

He had not argued with Aunt Nellie, because there was nothing to argue about. He sat at Suzanne's desk, Aunt Nellie lay on
Suzanne's bed smoking—with her hat on—and Adam watched the
lake through the window with his binoculars. Eventually Adam
broke the silence: "Here she comes."

Aunt Nellie told Adam to describe everything Suzanne did,
and Adam kept the binoculars trained out the window, giving
Aunt Nellie a running commentary—how Suzanne was walking
across the lawn to the water's edge, getting into the little rowboat, putting the oars into the oarlocks, casting off, and starting
to row toward her little island. Adam described it all, step by
step, just as if he were the track announcer at the races.

"Well, I suppose," said Enrique, "Suzanne must have thought
she would be safe in her temple. It was her secret hideaway,
after all."

When Suzanne had rowed about halfway out into the middle
of the lake, Adam called out: "Here comes Mr. Brown!"

Enrique was quite sure about it: Adam had clearly said his
name was Mr. Brown. "I simply had no idea who this Mr.
Brown might be. Not a clue, really!"

Aunt Nellie had said nothing, Enrique was sure of that. She
made no comment one way or another.

Adam continued the play-by-play from his post at the window.
Suzanne was rowing out into the lake toward her temple, and
Mr. Brown was walking up and down the shore. "Of course,"
said Enrique. "You'd have to be a dummy not to figure out that
Mr. Brown was chasing Suzanne."

"Well, for example, it took Mr. Brown quite a while to realize that the barge tied up at the dock was what he was looking for. I mean, if it had an outboard motor on the back, it was what he needed. When he finally went for it, Adam reported to Aunt Nellie something to the effect that he'd seen it at last."

Aunt Nellie, according to Enrique, still said nothing. Perhaps she grunted. He couldn't remember. In any event, from the window Adam continued his play-by-play, describing how Mr. Brown pulled and pulled at the starter cord of the outboard, and when he finally got it started the barge went sailing forward against the dock with a crash, because Mr. Brown had not yet untied it.

Mr. Brown apparently didn't know too much about outboards. There was another delay while Adam described Mr. Brown casting off at last, getting the barge turned around, and finally setting a course toward Suzanne's *musée*, out in the lake. "Asshole," is what Enrique remembered Aunt Nellie saying. She then asked Adam where Suzanne was, and he answered, "She's just going into the temple, right now."

As the designer, architect, and builder of Suzanne's *musée*, Enrique was confident she was going to be completely safe, once she was inside. "Completely. First of all it would be dark—pitch black. Suzanne would know where the light switches were and that Mr. Brown character would not. She could switch off the lights as she entered—the main switch was just inside the door. On top of that, Mr. so-called Brown would never find her in there, because inside it was built as a labyrinth. That was the whole point, don't you see? It was a maze. Actually, if you know anything about mazes, they are easy to solve. You just keep your left hand always touching a wall, but an uneducated person like that Mr. Brown, or whatever his name was, would not know something like that."

The labyrinth inside Suzanne's temple was a circular maze, built on the same plan as the outside wall. Enrique explained that the semicircular corridors that switched back and forth into the center chamber were about four feet wide, but only one path led to the center chamber. The others were blind alleys. "Unless you knew exactly where you were going," in Enrique's opinion, "you could be in there forever. Especially in the dark. My judgment was that Suzanne was completely safe in there. That's what my judgment was."

When Aunt Nellie demanded to know where the keys were that worked the sluice gates of the dam, Enrique claimed, he had refused to answer her. Even if he had answered her it wouldn't have made any difference anyway, he said, because the keys were right where they belonged, hanging on a hook on the wall beside Suzanne's correspondence desk. They were actually a set of keys—a sort of fail-safe device. One key worked the lock to the drawer in Suzanne's desk; two more keys were necessary to unlock the toggle switches that activated the electrical switches on the panel in the drawer. The panel looked like one of those model-railroad control panels: not much different—two rheostats, and then little red lights above each switch to confirm its activation. "The keys were different for the drawer and the panel itself," said Enrique, "because it was eventually to be a two-step operation, but Suzanne kept all the keys together anyway, and a child could see which was which."

Enrique swore he did not touch them. "It was Adam who took the keys down from the wall."

But then Enrique turned evasive about whether Aunt Nellie had ordered Adam to turn the keys and start the sluice gates closed. He would not be pinned down. He couldn't recall. He couldn't remember that. His final line of defense was "You'll just have to ask Aunt Nellie yourself.

"And you'd better keep in mind," he continued, "that the flooding of the *musée* might actually have been the most reasonable means of helping Suzanne escape. You'll have to make up your own mind about that."

He had no idea why Aunt Nellie would hire a "hit man" to pursue Suzanne. With considerable coolness, Enrique replied that he could not think of a single reason. It was all high finance, and as far as he was concerned, beyond him. The moment Mr. so-called Brown landed upon the island in the center of the lake, Adam left the window, went to the desk, turned the keys, and started the sluice gates of the dam up on their winches. "Of course, Brown heard them. The gates make a frightful grinding noise as they come up, and a kind of screeching as the steel is winched up against steel. And he must have seen them before he

went into the *musée* after Suzanne. As those gates come up, anyone can see that since no more water can go over the dam downstream, the lake is going to rise. You've seen it—it's obvious. It
just starts coming up right away, and it comes up fast."

Enrique's conclusion was that Brown must have been too
dumb to understand what the sluice gates did, or how things
worked, "until he began to feel the water around his socks in the
dark in there. Then I'll bet he knew," Enrique said with satisfaction. "Then he surely knew."

The next day, when they lowered the sluice gates again and
drained the lake, Brown was found in a blind alley. "Which
proves, as far as I'm concerned," Enrique said, "that Suzanne
knew what she was doing. That was my judgment all along."

But a coroner's report concluding that Suzanne had also
drowned did not quite cover all the facts. "No, of course not,"
was Enrique's self-assured reply. "Accidental death by reason of
drowning, but no body to prove it. But, you see, there's no
changing that now—that's the law."

Then, Suzanne could still be alive.

"Obviously."

I wondered how long Aunt Nellie and Adam Shepherd had
watched the lake rise.

"Not very long. It doesn't take long, as you know. It was getting dark by then anyway, and there was not much to see. When
the level of the lake rose over the temple—once it was completely
inundated—you could look out there and there was no sign of
anything. Just a lake. Not a ripple on it. The two boats—the rowboat Suzanne had used and the barge with the outboard that
had given Brown so much trouble—drifted away from the island
on their own and fetched up against the dam. The current carried them there, of course. . . .

"No, of course not. No sign of Suzanne."

Enrique guessed that by then it was nine-thirty, perhaps
nearly ten o'clock. Aunt Nellie announced it was time to go, ordered Enrique to fetch her blue shoes for her—they lay on the
floor where she had kicked them off before she had settled on
Suzanne's bed. Then she drove away to her own house with
Adam. Within twenty minutes, Agent Tallman of the FBI arrived, and asked Enrique if he knew of Suzanne's whereabouts.

"One thing led to another, more or less," Enrique said, "and I told him what happened—substantially the same thing I've described to you."

Not much could be done in the dark. By seven the next morning, however, Tallman had given orders to drain the lake, and as Enrique described it, "there was a virtual army of police around the place—county, state, federal and what not—all tramping about and taking notes and trying to look busy."

It was Tallman who entered Suzanne's *musée* first; then, after they had brought Brown out on a stretcher, they all went in and had a look. Enrique showed them where the switches were, and how the lights worked. "Well, first of all, as you already know, the labyrinth was circular. As soon as you entered, if you turned right, the maze ended in a dead end. So, the first move was to turn left. Although that appeared to end too, you just had to follow your left hand, as I've explained, and follow the corridor as it doubled back."

The corridors could be flooded by overhead lights when it was necessary to get work done inside, but normally the overhead lights would not be turned on. Normally the corridors were dark. A different set of lights came on, "as long as you had chosen the right corridor. Electric eyes sensed your feet as you passed, and the panels lit up automatically.

"Let me explain," Enrique continued. "Haven't you ever been to the Museum of Natural History? And seen the displays they have there? There are the animals from Africa, or Kenya, or wherever it is. They are behind glass, and stuffed, but they look completely natural, just as if they were standing in their natural environment. The sky is painted to look just like the real sky. There's grass and bushes for them to nibble on, and so forth. Suzanne's panels were like those." Enrique giggled. "Except they showed her in *her* natural environment—which was usually someone's bedroom."

I waited for him to go on.

"They were like doing store windows for Bendel's or Bloomingdale's. It was her idea, but I carried it out. We had great fun getting them just right."

I only needed to remain silent. His enthusiasm was carrying him on.

"Each one showed Suzanne up to something marvelous. There were twelve altogether."

He seemed to be re-creating the details he had provided for Suzanne's museum. He obviously recalled them fondly.

"She was always the woman who was masked, but you knew it was her. Some of the others may have been people you would have recognized. We made models from photographs of everyone we wanted. Absolutely lifelike, really. The mannikins were completely articulated, and very well done. We could put them in any position we pleased, and let me tell you we tried out a number of amusing ones."

Miss Freddy dominated one window. Lydia Hopkins, Nan Kaufman, Gail Fowler and Diane Miles made up a foursome in another. Aunt Nellie sat upon a throne—it was a bishop's chair, actually—with four masked men waiting upon her. Suzanne peered around the corner of a damask curtain. She was half hidden, "But you knew it was her, all right."

It seemed to me that the displays were apparently not much different from the kinds of dramas Suzanne had created in her brownstones as Snow White. From Enrique's description, I supposed that, taken together, the twelve panels made up a kind of catalogue of Krafft-Ebing's deviations.

"I wouldn't say you could call them grotesque." Enrique was indignant. "Not at all. Surely you've seen windows like that? They are very popular these days—all the best stores have done them. That's what's done these days—it's just a joke, really. They're *tableaux vivants*—everyone loves them."

Perhaps I had misunderstood, but the windows I had seen like those were sinister, and often suggested violence.

"You are entitled to your own interpretations. If that's what suits you, then fine. You like to think a woman should always be tame—agreeable, cheerful, kind, loving and patient besides. Somebody's mommy. Might as well be dead. Let me assure you that in each of those deviations, as you so confidently put it, although Suzanne was masked you could see she was absolutely happy. She loved it. Her *musée* was a temple, don't you see, to some other possibilities."

23

Ghosts

1977

IN SEPTEMBER 1977 I telephoned Senior Agent John Tallman. By then he had been transferred from the Albany office to the FBI headquarters in the old Lincoln Warehouse building in New York. We agreed to meet for a drink at J. G. Melon's on 74th and Third Avenue, about five blocks from his offices.

Sitting at the bar, we compared notes. "What you've got there"—Tallman smiled—"is nothing; am I right?"

Tallman could laugh at my loose ends, because he had a few of his own. "No, we did no better than you. In the first place, there was no way to hold up the coroner's report, no way to slow it down, because we couldn't show that any crime had been committed."

Shaking his head like a man who's been the butt of a practical joke and who has no alternative except to laugh at himself along with everyone else, John Tallman checked off his difficulties. Just imagine, he said, getting an upstate district attorney to bring a murder charge before a grand jury, and asking them to believe that Mrs. Ellen Burns, or maybe one or another of her two interior decorators, had perpetrated a murder by pushing some buttons, or turning some keys, which in turn worked a dam, and so

forth. Even if the D.A. could convince a grand jury—Tallman
was willing to admit that most grand juries can be convinced of
anything—what then? The district attorney who wanted to bring
Mrs. Burns to trial for murder, or even attempted murder if he
believed he could show some connection between Mrs. Burns
and the hit man from Detroit, would have to be crazy. Especially with no body.

"Tell you the truth," Tallman said, "we had another problem."

I had to wait while he examined the bottom of his glass of
scotch.

"My own opinion was that your lady love didn't drown. If
there was any crime going, it was hers. It was time for her to go
missing person, and everyone else could deal with it any way
they cared."

Did he have any evidence that Suzanne was alive?

"Yes, sir, I sure do. I've been with the Bureau over twenty
years now, and I've seen maybe a thousand cases, all kinds of
cases. I've been on investigations you wouldn't believe."

And the FBI, as I understood it, always got their man. Sooner
or later.

"On television, sir. Only on television."

Two months later, I visited Count André de Montreuil at his
house in Palm Beach, Florida. He was voted off the board of directors of The Bank after a tenure of exactly six months.

His sentence—if that's how his retirement should be viewed—
was to serve his time in a Spanish-style mansion with a red tile
roof not far from the Bath and Tennis Club. The house had cost
him $855,000. He also had a forty-year-old mistress with black
hair and good skin to keep him company, as long as he would indulge her tastes for collecting second-rate Impressionist paintings and giving big cocktail parties during Palm Beach's winter
season. In the summers, Count André de Montreuil planned to
spend his days in a house he had purchased on Lily Pond Lane,
in East Hampton.

He would not comment upon any differences in the style of
the parties managed by his current good friend and those of
Suzanne. He said he was playing a great deal of golf, and that he
enjoyed it. He denied that Palm Beach was a kind of limbo for
retired business executives from the Midwest who had made a

lot of money. On the contrary, he said, although he was no longer involved directly in any of The Bank's affairs, or those of Providence Holding Company, he had a great many interests of his own. I came away with the impression that he was constantly on the phone to New York, to Washington, to Geneva and Nassau, proposing new schemes that might be profitable. None of them would ever get started.

"If Suzanne were alive," André said, "I'm sure I would know something about it."

Miss Freddy had also retired. She lived in an attractive four-story brownstone on Jane Street, in Greenwich Village, with another woman about her own age. Together they attended the Friday-afternoon concerts of the New York Philharmonic at Lincoln Center. They kept up with the latest Broadway and Off Broadway plays. They had season tickets to the Metropolitan Opera. If they could find someone to mind their three Persian cats, they might rent a car and drive up to Saratoga for summer performances of the ballet, or follow the development of John Houseman's Acting Company—a repertory group of young actors and actresses that had caught Miss Freddy's enthusiastic, and generous, support.

"If Suzanne were living"—Miss Freddy's smile was tolerant— "I'm sure she'd contact both of us somehow."

With Aunt Nellie's approval, John Putnam remained a director of The Bank. In addition, John Putnam was required to deal with a considerable increase in the trust and estate business that came his way. In January 1978, Putnam's favorite pupil, Billy G. Fenn, was named executive vice-president in charge of all administrative operations, and in addition received the assurances of The Bank's chairman, Mr. Thomas G. Phelps, that he could "expect a shot" at The Bank's top executive post if he "continued to keep his nose clean." Neither John Putnam nor Billy G. Fenn had any comment to make on Suzanne's death.

The sons of Mimi Benson Hutchinson were students at the best colleges that money could buy. By coincidence, Mimi's eldest son was a member of the same class at Harvard as the grandson of Amedeo Scutari, and as the great-great-nephew of Hermes Antoniadis. At Harvard, young Scutari was known as

Anthony Scott III. Mimi Hutchinson's conclusion was firm. "I don't expect to hear from my sister. She's dead."

"Look at Suzanne's record," Sam Harper insisted. "She was always the donor of unexpected gifts. Sometimes her beneficiaries were astonished by what they received, but Suzanne's gifts were always what her victims needed, if only they had realized it.

"Hell," said Sam Harper, laughing at the world itself. "John David Garraty is virtually a king in the box seats at Madison Square Garden. Those people at The Bank were convinced by Suzanne that their position was impregnable, which was all they wanted to know. Now the managers employed by Aunt Nellie expect that as soon as Aunt Nellie dies they will answer to no one but themselves—the Billy G. Fenns of American Syrup and The Bank will have arrived at last in managerial heaven!

"For that matter, when Suzanne started stealing precious eggs, and wrapping them up, and giving them away as Christmas and wedding presents, they were unusual gifts. It had never occurred to anyone before to have wanted the damn things. Sure, the stores were probably furious that someone was boosting their eggs. Now you see them everywhere. All the beautiful people got to have stone eggs. You can see them on cocktail tables and mantels and displayed casually on some fathead's desk. He wants you to know how discriminating he is—he's got a sterile egg! But it's expensive, by God! It really costs. The stores should have paid Suzanne a marketing fee."

Sam Harper chuckled to himself, savoring his own analysis. "Yes," he agreed, "she gave away people too. Just as soon as she had no further use for them. Don't we all?"

Would she give away herself?

"That," said Sam Harper, "is the kind of clever question I've learned to refuse. It pretends to sophistication, but behind it is a determined stupidity, a make-believe innocence, a tattle-tale morality I no longer tolerate. In the first place, every woman is required to give herself away all the time. Suzanne did it over and over. Why not?"

Then his rueful smile returned. "Maybe she still is. Just suppose," he continued, "you knew that at this very moment some suburban housewife with three darling children was shacked up in room eight-five-six of the Plaza with a twenty-two-year-old unemployed actor. She would have reasons of her own to have picked him up. Do you really believe you could ever know what they were? And at the moment she surrenders and screams for that punk, and rakes her nails across his beautiful shoulders, do you think you have any idea about why? If I knew—and I assure you I don't—that it was Suzanne who was in room eight-five-six, would you really want me to tell you?"

To be fair to Sam Harper, Suzanne was never reported to have been seen again at the Plaza. There were, however, rumors of her passage through extraordinary places. Having taken up with a Prince of Iran, she was to be seen in the skiing party of the Shah at Gstaad every winter—which was sheer nonsense. She was simultaneously said to be operating a charter-boat service in the Virgin Islands, and drinking heavily.

There were those who knew, without a shadow of a doubt, that it was Suzanne who was the administrator of a Zen monastery in Japan. There were others who were equally positive that Suzanne was now a high-level "auditor" of the Church of Scientology in New Zealand. Still others had heard from good sources that Suzanne had reappeared quietly in San Francisco as a priestess for the Church of Satan. These miraculous reappearances were easy to scoff away. Other certifications that Suzanne had been born again touched so neatly upon the popular faiths of the day that the truth of Suzanne's revisitation was not so easy to dispel.

It was said, for example, that she had disappeared behind the Iron Curtain, just as Kim Philby had done; and the proof of her value to the KGB was that she had a two-bedroom apartment in Moscow, which would otherwise be impossible for any outsider. She was also reported to have taken up residence in Jidda, where she published an oil newsletter for the sake of the Persian Gulf states, and the price of its subscription, at one hundred thousand dollars a year, was an accurate reflection of its impeccable sources. Simultaneously she was said to be gambling heavily again at The Claremont Club, in London, on the proceeds she earned as a courier for the diamond syndicate. She was also said to be the private art dealer for a former Mexican president, trading stolen masterpieces and living in the hacienda El Presidente had provided on the bay in Puerto Marqués. She was a spy, an assassin, the minister of finance for the Baader-Meinhof gang. She was the proprietess of a mail-order pornography business in Los Angeles with a half million subscribers. She was actually in a nunnery in northern Italy, had taken a vow of silence, and spent her days doing needlework upon linen sheets.

None of these fables reflected anything more than the substance of what some member of the congregation understood to be the central revelation of the day. They were tales believable only to the devout. To these follies I must add one of my own: the lessons of a field trip I made in December 1977, for urgent reasons I cannot now entirely explain. One Saturday afternoon not long before Christmas, I drove upstate to Saratoga. I drove straight through, as fast as I dared, arriving at the turn in South Corinth for the climb toward Suzanne's farm at about three o'clock. As I was making the turn, the first snowflakes flickered down upon my windshield from a gray sky. The road was full of potholes and frost heaves from winters past. On both sides of the road the remains of old slate walls served as containers for abandoned fields overgrown with scrub oak, volunteer birch, balsam and Scotch pine. I passed the signs that advertised upstate preoccupations: J. B. RICELAND, JR.—HOME OF SEEDS WE ARE PROUD TO SELL; and THE METHODIST CHURCH—MEETING 10:45 A.M. SUNDAY—GOD'S LOVE OF THE EARTH; SARATOGA COUNTY FAIR—SEPTEMBER 13–19. At the covered bridge the sign read: FIVE DOLLAR FINE FOR DRIVING FASTER THAN A WALK. As I crept across, old timber beams rumbled and jumped under the car.

Beyond the covered bridge, the road was dusty gravel, but it turned smooth again when I passed through the granite gates that marked Suzanne's entrance. I drove the long sweep up to the house through a carefully trimmed park of apple trees. They were bare of any leaves, but I was passing through an orchard of picture-book neatness; with real trees, where real deer might come to feed when the apples ripened and fell and rotted.

Since Suzanne's farm was not a real farm, the purpose of her orchard had been to add dashes of red to the green grasses upon which apples would surely fall. Similarly, she had planted the farm with about two hundred acres of rye and alfalfa each year, and had it all solemnly harvested, then piled by the bale into a magnificent white barn set beside the horse barns it was her pleasure to keep. The heaving work she required to be done was performed with gleaming yellow tractors and balers and reapers so bright they looked as if they had been delivered from a toy store. The neat post-and-rail fences enclosing the meadows gave the impression that the horses that had posed within those enclosures were as real as any raised in Kentucky. Unfortunately, when Adirondack winter approached, the horses had to be removed from the pretty postcard in which they had browsed to a climate like Kentucky's—warm enough for their survival.

At the end of the long, curving driveway, centered upon a small ridge in this pastoral, stood Suzanne's "old farmhouse." Its windows were blank, dark, empty of any signs of life within. In the house's original core there was much of the classic outline of American Federal; but additions had been built on, one after another. Although each addition had been constructed in the same red Federal brick—and even set in the old Federal pattern, with its butted ends showing—the extension of wings and walkways, screened porches, attached greenhouses where Suzanne had once ordered orchids to be grown, and barns whose ridgepoles did not sag even by a mite—all this would have baffled any Federal farmer's simplicity.

By the time I could park my car and walk around the corner of the deserted house toward the lake, the snow was coming down heavily and the wind was rising. I knew I had very little time left, and so against the bite of the wind I hurried to the back of the house and the view from the top of the lawn down toward Suzanne's lake.

Now I am not sure what I expected to see. The lake was filled to its brim at the lip of the dam, but of course it was frozen solid at that time of the year. I do not know why I had forgotten that by December a lake in Saratoga would be frozen. The blizzard was coming on, but the snow was not yet sticking. It blew in long spirals across the lake's glassy surface. I should have known there would be no trace of Suzanne's temple. There was nothing at all to see; gray ice streaked with snow upon a deserted landscape.

Winter's light was dim enough as it was, and a vicious blast of arctic cold made me shiver. I turned my back to it, cupped my hands around my ears to protect them, and tramped back to my car to start the long drive back to the city.

24

Gallery

It was snowing again in New York, Friday evening, February 17, 1978. As much as another foot was predicted, and by six o'clock it was apparently well on its way. Office workers had been let out early. Most of the city's taxis had already given up and gone home. Except for an occasional bus laboring from stop to stop, upper Madison Avenue was nearly deserted. Filtering down through the yellow cones cast by the street lamps, which continued to stand guard, a thick layer of powder was accumulating—only to be driven up again by boisterous gusts and sent whistling down the darkened side streets.

A one-man show of Michael Hassett's paintings was opening with a cocktail party at the Pryor Gallery, on East Eighty-fourth Street just off Madison Avenue. Inside the gallery's doors there was an odd aggregate of galoshes, Frye boots, rubber shoes for duck hunting probably ordered from L. L. Bean. Two coat racks accumulated a mixture of Abercrombie down ski parkas and more-traditional minks. Upstairs, the light was warm and brilliant. A handsome crowd of the *haute bourgeoisie,* necessary for a successful opening, circulated through the rooms. They posed upon polished hardwood floors, sipped from scotch and white wine on the rocks, exchanged kisses with each other on both cheeks, traded dazzling smiles and snatches of gossip, and while appreciating each other's reappearance on "such a hopeless night"—a phrase that seemed to be the evening's password—they even found time to glance occasionally at young Michael Hassett's oils. "Fine talent," everyone agreed.

There were, as a matter of fact, several examples of Hassett's most recent work, which showed a great deal of strength, but one of these, more than any other, had caught the attention of the party: Hassett's portrait of Suzanne. Not one of those present failed to stop before it, and there were few who did not claim how well they had known her, what good friends they had been, and then begin to pass on some delicious anecdote they swore was absolutely true. I stood against the opposite wall, in such a way as to eavesdrop on as many of these fairy tales as I could hear, pretending to sip at my drink, with my gaze fixed upon Hassett's interpretation.

The background behind Suzanne was not at all unusual. Hassett had painted in the deep browns and near blacks of traditional portraiture. Yet he had expressed other energies, much like those of autumn. The deep browns and hidden blacks of a forest turning color before the leaves fall were also flecked with the brilliances of red beech, golden oak, orange birch and yellow maple. Against this dark but at the same time shining field, the figure in the foreground was almost full length, but framed curiously. At the bottom, the figure of the woman could be seen to below her knees, but at the top the frame cut off her eyes just at the bridge of her nose.

What remained therefore was the body of a woman, undeniably Suzanne, facing out at her audience. She was costumed in a boat-neck sheath of silk threaded with gold lamé. At her throat the bone structure was strong, the chin firm above a muscled neck. The mouth was full and generous and half open; and it was Suzanne's thick red hair that flew, just as if she had at that very moment turned toward her observer. Yet her hands had not moved. Her left hand was settled quietly upon her left thigh, and her skirt was gathered at her right side, raised slightly between sure fingers. The observer was given no alternative but to travel upward along the lines of her body, raising his own glance until reaching the point where her eyes should have been, except that the top of the portrait cut them off. Hassett had denied us her eyes. No ghost stared back. Absorbed by the artist's omission, I suppose I did not realize that Angelique was standing by my side. I was startled by her interruption. "Hello, Professor. Still studying the lessons of history?"

I was immensely glad to see her, and told her so in more ways than necessary. I eventually got around to asking if she was living with Michael Hassett. "Oh, no," she said. "He is much too young, but you are forgiven for having asked such an awkward question. I am presently the mistress of an Iranian prince."

Angelique's reply was advanced in a matter-of-fact tone, much as if she had said she was studying sociology at Columbia. She said it with a flippancy that could have been a mimicry of her mother's. It was then I noticed she had hung about her neck an egg-shaped diamond of at least forty carats, one that could easily have been mistaken for the Montevideo.

"It looks," I said, "as if you have inherited the famous Montevideo."

"Yes, it certainly must look as if I have. Too bad it's glass." Angelique smiled tolerantly. "What a shame it isn't real."

7
D/
B

Mooney, Michael M
  Memento

DATE DUE

JUN 28 79			
SEP 20 79			
NOV 1 79			
NOV 23 79			
DEC 20 79			
JAN 10 80			